THE WRONG WIFE

L. STEELE

*For the good girls
who prefer Draco over HP,
this one is for you!*

SUN SIGNS

Knight – Leo

- You have a large ego.
- You don't respond well to criticism.
- You're self-centered.
- And domineering.
- And stubborn.
- You also demand lots of attention.
- You want to be in control.
- You're very loyal to the people you care about.

Penny - Aries

- You can be impulsive.
- You might make decisions that you'll regret.
- Act first and think later is your motto.
- You're impatient and want to excel at everything.
- And tend to behave recklessly.
- You are honest and optimistic.

- You want to satisfy your needs.
- You're sensitive and will do anything for your friends and family.

PENNY'S BUCKET LIST

- ~~Type 250 words a minute (done!)~~
- Have 5 O's in the course of 1 night (I'll settle for 1 tbh).
- ~~Learn to cook a gourmet meal. => I wasn't very good at it, but it's the spirit that counts, right?~~
- ~~Act in a movie or a play — I'll take a street act => It didn't go down that well. :(~~
- See the London Ice Kings play a game.
- Swim with dolphins.
- See the Northern Lights.
- Climb Uluru in Australia.
- Eat a chocolate croissant in a sidewalk café in Paris.
- Be d0minated. (Uh, maybe this should go up to the top?)
- Find a man who cares for my mother as much as I do.
- Be proposed to by the man I love.
- Explore ana1. (I'm chicken so this is right at the bottom — pun intended. Hahahaha!)

1

_____

Penny

"You're home!" My friend, Abby, throws her arms around her brother, Knight, who's prowled into the room. His hair is overgrown, and his beard is threaded with a few gray hairs. Huh? Knight definitely didn't have gray hair the last time I saw him. But then again, he hadn't been captured by the enemy and held for six months as a captive, either. Not that he looks any less desirable. He's lost weight, but that only adds to his appeal. There are hollows under his cheekbones, and a bandage over his left cheek that only adds to that dark and dangerous look he always carries around with him like a coat of armor. He's tall enough to tower over me.

At six-feet five-inches, and with shoulders that block out the room behind him, Knight looks mean and lethal. He looks like the soldier — or maybe secret agent — he's supposed to be. Abby told me he works for the British government. A real-life James Bond meets Jack Reacher with thick, dark hair, brawny biceps which stretch the white button-down he's wearing, tailored slacks and formal shoes.

The last and only time I saw him was when he was about to ship out on his mission. He was dressed in army fatigues, and he kissed Abby on both cheeks and hugged her tightly, his affection for his sister apparent. He promised to be safe and held her tenderly as she held back her tears.

His tenderness seemed so much at odds with his thick muscles and larger-than-life persona that I melted. I haven't been able to get his piercing green eyes out of my mind. Or the strength in his shoulders, the sculpted planes of his chest, barely contained by his shirt, or the way his pants molded to his thighs, not hiding the bulge at his crotch.

No, I wasn't looking at my best friend's brother's crotch. Maybe I was. But it was a fleeting glance. I only peeked, promise. But—oh my—the size of that impressive package between those tree-trunk like legs sent a pulse of heat straight to my core. I swear, I drenched my panties, then pretended it didn't happen. Not that he noticed any of it. He consoled Abby, then left.

Within weeks, I heard of his being captured on his mission and held behind enemy lines for six months, before being freed.

Now, Abby buries her face in his chest and weeps, but Knight doesn't make any moves to console her. He stands there with no change of expression on his face.

Cade gives a subtle shake of his head, then approaches the brother and sister. "Shh, babe, your brother needs time to acclimatize." He places his hands on Abby's shoulders and coaxes her back.

"I'm sorry I broke down like that—" She wipes her face. "I'm happy to see you, big brother."

Knight's expression softens. He clears his throat. "It's good to see you, too, Abby."

Abby makes a choked sound. "I was so worried about you. I thought I'd lost you, I—" She begins to weep again, and her husband Cade pulls her around and into his arms. She wraps her arms about his waist and begins to sob. Cade pats her hair. He glances up at Knight, who's watching the proceedings with a slightly confused look on his face. Finally, Knight shakes his head, then reaches over and pats Abby's shoulder.

"Cade is right. I need a little time to adjust back to civilian life." He winces, then adds in a hard voice, "Permanently."

"Permanently?" I cry out. Then flush as every single person in the room turns to look at me.

We're at our mutual friend Solene's engagement party, so I know many of the people in the room. Not that it stops me from wanting to slap my hands over my face and pretend I didn't say that. Instead, I draw in a breath and flash a bright smile at my audience, because, uh, that's basically what they are, and that's basically what I do when things aren't going my way. I curve my lips and draw on every last sliver of positivity inside me because when you think positively, positive things happen. Right?

"I mean, uh… Of course you want to leave the force after what happened. I mean, it's not easy being a prisoner of war." I cringe. "Did I say prisoner of war? That is the official term for what you were, eh? Oh gawd, now I'm putting my foot in my mouth. I mean, I have verbal diarrhea. Ugh, those two scenarios don't go that well together."

I shake my head, then square my shoulders. "Let me try again. What I was trying to say was, you must have loved the military, surely, and thought of it as your calling to join it, so to leave it? That must be agonizing, no matter the circumstances."

Silence follows my outburst. Everyone stares at me with varying degrees of shock… Horror… Pity? My cheeks feel like they're on fire. "Oh, my gawd, somebody kill me."

This time, it's Knight who winces.

Ugh, nice one. I slap my forehead. "Oh, shoot, what am I thinking about, prattling on about killing and dying and—" I wave my hand in the air. "Forget I said that. You probably have PTSD from hearing me blathering on like this, huh?"

His features darken.

"Oh, no, no, no. Did I say the P-word? I'm not supposed to say the P-word." I shuffle my feet. "No, no. Forget I said it."

Knight glares at me. If I thought he couldn't appear more pissed off, I was wrong. His shoulders swell, the veins on his neck pop, his hair seems to thicken and stand on edge. Waves of rage vibrate off of him. Cold rage. The kind that, surely, heralds the coming of a storm or a nuclear explosion. The air between us thickens. The hair on the back of my neck stands on end. An arrow of heat zips straight to my core.

Huh. Do I find his anger hot? Why do I find his show of rage hot? And sexy. And erotic. Surely, it's because I'm tired and on edge, since I barely slept most of last night. Knowing your short-lived career as a junior chef is over and wondering how you're going to pay your bills can do that to a girl.

Then, because I never did know when to shut up, I prattle on, "What are you doing here anyway? Shouldn't you be in a debriefing or whatever it is you have to do once you're rescued?"

His features grow hard, then he seems to force himself to relax. "I debriefed with my superiors before I flew in."

"O-k-a-y..." I swallow. "And therapy? Shouldn't you have gone straight into therapy?"

His eyes narrow. "What did you say?" he growls.

His hard voice lights up my nerve endings. Every pulse point in my body seems to drum in tandem. I shift my weight from foot to foot, then tilt up my chin. "It's just... I wondered if you shouldn't acclimatize to people in phases and—" my voice peters off. Utter silence descends upon the room.

I hunch my shoulders, try to imitate a turtle tucking its neck back into its shell. Although, by the way his gaze is locked on me, I know I'm very much visible. I turn up the wattage of my smile. "Sorry, sorry, I'm so sorry for being so indiscreet. I don't normally have such a non-filter. I mean, no, I normally don't have much of a filter, but I'm being especially filterless today. It's all your fault."

Knight blinks.

I stab a finger at him. "Yes, sireee, it's your fault. You make me nervous. Am I the only one who's nervous?"

I glance around, taking in the various expressions of surprise and amusement that the rest of them wear. "But seriously,"—I turn on him—"isn't therapy the best way to give yourself a chance to adjust back to civilian life?"

"Are you saying you'd rather I had not come to meet you and"—he jerks his chin in the general direction of the room—"our friends?"

"No, no, I was only concerned that it might be too much for you to have descended here in the middle of a group of people, when you've spent the last six months being tortured and—" I squeeze my eyes shut and flatten my lips, then count from five-four-three-two-one. When I open my eyes, everyone's gaze is on me.

"Oh, my gawd! That's it. I have officially reached the end of my tether. Can't take me out anywhere, eh?" I laugh weakly.

Someone in the room begins to chuckle—it's Cade, Abby's husband. I scowl at him, and he turns it into a cough. Another man guffaws loudly. When I look at him, he shoots me a thumbs up sign. Huh? He's older than the rest of us and a friend of Cade's. Guess he must see some-thing I don't? The man standing next to him, also tall and broad, with intense looks—Abby mentioned he's the co-owner of the leading finan-cial services company in the country—looks between me and Knight, then smirks.

That seems to annoy Knight further. His gaze intensifies, and his jaw tightens further. Jesus, he might crack a molar, or ten, at this rate. He folds his arms across his chest, and those massive biceps of his stretch the sleeves of his shirt. And this is when he's leaner. He was an absolute beast when I first saw him. The kind who'd gift Beauty a library because she likes to read.

I've set my standards high for what I want in a man, but lord above, this man tempts me. He does look like a beast, though. A very mad, very grumpy, very sexy beast. I widen my smile—mainly to hide the fluttering of my heart and my pussy, which seems to have developed a sudden plumbing problem, what with all the moisture sliding through my slit.

Ignore it. Ignore the little fires that have popped up under my skin. Ignore the bead of sweat that runs down my spine.

I tip up my chin and glance around at my friends. "Right, then. Now that I've made a complete earthworm of myself, can someone point me in the direction of the door?"

Mira's lips twitch. "Uh, Penny, did you say, earthworm?"

"Yeah, you know, since I don't like to swear. And I'll take my torn Chucks—which, by the way, are the same as Converse. Did you know that? I didn't. I had to, uh, Google it and— Oh, my god, I'm doing it again. I'm jabbering on." I hunch my shoulders. "Can we pretend that didn't happen?"

A nerve pops at Knight's temple. "To answer your question, I'm good. I might have been locked up and tortured for six months—"

I swallow.

"—but that's only made me stronger. It's what my job prepared me for. A job I've since given up. And now, I have a question of my own." He looks me up and down. "Who the fuck are you?"

2

Knight

"Penny." She flashes me a big smile, her blue eyes sparkling. She thrusts out her hand and approaches me. "I'm Penny."

I purposely cross my arms over my chest. Her face falls, then she lowers her hand and manages to smile again. *Fucking hell, did she swallow sunshine and rainbows today?*

"It's fine, I know who you are."

I glare at her.

Some of the color fades from her cheeks. Her smile switches off, *thank fuck.*

"It's fine, you don't have to talk or anything. My ma says I can keep a conversation going all on my own."

No shit.

She pushes a strand of pink-colored hair behind her tiny ear. Her heart-shaped face has high cheekbones, a turned-up nose and a plush bow shaped mouth that's currently moving again. I tune her out and focus on the dress that drapes over her narrow shoulders—also pink. What a surprise, eh? It dips low enough at the neckline to hint at her ample cleavage.

Cleavage I've been trying to keep my gaze off of since I slipped in the door. The only reason I'm here is because I knew my sister would be anxious to see me.

It's been forty-eight hours since I was extracted from hell. During that time, I was flown to a military base in Germany and debriefed. After a quick shower and five hours of sleep, I was ready to be transferred home. They insisted I speak with a shrink, which I initially refused. I agreed to it after being told I couldn't return home without doing it, since they needed to ensure I was of sound mind.

Gaining the confidence of the shrink took no time at all. Once he'd signed off, with the caveat that I continue the sessions when I returned home — unlikely — I sat through a debriefing meeting with my superiors.

I must have said enough to convey to them that I was quitting. They were not happy about it. I'm one of the few soldiers to escape from being held by the enemy. I was their prized horse, the one who survived incredible odds and made it back home. A shining example of the resilience and survival skills of what the Royal Marines stood for. Only they didn't realize the true extent of what I've been through. Only I know the guilt I carry with me. The pain and helplessness and fury at seeing my team members killed in front of my eyes.

I had a bad feeling about the mission, but orders are orders. One doesn't disobey them when they're handed down from the highest authority in the country.

Like a good soldier — and ultimately, that's all I was, regardless of the fact that I was part of the secret service — I answered the call of my motherland. And almost died. That I'm standing here today is, in no little part, due to the crack-extraction unit my friends put together to get me out of the purgatory I was trapped in. Black, darkness, pain, and a sense of hopelessness were my constant companions. In some ways, I'm stuck in that hole they stuck me in. In some ways, I'm stretched out on that table while my enemies waterboarded me, before sticking electric rods onto my extremities and —

"Hey, you all right?"

I scowl down at the slip of a woman who's waving her hand at me. "You, uh, you blanked out there for a second."

I glower at her. Upturned nose, big blue eyes, skin that looks soft enough to give way under the impact of my palm. Plush lips which, when parted, would reveal a heart-shaped hole that would be perfect for my cock. I blink.

Where did that thought come from? Women like her, who seem to be made from spun sugar, usually dissolve when faced with a light rain. With her ample breasts, tiny waist, and hips the perfect size to hold onto when I bend her over and fuck her... She's the kind of woman I need to avoid.

She'd never understand the darkness I carry within me. The agony that comes from having your life ripped apart. My ideals shattered. My goals revealed as a mistake. Everything I believed in, every opinion I've held, every interpretation of my hopes, my resolves... All of it, a mirage.

I wasted my life for the greater good. I wanted to contribute to my community, to my country, to my fellow humans. Something I held close to my heart since the day I became conscious I had the capacity to make a difference. All bullshit. All of it a mistake. A fallacy. I was fooled; I deluded myself. It took a stay behind enemy lines for my blinders to be removed.

From now on, I live... For myself. I'm going to join the ranks of those who pursue power, who make money. It's the only tangible thing, a stake in the ground. There are no shades of grey when it comes to money. It brings with it the influence and the power I crave.

Never again will I be as helpless as the way I was in that hole in the ground. I'm going to live life in complete control. And that means never allowing anyone or anything close enough to make me feel again. Emotions are raw, and real, and have no place in my future. There's only me and my born-again vision. Which definitely does not include the likes of a curvy, wide-eyed, innocent-gazed vixen.

I turn away from her, then walk over to my sister. I take Abby's hand in mine, then bring it to my mouth and kiss her knuckles. "I'm sorry for what I put you through. I'm sorry I missed your wedding. I'm sorry I spent so much time away from home. All that is in the past. I'm back now, and I intend to make amends."

Abby smiles through her tears, then she pulls her hand from my grasp and hugs me back. "Oh, Knight, I'm so happy you're safe and in one piece."

Am I though? I manage a tight smile, which seems to convince her enough that she steps back. She pats my cheek. "It really is wonderful to see you, Knight."

Cade, her husband and my best friend, pats my shoulder. "Good to have you back, mate."

I tip my chin in his direction, then turn to JJ. "Thanks for helping to put together the extraction task force."

"Sinclair and Michael also played a part in that." He's referring to the two men who stand on either side of him. Sinclair Sterling is one of the Seven who co-owns 7A Investments, and Michael Sovrano is the ex-Don of the *Cosa Nostra*. Perhaps still is, though he claims to have gone legit.

JJ himself is the head of an organized crime syndicate in the UK who also professes to have moved to the right side of law. The three of them represent the kind of morally grey men I once detested. Men like my father. Men who are ruthless and exploit the system for their own selfish ends. Men who value power and money over anything else — other than the women in their lives, and apparently, their friends. I mean, they came together to help me.

Once upon a time, I'd have passed judgment on them. I'd have said they were the reason people lost hope in each other and the future. Now, I understand this is the only way to be. I might have had a vision about contributing to the greater good. Now, I know the only good that makes sense is the kind that benefits me directly. Sure, I'll extend it to include my sister and those who'd helped me out, but that's where I draw the line.

Money, power, control of my own fate. Those are my ultimate goals. Good thing my father's a billionaire and can't wait for me to take over his company. "I owe you both." I tilt my head toward Sinclair and Michael.

JJ searches my features. "Did the crew arrive too late to save you?" he asks slowly. He seems to see something I've been desperately trying to hide from everyone else. He's a bit too observant for my tastes.

I scowl, then pretend I don't understand what he's implying. I widen my stance and shove my hands into the pocket of my slacks. " Adam and I — the only other surviving member of my team — had escaped from where we were being held. It was perfect timing when we ran into them. If not" — I raise a shoulder — "we wouldn't be having this conversation."

Silence descends on the group, then JJ nods.

"Anytime you need to talk..."

A-n-d so it begins. Everyone I meet feels the need to contribute. They all think they know what I went through, that their words are going to help fill the gaping hole where my soul once used to be. They have no fucking idea. He probably means well — and these are my friends, and I should be polite — but fuck that. If they really are my friends, they'll know I'm not in the right space for niceties. I grunt before turning away and raising my hand at Abby and Cade. "I'll be in touch."

Then, because I can't push back the noise that fills my head anymore, I turn and stalk through the door, down the hallway, past the uniformed staff who're placing drinks on trays, toward the front door. Shouldering it open, stopping myself from taking the stairs two at a time, I walk down the steps at a steady pace and turn toward where my car is parked. I lean against the trunk, draw in a breath, then another, and will my racing heart to slow down. Coerce my pulse to climb down from the insane speed at which it's galloping.

I've come to realize something very quickly; I don't like being indoors or in any kind of space with a crowd of people. Not that the room inside was crowded. Indeed, I know most of the people there. I saw the concern on their faces. Noticed the questions in their eyes. Their worry was a thrum in the room, and it repelled me. I don't want their pity. Their scrutiny. Their agitation on my behalf. I want to deal with what I've been through on my own terms. As I feel is right.

Leaving the army was the first step. I need to keep going and assume the reigns of the empire I turned my back on for so long. I —

"Hey, soldier?" That same cheery voice that grated on my nerves earlier has, apparently, followed me out here.

I square my shoulders. Turning my back on her, I round my car. My chauffeur appears and holds the door open for me. I'm about to slide in when there's a tug on my sleeve.

"Uh, can I call you Knight?"

3

Penny

"I mean, you're my best friend's brother, so I assume it's okay to call you by your name?"

He pauses but doesn't turn around. He also doesn't get into the car, which I take as a positive sign. *And why am I here? Why didn't I let him leave? What force compelled me to run out of the room, follow him outside, and try to engage him in conversation, when he barely acknowledged me earlier?*

Maybe it's the fact that he barely spent a few minutes in that room. Enough to let everyone know he's safe and to thank his friends for their help rescuing him. He acknowledged Cade and Declan—his closest friends—and then he left. He might be out of the war zone physically, but mentally, it's obvious he's anything but in the clear.

He cut a solitary figure as he turned and stalked out, taking with him that strange edginess that's gripped me from the moment he locked his gaze on me. It was like being at the business end of a tractor beam. One that pinned me in place, robbed the breath from my lungs and the moisture from my throat, sending it to other parts of my body. One that also sent a pulse of exhilaration up my spine. A sure sign that I hate him. But it also made me feel alive. Like I was coming out of a prolonged holding pattern. Like I only ever existed before, biding my time, flitting from one interest to the next, trying to forge a career, trying to find something that caught my attention. Then I saw him.

Maybe it's fanciful thinking. I mean, the man doesn't even like me. But that inherent need to soothe tumbled to the fore. He's in pain. He's lonely. He's in a state of shock. I'd go so far as to say he's a prisoner, and I can't let him leave. Not yet.

So, I followed him out and caught him as he was about to step into the car. Which he hasn't yet done. But he hasn't turned around to face me, either. I shift my weight from foot to foot. The grey-haired chauffeur looks between us, a question on his face.

"Hi, I'm Penny." I flash the chauffeur a wide smile. Because that's what I do. When I'm embarrassed, I smile. When I'm angry, I smile more. When I'm in the wrong place at the wrong time, like right now, I smile the biggest smile I can muster. Because isn't being optimistic and happy supposed to make things better?

"Rudy." The older man takes my hand. "Are you coming with us, Miss?"

"No," Knight snaps, before I can reply.

It speaks! So, all he said was a single word. And it's that one word in the entire English language that's the epitome of negativity. Still, that's progress... Of a sort. I think. It's how I choose to take it, anyway.

Rudy steps back, looks between us again, then nods. "I'll give you two some privacy." He sits down in the driver's seat and closes the door.

Knight makes a growling sound at the back of his throat. My toes curl. All of my nerve endings seem to spark at the same time. All because this monster of a man makes a sound like a rabid beast. *No, no, no, I can't compare him to Beast.* That's my very own secret fantasy, and I'll never find anyone who can fulfill that. Certainly not this bad-tempered, angry, snarly savage of a man. *Oh, but barbarians give the best orgasms. Eh? Why did my mind go there? Also, he's my best friend's brother, so that makes him off-limits or something, right?*

Of course, Abby is married to her brother's best friend, which is slightly different, but in the same territory.

I clear my throat. "I'm gonna leave. I don't know why I came after you. I mean, not *after you* after you, but just... After you. It's just... You seemed a little lonely, and maybe that's my imagination, and really, it was stupid of me to come and ask if I can do anything to help. Not that I've asked you yet. But I couldn't stop myself from following you out. Not *follow you* follow you, just... I was right behind you and—"

I gasp, for he's pivoted around and is glaring at me again. Green, green eyes. Sparks of green and gold and blue circling each other, chasing and ebbing and flowing like the Northern Lights. I've never seen the phenomenon in real life, but if I did, I'm sure it would look like the vivid green that pulses and throbs and storms in his irises. Then, it's gone. Banked. Vanished. To be replaced by a sheet of emerald so hard, surely, it could cut me off at my knees.

The impact of his gaze is so intense, it's like a ten-ton truck slamming into my chest. I stumble back and would fall, except he shoots out his arm and grabs my shoulder. The heat of his touch sizzles to my core. My fingers tremble. My pussy clamps down and comes up empty. My nipples are so hard, they hurt. *They hurt.*

I'm certain he reads my mind, for he drops his gaze down to my chest. Instantly, I blush. I chose this dress, knowing it shows off my tits. I'm a big girl, and I've never hidden it. I like my size. I like my hips. My fleshy thighs. The little rolls of fat around my middle. Most of all, I like how my tits are perfectly round and how they jiggle when I walk. I'm a plus-sized girl, and no one is ever going to make me feel bad about it.

He stares for so long, a million butterflies take flight in my stomach. I try to pull away, but his grip tightens. Slowly, he raises his gaze to mine. I see a mirror of my surprise, and something like… Loathing. Something so intense, I take another step back.

His eyebrows draw down, then he releases me so suddenly, I stumble again. This time, he doesn't right me. Instead, he pulls a hand-kerchief from his pocket and dusts off his hand. *He. Dusts. OFF. His. Hand. What a… Cretin.* He makes that growling sound at the back of his throat again, and my panties dampen.

He's mad. I get it. I'd be, too, if I'd been taken prisoner by my enemies. And then come home, only to be harassed by a woman like me who talks too much. And yeah, he's a hero. Media speculation is that he's going to be knighted by the monarch of England. *Which would make him Knight Knight? Would he be called Sir Knight?* I chuckle.

He scowls at the amusement on my face, and his green eyes blaze. That nerve that throbs at his temple is joined by a vein. The muscles of his shoulders bunch. He looks like he's going to burst out of his shirt any moment. *Would that make him Knight Hulk?* My lips quirk. *Don't laugh. Do. Not. Laugh.* Instead, I say, "It's not good to bottle all that rage inside, you know. It can lead to an early grave." The words are out before I can stop them. *Oh, my gawd! What's wrong with me?*

I lick my lips. His gaze drops to my mouth. Something flashes in those dark eyes. Something that sends a pulse of heat shooting through my veins. I shift my weight from foot to foot.

"Uh, I'm sorry, I didn't mean to talk about dying again. Honestly, especially because—"

He abruptly turns away from me, ducks his head in the car, slides inside and pulls the door shut. The car drives off, leaving me gaping after him. *What the— He drove off? And without saying a word to me? Did I mistake that flash of lust in his eyes earlier?* There's no mistaking the hate I glimpsed there, of course. He doesn't like me—I sensed it in the room, and the way he glowered at me, you'd think he had something personal against me. Except for the fact I've only ever seen the man once before today. Which begs the question: *Why did I feel so compelled to follow him out?*

"What are you doing out here?"

I turn to find my friend Mira walking toward me.

"I— uh—" A gust of wind blows the hair back from my face. A chill of foreboding slithers down my spine. "I—uh—thought I forgot something."

"You mean this?"

She holds up a bag. I stare at it for a second, then realization sinks in. "Yes, exactly. I forgot my handbag." I take it from her and hook it over my shoulder.

"You ready to leave?"

"You're no longer training to be a chef?" Mira takes a sip of the hot chocolate, then places the mug on the tiny breakfast counter which demarcates the living room from the kitchenette. We shared a ride here and decided to have a drink and decompress. Neither of us wanted to go out, so we opted to come back to Mira's tiny apartment. When my last landlord asked me to leave with less than a month's notice, Mira—who'd been looking for a flat mate—asked me to move in, and I agreed.

"Turns out, the hours are too long, the pay is shit when you're starting out, and not much better later, and you don't even get weekends free." I glance down into the depths of my herbal tea. Why the hell did I choose chamomile? I hate the taste, but it's supposed to be soothing, and I could do with a little of that right now. I squirm around on the bar stool, trying to find a more comfortable space.

Mira looks at me with curiosity. "You okay?"

"Why wouldn't I be?"

"You look a little peaked."

"It's the changing weather. Summer into autumn, the days drawing to an end earlier. I mean, I do like the turning of the leaves, but I much prefer when it's warm and sunny."

"Hmm…" She taps her fingers on the table. "You're a shit liar."

"I'm not lying. I do prefer when it's warm and sunny. " I take a sip of the chamomile tea and almost gag.

She looks at me skeptically. "You don't have to drink that, you know."

"I do." I hunch my shoulder. "My ma always used to say there was nothing chamomile tea couldn't make better."

Her gaze softens. "How is she doing?"

"Well, she recognized me the last time I saw her, so it was a good day." The slippery sensation of chamomile fills my mouth, and I force myself to swallow it. Maybe the more I do the things I don't like, the more God will reward me with the things I want. It's a strange logic, but one that has been drilled into me, thanks to the nuns who ran the school I attended. The same nuns who forbid swearing and thinking about sex and boys. It was a strict upbringing, but a happy one.

For all the singing of religious hymns at morning assembly, and the talk of sacrifice, it was an innocent, carefree childhood. My father passed when I was fifteen, and my mother picked up a second job. She ensured I never wanted for anything and was my best friend. Growing up, I remember my mom always keeping lists so she wouldn't forget things. She'd say, "I have a lot on my mind. I can't be expected to remember everything."

After my father's passing, she became more absent-minded, forgetting where she left her lists, sometimes forgetting to even make one. On occasion, I'd notice her hands shaking as she made dinner, but she always had a ready explanation. She was too tired. She was missing my father and coming to grips with it. Work had been stressful, etcetera, etcetera. I never pushed her for an explanation, as involved as I'd been with my own changing body and hormones, and then the race to get accepted into college. Then, I came home one day to find her searching for something she'd given away long ago. Concerned, I persuaded her to see a doctor, just for a general check-up, and she was diagnosed with early-stage dementia.

I was eighteen and had won a scholarship to study drama at UCLA. I wanted to put off going to university so I could support her, but she insisted I go. By the time I completed my degree, her dementia was advanced. I'd been offered a role in a play in London. She refused to let me turn it down. Instead, she spent her lifesavings moving from America to be with me.

I managed to get help from our local council—something I don't think we'd have been able to get in the States—and was able to admit her to a home where she's been the last three years. Her condition has been deteriorating, and at the same time, the council underwent budget cuts and can't cover her costs anymore. So, I need money. Fast. And here I am, unable to hold down a single job. I wasn't even able to continue my acting career—because I found it wasn't for me, after all. All that sacrifice of being away from her was in vain.

"I'm sorry, Penny." Mira reaches forward and grips my hand. "I wish there was something I could do to help you."

"You're allowing me to stay here and pay a fraction of the money I should be paying in rent. I think you're doing a lot already."

"I have a job. I can support us." She raises a shoulder. "Besides, if I'd refused to accept any money from you, would you have moved in here?"

I begin to object when she stops me with a raised brow.

"That's what I thought." She lifts her mug of hot chocolate and slurps it up. "You make a mean hot cocoa. Also, I'm the beneficiary of your cooking experiments, so I'd say I got the better end of the deal."

"That's you being generous. I'd hardly qualify my little cooking forays as sufficient to afford this apartment in London." I glance around the tiny flat. What it lacks in space, it makes up for in light. It's on the top floor of a two-story block, with skylights that allow the sunshine to stream in. And it's in the heart of Soho, which is as prime as you can get, in terms of real estate locations.

"You don't give yourself enough credit."

I laugh. "If you mean the cooking, I really do like it. But I prefer it as a hobby. I like to cook at my own pace, rather than being packed into the pressure-cooker environment of a kitchen run by a professional chef."

"That bad, huh?" Her tone is sympathetic.

"It took the joy out of cooking. I realized, very quickly, it's not for me."

"It's good you realized it early, huh? This way, you can move on, instead of investing your life in a career you don't like."

I take in her features. "Are you referring to yourself when you say that?"

"Who, me? Nah!" She places her palms together in front of her. "I mean, the big boss of my company is a jerkass, but I don't have much to do with him, so it's all right. I like what I do, so that's a positive."

"I wish I could find a career I love. I'm twenty-three and trying to work out what I want to do with my life."

"You have plenty of time to work that out," Mira assures me.

"But my mother doesn't." I swallow down the ball of emotions that blocks my throat. "I need to find a way to keep her in the home. She's comfortable there. Everyone knows her and is kind to her. If only I could find a job that I could hold onto, I—"

As if summoned, my phone buzzes with an incoming text message. I glance at it. "It's from Abby," I murmur.

"Oh, what does she say?"

I read the message again, then hold up the phone for Mira.

Abby: I have the perfect job for you.

4

Penny

"No, absolutely not." I cross my arms across my chest. "I'm not going to work for that...that..." *moron.* "Man." I shuffle my feet. "He's your brother and I know he's been through a lot, but he wasn't very warm when I saw him last."

"He's just gotten back from a traumatic experience." Abby bites the inside of her cheek. "I know he didn't speak much when you met him, but really, he's not a bad person, once you get to know him."

Which I don't intend to do.

I slouch into her office armchair. It's been a week since Knight returned. I haven't seen him or Abby since. When she texted me to say she had a job for me, I was intrigued, but this was the soonest we'd been able to meet. I'd spent the time looking for a new job but had come up with nothing. In all honesty, this possible opportunity she's offering me is my last resort. I'm running out of options. But now that she's told me who I'm going to work for, I'm sure it's not right for me.

"I'm not here to pass judgment on him, but our personalities are so different. He barely speaks—"*except in grunts and growls, which, admittedly, has a certain appeal. If you go in for the alphahole type of man... Which I do not.*

I don't. "He barely acknowledged me when we met. And even then, he spent all of that time glowering at me. I, on the other hand, like to be friendly to people. I want to be positive. I prefer to believe in the goodness of others. While he seems to expect the worst from those around him."

"Which is why you're perfect for him."

"Which is why we're all wrong for each other," I scoff.

She rises from her seat behind the desk and crosses the floor to sit down next to me. "Look, Penny, Knight wasn't always like this. He was an idealist. He believed in the greater good."

"This, from the man who now wants to join your father's organized crime business?"

"He wants to join my father's *legal* business," she corrects me.

"Which was built using the money that came from the illegal activities your father was involved in, as you've told me many times."

She winces. "Not denying that. But if that's what he wants to do, I can't stop him."

"It doesn't make sense. He was on a mission for the government, and from everything you've told me, he was a patriot. A believer in wanting to contribute to the greater good. Now, he wants to embrace capitalism and make money?"

"And grow the company to become the foremost in the world in its field." She lowers her chin to her chest. "He's changed. Something happened to him when he was taken captive by the enemy."

"Yeah, well, he was a prisoner of war; can't imagine that'd be an enjoyable experience," I murmur.

She locks her fingers together. "He was there for six months. Whatever they did to him killed the humanity inside him." She presses her knuckles to the space over her heart. "I don't recognize my brother anymore. He used to be warm, and even though being a soldier is not the easiest job in the world, he loved it. It was his calling, you know? There was not a day when he didn't want to make the world a better place for everyone. But now... It's like all traces of that man are gone. I don't recognize who he is anymore."

I lean forward in my seat. "He's only been back a week. As long as he's getting help, that should get him through the aftermath of what happened, and hopefully, he'll go back to leading a normal life."

"That's just it. He refuses to get help."

"Eh?" I blink. "So, he's not seeing a therapist."

"Forget about a therapist. He's refusing to meet me or his friends. He, Cade, and Declan were always so close, but he's been refusing to talk to them or see them since the day he briefly saw everyone at Declan's place."

"And your parents?"

She grimaces. "My ma's worried about him but she's more concerned about her society events, so she's not going to push it if he says he doesn't want to see a therapist. My father's happy he's returned back to the family business, so he's not asking too many questions." She locks and unlocks her fingers. "Honestly, I'm at my wit's end about what I can do to help him. It's one reason I agreed to help him out with his PR. I thought I could keep an eye on him, but I have Cade to think of now. I can't spend my time trying to make sure he's okay."

"Whereas I can because I'm single?"

She flushes a little. "I didn't mean it that way. If you work with him, you'll have a better idea of how he's doing. Besides, I'm his sister. Perhaps he doesn't feel too comfortable talking to me, but he might with you."

I roll my eyes. "That man probably wouldn't recognize his own voice if he heard it; that's how little he spoke that day."

"Which is good, right? There's less for you to contend with. You only have to do your job and make sure he doesn't do anything stupid."

I frown. "Anything stupid like—?"

She looks to the side then back at me. "It's just, you know, he's retired from the military. That was his whole life. I thought he'd be a career military guy. But what happened made him lose his faith in his beliefs, in a way of life he had subscribed to whole-heartedly. He's someone who doesn't know what he believes anymore."

"Well, clearly, he believes in this company." I look around her plush office. It's almost as big as the entire flat I'm sharing with Mira. Sometimes, I forget that Abby's a Mafia princess. As was Solene, which is how the two of them met. They have a lot in common, as do Mira and me. The four of us hung out a lot over the past year while Abby and Solene went through their respective romances and heartbreaks, only to get back together with Cade and Declan. The two of them have their happy endings, and I'm so happy for them. I truly am, even if a part of me wishes I could find someone as devoted to me as Cade and Declan are to their women.

"He wasn't always like that. In fact, Knight and I hated what our father did for a living."

"You mean, because your father used to be in the Mafia?"

"And because he was so focused on growing his business, he never had time for his family. We swore we'd never be like him. But since Knight has come back, he's spent hours closeted with our father. A man he refused to meet earlier. It's very confusing." She bites the inside of her cheek. "Which is why I think having you on his team will help me find out more about where his mind's at."

"You want me to spy on him?"

"Oh, Penny, you make it sound so bad. I'm just worried about him and want to make sure he's in a good place, mentally, you know?"

"Hmm." I lock my fingers together. "You're sure the business is legitimate?

She tilts her head. "My father runs one of the largest media conglomerates in Europe, so I have to answer yes to that."

"And you think that's what your brother wants to do now? Run the company?"

She glances at the door to make sure we're alone, then turns her gaze on me. "I think my brother is confused. I think he's trying to find something to believe in. And yes, I think he wants some kind of revenge for what happened to him. He's searching for a cause after losing the one he was so passionate about, and he found it in my father's company."

I purse my lips. "And you want me to work for him?"

5

Knight

"You want to work for me?" I lean back in my armchair. My jacket stretches across my shoulders. The collar of my shirt digs into my throat. My fingers tingle. I want to rip off the tie and fling it across the room—or perhaps, use it to blindfold the wide-eyed gaze of the woman who's staring at me from the doorway of my office. Her blue eyes are large, round, and surprised, her pink lips slightly parted. Her blonde hair is streaked pink and halos her heart-shaped face. She's wearing a suit—which is, you guessed it, pink—with a skirt that comes to above her knees. It hints at her plump thighs. Thighs which would be creamy and soft and perfect for marking with my fingers. My dick twitches. The first sign of life I've felt there since my escape from the enemy.

Darkness. Black. Pressing down on me. Sweat. The acrid scent of my body odor, the thick stench of my own piss and shit. The cold wraps its arms around me, my muscles quivering and twitching under my skin to generate some warmth. My arms are pulled up and tied to a rope attached to the ceiling, and I'm balanced on tiptoes. Every time my eyelids close and I nod off, I stumble forward, and my restraint stretches tight. I jerk upright. Don't open my eyes. Let the quiet settle around me, except for the drip-drip-drip of water in some corner of the basement

I'm being held in. Then with a clang, the door to my prison squeaks open. A shudder grips me. My guts churn. My heart jackhammers against my ribcage. No, not yet. I'm not ready, I —

"Hey, you okay?"

The noise in my mind retreats enough that I can focus on the pint-sized woman who's staring at me. I glare at her, and some of the color fades from her face.

I keep staring at her, and for a few seconds, she meets my gaze. Then, she shuffles her feet and secures her handbag—also an eye-watering shade of—y-e-a-p—pink—over her shoulder. The silence stretches. I continue to take in her features, the pointed edge of her chin, the soft skin of her throat, which seems like it's never been touched by anyone except her.

I'd be the first. Her first. A flare of lust unfurls down my spine. In the days since I escaped, I've been sure I'd never be interested in sex again. The sight of anyone else made me want to yell at them to get out of my way. In the forty-eight hours I've occupied this office, I've alienated my staff. Not a great start.

Working on the kinds of missions I did, I had the eyes and ears of an entire team behind me to help me navigate. I owed every successful operation I had to them. When I was captured, it was due to my own carelessness. My unit had never failed me. No one knew the importance of building relationships and fostering loyalty among your crew more than me. Considering that's not going to happen as long as I'm coming to grips with the events of the past six months, it makes sense to have someone act as a buffer between me and the organization. But is that person this curvy Barbie-doll lookalike? I'm not sure.

"Hey!" Her fuchsia heels sink into the carpet as she crosses the floor. "Are you okay? Should I call Abby?" She pauses in between the chairs pushed into the opposite side of my desk. "You seem like you're in a daze." She laughs, a high-pitched wheeze. Nervousness undulates off of her. I draw in a breath and the scent of roses—her scent laced with the sugary-sweet notes of... Her arousal?— fills my senses. I narrow my gaze on her.

"Ah... if you don't want to talk. I understand. It must be tough for you to adjust back into civilian life, after all." She scans my features. "You took off your bandage."

I stare at her.

She giggles, the sound nervous. "Sorry, I'm stating the obvious. That scar looks good on you."

I resist the urge to raise my hand and trace the outline of the slash across my left cheek. Too bad the wounds inside are not going to heal as quickly.

She continues to study me. "Your jawline does look more pronounced since I last saw you, and you have dark circles under your eyes. Have you been sleeping well?"

My frown deepens.

She opens and shuts her mouth. "Oh, my god. That was such a stupid thing to say."

Ya think?

"Of course, you're not sleeping. In fact, if you've gotten any shut-eye since you returned, my carriage will turn into a pumpkin at midnight."

I scowl. *What the hell is she talking about? Have I wandered into an alternate reality filled with blonde, curvy women who shoot their mouths off while looking like plus-size-Barbies?*

"That was Cinderella, though. My personal favorite is Beast and the Beauty. I mean, Beauty and the Beast. Not that you're the Beast, or I'm the Beauty. No, I certainly didn't mean to imply that you're the Beast, even though you don't smile, and you certainly are large and tall and broad and have the most massive shoulders I've seen on anyone—and this, after you lost weight since I saw you when you came to bid Abby goodbye before you left to wherever you did. And I didn't ask Abby about your mission, no siree." She shakes her head. "Nope, not me. And I certainly didn't probe her about you. I mean, I'm not interested in you that way. Not at all."

Maybe she didn't probe Abby about me, but I'd like to probe her. I arch an eyebrow.

She chews on her thumbnail, and when I stare at it, she reddens further. She lowers her arm, then shoves it behind her back for good measure. "Bad habit, sorry. Don't know why I'm apologizing to you for it, anyway." She straightens her spine. "Also, I shouldn't have said that, should I? I shouldn't be talking at all, but you don't speak, though you did ask me when I arrived if I wanted to work for you, and—" She shuffles her feet. "I'm not sure I want to. You're a grump and I'm a people-person—"

No shit.

"We're too different. We can't possibly get along. I told your sister as much, but she thought it would be good for you to, uh"—she glances away then back at me—"uh, to have a friendly face on your team. But I really think it's a bad idea." She straightens. "No, I'm *convinced* it's a bad idea. So, I guess the answer is no, I don't think I want to work for you."

She stares at me, expectation writ large on her features. Did she honestly think I was going to stop her stream of consciousness before she tied herself into a knot? It was too entertaining to watch her stumble into a hole then pull the hole in after her. I continue to watch her with a steady gaze. My breathing is even. And if my pulse rate becomes slightly elevated, and my engorged dick indicates my body is attracted to her, fact is, she's not my type.

Even before the months spent in that hellhole, I preferred my women quiet and ready to spread their legs when asked. And while I'm not in any hurry to entangle myself in a relationship, my time away has ensured I'm not fit to be in any kind of liaison with someone of the opposite sex.

Also, she's not tough enough to last one day in my presence. Even if I gave her the job—which I'm not going to— she'd run screaming out of the office within the hour. And she's Abby's friend, which would make it all very messy. And her non-stop chatter would only drive me insane. Nope, this job is not for her. I continue to hold her gaze, and when she realizes I'm not going to say anything, she hunches her shoulders.

"Okay, I get it. I knew this was a bad idea. I don't know why I allowed Abby to talk me into it. Anyway—" She flashes me that bright wide smile of hers. "It was, uhh, a pleasure." She shakes her hair back from her face and waggles her fingers at me. "Toodles, Abby's bro." She takes a step back. The next second, her body arches, a small cry escapes her mouth, and she begins to pitch toward the floor.

I jump up and throw myself across the desk.

6

Penny

One second, my heel catches in the carpet and I begin to pitch back. The next, something—no, someone—Knight, grabs the collar of my jacket and pauses my descent. He tugs and I stumble forward. My heart slams into my ribcage. My pulse rate spikes. I come to rest at eye-level with him, bent over the desk. He's stretched over it, more than halfway across the span of the considerably wide space. Only, the man is so tall that stretched out over it, he manages to make its expanse seem slimmer than what it is.

This close, his green eyes are a sheet of glass. A lighter green than I'd realized. They're almost a pale blue. Icelandic, icy. There's no emotion there. A chill grips me. Goosebumps pop on my skin. If I'd hoped to see through that frozen barrier he seems to have slapped down between him and the world, I was sadly mistaken. There's nothing there. No emotions. Definitely no empathy. Not even a streak of meanness. There's simply a blank canvas. It's as if he's wiped out his feelings or— he's hidden them deep down to protect himself against what happened.

I draw in a sharp breath, and the scent of sea-breeze laced with pepper—his—fills my senses. Oh, my god. The contrast to that vital, sexy, erotic scent of his body and the bleakness I glimpsed in his gaze is a sea-change. My head spins. My pussy clenches. My nipples tighten into points of desire. He must sense my response, for the spider web of lines fanning out from the corners of his eyes deepen. His nostrils flare. Then he begins to straighten slowly, without letting go of me.

I find myself pulled across the desk. My chest flattens against the surface, and he pulls me forward until I'm flat on the surface on my front, my legs dangling over the side of the desk opposite him. He sinks down into his chair and releases his hold on the collar of my jacket. Only, he curves his fingers around the nape of my neck. He applies enough pressure, and I lower my cheek into the table. For a few seconds, he keeps his fingers there, and it's strangely calming.

The adrenaline empties from my blood stream, and he doesn't let go. I might as well be a feral cat and he my new owner, with the way he communicates with my body without saying a word. Then, he releases his hold, rises to his feet and rounds the desk. I hear his footsteps as he prowls around to stand behind me. There's silence. The kind that pushes down on my back and pins me to the table.

I should look over my shoulder and see what he's doing. I should push up and off this desk and ask him what he means by pushing me down into it. I should... definitely not be sprawled out on his desk unable to move, with the anticipation building in the pit of my stomach. With my thighs clenched, my breath coming in pants. My nerve-endings stretched, my pulse beginning to race again.

I—I gasp, for he's palmed my butt through my skirt. The heaviness of his hand, the heat which sinks through the fabric and into my skin seems to brand the print of his fingers into my ass. I inhale a shaky breath. Heat shoots up my spine. My belly trembles. My breasts hurt. Then, the weight of his hand is gone, to be replaced by his grip around my hips as he slowly drags me back across the desk, stepping between my legs as he pulls, until my feet touch the floor. *He treats me like a rag doll he can throw against the wall or on the floor on my back and push aside my legs and—*

The heat of his body is a furnace behind me. I want to wiggle my bottom back against his crotch, but he slides his hands up under my arms to pull me upright. The solidness of his physique is a reassuring presence. His hands slide down again, his touch possessive on the curve of my hip, the part that almost forms a handle to grab onto when he... pulls me back. The scent of him is potent. I feel... owned, possessed, branded… And all without his having said a word. His hold tightens on me—then he releases me and steps back. A shiver runs up my spine.

He walks around to stand behind the desk once again.

"Leave." He sits down in his chair, then pulls out his phone and begins to tap on the screen.

"Excuse me?" I gape at him. Is he going to ignore what he did? He touched my ass. I didn't imagine it. As if that weren't enough, he grabbed a hold of my hips like… like a lover would do. And then, he slid his hands up my body, his fingers reaching the top of my chest as he reached under my arms and lifted me, before dragging his fingers back down to my hips. I liked it, but that's not the point. He patted my butt, then manhandled me as he, he *put you back on your feet. And stood there with his hands on your hips. And you didn't say a word. Nope, nah. Not a peep out of you, missy. So, are you going to tell him off?*

I open my mouth, but what comes out is, "You're not giving me the job?"

"Thought you didn't want the job?" He doesn't look up from his phone as he speaks.

"I… I… Uh, I changed my mind."

He continues scrolling on his phone.

"I… ah… realized I would be stupid to turn down this opportunity." *Also, the touch of your hand on my body sent me into a tizzy. Can you please, please touch me all over, especially in that place between my legs which, right now, is so empty? Gah, stop thinking about him in that fashion. He's going to be your boss, remember?*

I shuffle my feet, stare at his bent head, but he shows no sign of having heard me.

"Hello, Knight—"

"Did I give you permission to call me by my name?"

I swallow. "Mr. Warren, uh, are you not offering me the job? Was this an interview?" I laugh, but the sound is so nervous, I wince. I hunch my shoulders. "Uh, I thought I had the role when I came here and—" I promptly forget what I'm going to say, for he's looking up from his phone. Those green eyes—now, a cold emerald with no hint of the gold or silver flecks I saw earlier—bore into me.

"If this had been a real interview, you'd have never gotten through it. That was *not* an interview. Congratulations, you managed to fail that, too. And no, you didn't have the job when you walked in here. In fact, you still don't have the job."

"B-b-but Abby said—"

He sighs. "Yes. There *is* that. I trust my sister's judgment, and for some reason, she feels it's a good idea for you to become my assistant."

"So, you *are* giving me the job."

"I never said that."

"Th-th-then…"

He yawns. "Do I have to spell it out for you?"

"Spell what out?"

"If I were to give you the job, you'd fall for me. And that would be unfortunate—for you, not me. You understand? So, it's best you leave." He jerks his chin toward the door, then turns back to his phone.

I'm gaping again. My mouth is wide open. If my jaw could physically hit the floor, that's where it'd be. The ego of this guy! "I'd fall for you?" I snort. "I have a line of men queuing up to date me, and trust me, they are all much better looking, and far more personable, and much more gentlemanly than you."

He arches an eyebrow. "You don't want a gentleman."

"Eh?" I blink.

"You want a man who'll throw you down on the floor, tear off your clothes, lick your pussy and keep licking it while ordering you not to come. Then, when you're drenched and trembling, you want him to order you to crawl to him and suck his cock like a good girl."

A shudder oscillates up my body. Fires seem to light up in each and every cell. Heat flushes my cheeks. *Oh god, oh god, oh god. Did he talk dirty to me?* I should admonish him, yell at him, then leave. So why am I standing here trembling, with my pussy clamping down and coming up empty?

His gaze narrows. For the first time since I walked into the office, there's a flare of something in his eyes. He puts down his phone and tilts his head. It's the gesture of a predator who's caught a whiff of his prey. Then, he jerks his chin toward the door, before he looks down at his phone again.

That's it, I'm dismissed?

I blink, pivot on my heel, walk toward the doorway, push open the door, then pause. I turn to glance at him over my shoulder. "Oh, Mr. Warren?"

I wait until he raises his gaze to meet mine.

"Don't blame me when *you* fall in love with *me*."

7

Knight

Fall in love with her? As if that's going to happen. She has a certain innocence about her which is appealing. And her curves are alluring. And her eyes—fuck me, but her eyes are like the bluest of lakes which mirrors the skies overhead with not a cloud to be seen.

I looked into them, and it was as if I could see the man I once was. The man who was dedicated to his country, for the greater good, to give himself up for a good cause. The man who believed in right and wrong, good and bad. Who wanted to make this world a better place for future generations. The man who didn't hesitate to sacrifice himself for his motherland.

That man is gone. And in his place is someone who knows everything he once believed in was wrong. A man who is focused on only one thing, his survival. Power, money, influence—the things I once abhorred are my new friends. The weeks and months of solitary confinement and torture at my enemy's hands stripped me of any veneer of civilization. It revealed that I'm no different than the people I once looked down on. People like my father, who'd always been clear their lives were dedicated to the pursuit of material possessions. That power is the only thing that matters. And the man who has money wields power.

Then, it comes down to how strategic you are in wielding it. How you use power to get what you want. Funny how I'd been too busy delivering on my responsibilities and my duties to truly ask myself what I wanted. Turns out, what I hankered for was absolute control. Over my future. My fate. My destiny. I'm the master of what's to come. Of how I live my life from now on.

No longer will I be following the orders of someone I can't see. Someone at the top of the food chain who decreed that I was the right person for that mission, and whose command I followed without question. And it left me with my entire life turned upside down. Though, perhaps, I should be grateful for what that person did, for the blindfold over my eyes is gone.

All that drivel I filled my head with—*Better to Die than Live a Coward*, *Ready for Anything*, and of course, that slogan that was drummed into me, *Death or Glory*. Well, I choose glory. And power. And money. Death is no longer an option. I cheated the grim reaper, and I'm going to ensure that I live life to its fullest, and in its basest forms, before I punch my ticket off this earth.

Which is why I'm standing inside The 7A Club, of which I'm a member. Situated in the heart of London and owned by JJ Kane and Sinclair Sterling, the first floor of the place recently added a bar open to everyone, as well as a Michelin-starred restaurant run by Chef James Hamilton. It's attached to a private member's club where I've met my friends in the past.

Another new addition is the exclusive BDSM club housed on the higher floors. The venue is dedicated to BDSM and the pleasures that those who enjoy the erotic practice of roleplaying, bondage, dominance-submission, and masochism—as well as some other kinds of fetishes not spoken openly about—come to. This is the kind of place I might have once expected to see my friends. All of whom are now married or in a long-term relationship. Ergo, they are ensconced at home with their other halves. I, on the other hand, have no such constraints. It's been months since I've been here. Strangely, this is the one common trait with the person I was before my captivity and the one I have now become.

Only, my tastes seem to have been enhanced. My needs are sharper, darker, more vicious. The yearning to possess, to dominate, to master and subjugate is far more powerful in me. It's as if the torture that stripped me of my humanity also sheared off any urge I had to conform.

Perhaps, I was never really the kind of person who'd follow rules willingly. Perhaps, that was what attracted me to the military. Knowing the discipline would keep that animal inside me at bay. The beast that has now been unleashed and is ready to show its true self.

I walk up the steps of the club, past the first floor, where novices test out their fledgling erotic fantasies, and the second, for those who are ready to get more adventurous in the exploration of their desires, to the third, where the more experienced players can indulge their depravities. A steward in his dinner jacket steps forward. "This way, Mr. Warren."

I called ahead to let them know about my preferences, and they were all too happy to cater to my requirements. While I hadn't earned enough on my military paycheck to spring for a membership here, and I'd have never dipped into my trust fund to spring for the membership fees — thanks to my friends, Cade and Declan, I've always been welcomed here. It's an indulgence I allowed myself when the tendencies inside me needed an outlet.

Now that I've been appointed CEO of my father's group of companies, I have no compunction paying what's necessary to ensure my needs are fulfilled. I don't need to depend on my friends anymore. I have my own means — and my trust fund, which I plan to access very soon. But first, I need to take the edge off that darkness inside of me. That insistent urge that's been chipping away steadily at my guts. That nothingness occupying the place where my heart once was. That...compulsion unleashed by the atrocities committed upon me, which I can no longer hold in check.

The steward leads me to a room at the end of the corridor. "All your requirements have been met, Sir. Your submissive has been carefully vetted, and we believe she will meet your requirements."

He opens the door. I step inside, and he closes it after me. My phone buzzes in my pocket. I pull it out and read the message.

Adam: Got your earlier message buddy. Sorry it took me a while to reply. Was volunteering at the hockey camp. Also, you know the Club is not my scene but if this is what you need to find some peace, then don't deny yourself.

. . .

I stare at the screen for a few seconds, then mute the phone and slide it back into my pocket. Of all my friends, Adam is the only one who knows what I went through. He was there with me, after all. He got off easier though. He didn't have to watch his teammates being killed, one by one. He was unconscious through most of it, and his awakening is what spurred me on to escape.

After being confined to a six-by-four-foot coffin-shaped cell underground, where I had to curl myself to fit in, and with no light or food for forty-eight hours, my captors pulled me out. I managed to survive by drinking from the rainwater trickling in. I was too weak, my spirit almost broken. I was ready to give in. That's when Adam, having broken free of his restraints, reminded me of my promises. He reawakened in me the strength to fight back. Together, we overpowered our captors and escaped.

And as we raced through the forest surrounding where we'd been held, he kept my spirits up. I was weak after months of torture and lack of nourishment, but Adam spurred me on.

If it had been only me, I might have given up. But thanks to Adam, I made it. I respect his decision not to come with me to the club. And that he doesn't judge me for what I need to fill that emptiness inside me. If I were a better man, I'd accompany him in coaching the boys at the hockey camp, but I'm not like Adam. There's no shred of the man I once was left in me. All I have is this... aching need to feel... Something. Feel some part of the humanity that once resided in me. Feel alive and connected to something—someone, other than the hate that resides in me. It's what led me to specify the exact kind of experience I was looking for.

In the center of the room is a padded spanking bench, complete with restraints. A door at the opposite end of the room opens, and a woman steps in. The spotlight shining on the bench throws the rest of the room in darkness and prevents me from making out her features. That's what I asked for. I need a faceless body. Warm flesh on which I can slake my thirst, without seeing the face. This way, I don't need to have a conversation, or pretend an empathy I don't feel. This way, I can get rid of the pressure building deep inside me and move on.

The woman takes a few steps toward me, and I call out, "Stop."

She pauses.

"Now turn around."

She hesitates for a second, another, then slowly turns around to face the door she came through. That will not do at all. She needs to be taught to obey my rules without reserve. Assuming she lasts through today's session.

I glance around, then spy the remote control that manages the lights in the room. It's on a table by the only other piece of furniture, a couch facing the bench. I head for it, then manipulate the device so the spotlights train on her instead. Tossing the device back on the table, I prowl toward where she stands with her back to me.

When I'm within arm's length behind her, I stop. She hears me approach, for she stiffens. I take in her slim shoulders, the straightness of her spine, the tiny waist, the flare of her butt, all clad in a white dress that clings to every dip and hollow in her body and comes to mid-thigh. She's wearing over-the-knee boots with four-inch heels that squeeze around her fleshy thighs. Creamy skin, perfect to be marked.

My fingers tingle, and my scalp tightens. A pulse flares to life at my temples, and I raise my gaze to where her blonde hair is piled up in a messy bun. She's short enough that she comes to the line of my heart. Perfectly tiny. Perfectly curvy. Perfect to be broken by me. Before I can stop myself, I reach down and pull out the single clip that holds up her hair. She gasps. Strands of white-gold hair pour down her back. The color is lustrous, pure, shining pale in the dim light that bathes her. A tremor grips her. Her fear leaches out into the air, laced with something sweet and complex... The scent of her arousal. I'm instantly hard—what the—! That's only my second hard-on since I returned. The first was when I saw *her*.

I rub my chin, then grip her shoulder. Electricity zips down my arm, straight to my balls. She must sense it, too, for a whimper escapes her. My cock stabs into my pants, and fuck, if I don't come right then. I bend my head and sniff the air next to her neck. Roses. Definitely roses, tinged with something sugary-sweet. The unmistakable scent of her arousal goes straight to my head. I curl my lips, then straighten and thrust my foot between her legs. A small cry escapes her, then she slides her legs apart. I release her, and she trembles again. The air between us vibrates with her uncertainty, her heightened emotions, her anticipation about what is to come. *How far can I push you, little Dove, hmm?*

"Bend over and grab your ankles," I order.

This time, she instantly complies. In this position, her heart-shaped butt juts out in the air. Her silver-colored thong rides up the valley between her butt cheeks and nestles between her pussy lips. Moisture glistens on her inner thigh, and my mouth waters. My thigh muscles harden, sweat beads my forehead, a-n-d why am I having such a primitive response to this woman? I thrust my hand between her legs and cup her pussy. Her knees seem to give way, and were it not for my grip on the most intimate part of her, she'd fall.

With my free hand, I grasp her hip to hold her in place, then I slide my finger under her thong and inside her slit.

"Ohgodohgodohgod," she gasps.

"You like that, hmm?"

She nods, then pushes out her butt so my finger slides deeper inside her hot, tight, wet cunt.

"Are you hungry for what I'm going to do to you, my little Dove?"

A low, keening whine emerges from her lips. I pull out my finger and suck on it. The popping sound as it leaves my lips sends another shiver racing up her spine. That's when I tear off her panties.

She cries out.

I stuff the piece of silk into my pocket. Then, holding her hip, I step back to the side, widen my stance to brace myself, and bring my hand down on her arse. The sound of flesh meeting flesh echoes around the room, and she yells. "What the—" She tries to pull away, but I hold her in place.

"Did you like that, little Dove?"

"No, you jerk hole, you bastard, you, ahhhh—" She bites off whatever else she's going to say as my palm connects with her butt, this time, on the other cheek.

"It hurts, you maniac, what are you doing?"

In answer, I spank her arse cheeks again. She moans. I step back and survey the prints I've left on those fleshy globes. My dick thickens even further. A bead of sweat runs down my spine. I massage the reddened skin, and she whimpers. A fat bead of cum trickles down her inner thigh. I scoop it up and bring it to my lips. The taste of strawberries fills my palate. Interesting.

"So, tell me, little Dove, should I tie you up, then whip you, and then tear into your pussy? Or should I tie you up, then take your pussy, and then whip you?"

She freezes. "Wh-wh-whip me?"

"Does that bother you? Maybe you'd prefer I dispense with all the niceties and take you up the arse directly, hmm?"

"Up the... Up the-the..."

"Arse," I supply.

"What the—" Her arse cheeks clench. She tries to pull away, but I don't let her.

"Or perhaps you prefer something more hardcore?"

"M-m-more hardcore?" she yelps.

"Hmm, let's see. I take you up the arse, then use a vibrator on your clit, and stuff my fingers in your mouth. All of which drives you out of your head and makes you want to orgasm, but I won't let you. So, you try to beg me for release—*try* being the operative word—because you can't speak, as your mouth is otherwise occupied. But from the sounds you make, I'll gather that's what you want—because I'm good that way—and also, because your pussy is so saturated with your cum, and your inner walls are clenching down on your emptiness, and you're frustrated enough that the keening sounds which emerge from you grow in intensity, and your breasts ache for my touch, and every part of you is heightened and ready for that release, but I don't let you come. And then I pull out and plunge into the forbidden hole between your butt cheeks and—"

"Stop—" she cries and tugs on my grasp. I release her. She staggers forward, straightens, then spins around and raises her arm. I catch her wrist. When she takes in my features, her blue eyes widen. "You?"

8

Penny

"What are you doing here?" I cry.

His lips curl. "What are *you* doing here?"

"I... I..." I swallow. *What am I going to say? That I loved what you did to me earlier? Was so turned on by how you spanked me? When you kicked apart my legs, it sent a primal thrill through me, and when you tore off my panties I almost spontaneously orgasmed? And that was before I knew it was you. Now that I know it is you, please, please, please can you throw me down on my hands and knees and fuck me, please?* I tip up my chin, then straighten my shoulders. "I'm here to do a job."

"Job, hmm?"

"Yes, a job. You know, the kind where you earn money by the hour."

"And have you done this kind of job before?"

I blink, then slowly shake my head.

A furrow appears between his eyebrows. "This floor is for the more experienced players. How did you get in here?"

I bite the inside of my cheek and glance away, but he pinches my chin, so I have no choice but to look at him.

"Tell me. Now," he snaps.

"I lied to the bartender. I told him I was desperate for a job, and he pulled some strings with the recruiter to get me up here." The words rush out of me before I can stop myself. *Jesus, why don't you tell him your entire life story while you're at it? Funny thing? If he commanded me to do so in that hard voice of his, I'd do it, too. And that's scary. It's also sexy. But really, really scary.*

His eyes flash, and a vein pops at his temple. He looks like he's about to lose his temper—which has a certain appeal, given how controlled he's been so far, but I'm not sure I'm ready to face the consequences when that happens... Yet.

I swallow, and his gaze drops to my throat. His jaw ticks. For a second, I'm sure he's going to wrap those thick fingers of his around my throat and squeeze. My breath catches. My pussy clenches. What kinky fuckery is this that I find every move of his such a turn on?

He leans in close enough that his rich, spicy scent invades my senses. My nipples harden. A million little fires light up my nerve endings. A moan escapes my lips. Instantly, he looks up and into my face. He seems to remember where he is and who I am, for his gaze clears.

"What the fuck is this asshole's name?" he growls.

"I... I don't know his name."

"You don't know his name?"

"I, uh, flirted with him and got what I wanted. It was one meeting and very innocent. He also discounted my drink, so you know, all in all, it was worth it." I bat my eyelashes at him. It only serves to make his lips twitch. And now, I feel like an idiot. You know, 'cause I didn't earlier.

"Innocent, huh?" He asks in a lazy voice which does weird things to my insides. Jeez, there's no winning with him. When he's all forceful, I adore it. And when he goes all laid back, I crave whatever it is he wants to do to me. My thoughts are definitely not innocent. I manage not to blurt that out and firm my lips, which light up those green eyes with a dangerous gleam.

"So, you've never been someone's submissive?"

"Submissive?" I squeak.

He releases my chin, only to press his thumb into the pulse that's beating at the hollow of my throat, and oh, my god, it's as if he's branded me there. My mouth dries. My toes curl. I stare up at him, unable to look away as he holds me pinned in place.

"Tell me, Miss Innocent, did you know you were here to be *my* submissive?"

"I didn't know it was going to be you—" *In which case I'd have stayed away. Nope, I lie, in which case I wouldn't have been so ashamed to be aroused by what you did to me.* Somehow, the fact that it was Knight and not some strange man makes it all better—not the part where he threatened me with anal, but the earlier part when he was spanking me, which I, strangely, liked. A lot. "Also, I know what a submissive is."

His gaze intensifies. "You do, huh?"

"Of course, I do. I'm not stupid." And I've read enough smutty books to be somewhat of an expert on the topic. Not that I'm going to tell him that...

"And yet, you're here, in this room, with me?" he murmurs in that silky voice which seems to slither down my chest and coil in my belly.

I squeeze my thighs to control the ache that flares there and tip up my chin. "Yeah, uh, I needed a job, and the bartender said they were looking for someone who—"

"Who?" His voice is low, almost deceptively soft, but the skin around his eyes creases, and I know then, he's not anywhere as composed as he's pretending to be. "What did he tell you?" The command inherent in his words causes a spurt of something to twist my belly. *Oh, god, why is the simple act of talking to him an erotic dream come true?*

"Don't keep me waiting. Tell me. Now." He lowers his voice to a hush, and something inside of me loosens.

"He mentioned they needed a woman to entertain one of their clients with specific tastes and that whoever was chosen for the gig would be paid a lot." The words rush out of me.

His jaw ticks. "Specific tastes?"

I nod.

"And you didn't think to ask what that meant?"

"Uh, I thought, you know, that it'd be like *Fifty Shades of Grey*." And I've always wondered what that kind of a relationship would be like. Again, not something I'm going to tell him.

"You. Thought?" A nerve pops at his temple.

"Y-yes."

"Do us both a favor and stop thinking, because clearly, it makes no difference, even when you do." A coldness pours off of him. This man... Even his anger is like being dropped in the middle of an iceberg. I shiver. Goosebumps pop on my skin.

"No need to be rude." A shiver runs down my spine. "Also, I'm cold."

He looks me up and down. "And you're surprised, why?"

"Hey, this is what I was told to wear."

"And you always follow what you're told to do?"

"Not... Always, but this was a paid gig, so—" I raise a shoulder, and his eyelid twitches. Somehow, that feels so much more ominous. The cold vibes pouring off of him drop the temperature until I feel like I've shut myself up in a freezer. Strike that; freezers are warmer than the glacial frigidness of his expression.

"And it didn't occur to you to check into what was going to be expected of you? Did no one warn you about what goes on within these walls?" His voice is tight, the tone ominous. I swallow, then slowly shake my head. "I-it's not their fault. I may have, uh, slipped through the checks. I, uh, may have coerced him into doing me a favor."

"A favor?"

I nod again. "He wasn't going to, but I pulled the sympathy card and told him how broke I was, and that this was my last chance to pay for"—I glance away, then back at him—"pay my rent. Also, we agreed that he'd be right outside the room, and if I yelled, he'd come to my rescue."

He blinks. "You'd yell, and he'd come to your rescue?"

I scowl. "That's what I said."

"I see." He releases his hold on my wrist, then steps back. "Spread your legs."

"Excuse me?"

"You heard me."

I scan his features and the expression on his face is bored. He holds my gaze, and the seconds stretch. A hollow sensation yawns in my belly, a melting sensation grips my thighs, then I slide my legs apart.

He moves so quickly that, one second, he's standing there; the next, he slaps me between my legs, right on my swollen, sensitized pussy. I yell. I can't help it.

"What the hell was that?" I snap.

"These walls are soundproof. You can scream all you want—indeed, it's expected that you will—and no one is going to help you."

My throat closes. That hollow sensation in my belly spreads to my chest. "Oh. Right."

He tilts his head, and of course, I feel a flush coming on. I glance around, then point toward the corner of the ceiling. "Security cameras—"

"Are not allowed in private playrooms. Here, only my word goes, as the Dom; and you, as the sub, are expected to fall in line with it."

I swallow. "So, I am—"

"You are under my control. I hold absolute power over you. When you walked in that door, you left all choice behind."

My pussy clenches. I squeeze my thighs together. *I didn't like the sound of that, did I?*

"O-k-a-y." I laugh, but the sound is so uncertain. I flinch. "Look, you've had your fun. You've proved your point. It was a mistake to take this job. So, guess I'll say goodbye now and be on my way." I begin to slide my legs together, but he plants his foot between mine.

"Wh-what are you doing?"

"I didn't say you could move, did I?" His words are said in a conversational tone. In fact, from the expression on his face, you'd think we were having a conversation around the office water cooler. Not that this man would ever be seen near the water cooler, but you know what I mean. There's a very attentive look about his eyes. He's looking at me with keen interest. Like I'm a lab specimen, or like he's a predator and I'm a little animal he's toying with for his pleasure, before he moves in for the kill.

Don't be a stupid little prey who's going to be hunted down; stand up for yourself. And I'm not a simpering, ditsy blonde. I'm not—okay, so I do have my blonde moments—but honestly, I have learned to fight back when I'm faced with a challenge. I've had to with the cards I've been dealt in this life. *So why is it, in this man's presence, I seem to reduce to a stereotypical, hot mess?* I tip up my chin. "I don't have to do what you say."

"Oh?" He tilts his head.

My scalp itches. My hindbrain screams it's not good to provoke someone like him. Someone who's lethal and, clearly, dangerous. The suit he's wearing and the veneer of civilization he's cloaked himself in is a front to make people comfortable, but I'm not buying it.

"I told you it was a mistake I made coming here. Now, if you'll excuse me—"

"I will not."

I gape. "Sorry? What did you say—?"

"No mistake can go unpunished, Little Dove. It's time you learn that."

My nipples tighten. My heart seems to sink down to the space between my legs. I swear, every part of my focus is concentrated there right now.

"Wh-what do you want from me?"

"What can you give me?"

What can I give him? Let's see. I don't have money to pay for my rent, and all my savings have been used up in taking care of my mother, so that leaves me with— I blink. He must see the expression on my face, for his attention sharpens.

Nope, not going there. This is dangerous territory. And stupid. Really don't say it. Don't.

"Say it," he snaps.

I say it. "My virginity."

9

Penny

"You told him whaaat?" Mira spits out her vodka across the bar. The man on the barstool next to her moves out of the way, then scowls at her. Mira raises her hand. "Sorry, sorry. My friend announced to the man she has a crush on that she's a vir—"

I clap my hand over her mouth. And I thought *I* was filterless. "Why don't you announce it on social media, huh?"

She looks at me and says something, but her words are muffled by my palm.

"I'll release you if you promise to stay quiet."

She nods. I lower my hand. She grabs her drink and takes another sip. "Sorry, I didn't mean for that to burst out like that. You took me by surprise, is all."

"You mean the fact that I'm a virgin, or that I blurted that out to him?"

"Both?" She leans an elbow on the counter.

We're at the bar at The Club the day after my announcement to the grumphole that I've yet to lose my V-card. And the only reason I'm here is because I thought I could coerce the bartender—the very same one who snuck me inside, and thanks to whom that entire disastrous meeting with Knight had happened— to give me a discount on my drink again. But when I arrived, that particular bartender was not to be found. He'd been replaced, which means I didn't get my discount. As for the recruiter, I'm sure she no longer works here, either. Knight was livid enough to get them fired. It's my fault they're out of jobs. I hunch my shoulders. Can't do anything right, can I?

I reach for my glass of whiskey—full-price, now that I have no way of getting a discount.

"You should have seen how quickly he got away from me once I said that. I guess it was one way to ensure he never wants to see me again." I take a sip, and the liquor leaves a warmth in its wake. It's thanks to my Dad that I developed a taste for whiskey. My earliest memories are him and my ma sitting on the patio in the evenings after dinner, each of them nursing a drink of their choice. My Dad's was always a whiskey, and my mother's a white wine. They'd sit on the swing, and I'd sit at a table on the other end of the patio. I'd work on my homework, and they'd catch each other up on the day's happenings. Their voices would be a hum in the background, along with the buzz of crickets and other insects in the fields surrounding our home in Gainesville, Florida.

As the night drew in and it got chillier, one or the other of them would urge me to go inside and finish the rest of my assignments. I'd ignore them until my father would come over and lead me inside the house. I could never say no to him. I was my father's daughter in every way. As I grew older, my relationships with my parents grew deeper. We were a unit, the three of us, and outside of school, I hung out with them a lot. Most teenagers rebel against their parents—me, I was more than happy to do as they wanted. I liked spending time with them and found their discussions about movies and music so very interesting.

My father taught violin at the local community college, and my mother taught piano. They were talented in their own right, and it's what made me want to try my hand at the arts, too... Only, I don't have any such inherent aptitude to speak of. I can't sing—not even in the shower—play no musical instrument and have two left feet.

The only thing I was good at was typing... Go figure. I could type really fast and won a few local competitions. Clearly, my future would have something to do with a keyboard—just not the musical variety. I turned my back on that particular talent. I'd thought I could use my skills in the role of Knight's assistant, but that's out. In fact, I can't even use my body to earn money, if yesterday's botched effort at being a submissive is anything to go by. Now, I'm really out of options.

Mira must see the desperation on my face, for she flattens her lips. "Shit, I really am sorry. I'm being indiscreet. I know how much you were hoping for that gig to work out—though you have to admit, it was a far shot."

I lower my chin. "No shit."

"I could loan you money, you know—"

I shake my head. "Nope. Absolutely not. I'm not taking money from you, or Abby, for that matter."

"So, I guess you're not going to tell her about your run-in with her brother?"

I stare at her. "What do you think?"

"I guess you're not going to do that but—" She stares over my shoulder and her gaze widens. "I think you might have to talk about it with Knight."

A tingle races down my spine. My pussy clenches. Strange, even his name seems to elicit a weird response from my lower regions.

I flick my hair over my shoulder. "Don't say that bastard's name in front of me. Once I told him I had my V-card, he couldn't get out of there fast enough."

First, he took off his coat and placed it around my shoulders . Then, he walked me out of that room and to his waiting car, where he asked his chauffeur to drop me at home. I was too stunned by the speed of things to protest. Before I knew it, I was back at Mira's apartment—and broke.

"He could have, at least, paid for my time," I take another sip of my whiskey. "In fact, if I had taken a picture of his face with the expression he wore when I told him I was a virgin, I could have hawked it on the internet. Or made T-shirts with the print of that picture and sold it on Etsy with the caption, *'How to shock a douchebag? Show him your V-card.'*" I trace a rectangle in the air with my fingers.

Mira swallows, her gaze trained over my shoulder. "Umm, Penny, I think you should—"

"Go ahead with it? I think so, too. Only, I didn't take a picture of his face—"

"Probably because you were otherwise occupied," a voice says from behind me. A voice which is low enough that I shouldn't have heard it over the conversation in the bar, but I do because... it's *his* voice. Heat sears my back. Now, I know why I have goosebumps all over my skin. I stare at Mira with horror.

She winces. "Sorry, babe, I tried to warn you."

"You could have thrown something at me, or knocked me out cold, or—" I squeeze my eyes shut. "I'm never going to live this down, am I?"

I sense her shaking her head. She touches my hand, then reaches over and asks, "Want me to stay for this?"

I manage to gather my wits about me, then crack open my eyes. "Go, please, and let me die quietly, on my own."

She has a worried look on her face. "Are you sure?"

The heat at my back turns up to furnace levels, and I know he's moved closer. My scalp tingles. My toes curl. And all this, because I'm in his presence.

She glances up at the man standing behind me. "The only reason I'm leaving her alone with you is because you're Abby's brother and I know you won't do anything to upset her best friend."

My cheeks catch fire. "Mira, please."

She continues to glare at him. "Well, what do you have to say for yourself?"

I wince. *No, no, you can't talk to that alphahole in that tone of voice. He's going to say something hurtful to her and—*

"I promise I won't do anything—not without her consent." He holds up his hand, palm face up.

She blinks. So do I.

We stare at each other, then I lean in toward her and whisper, "He used the 'c' word and I find that hot." *But I'd find it hotter if he took without consent. No, no, no I did not think that.*

She cups her palm over her lips. "Real life is not like my spicy books," she hisses back.

"I don't read smut." Only Dramione fan fiction. Something I've never told anyone and am not going to start now. "Bet he looks better than any fictional book boyfriend you've come across."

She scowls. "He's more like a villain."

"Now you know my catnip," I murmur.

She gasps, "Oh, my god, you did not say that. Also, didn't the two of you get off to a bad start?"

I bite the inside of my cheek. "That was then—" I pop my shoulder.

"Thought you didn't like him," she says in a suspicious tone.

"I don't. But—I'm curious about him, you know? He intrigues me."

I glance sideways to find said grumphole dark-haired Draco fingering his phone. *Lucky phone.* What the—I am not envious of his stupid phone. Am not. He meets my gaze and I look away.

"I'm not comfortable leaving you alone with him." Mira chews on her lower lip.

"I'll be fine." I pat her shoulder. "He's Abby's brother and he dotes on her. He's not going to hurt her friend in any way and risk her wrath."

"Hmm." Her frown deepens.

"No, no more hmm'ing. I'm a big girl. I can handle myself. Also"—I gesture to the bar—"we're not alone."

She doesn't look happy, but nods. "You'd better text me when you are on your way home. If you don't, I'll be calling the cops."

"Okay, mother." I hug her. "Thanks for looking out for me."

"Always, babe." She glances up at the man who's been standing quietly. "I'm going to leave now, but remember, if anything happens to her, if you so much as upset her, you'll have me to contend with. Also, I have the cops on speed dial, and if she doesn't message me to tell me she's on her way home in a few hours, I'm calling them." She jerks her chin in the now-silent Knight's direction, then back at me. "Don't forget to text me."

Silent Knight? Yeesh, my mind is totally going around in circles. "I will, promise."

She slides off the barstool, grabs her bag, and with a last warning glare at Knight, she leaves.

I stay where I am. So does he. The seconds stretch. No move from him. Around us, the noise in the bar turns up a notch. There are groups of men with ties-loosened, shooting the breeze. A couple who are eye-fucking each other sits at one of the tables. At another, two women are holding hands and smiling at each other, and a group of four at another table burst into laughter. Jackets have been flung over chairs and bags dropped to the floor as everyone lets off steam after the day's efforts. I'd do anything to join their tribe.

To get a job, and bank that monthly check has never felt more out of my reach. My nose tickles, and a pressure builds behind my eyes. *Stupid, stupid. I'm not going to cry, and definitely not when he's hovering behind me like some angel of death.* I snatch up my glass of whiskey, drain it, then gesture to the bartender. He reaches over with a bottle of whiskey to top me up, only to glance over my shoulder. He pales, takes a step back, and another, then spins around on his heels and walks off.

"Hey, stop, where are you—" I gasp, for *he* brushes past me. And he hasn't even touched me. All that happens is he disturbs the air around me, but tell that to all the cells in my body that sit up and take notice. Knight slips onto the barstool vacated by Mira.

I don't look at him. I stare straight ahead. Maybe if I keep quiet, he'll leave. *Do I want him to leave? Yes, I do. I don't want to see him again. So, why is all my attention focused on him?* We stay like that for a few seconds more, then he leans in toward me. I flinch, but all he does is grab the seat of my barstool and spin it, so I'm turned toward him. I draw in a sharp breath, and that familiar sea breeze and pepper scent of his laces my nostrils. Oh, my god. I smelled him yesterday, too, but I was so worried about how I was going to hold up, and so distracted by what he was doing to me, that I shoved it aside. But knowing he's seated right next to me seems to amplify the impact of his scent on my body. My nipples pebble, and that yawning emptiness between my legs seems to multiply ten-fold.

He's cast a net over me. The more I struggle, the more I seem to entangle myself in it. I keep my gaze focused on his chest—his broad chest clad in the usual black sweatshirt, which stretches across those massive shoulders. He's so big, I can't see around him. His presence is so potent, the rest of the world might as well have vanished. He draws in a breath and the muscles under his sweatshirt ripple.

Then he leans in so his thighs bracket mine. The emptiness between my legs is replaced by a throbbing heaviness. He pinches my chin, so I have no choice but to look up at him. My gaze meets his piercing green gaze, and a trembling grips me. *Gah, stop it. You should slap his face for the way he retreated from you so quickly yesterday.*

I open my mouth, but he speaks first, "I have a proposition for you."

10

Knight

"Eh?" She gapes at me. "What did you say?"

I lower my hand to my side. "I understand yesterday must have been a little out of the ordinary for you—"

"You think?"

"—which is the only reason I'm going to repeat myself. I have a suggestion for an arrangement which might benefit you."

Her gaze widens further until her blue eyes seem to swallow up her face. With her blonde hair and a pink dress that barely contains her curves, she's definitely not the kind of girl I'm normally attracted to. But then, I've rarely noticed the features of women I've been with, let alone the shapes of their bodies. One hole was as good as another—except when it comes to hers. And no one had been inside of her. Fuck me.

When she announced that yesterday, it was as if a building had collapsed on me. The reverberations from her proclamation managed to cut through the wall I'd built around myself during those days in captivity. I'd divorced myself from my body—locked away my feelings, my emotions, my humanity in a corner of my mind which I'd then isolated behind a barrier. And she—had managed to get through it.

She surprised me, and I wasn't able to stop myself from reacting—by running away from her. The shock of feeling something other than that hopelessness inside of me sent me packing. *Like the coward you are. When it came down to it, tough guy, you weren't cut out to be a soldier.* And then, I walked into the bar today and spotted her. She drew me to her like a magnet. Before I realized it, I was standing behind her. I wasn't sure what I was going to say to her—but putting forward a plan to her was not on my list.

Now, she firms her lips, then juts out her chin. "If you think I'm going to listen to you after you ran from me like I had the plague, then you are so mistaken, you—"

"You're right in being angry with me," I murmur.

She blinks. "I am?"

She's surprised. I don't blame her. Hell, I surprised myself with that statement. But needs must, and all that. She's pissed off, and if I were my natural self, she wouldn't listen to me. So, I'm going to turn on my charm and try to convince her. My charm always works, after all. I curve my lips.

She frowns. "What are you doing?"

"Trying to demonstrate that it's a good idea for you to listen to me."

"Well, if you're going to wear that grimace on your face—"

I straighten my mouth. "It wasn't a grimace."

"I was on the receiving end of it, so trust me when I say, it was painful to look at."

I stiffen my spine. Fuck that pretense. It's not me. Might as well lay it all out in black and white. "You will work for me."

"Excuse me?"

"You. Will. Work. For. Me," I growl.

She folds her arms across her chest. "And if I say no?"

The fuck? No one says no to me. Not even the team who followed me on my last mission; *and look what happened to them? You saw them tortured; you saw them die. You should have died, too. Why did you escape, you—*

"Mr. Warren?" She touches my shoulder. "Hey, Mr. Warren, sir?"

Did she say *sir?* My cock twitches. I snap out of my reverie and look down my nose at her.

"Ms. Michelle Easton. Suffers from advanced dementia, which has led to her rapid degeneration. You moved her from Gainesville, Florida to London so you could take care of her."

The color leaches from Penny's cheeks.

"She's confined to a care home the last three years and—"

"Stop, why are you telling me this?" she cries.

"Because you need the money to take care of her."

She flushes. "Are you blackmailing me?"

"It was an order, actually."

"An order?" she asks slowly.

I resist the urge to bark at her to stop wasting my time when we both know it's only a matter of time before she complies.

"You're ordering me to work for you?"

"Yes."

"And if I don't want to?"

"Like I said, I don't think you have the luxury of choice."

She tips up her chin. "I have other ways of making money."

"If you mean by pretending to be a submissive, you can drop that idea; you're no good at it."

Her color deepens. "I... I can use my body."

Anger twists my guts; a physical pain stabs me in my chest. "No," I snap.

"Excuse me?"

I look her up and down. "If you think anyone is going to pay for that, then you're being truly optimistic."

She draws in a sharp breath. "You're a horrible, horrible man. After how you acted yesterday, I should have ignored you, but I thought, you're Abby's brother; you've been through a lot the last six months. Which is why I gave you a second chance. Now, I know I made a mistake. You're a born asshole. I don't know how you have a wonderful person like Abby for a sister. You don't deserve her." She slides off the bar stool and straight into the space between my thighs.

And do I let her go? Of course not. She thinks of me as a bastard. May as well confirm that impression, hmm? I reach forward and slap my palms on her barstool so I've bracketed her in.

Her chest rises and falls, and her breathing grows unsteady. "Wh-what are you doing?" Her voice is unsteady.

"You don't think I'm going to let you go without being compensated in some way for the time you wasted yesterday, do you?"

"Hey, I'm the one who didn't get paid for the pleasure you derived from my—" She snaps her lips together.

"From your—?"

"From my body."

"On the contrary, I'm the one who made you almost come with my expert handling of your pussy, so it's you who owe me."

Her lips part, and her pupils dilate. Interesting. Is it because I used the P-word?

"Does your cunt miss the touch of my fingers?"

The pulse at the base of her throat drums faster.

"Does your arse feel the prints of my palm on it?"

She swallows.

"Did it hurt when you sat down, hmm?"

A jolt travels up her body.

So, she likes dirty talk. That's good. Not that I'm keeping track of everything she responds to; nothing like that. But the thought of her not agreeing to my proposition... Is not acceptable. And when I tried to turn on the charm, she saw right through me. Which is why I'm being so heavy-handed, including using her mom's needs to coerce her... Which is a shit move and isn't helping my case. I need to back the fuck off here and be strategic.

I lower my face until my nose is positioned in front of hers. I draw in her sweet breath and my thigh muscles harden. Goddamn. Another few seconds here, and I'll throw her down and have my way with her—which is crazy. I need to get through this conversation and seek out company of the feminine kind. A hole... *Any* hole will do. All those months without sex has warped my brain; that's all it is. I push my feet into the floor of the bar and straighten. She blinks, then glances about the bar, and her lips part. "Where is everybody?"

"They left."

"They left?"

"I needed to have a conversation with you."

"So, what? You bought the bar and ordered everyone to leave?" she scoffs.

"I know the person who owns the building. I called in a favor."

"Of course you did." She shakes her head. "I can't believe I didn't notice the space emptying out." She glances about the space again, then pauses. "And the bartender. Did you have anything to do with him leaving, as well?"

"He recommended you for a role you were scant qualified or equipped to handle. He was no friend."

"You're right. He was more of an acquaintance, but I'm sure he had my best interests at heart."

"*I* have your best interests at heart."

She tosses her head. "*Actually,* you have only *your* best interests at heart. It's why you marched in here and ordered me to accept the job."

"I only want to help you." I hold up my hands. "But if you want to refuse the chance to keep your mother in that care home, that's your prerogative."

11

Penny

"I'm so sorry, Ma, I thought I'd find a way to keep you here but I'm at my wit's end. I could have accepted that assho— Uh, Abby's brother's offer, but he's such a bast— Uh, unpleasant man, that I didn't think it was right to give him the chance to manipulate me. And he would have. If I'd gone to work for him, he'd use it to his advantage. I know that. And you know I'd have done such a good job for him. Working as an assistant to a hot-shot CEO is probably the only thing I haven't tried. And I have a feeling I'd be good at it. After all, the only thing I'm good at is typing, and I'm organized—mostly—and given my last two, no, three career options"—*If you include my attempt at becoming a submissive*—"didn't work out, I'm kind of up against it." I drag the comb through her greying locks. I'm seated behind her at the tiny dresser in her room at the care home.

Last night, Knight insisted on dropping me home. I was so taken aback by first, his announcement that he had the bar emptied so he could talk to me un-interrupted, then, he all but accused me of putting my interests before that of my mother. After which, he stayed silent all the way to my place. Now, he knows where I live, but that's the least of my worries. This morning, I woke up early and came to see my mother at the care home.

I have another twenty-four hours until her time here runs out, and I'm no closer to finding a way to pay the fees for the next month. Maybe Knight was right. If I weren't so prideful, I'd have accepted Knight's offer. I hunch my shoulders.

I did look into selling my body. I checked out the website where I heard women could strip and make money, and promptly clicked out of it. No way, do I have the courage to pose naked in front of a camera. As for going through with using my body for sex... I'm not sure where to start. I suppose, I could look for another place like the 7A Club, but the thought of anyone else's hands on me made me so nervous, I began to feel sick to my stomach. I shut my computer and pulled the covers over my head at two a.m. this morning.

I barely managed to get a few hours of sleep before coming to meet my mother. It helps to talk to her. She doesn't respond, but saying my issues aloud makes them feel lighter. The sound of my voice always seemed to soothe her. She also loves her hair being smoothed out. I place the comb down on the bed, then twist her hair up into a bun and pin it.

"There, that looks good, eh?" I glance up at her reflection in the mirror.

"Thank you, dear," she smiles at me. There's a twinkle in her eyes, and she seems so like the mother I once knew.

Then her forehead wrinkles. "You look so much like my daughter. What did you say your name was again?"

My nose stings. Tears prick the backs of my eyes. *I will not cry. I will not.* "It's Penny," I manage to choke out. "My name's, Penny."

"That's my daughter's name. What a coincidence." She laughs. "I must tell her the next time I see her. I'd tip you for your help, but I don't have money. I'll have to ask my daughter when she comes by." Her lips turn down.

"It's okay; don't worry. You don't need to tip me."

She's silent for several minutes before her forehead furrows and she laughs. "Of course I don't need to tip you. You're my daughter, silly girl."

"Mom!" I burst out. "Mom, you recognize me?"

"Of course I recognize you. I'm so happy you're visiting us. Eric should be home very soon—" Her gaze grows vacant. She stares through me, and I know I've lost her.

I don't know if it's worse when she doesn't recognize me at all or when she's coherent for a little while, then forgets who I am. And she thinks my father's alive. Not an unusual occurrence.

On a good day, she's coherent enough for us to have a normal conversation. There have even been a few days when she's been her cheerful self throughout the entire visit, though those days have been dwindling, of late. She grows more withdrawn and confused as the day wears on, which is why I prefer to come in the early part of the day to see her. How much longer will I be able to do that? How long can I keep pretending that the mother I knew isn't all but gone in flesh.

The ball of emotion in my throat grows bigger. I swallow around it and scan her features—pale cheeks, thin lips, hollows under her eyes. Vestiges of her beauty cling to her features, and if I stare hard enough, I can still see the animated mother who'd drive me home from school, play the piano in the mornings so I'd always wake up to the sound of one of her favorite sonatas, hold my father's hand and mine when they took me to my first opera as a birthday surprise... She gave up so much for my happiness, even turned her life upside down to move to another country, just to be close to me in London. And how do I repay her? By not even making it as an actress. Not being able to pay for her to remain in the home she's grown to love.

"I'm such a selfish daughter." I swallow down the tears that threaten to overwhelm. "I'm so sorry, Ma, I wasn't able to help. I'm sorry I was too self-involved to realize the true state of your health. But I promise, we'll find a way. I'll take you home. It's a flat I share with Mira, but you can have my bed. I'll sleep on the couch and—"

A knock on the door has me glancing toward it.

The manager of the place, Sunita, stands there. There's a grim look on her face, and her lips are pinched. Oh, god, I thought I had another twenty-four hours before having this conversation, but there's no putting it off. I place the comb on the dresser, then bend and kiss my Mom's cheek. "Let's get you into bed, shall we?"

I urge my Ma to her feet, and once she's in bed, I pull the covers over her, then step out of the room. Sunita shuts the door. We stand in the hallway, and she opens her mouth to speak, but I raise my hand. "I know what you're going to say, and I did everything I could to avoid it, I promise."

She just looks at me without saying a word.

I square my shoulders. " Honestly, I tried everything. If there was any other way out, I'd have taken it," I lie. "I don't want to move her out of here, but—"

She blinks. "You don't have to take her out of here, but you insist you're going to. What is the rationale behind that?"

"I thought I'd find the money to pay and keep her here, but—" I blink. "Hold on, did you say I *don't* have to take her out of here?"

She raises a hand. "That's what I've been trying to tell you. You don't have to move her."

"But I don't have the money to pay to keep her here."

Her scowl deepens. "What are you talking about?"

"That I've been unable to find a way to keep her here."

She leans forward on the balls of her feet. "But her bills have been paid."

I freeze, open and shut my mouth, but nothing seems to emerge. I seem to have disconnected from my body and am looking down at the scene unfolding. So, this is what a brain fart looks like?

"Penny?" Sunita waves her hand in front of my face. "Penny, you okay?"

I draw in a breath and my lungs burn. "Her bills have been paid?" I manage to choke out.

"Yes, and for the next twelve months."

"B-by whom?"

Her gaze widens. "You don't know who paid your mother's bills?"

I open my mouth to agree, then give myself an inward shake. *Don't kick a gift horse in the mouth. Take it and move on. You want your mother to stay here, don't you?*

"Ohhh, I know who did. It was my new boss."

"New boss?" She tilts her head. "You found a new job?"

"Yes, yes, I'm going to be the assistant to the CEO of Warren Media."

"Warren Media?"

"Yes, he's my friend Abby's brother. That's how I got the job, and as part of the deal, he—I mean, the company—agreed to pay for my mother to stay here."

She smiles. "That seems like a generous offer."

I shuffle my feet. It's a guess on my part to say it's Knight who paid the bills, but who else could it be? No one else I know has that much money to spend. But why would he do that? And for the next twelve months? I pull my phone out of my pocket and pretend to gasp. "Look at the time. I need to go meet my new employer."

"You're meeting him at five p.m.?" Her forehead furrows.

"Oh, yeah. I officially start tomorrow, but it's a preparatory session. These big companies—" I roll my eyes. "They're so particular." And now I can't stop the lies that spew out of my mouth. I wave my hand at her. "Well, thank you again for being so helpful. I gotta go." I brush past her and walk down the corridor and out of the building.

My head is swimming. A strange floating sensation fills my limbs. It feels like I'm in a dream, walking through a thick syrup. I manage to make it to the tube and head over to Knight's office building. I enter, march up to the reception and announce, "I'm here to meet Knight Warren."

"Do you have an appointment?" The receptionist sniffs.

"I don't, but he'll see me."

She looks down her nose at me. "I'm afraid he won't be seeing you if you don't have an appointment, and—"

"Penny?" His rough, hard voice rolls down my back. Sparks of awareness flicker off my nerve-endings.

The receptionist in front of me jumps to her feet so quickly, her chair overturns. Her face is flushed a deep red, and her pupils are dilated. OMG, is she going to have an instant orgasm right now? Not that my thighs are not quivering. And the inner walls of my pussy are clenching. My panties are not so drenched, I can feel the wet fabric sticking to my inner thighs. But seriously, does he have that effect on everyone?

It must feed his already inflated ego to see women melt into incoherent blobs of goo wherever he goes. As if to illustrate my point, the receptionist swallows, then stutters, "M-Mr. Warren, she doesn't have an appointment to—"

"She doesn't need one. She's my new assistant, Penny Easton."

The receptionist gapes. "Y-y-your new assistant?"

"Put her on the list of people who have twenty-four seven access to me."

"Twenty-four seven?" It's my turn to gape. I stare at him over my shoulder. "But I don't need twenty-four seven access."

"Yes, you do." He locks his fingers above my elbow, and tendrils of

heat vibrate out from his touch, arrowing straight to my core. My
nipples harden, and I find myself swaying toward him to draw in his
sea-breeze scent. Then, he's steering me around the receptionist's desk
and toward an elevator set at the far side of the lobby. He stabs the
button, and the doors open. He pushes me in, steps in after me, then
presses his thumb onto a pad.

The dashboard illuminates with a green light, and the car rises
upward. It's so smooth, it's only the progression of numbers in the floor
display panel that indicates our upward movement. The elevator doors
are buffed to a high polish that reflects back both of us. He releases me
and moves to stand to the opposite side of the car, putting as much
distance as possible between us, and a shiver runs down my spine. How
is it possible to miss his warmth when he doesn't mean anything to me?
He's an egotistical, pompous bastard who thinks no one can disregard
his orders.

"If you think paying for my mother's stay at the care home means
you've bought me, then you're—" I firm my lips, for he's turned those
startling green eyes on me. My words stick in my throat. Am I going to
deny why I came to see him? Sure, it was to tell him off, but also to say
I'd work for him.

The relief I felt knowing my mother doesn't have to leave the home
made me understand my priorities. It doesn't matter what I have to do
to keep her in there. Doesn't matter that I'm going to work for the devil
himself. Nothing matters as much as making sure she's comfortable and
safe and content in her last days. And the bastard knows it. That's why
he paid for her for the next twelve months. Which means, I'm effectively
bound to this job for that much time, at least. The fight goes out of me,
and I glance away.

He notices it but doesn't say a word. He could gloat about how he's
been proven right about the job, but he stays silent. The elevator slides
to a stop at the top floor of the building. He couldn't have his office
anywhere else but where he'd be the lord and master of all he surveys,
of course. The doors open, and he gestures for me to step out, then leads
the way. This time, he doesn't touch me. The first time I met him here, I
was too nervous about the prospect of working for him to take in my
surroundings. Now, I follow him past the rooms with executives still at
their desks—apparently, people here work late nights—a small conference room with two other executives engaged in discussion, then two

larger ones which are empty, and a workstation set outside double doors. He opens one and ushers me in.

I walk into what I know is his office. I noticed how spacious it was the last time, but this time, the details sink in. It has to be triple the size of the apartment I share with Mira.

Floor-to-ceiling windows cover one side, and I can see the Thames and the large imposing building which houses the MI5 on the opposite bank of the river. In the distance, the London Eye gleams in the late morning sun. He props a hip on the massive desk that is set against another bank of windows. There's a laptop, three screens, and a couple of papers stacked one on top of the other in a neat pile. Other than that, the surface is spotless. On the far end of the room is a bookcase—or rather shelves of a bookcase which are empty—that lines a wall, and in front of it is a seating area. There's a sofa with its back to the bookcase, a coffee table in front of it, and two chairs on either side. Next to it is a door which I assume leads to an ensuite bathroom. In another corner is a long table with chairs, and a screen on the wall—a space meant for more formal meetings. Next to that is a wet bar, and adjoining the room is a kitchenette. Whoa, it's a self-contained unit. A self-contained, not very lived-in unit. There's no art on the walls, no empty coffee cup, no pictures. Except for the papers on top of his work desk. It's a sterile room, with a stunning view dominating the space. Unable to resist the view, I walk over to the window and glance out.

The hair on the back of my neck rises, and I know he's watching me. I tighten my hold on my bag and continue to stare ahead. If I turn to him, I have to face the fact that I'm at his mercy. *And would that be so bad? What the—! I did not think that. I did not!* And I can't hide away by looking at the view, either.

"So,"—I point at the MI5 headquarters—"is it true that, though you were in the army, you were on a secret mission for the MI5 when you were captured?"

The silence in the space seems to deepen. The temperature seems to drop until it's frigid in here. I wouldn't be surprised to see my breath forming puffs of condensation in front of me. Goosebumps rattle up my skin. I mentally slap myself. Nice one, you went and said the one thing that he didn't need to hear. The one thing that's probably giving him flashbacks to his capture and to whatever was done to him there, and I had to bring it up.

I draw in a breath, then square my shoulders. "Okay, sorry, I shouldn't have said that. I don't mean to constantly bring back memories of your time as a prisoner of war. It's just—"

Heat sears my back. I turn and gasp, for he's standing right behind me.

12

Knight

"You want to know why I have this unrestricted view of the MI5 building from my office?"

She gulps, her bag slips from her shoulder, and I catch it, then lower it to the ground next to her. When I straighten, the color bleeds further from her features. Her fear is a visceral scent that zips straight to my groin, and my cock grows harder than it's been since I'd first seen her standing at my reception. Fucking woman. Can't stop myself from thinking of all the dirty things I want to do to her. Not when I'm away from her, and not when she's standing in front of me, all big eyes and blonde hair and pink lips parted in surprise. "Do you, Little Dove?"

"Do... Do I what?" she stutters.

"Don't make me repeat my question."

She pales further; her eyes dilate. She glances at the door, then back at me.

"I'm not letting you leave without answering," I drawl.

She manages to get a hold of herself and draws herself up to her full height, which still means, she's only at eye level with my chest. Not a surprise, considering how tall I am. Most women are diminutive in front of me. But I don't want to drop to my knees and press my face into the apex of their legs and draw deeply of their pussy scent, the way I want to with her. And if she doesn't speak soon, nothing is going to stop me from doing it right now, either.

She must read some of the intensity on my face, for she takes a step back, only to freeze when her shoulder blades touch the windowpane. She gulps, "N-no."

"No, what?"

"No, I don't know why you have this unrestricted view of the MI5 building from your office." Then, she flashes me a bright smile because, of course, that's what Ms. Sunshine and Happiness does.

"Let me enlighten you." I twirl my finger in the air.

She blinks, then slowly follows my lead and turns around to face the window again.

"Good girl."

She shivers, then a small cry escapes her lips, for I've grabbed one wrist, then the other, and shackled them behind her with my fingers. I kick her legs apart—good thing she's wearing a dress with a wide skirt that allows for movement— then I fasten the fingers of my free hand around her neck and push her cheek into the glass.

A trembling grips her. "Wh-what are you doing?"

"Do you want me to stop?"

She hesitates.

"Say the word, and I'll release you."

"Can I keep my job?" she says in a breathless tone.

"Are you accepting the job?"

"Isn't that why I'm here?"

"Is that not why you're here?"

She huffs. "Why do you have to answer every question with a question?"

"You know the answer to that."

She groans. "Okay, fine. I admit it. I came here to accept your job offer, though it was presumptuous of you to expect that when you saw me and"—her chest rises and falls—"and I don't want you to stop," she mumbles under her breath.

"What was that?"

She narrows her gaze and looks at me from the corner of her eyes. "You heard what I said."

"I need you to state it clearly."

"You're a bastard."

"Not legally, but in every other way, yes."

"I hate you."

I yawn. "Still not hearing the words, Little Dove."

"Don't call me that," she protests.

"I'll call you want I want, when I want. Better get used to that."

"You're not selling this—whatever it is—so you know."

"What I do know is that your breasts are aching, your nipples are hard enough to cut through the glass against which you're plastered, and if I cup your pussy, your panties will be wet from the evidence of your arousal. So, can I hear from your lips that you want me to continue manipulating your body? Otherwise, I'm going to release you on the count of three, two, on—"

"Fine, I don't want you to stop," she bursts out.

"And what is it you want me to do you?"

She squeezes her eyes shut. "Why are you making this so difficult?"

I lean in until my breath raises the hair on her head. "The more difficult things are to attain, the sweeter the reward."

The pulse at the base of her throat beats faster. "Is that a military saying?"

"Doesn't matter. The only thing of relevance is that you put yourself in my hands and now, you will be rewarded." I push my knee forward so the ridge of my thigh chafes against the crotch of her sodden panties.

She gasps, "Oh, god."

I release my hold on her wrists, only to flatten one of her palms against the glass, then the other. "Hold on."

I grasp her hips, pull back my leg, then slide it forward again. She pushes her palms into the glass, then bends her knees so she's seated firmly on my thigh. "Good girl. Now, let me take you to the edge."

I increase the pressure around her neck enough for her to pant. Then, I begin to saw my leg back and forth between her thighs. Each time I thrust forward, I increase the pressure on her clit. Each time I pull back, I slow down to ensure she feels every tendon of my thigh. She moans and whines and tries to wriggle away even as she pushes down her butt and tries to increase the surface area of contact between us. She arches her back, her legs quiver, and I know she's close. "Mr. Warren, I'm so close."

"Sir," I growl.

She hesitates.

I lick up her cheek. "Sir. You call me Sir from now on, understand?"

She shudders. "Yes, Sir, Mr. Warren, Sir."

The sound of her voice in that subservient voice sends my pulse rate spiking. The blood thuds behind my eyes, at my temples, in my balls. She arches her spine, her hips jerk and that's when I know she's close, so close. I press my cheek against hers. "You ready to come?"

She nods.

"Open your eyes. Watch how the world out there watches you hump my leg as you're poised to fall apart in front of them."

She cracks open her eyelids and peers outside from under her heavy eyelids.

"Good girl."

She moans, and her entire body constricts with a tension that radiates out from deep inside of her. She's at the edge. That's when I release her. I step back, keeping my hand on her shoulder until I'm sure she's capable of standing on her own. Then, grabbing her bag and spinning around, I walk over to sit down at my desk. I place her bag on the top and watch as she stays plastered against the window for a few more seconds. Then, as understanding dawns that I'm no longer holding her up, her entire body grows rigid. She turns and realizes that I'm seated at my desk.

"What..." she croaks. "What are you doing?"

"Attending to my work. Which, if you want to keep your job, is what you'd do, too." I lower my gaze to my phone and swipe down the screen. *Wait for it. Wait for it. In 3-2-1...*

She stomps over to my desk, then swipes the few pieces of paper on it to the floor.

13

Penny

"You asshole. How dare you toy with me?" I snap.

He yawns. Bastard yawns and continues to study the screen. Anger blasts through my veins. I reach forward, grab the phone from his hand, and throw it over my shoulder.

His jaw hardens. He raises his gaze slowly to mine, and a pulse ticks at his jaw. *Uh-oh, what I did wasn't very wise, eh?* I take a step back, and another. He rises to his feet and keeps rising--because he's so freaking tall—and I have to tip my head back to see his face. He holds out his palm. *What? Oh.* I turn, scamper to where the phone lies face down and bend to pick it up, then gasp when his big hands grab on my waist and hold me in place. "You shouldn't have done that, Little Dove."

"It's your fault! You drove me to it, you unfeeling brute, you piece of — Ah!" I cry out as he spanks my backside. Not again. He wraps his arm about my waist and hauls me up to my feet because, of course, I weigh nothing to him, then turns and walks over to his chair. He sits down and splays me across his lap. I wriggle around, try to escape and come in contact with that solid column in his pants. Instantly, I stop my movements, but my pussy recognizes that I'm very close to the one thing that can put me out of my torment. *Damn him, damn him for always getting the upper hand.*

"You're a bully, a horrible man who's intent on torturing me and—" I squeal as he flips up my dress and brings his heavy hand down on my butt cheek. Not again. What is it with this man and my ass? He seems to constantly find ways to touch it and tap on it and oh—He massages the butt cheek he hit, and the heat of his palm sears me through my panties. He rubs the ache through my asscheek, and it sinks through my blood and circles my clit. I can't stop the whimper that leaves my mouth, can't stop myself from squeezing my thighs together to clamp down on the ache that blooms between my legs.

"You like that, hmm?" His hard voice rumbles over me, and that only sends my nerve-endings skittering in delight.

"You know I like it. You know I want your touch. You know also how much I hate that you can get my body to respond to you. And you know I need this job, and yet, you're intent on breaking every possible rule of etiquette between us."

"Etiquette?" His voice sounds almost puzzled.

I shove my hair out of my eyes and glance up at him over my shoulder, "You're my boss, and I'm supposed to be your assistant. There's meant to be a professional relationship between us, but you've been overstepping that line—no, trampling all over that line—since I walked into the room. In fact, you've been coming onto me since we met and—" I swallow the rest of my words as he lifts me up and plants me on my feet next to his chair. The fabric of my dress flows down over my thighs. He holds his hands on my waist long enough to ensure I'm not going to stumble. Then, he lowers his arms, and jerks his chin toward the table.

"What?" I scowl.

"My phone."

"Oh, right." I place the phone clutched in my hand on the table.

"You may leave now, Ms. Easton."

I gape at him, too shocked to move. Did he dismiss me after what he did to me? Can I expect an apology from him? No. Can I report him for his misconduct... To whom? He owns this company, so the HR person would answer to him. Besides, I need this job. So, I'm going to put up with everything he did because— He's my best friend's brother, and a complete dick, and *his* dick had felt so good when I'd felt it pulse against my pussy.

He places his phone face down on the desk and turns to his laptop. He begins to tap away at the keyboard, and I'm sure he's forgotten all about my presence. I shake my hair back from my face, then grab my bag from his desk and head for the exit.

"Also, I'm sorry."

I pause, then turn around to face him. "Did you say what I think you did?"

He raises a shoulder. "I seem to forget myself around you, but you're right. I need to maintain a professional relationship, now that you're my employee. It won't happen again. Not unless you want it to, that is."

So that wasn't really an apology. What a piece of work he is. I don't want anything to do with him. I don't.

I turn to leave again, and he calls out, "HR is on the floor below. Have them onboard you, and I'll see you at your desk tomorrow at eight a.m."

"So that's it? You're working for him?"

I pull up my legs and wrap my arms about my bent knees. "I guess?" I slouch into the sofa and watch as Mira rustles up dinner for us. The HR induction had gone okay—I guess. Except for the pitying look I got from the HR manager. When I asked her what the problem was, she let slip that everyone tends to give Knight a wide berth. He's only been in this position a few weeks, but his reputation as being very difficult to work with has spread throughout the building—which his family owns. Also, he's been through an assistant a day since arriving. Not one has lasted past lunch time. And yes, there's a betting pool going on for how long I'm going to last. They don't realize I don't have a choice. I have to grit my teeth and bear it because that's my only option. I'm already in the asshole's debt.

Mira plates out the spaghetti, then slides one across the breakfast counter. "Let's eat."

"I'm not hungry."

"You need to maintain those curves—"

"That's what he said."

She frowns. "What are you talking about?"

"Nothing." And no, I'm not insecure about my plus size figure. I like how I look. I'm a big girl, and although I'm not tall, my curves compensate for my lack of height. Certainly, Knight hasn't complained once as he's squeezed my ample butt. Also, I like to eat... Normally. So, why have I lost my appetite? I unfold myself from the sofa then walk over to take my place on the barstool. "Do you think I'm making a mistake?"

Mira waits until she's swallowed the mouthful she's eating. "A mistake?"

"Agreeing to work for Knight?"

I nod, then twirl some of the strands of spaghetti around my fork before sliding them inside my mouth. The tart flavors of tomato and the tanginess of the garlic seep into my tongue. "It's delicious. Thanks for making dinner."

"Of course, sweetie." She eats some more of her food, then eyes me closely. "I've never seen you this disturbed. Not even when you thought you had less than twenty-four hours to find a solution for keeping your mother in the care home."

"I never lost faith that I'd find a solution. I just didn't think the solution would be this one."

"So, you go to work for him. What's the problem?"

"I feel beholden to him. He paid for my mother staying on in the care home and now, I feel I have no option but to work for him, you know? It's not a feeling I like. I feel like I'm not in control anymore, like I have no option but to continue working for him, even if I don't want to." I place my fork back on my plate.

She pops a shoulder. "Maybe this will force you to stay focused and see this job through."

I blink. "Are you saying I can't focus? I know I'm not good at seeing things through. I like anything new and shiny and can't stop myself from chasing them." I hunch my shoulders.

"Oh, honey, I didn't say that to make you feel bad." She leans over and puts her arm around my shoulders. "All I'm saying is, since it cuts down on choices, you'll have to double down and concentrate on the job, which might help ground you."

Only, he'll be there. Seeing him, working with him, watching him, smelling him, trying not to stare at him all through the working day... It's going to be torment—sweet torment, but torment, nevertheless. And how am I going to get through my time working for him, without sleeping with him, or worse, falling for him? Because I'm not so good at separating my emotions from the physical. And he doesn't seems capable of reciprocating any sentiments, either.

Something of my thoughts must show on my face, for she stares. "Did you sleep with him?"

"What? No!"

When she narrows her gaze, I lower my hand to my side.

She steps back then surveys my features closely. "You *did* sleep with him."

"What? Of course, not." *Not yet, that is.* Not ever, if I have my way, which doesn't mean anything. When it comes to Knight, my ability to say no is non-existent.

"Penny!" Mira warns.

"What? It's the truth." I bring more spaghetti to my mouth, then begin to chew.

"You told me when you met him at the club, nothing happened."

"Nothing happened then," I insist.

"But something did happen, since?"

I widen my gaze. "I'm not lying, I didn't sleep with him."

"But you kissed him."

I choke, then cough. Mira slaps my back, and I reach for the water and swallow down the piece stuck in my throat.

"Not exactly... I might have, uh, crossed the boundary of what's professional, but he's the one who initiated it."

"Hmm." She has a speculative look on her face.

I wipe the tears that have rolled down my cheeks due to my coughing fit. "No, seriously, the man's an animal."

"I see." Her lips quirk slightly. "I mean, I'm all for you riding that grumpy, gloomy, wounded warrior of a stallion. The sex will, surely, be an experience."

"He's my boss. That would make things very uncomfortable."

"It's not like you're sleeping your way into a job or anything."

I blush harder.

"Oh, my god! Did he offer you a job because you and he—" She pinches the fingers of her hands then brings them together. "Is that why he paid for your ma to stay on in the care home?"

"First, when it comes to Knight, it's not like I have a choice. He, uh, made a move on me, and I couldn't resist him. And he paid my mother's bills because he likes to have a hold on me. He likes to manipulate people. That's what he does. Also, this conversation is now giving me a headache, so can we change it?"

A line forms between her eyebrows. "But, Penny, you—"

My phone rings, thank god. I scramble off the barstool and walk toward the coffee table where I left it. "It's Abby."

I bring her up on FaceTime.

"I'm so happy you're taking the job." Abby's features are wreathed in a smile. "This is going to be great! I know it."

Not sure she'd feel that way if I told her about all that transpired between her brother and me. Not that I'm going to... yet.

"Uh, yeah, I'm excited." I flash her a smile.

"You're going to be good for him, Penny, I just know it."

"Um —" I clear my throat. "It's not like I've been an assistant before or anything."

"But you've held down so many jobs, you have the experience to roll with the punches, you know?"

I wince.

She purses her lips. "I know Knight's not the easiest person to be with, which is why you're going to be great at being the intermediary between him and the rest of the office."

Mira walks over to glance over my shoulder. "Hey, Abby!"

"Hey, Mira. Gosh, you girls are hanging out together, and I'm so envious. I wish I could be there."

"You're with your hot husband. Please. I'm sure you'd rather be there than with us," Mira scoffs.

A man's voice calls out to her from off screen. Abby blushes a little, then turns to us. "Sorry, guys, Cade can be a little possessive."

"A little?" I laugh.

"Okay, okay, a lot." She chuckles. "Before I go, I wanted to invite both of you to our place tomorrow evening. We're having a small get-together to welcome Knight back. Nothing fancy. Just a way of showing our thanks to everyone for standing with us while he was away, and... Uh... Also, so he can meet his friends again, you know?" She bites down on her lower lip. "He's been spending so much time on his own. All he does is go to work, then go running or hit the gym, and come back home. He doesn't socialize. Not even with Cade or Declan, and these are the guys he'd hang out with almost every evening. He's changed so much." She hunches her shoulders. "I'm worried about him."

"You're a good sister, Abby," I say softly.

She shakes her head. "If I were a good sister, I'd push him to go see a therapist, but if I do, he'll only get upset and stop talking to me. So, I'm taking it step-by-step with him. Also, he works too much. He needs to unwind a little and take time off to relax, you know?" She nods at me. "I'm hoping you can help with this, Penny."

"Me?" I ask, surprised.

"You'll be working with him, so perhaps, you can make him see sense?"

14

Knight

"I'll meet the salesforce at noon. Cancel my one o'clock, bring forward my two o'clock, then I'll meet the programming personnel at two p.m., followed by the meeting with my father at three, and—"

"Wait, was that to change your meeting to two p.m. or bring it forward, or—" She glances up at me and pales under the weight of my glare. "Uh, bring it forward. Got it."

Her hair has come undone from her messy bun and hangs in tendrils around her features. She's wearing a skirt and jacket—pink, of course—which fits her curves like it was painted on. The buttons of her jacket strain across her ample bosom. The neckline dips enough to hint at the valley between her breasts. It's a functional office suit, but on her, it might as well be a seductive evening gown. Clearly, she wore it to taunt me. She wore it, knowing I was going to be hard as soon as I saw her. In fact, my cock has been in a state of painful arousal since she walked into the room this morning—late, by a full five minutes.

Before I could tell her off, the scent of roses wafted over to me, and my heartbeat had spiked. My pulse rate galloped, and I was unable to do anything but stare as she sashayed over to me with her tablet in her hands and began reading out my day's appointments.

"What about lunch?" she stops typing into her tablet long enough to ask.

"What about it?"

"Don't you need time off for lunch?"

"I don't eat lunch."

"Oh, well, I need an hour off from twelve-forty-five to—"

"Not happening."

"Excuse me?" Her lips twitch as if she's trying not to smile, and not succeeding. "Did you say—"

"You heard me. Don't pretend otherwise. We work non-stop in this office."

"That's illegal; you can't do that."

"Tell that to the employees who're happy to be compensated for working through their lunch hour."

She sets her jaw. "We're humans, not machines."

I'm not. I lost my humanity somewhere after I was hit for the hundredth time. You bet, I kept count of it, and returned it with interest. I made sure they saw my face, made sure they knew who had come for them. Made sure they saw my intention in my eyes when I grabbed my captor's gun and shot him down, along with everyone else in that facility. Then Adam and I ran out of there and—

"Uh, Mr. Warren, Sir?"

Her husky voice cuts through the noise in my head. It recedes, leaving behind a calm. *How the fuck is that possible?* I ran half the night, trying to stop the voices in my head. When that didn't help, I called Adam who was only too happy to meet up to work out with me at my home gym this morning. By the time I got into work, every muscle in my body hurt, but my mind had not ceased its chatter... Until she called me by the title I asked her to.

Is she even aware of the impact she has on my body?

"Are you okay?" she asks softly.

I turn away and focus on my computer screen. "Get me my coffee, and starting tomorrow, don't come to my office without it. And you need to collect my suits from the dry cleaners and have them delivered to my apartment, and—"

"Hold on, I'm your assistant, not your housekeeper."

I shoot her a look from under my eyes. "You're in my debt for the next twelve months. You'll be anything I want you to be."

Color flushes her cheeks. "This is insane. You're infringing on all kinds of human resource regulations here, surely, and your team needs to eat. If they take a break, it only increases their productivity. Just because you thrive on working and feed off adrenaline and like to feed on human blood and tears, doesn't mean the rest of us have to follow the same schedule." She stops, her chest rising and falling. The buttons of the jacket across her bust stretch, and I eye them with interest. *Can I make her angry enough that she draws in a breath and one of them might pop, giving me more of an eyeful of her sweet curves, I wonder?*

"Hey, my face is up here."

"But my interest lies in what you have below."

I gape then recover myself long enough to scoff, "That's such a sexist thing to say."

I lean back in my chair. "I'm that and much worse, as you're aware."

"You seem to wear your misogynistic tendencies on your sleeve like you're proud of it."

I raise a shoulder. "I don't care either way. Also, save your righteous indignation. The staff are allowed to take an hour off for lunch, just not you."

She stares. "That's insane."

"Welcome to my world. Now, get gone, I have work to do."

She opens her mouth as if to say something else, then pivots with such force, the device slips from her hand and falls to the floor. She bends, presenting me with the perfect view of her heart-shaped, curvaceous behind. The skirt stretches across the expanse of that gorgeous arse, and I almost come in my pants. A groan swells my throat, and I reach for my bottle of coke and empty it. It only fuels that fire inside of me, so I feel like I'm being consumed by an inferno of need, of lust, of such craving to be buried inside of her that I know I need to do something about this ache, fast.

She wriggles her butt as she straightens, and my balls harden. *F-u-c-k, she did that on purpose.* She pushes out her chest, then heads for the door, seemingly unaware of the destruction left behind. Before the door snicks shut, I push up from my chair, and stalk into the ensuite toward the sink.

I stare at myself in the mirror, grip the edge of the counter, and undoing my belt and zipper, shove my pants down. My dick springs free. I grab it and squeeze from base to crown, and again. A vein pops at my temple, my cheeks are flushed, and my eyes blaze with a desire I thought I'd never see in them again. I thought they'd beaten every emotion out of me, squeezed every last drop of humanity through my pores, electrocuted the will to sense passion, intensity, fervor, ardor— I was sure I'd never feel halfway human again. But as I take in my reflection and see the life-force pulse through the veins of my throat and my face, and feel it pump through my cock, I know, I'm slowly coming back to life. *Thanks to her.*

The pressure builds at the base of my spine. I drag my fist up my rigid shaft, squeezing the precum out so it overflows the sides. "Bloody hell," I growl. "Bloody fuck, Penny, I'm going to come."

A prickling sensation seizes my skin. I glance to the side and spot her watching me from the entrance of the bathroom. Her lips are parted, her chest rises and falls, and her cheeks are almost as pink as her jacket. Her gaze is wide and lowered, and I know she's watching me knead my cock. Down to the base and up, again and again. I increase my pace, and the slap of flesh against flesh fills the room. My balls draw up, and with a growl, my cum sprays across my shirt. I jerk my chin at her. "Come here."

Without hesitation, she walks to me.

"On your knees," I growl.

She sinks down, and I paint my cum over her lips. She slips her tongue out, licks it up, and it's as if tasting me on her mouth brings her to her senses. "Oh, my god!" She flushes, then jumps up and scampers off.

I admit I don't take my gaze off the twitching of her backside until she's out of sight. Then I clean myself up, change out my shirt and pants, and toss the used clothes into a laundry basket in the corner, before walking out to my desk.

"There you are." My father looks up from where he's standing by the window. "I need to talk to you."

15

Penny

"I... I... I saw him jerk off." There. I said it aloud. So what if it's only to myself in the ladies room? I had to get it off my chest. The worst thing? It was so hot. Soooo hot.

I went back to ask him something—what it was, I can't remember, and you can't blame me for that. I saw my boss wank himself off, and it was the most erotic experience of my life. *How pathetic am I?*

I stare at my face in the mirror. My cheeks are flushed; my lips are parted and seem swollen, as if he's been kissing them. Though he hasn't. Fact is, we've never kissed. He seems to be attracted to my body, but clearly, it has nothing to do with tenderness or feeling. It's purely lust that draws him to me. And the only reason my lips are puffy is because of my state of arousal. *It's not because he painted my lips with his cum, and I licked it off. Then found the taste so enticing, I licked them again and again. Nope, nah I did not do that.* I totally did that. Seeing him squeeze his monster cock—P.S. that massive ego of his is justified— the way his fingers wrapped around his shaft, and his biceps stretched the sleeves of his shirt as he wrenched his hand up to the crown and down, is a sight I'm not going to forget for as long as I live.

Each time he squeezed down, his entire body went rigid. The muscles of his thighs strained against his pants. The tension shimmered off of him. The heat of his body reached out to me, even though I was standing a few feet away. And I smelled the sea-breeze of him, laced with the scent of his sweat and something more complex, more musky and earthy, which could only be his arousal. I knew I should leave, but not even a bomb going off next to me could have tempted me to drag my gaze away from the lewd act of my boss pleasuring himself.

And watching him take care of himself had seemed dirty, and obscene, and it made my pussy drip like a melting ice-cream cone. The emptiness inside of me amplified until every part of me felt needy and wanting, and so very desolate. Everything in me wanted to go to him, drop to my knees in front of him, and take him down my throat so I could taste him.

So, when he indicated I should go to him, it was as if he had a chain attached to my cunt and yanked on it. I scurried over, and he rewarded me with his cum on my lips. I flick out my tongue and lick my lips, and oh, god, the salty, earthy, musky taste of him fills my senses again. I allowed him to smear himself on my lips before he kissed me— If only he kissed me. *What's this obsession with wanting him to kiss me? But why hasn't he wanted to kiss me yet?*

I scowl at my reflection. There you go, building dreams about a man who only sees you as a plaything. A man who has too many devils of his own. A man suffering from PTSD from whatever he went through, and who refuses to acknowledge it. A man who is now focused on building his empire to the exclusion of anything else. A man who, certainly, does not do relationships—except for the carnal kind. *And would I be happy with that? Would I be happy as his fuck-toy?* My breasts seem to swell, and my nipples tighten. My body is very clear about its response. My mind and my logic, however, are waving red flags. I need to...

Move on from the sex-starved dreams I'm beginning to have about my boss. Except now, the image of him wanking off is burned into my brain. It's a tableau I'm going to pull out every time I need to orgasm. In fact, thinking of it now is turning my knees to mush. I grip the edge of the sink and take a few breaths. Count back from five-four-three-two-one.

I draw in a breath, then another, getting a hold of myself. Then, I lean forward and run water over my hands, dry them, and walk out, up the corridor to my desk. As I take my seat, an older gentleman walks out of Knight's office. His jaw is set, his steps determined. He strides off without noticing me. Something about the set of his shoulders and his gait reminds me of Knight. Guess that must be his dad, the man who started this company.

There's a loud bang. I jump and turn to find the doors to Knight's office are now closed. He must have slammed them shut. Guess there's something—or someone—who ruffles his composure, huh? For the next hour, the doors to his office stay that way. The entire floor is silent. The other executives in their offices must also be focused on their work.

I shift around Knight's appointments and reply to his emails, to the extent I can, and flag the ones on which I need his input. After another half hour of concentrating on the screen, my vision begins to blur. I roll my shoulders. I need some caffeine. I'd prefer a chai tea latte, but since I don't dare step out to a coffee shop, I guess I'll have to make do with the coffee machine in the kitchen. I grab my phone, then head toward the kitchen, which is at the other end of the floor. The walk is welcome, though. I pass by the conference rooms and the offices of the few other executives on this floor before I reach the coffee machine. As I wait for it to fill my cup, I message Mira.

Me: You have no idea what happened today.

She replies at once.

Mira: Let me guess. You ran into your dishy boss and then he pushed you over his big executive desk and the two of you had office sex?

Me: You think I'm living in a smutty office romance, don't you?

Mira: Hey, I'd give anything to live in a smutty office romance with a sex-on-sticks boss.

Me: It's nowhere as smutty as your books.

It's smuttier. But I'm not going to tell her that.

Mira: Ha, somehow with that eye-candy in your face all day I doubt it. But what were you going to tell me? What happened today?

I begin to type out the incident, then erase my words. Can I tell her I saw a glimpse of my boss' pecker, and that he was jerking off to thoughts of me, and yep, that was sensual and carnal and raunchy, and I'd want to have him come all over me next time? I squeeze my eyes shut. *No, no, no I can't say that.* It's bad enough I'm admitting it to myself. To tell her would be akin to confessing how much of a slut I am.

My phone buzzes, and I yelp. I glance at the screen, and it's an unknown number, so I decline it. It rings again; I decline it again. Then, another message pops up.

Unknown: How dare you not take my calls?

Unknown: Also, why aren't you at your desk?

Unknown: My office. Now.

Of course, it's him. And how did he get my number? Probably from HR. I change his name in my contact list, so the message now reads:

SirKnighthole: My office. Now.

Okay, so that was childish. But it makes me feel better. The three dots at the bottom of the message move again.

SirKnighthole: Why are you not here?

. . .

SirKnighthole: Don't keep me waiting.

Oh, my god! This man is certified. I message Mira.

Me: Gotta go. The bosshole is calling.

The phone begins to ring again. I grab my coffee, flavor it with pumpkin spice syrup, then add some cream and a spoonful of sugar. I take my time mixing it all in, then walk back to Knight's office.

The double doors to his room stand open and I enter, holding the coffee in one hand, and my phone in the other. "What's the hurry? Where's the fire? Why are you—" I spot Abby seated in one of the chairs in the seating area with Knight standing opposite her.

"There you are." Abby's face lights up. I walk toward her, and she embraces me. "Hope we didn't pull you out of anything important?'

"Whatever it was, this is more important," Sir Knighthole growls.

Abby scowls at him. "That's not very nice."

"No, it's not," I say sweetly in his direction.

Knight ignores me and directs his words at his sister. "Anyway, this entire scheme is not going to work. This is not something she can deliver on. She's barely managed to juggle my appointments for the day, and you think she's capable of drawing up a list of likely candidates for the role?"

"Oh, shush. Penny has the patience and the temperament, and she'll be able to interview the candidates without pissing them off. Unlike—" She narrows her gaze on him.

Knight snorts, then he folds his arms across his chest and widens his stance, impatience written into every angle of his body.

I look between them. "What are you talking about? Draw up a list of candidates for what role?"

"Uh, it might sound a little unorthodox, but this is going to be the only way out." She wrings her hands. "My father isn't the easiest person to get along with, as I've told you before. And he was never happy that Knight joined the military. Of course, he's thrilled that he's back now, but there's a problem."

"Clearly, he's not that happy, since he's trying his best to kick me out of the company, but I'm not having any of it." Knight leans forward on the balls of his feet. "Nothing is going to stop me from taking over from him and making more money than he ever did in his lifetime. And I'll do it in less than half the time it took him, too." He shoves a hand inside the pocket of his slacks—his new slacks.

It didn't skip my attention that he's changed his clothes since I last saw him. My cheeks heat at the reason for that. Images of him fisting his gigantic cock as he groaned my name crowd my mind. He must sense the direction of my thoughts, for his lips curl. His green eyes, though, are chips of glacial nothingness. Whatever I glimpsed in them as he orgasmed is gone. It's as if the only time he feels something is during sex —whether he's pushing me to the edge or masturbating.

"So, what do you think, Penny?" Abby's voice cuts through my thoughts.

"Think about what?" I turn to her.

"About what I told you?"

"Oh, sorry, my mind drifted for a second. What was your question?"

"Will you help Knight find a wife?"

16

Knight

Her eyes widen. "Did you say *a wife?*"

Abby nods, and Penny starts laughing.

Abby chuckles, then says, "It sounds ridiculous, but it's the only way Knight can take over the company from my father."

"Did I miss something?" She blinks rapidly. "He needs a wife in order to take over the company?"

"A condition my father only saw fitting to tell me just a little while ago." I manage to school my features into a bored expression. My father caught me by surprise. I'd anticipated he'd make me pay for the years I spent away in the military and for turning my back on the company he built, but this stipulation of his was not something I could have seen coming.

"Wait, I'm confused." Penny shifts her weight from foot to foot. "Aren't you the CEO of this company?"

"The CEO looks after the day-to-day running of the company. The Chairman of the Board has the final say on all decisions of the company," I say in a voice that's meant to sound condescending.

And it does, for she scowls in my direction.

"The position of Chairman is currently held by my father, and for me to take over from him, I need to be married."

"And within the month," Abby chimes in. "Also, he has to produce an heir within the year."

"Wha—?" Penny shakes her head. "I'm afraid this is all waaay over my pay grade. You'll have to explain to me what your being married has to do with your becoming the head of the company."

"My father believes whoever is at the head of the company needs to be someone settled in life, someone who's a family man, in order to prevent any scandals from rocking the future of the corporation." Abby places her fingers together. "Our father refuses to concede on this point."

She glances in Abby's direction. "So, why don't you take over?"

Abby laughs. "And inherit the ton of problems that go with it? No, thank you. I'm happy focusing on PR—and for the time being, helping Knight with the PR of this company, and then I have Cade. Call me old-fashioned, but I want time to focus on my marriage and Cade and our future together." Her features soften, her eyes shine, and for a few seconds, I'm envious of the happiness my sister has found.

Sure, Cade was an asshole, in terms of how he got her to fall in love with him. But apparently, they're happy now. And my sister is content. I've seen how Cade looks at her, how they look at each other. They are soulmates, despite needing to get past their checkered history to get there. And now, they have each other's support; they are each other's best friends and life partners. Something I will never have, for not another soul will understand what I've been through.

"Of course, it's not like someone getting married means there are no scandals that follow, but that's my father's archaic thinking for you." Abby rolls her eyes.

"Okay, fine, so he"—Penny jerks her chin in my direction—"has to get married to hold onto the company. That's his problem."

"You're my employee, so it's your problem," I insert smoothly.

She blinks rapidly. I glare at her, and she pales, then ducks her head, and takes a sip of whatever she has in her mug. "I think, uh, I need to sit down." Then, before I can give her permission, she walks over to the sofa and plonks down on the corner nearest to Abby. Of course, her cup sways, and some of the liquid sloshes over onto her skirt. "Oh, no, and this is my favorite, too." She places the mug on the coffee-table, then glances around.

"Here—" Abby reaches into her bag, pulls out a packet of tissues and hands it over. Penny pulls one out and dabs at the blot on her dress. "No, no, no, why do I always spoil my clothes like this."

Because you are adorably clumsy?

Did I use the word adorable*?*

I shake my head. "Leave it, woman, you're only making it worse."

"But the spot stands out against the pink." She balls up the tissue in her hand, and her lips droop down.

Of course, you could take it off and work the rest of the day with your panties and your gorgeous thighs on display — in my office, of course. Wouldn't let you show that to anyone else.

Fucking hell, the lack of sleep is getting to me, clearly.

I straighten. "So, it's settled. You'll draw up a list of eligible women who meet the criteria, and I'll choose one from them."

"Wait, what?" she yelps. The phone slips from her hand and falls to the settee next to her. "How do I know what the criteria —"

"Because you're going to draw it up for me."

She begins to shake her head. "I wouldn't know where to start."

"I'll help you." I allow my lips to curve a little.

She scowls. "Uh, I'm not sure that's such a good idea."

"Nonsense, it's a great idea. We'll get dinner tonight, and I'll walk you through my requirements."

"See, I knew this would work out." Abby rises to her feet. "The two of you work so well as a team."

Penny scowls.

I nod. "Thanks, sis." I walk toward Abby and take her arm to guide her toward the door. "I knew I could count on you."

"Wait, wait, I'm coming, too." Penny jumps up and dashes in our direction.

I see Abby out, then shut the door, turn and push my shoulders against them. "Where do you think you're going, Ms. Easton?"

"Uh, I have work to do." Penny slows to a stop a good four feet in front of me. Like that would stop me from touching her, if I wanted to. But I'll allow it, considering I need help in locking down suitable candidates to fulfill this damnable stipulation my father has concocted.

"Put everything else on hold. Your priority is to find me a wife."

"This is crazy. Are you hearing yourself? I cannot find you a wife. This is the twenty-first century. One doesn't go sourcing wives in the market."

"You're right about one thing. It is a market."

She shuffles her weight from foot to foot. "I've no idea what you're talking about."

"I'll pay a million dollars when the woman marries me, and then a million for every year we stay married. Plus, I'll add two million for every kid she produces—once I confirm the offspring is mine, of course, via DNA testing."

She gapes at me. "Do you think you can buy anything?"

"Do you think I can't buy everything?" I step forward; she skitters back. Damn, but I find her skittishness around me so damn alluring. The fact that she, clearly, dislikes me and hates that her body responds to me but is powerless to stop it sends a jolt of adrenaline shooting through my veins. I advance on her, and her big, blue eyes grow enormous. She slides back, and when I don't stop, turns and darts forward and around my desk.

"What do you think you're doing?" I drawl.

"Uh, just, uh, the view." She stabs a finger at the window, and when I round the desk, she slips around the other side and toward the door. She's almost out the room when I call her name, "Oh, Ms. Warren."

She flinches.

"Don't forget your phone."

17

Penny

I wish I'd left my phone behind. That way, I wouldn't have to read the barrage of excited messages from Mira, who's under the impression Sir Knighthole is taking me out to dinner. I tried to correct her misconception and explained that it was a working dinner, but this only elicited a bunch of more excited messages from her.

We're in his car with Rudy driving and the partition behind him raised for privacy.

At seven p.m., when I was sure I'd keel over with hunger, he marched out of his office, snapped his fingers as he passed me, and expected me to follow. I stuck out my tongue at his back, and he commented without turning, "You done with making childish faces, or should I take this as a sign I need to spank the brattiness out of you?"

Oh, my god. My pussy clenched so hard, my toes curled, and I almost dissolved into a slobbering mess right there on the spot. I managed to find a measure of composure enough to scramble up, grab my coat, and race to keep up with him.

The ride down in the elevator passed with him glued to his phone and me aware of how he seemed to dwarf the space. Every pore in my body was alert to his every breath, the way his big fingers made the phone seem tiny in his palm, the way those thick fingers of his had been inside me and taken me to the edge and —

My phone vibrates with another incoming message. This time, I move it over to my other palm and peek at the screen.

Mira: Okay okay. Sorry I'm so excited about your dinner. Make sure you share all the details with me once you're back.

Me: Will do but there won't be much to report. It's a boring dinner to discuss his new hire.

Which is true. After all, Knight's going about this entire exercise of finding his wife like it's a business merger.

Mira: Eggplant emoji. Pussycat emoji. Sweating emoji.

Me: Sleeping face emoji.

"If you're done playing with your phone, Ms. Easton, perhaps we can get some work done?" he drawls.

Ha, told you he thinks of this exercise of going bride-hunting as some kind of investment strategy. In a way, it is. It's his route to consolidating his position in his company, so I guess he's not completely wrong. Only the rich would connect their need for power and their personal lives so closely. Of course, from what Abby has told me, Knight wasn't always like this. Does what he went through justify what he's become now? I suppose, I don't know because it didn't happen to me. But... it's something I'm not able to get my head around.

"Ms. Easton, I asked you a question."

I blink, then give him my full attention. "The answer is no."

"Did you even hear the question?" He scowls.

I resist the urge to roll my eyes. "I wouldn't dare make you repeat yourself, Mr. Warren, Sir."

His eyes flash, and heat spikes in my lower belly. In the next second, he banks whatever momentary lapse in composure he displayed. In fact, maybe I mistook the streetlight shining through the window and in his eyes for that crack in his self-control.

"No, I don't need to use my phone, and sorry I was distracted. It was, uh, my friend Mira. I was letting her know I'm headed out for dinner so we can't meet this evening."

"She a good friend of yours?"

"Oh, yes." I allow my lips to curve in a genuine smile. "I've only been in London a few years. Not long enough to meet that many people, and of course, with my mother's condition deteriorating—" I look away and swallow, "Uh… it hasn't been easy to socialize. But thanks to Abby, who I met through a mutual friend, I also met Mira, and now the three of us hang out a lot. Or rather, we used to, now that Abby is married and all." I hunch my shoulders, force myself to keep the smile on my face. "It's fine. It's life, you know? The only constant is change."

I glance up to find he's staring at me with a strange look in his eyes.

"What?" I half laugh. "Do I have a spot on my face or something?"

"You have a—" He reaches out and tucks a strand of hair behind my ear. "It had come lose from your hairdo."

"Oh, thanks." I swallow. A slow, melting sensation coils in my chest. It's different to the explosive chemistry that always stretches between us. Even now, in the car, the air is heavy with unspoken needs, wants, cravings, desires… All those things we're taught to never voice but which, the more you don't acknowledge them, the more they grow bigger in the space. But this—whatever this nascent, fragile emotion is that curves around my heart—is different. We stare at each other; the silence stretches.

Then, there's a screech of brakes being applied, and the car lurches to a stop. My heart jumps into my throat. I'm thrown forward and against the seatbelt—and into a heavy barrier that's been slapped in front of me. An immovable barrier that holds me in my place. It's his arm. I didn't even seen him fling it out, but it's there. His arm, encased in the sleeve of his jacket and attached to his large, powerful body, which is vibrating with so much tension, the fabric strains at the seams to hold in the muscles of his shoulders.

His chest rises and falls, the veins on his throat bulging with such tautness, surely, it must be painful. His cheekbones stand out in rigid angles that cut through the air, and his gaze is fixed straight ahead on a spot I can't see. I touch his hand and the sinews under his skin jump. He's so rigid, so impenetrable, something inside me softens in direct contrast.

I unsnap my belt, and before I can stop myself, I've slid out from under his arm and straddled him.

He lowers his gaze to my face, but he's not really seeing me, so I throw my arms about him and reach up and fix my lips on his. He goes rigid; the muscles of his shoulders jump under my touch. His chest rises and falls, but otherwise, he's still. So still. His mouth is hard, unmoving as I brush mine over his once, twice. There's no response from him, nothing to indicate that I'm in his lap and kissing him and — something thick stabs me between my legs.

Aha! He's not as unmoved as he's trying to pretend he is. I tilt my head, deepen the kiss, and the column between my legs jumps. My stomach clenches. My pussy begins to weep. I bite down on his plush lower lip, and a low growl rumbles up his chest. I slide my fingers up the back of his neck, wind them through the short hair and tug. His chest-planes vibrate, and his entire body seems to turn into one solid mass of immovable granite.

There's a second during which I stare into those emerald sheets of his eyes. The next, flames ignite behind them. I gasp as he plants his big hands on my hips and yanks me close enough that my breasts are flat-tened against his massive chest. He pushes me down firmly onto the thickness between his thighs, and without blinking, he licks the seam of my lips. The moment I part them, he thrusts his tongue into my mouth and deepens the kiss. He draws of me, sucks from my life force, drains me of every thought.

My entire body has turned into a mass of writhing, yearning, a melting sensation that strains to be one with him. And still, he holds my gaze captive. It's as if he's looking right into me, as if he knows my innermost desires, my most secret shameful inclinations, how I hunger for his touch, his lips, his tongue, his cock, which seems to have grown bigger and heavier and thicker against my core, as we speak. He drags his hands down from my hips to the expanse of stocking-covered thigh exposed when I drew up my skirt.

He squeezes down on my skin, and my entire body goes into a tail-spin of longing. My heart slams into my ribcage, and the blood thunders at my temples. Something inside me snaps, and I crawl closer, pushing myself into him, rubbing myself up against him, aware I'm making small whimpering noises in my throat and unable to stop myself. Aware that I'm humping that thick rod between his thighs through the crotch of my stockings and his pants and unable to stop myself. As for Knight?

He continues to kiss me, continues to ravage my mouth, and continues to thrust his tongue in and out between my lips in an imitation of how he'd, no doubt, shove his dick inside my pussy. He drags his palms up to my butt and squeezes it hard. I yelp, but he swallows the sound and pulls me even closer, until the heat of his body surrounds me. It wraps around me like a caterpillar in a cocoon that it's woven around itself and is never going to be able to shed.

The air thickens, pulses, pushes down on my shoulders and holds me in place as surely as his hands that cup each butt cheek as if he'd like to imprint himself on my body. In me. All over me. A trembling screeches up my spine, and oh, my god, is it possible to orgasm from a kiss alone? Surely, I'm going to—

The muted sound of a horn cuts through the charged space, then Rudy's voice comes over the intercom, "Sorry about that, Knight, but we're clear of the traffic now."

We break apart. My chest heaves, my lips throb, and a thousand little fireflies spark through my veins. Knight's eyes blaze at me for a few seconds, then that emerald curtain descends over them. He lifts me up, deposits me on the seat next to him, then leans forward to push a button on the panel. "Change of plans. We're dropping Ms. Easton home."

"So that's it, he dropped you home?" Mira blinks up at me from the couch in our living room.

"Maybe something came up... I guess?" One minute, we were kissing. The next, he couldn't wait to get away from me. He immersed himself in his phone, told me we'd discuss things the next morning in the office, and didn't give me any other reason for the abrupt change in the evening's proceedings. Of course, I'm pretty sure I know the reason. "He's a busy man; perhaps, there was something urgent in the office?"

"You're his assistant; you'd be aware if that happened," she points out.

That's true, and I checked my inbox on the way home. Even though there were a hundred emails since we left the office—I wince—there was nothing that needed his immediate attention. Nothing that pointed to the real reason behind his hurry in dropping me off at my home before he took off. Which leads me to conclude, it has something to do with my V-card. He must have been reminded of it when we were interrupted.

I reach for the box of wine Mira took out and pour some into my glass. I take a sip, then make a face.

"I know, sorry, it's all I had."

"Oh, please don't apologize. You put your evening on hold for me."

"Now that you mention it..." She pushes a finger into her cheek. "Let's see. I had a hot book boyfriend, a bubble bath, and a vibrator ready to go with this wine, so yeah, I could be having multiple orgasms with my fictional crush and my Hitachi." She laughs. "But instead, I'm here, listening to how your hot boss kissed the hell out of you, then realized he was so in danger of falling for you that he promptly decided to turn tail and run."

I huff out a breath. "He's not falling for me. He's not even in the vicinity of noticing me—"

"—just touching you every chance he gets?"

"It's not quite that way."

"What else can it be?" She reaches for the box-wine, eyes it with skepticism then pours some into her glass anyway. "He's attracted to you, but he's fighting it."

"He's certainly fighting something," I muse.

"Do you think he was injured when he was prisoner of war, and now, he can't... You know—" She holds up a finger.

This time, I chuckle. "Oh, trust me, he can... Very much—" I hold up my fist.

"Ah." She nods, then gapes when I hold up my other fist next to my first.

"Like that, hmm?"

"He's, ah... hung, all right." My cheeks flush. "And I'm not talking about this with you anymore."

"Aww." She pouts. "At least, you're getting some action."

"More like, I get *re*-actions from this man. He's battling something inside of himself."

"His lust for you." She makes a slurping sound. "He's fighting to keep his python in his pants."

I stare at her. "Did you call his whatchamacallit a python."

"Or perhaps, I should say mamba."

"Mamba?"

"You know that phrase 'milking the mamba'?" She makes air quotes with her fingers.

"Ugh, whatever. How do you know all these euphemisms?"

"You mean, how do I know that you can also call that particular act choking the chicken, bashing the bishop, flogging the dong, beating the—"

"Stop." I laugh. "Enough. I can't decide if I should be impressed you know all these urbanisms or worried?"

"That's what comes when you gorge yourself on smut. I'm a smut-head. What can I say? And as things go, it's a fairly innocent thing to OD on, don't you think?"

"I think you should —"

The intercom buzzes. We look at each other. "Were you expecting someone?"

"No, you?"

She shakes her head, then walks toward the intercom and presses the buzzer. "Delivery for Ms. Easton."

"Eh?" I blink. "I didn't order anything."

There's silence, then the man says, "It's definitely for Ms. Easton."

I exchange a glance with Mira, then place my glass on the coffee table. I walk past her, head out the door and down the flight of steps, with Mira on my heels. I open the door to find a man standing there with his arms full of paper bags.

"What's this?"

"It's a delivery from the restaurant of James Hamilton."

"But I didn't —"

"James Hamilton?" Mira squawks from behind me. "The Michelin-starred, celebrity chef who has his own show? *That* James Hamilton?"

The man grins. "Yes, Miss. May I bring this up to the apartment? There are a lot of bags."

I begin to protest, but Mira steps back and gestures for him to come up. I move to the side, then follow him up. He walks into the apartment, and we direct him to place the bags on the coffee table.

"Oh, I had strict orders to plate these out for you, ready to eat." He glances around and spots the breakfast counter. "May I?"

I frown.

Mira steps forward. "Oh, yes, please," she gushes.

He walks over, spreads a white cloth over the countertop, then sets out the carriers of food, and a bottle of red wine, which he uncorks and pours into two wine glasses which he places next to two plates arranged on the surface.

"Enjoy yourselves." He half bows and leaves.

Mira and I look at the spread.

"Wow!" She heads for the bar, then removes the covering of a dish.

The scent of something tangy tickles my nose. My stomach grumbles. She sets the cover aside, then snatches up a folded note.

"Let me read that." I reach her, and before she can open the note, snatch it from her.

She glances over my shoulder, and I step away so she can't read it. "Is it from him? Don't keep me in suspense. Is it?"

18

Knight

"Thank you for the dinner last night, but you didn't have to do it," she murmurs from across the expanse of my desk.

I place the tips of my fingers together. "I deprived you of your dinner. Least I could do."

Her features soften, and her lips part.

"I'd have done it for any other employee."

"Right." The light in her eyes dims.

Something stabs into the space behind my breastbone. *Don't catch feelings for her. Don't. It's strictly business. It has to be.* Last evening, when she climbed into my lap and pressed her lips to mine—I was taken aback, and that's saying a lot. I should have pushed her away at once, but her scent had gone straight to my head. And my balls. And the feel of her lips on mine was like the first rain on parched earth. Like the first snowfall that covers the earth in a carpet of virgin white, so everything is muted, and hushed and waiting… Waiting…

I couldn't have stopped myself from grabbing her and bringing her closer, deepening the kiss and taking from her. She opened herself up and allowed me to draw from her—to use her innocence, her response, her softness to repair that wound inside of me. I felt myself healing from trauma I haven't even fully processed yet—and that scared me. Enough that I set her aside and decided to drop her back home instead of spending another moment in her presence. Then, I called Adam.

We met up and ran five miles together before he had to take off. By the time I reached home, I was drenched in sweat. So, I took a quick shower, then managed to get four hours sleep, which is unusual but welcome. Most nights, I've been averaging about two hours of sleep, if I'm lucky. The result of my marathon sleep session is, I feel rested, despite being up and awake since four a.m. Now, I reach for the coffee she placed on the desk.

"Have a seat, Ms. Easton."

"Uh, I'd rather stand." She sets her jaw.

"Suit yourself." I push a sheet of paper in her direction.

She picks it up and glances at it. "It's blank."

"Indeed."

"What do you want me to do with it?"

"Make a list."

"A list of—?" She taps her foot, clad in three-inch stilettos which are another shade of pink. Her skirt is purple, the shirt she's tucked into it a pale lavender. Her lips are painted fuchsia. Perfect to wear on my dick. She chose the color to taunt me, no doubt, with visions of how soft her mouth had been, how her lips had clung to mine, how the outline of her nipples against my chest and the heat of her pussy as she rode my cock through the layers of clothes we were wearing had made me almost shoot my load in my pants.

"Mr. Warren, Sir?"

My cock stiffens on command. *Fuck.* Maybe it was a bad idea to encourage her to address me by that title. I shake my head to clear it, then focus on the task at hand.

"Make a list of attributes my future wife should have. Then, use it to find someone for me by the end of the week."

She laughs. "You want me to make a list of attributes for *your* future wife?"

"Don't make me repeat myself."

She draws in a breath. "I have no idea where to start."

"How difficult can it be?"

"If it's that easy, why don't *you* do it?"

I scowl; she scowls back. My lips almost twitch at her show of defiance, but I manage to hide it. My Little Dove is learning how to hold her own. This makes things more interesting.

"Virgin."

"What?"

"She should be a virgin."

She scoffs, "Of course, she should. Not that you are, but she should be."

"She's the mother of my future spawn; she needs to be untouched."

She stares at me. I skim a pen in her direction. She picks it up then, plants herself in the chair and begins to write. "Virgin, got it."

I frown. "Don't sass me."

She widens her eyes at me. "Like I would dare."

My lips twitch again, and she stares. "OMG, did you smile? Did the big, bad, macho, scary alphahole forget to act all grumpy and growly and curve his lips?"

"Alphahole?" I blink.

Her cheeks redden. "Just a slip of the tongue, is all."

"I like it."

She rolls her eyes. "Of course, you'd take it as a compliment."

I lean further back in my chair. "Keep them coming."

"That's it. That's all you're getting out of me." She pretends to zip her lips. "Also, you're the one who should be speaking. It's your list."

"And I pay you to do as I tell you, so why don't you put down the attributes my wife should have?"

"Hmm, let's see. Must be thick-skinned enough to put up with your crotchety temper, your general lack of politeness and your disagreeable nature. Must be meek and bow to your will. Must not have a single original thought of her own. Must do as she's told at every turn." She peeks up at me from under her eyelashes. "How am I doing?"

"You forgot must bend over and let me fuck her whenever the need takes hold."

She swallows, and the pulse at the base of her neck speeds up. "You don't mean that."

I raise a shoulder. "What's the point of being married if there's no sex-on-tap?"

"Why do you want to get married for that?" She tosses her blonde ponytail—yep, the woman has her hair tied up in a cheer-leader's version of a hairstyle that has all that golden goodness fountaining down her back in a spring of curls, and fuck, if I don't want to wrap it around my hand and tug her head back and bite down on the skin where her shoulder meets her throat and —

"You have enough women lining up and willing to let you into their beds for that." She scowls.

"Ah, but only my wife gets me bare-back. No barriers between us, just skin on skin, and the closest I'll ever be to any woman."

Her flush deepens. She shifts in her seat. "You're talking dirty to shock me."

"No, I'm talking dirty to arouse you."

She looks away, draws in a breath, then seems to compose herself. When she turns back to me, her gaze is shrewd. "Hidden behind all that crude, vulgar, sadistic behavior of yours is a romantic."

I allow my lips to curl. "Hidden behind that curvy, Barbie doll persona of yours is someone who's attracted to the dark side of sex."

She tips up her chin. "I'm not denying the foray into BDSM at the club got me curious about the kinky side of making love."

And she calls it making love, which is so fucking cute. I prefer to call it an exchange of bodily fluids, a transaction, a way to get rid of this need that's crawling inside me and waiting to break through my skin.

"At least I'm honest." She squares her shoulders. "Which is more than I can say about you."

I scowl. "What are you talking about?"

"That underneath all your bluster and overbearing personality, you're lonely. You're hurting. You're wounded from what happened to you when you were taken by the enemy."

My muscles bunch. My stomach tightens. I glare at her, but for the first time, she doesn't look away.

"Perhaps these are injuries you had even before, and likely, didn't get a chance to address. And then, with the pressure you came under, all of it came to the fore."

"What is this, pop psychology 101? Or maybe it's a quiz you read in one of your fluffy women's magazine and now you think you can gauge what I went through based on it?"

She firms her lips. "That's your fallback option, isn't it? When you're scared or you feel vulnerable, you strike out like a cornered animal."

"And when you're scared, you get turned on."

"What?" She gapes.

"It's true, isn't it, Little Dove?" I use my nickname on purpose and am rewarded when her pupils dilate. Oh, she responds to my pet name so beautifully. How would it be to make her respond to my cock, hmm?

"What do you mean?"

"I mean, if I dropped to my knees and pushed my nose into your crotch, I'd find you gloriously aroused and dripping all over my chair. You've oozed cum all over your panties, haven't you? Hearing me talk about fucking without a condom has your clit throbbing, your pussy squeezing down and coming up empty. You can't wait to leave here and use your fingers to find relief."

"That's not true."

"Oh?" I allow my lips to curl. "Want me to put it to the test?" I push up as if to rise to my feet, and she jumps up. "No, no. Stop. Don't come near me."

"Then admit that you're turned on when I use explicit words."

"I... I—"

I begin to rise to my feet, and she yelps. "Fine, fine. I do. When you use obscene words it, uh, does something to me."

"Describe it."

"What?"

"Tell me what it does to you."

Her eyes round. "No, I won't."

"In which case—" This time, I do rise to my feet, and she throws up her hands. "Fine, it does weird things to my lower belly and between my legs, and my nipples tighten, and my breasts seem to swell, and my scalp tingles, and my toes curl, and moisture seeps out from my—"

"Cunt?"

She nods.

"Say it."

She shakes her head.

I glare at her, she pales, then squeezes her eyes shut. "Cunt."

"Didn't hear you."

"Cunt!" she yells.

That's when the door opens, and Abby walks in.

19

Penny

"Excuse me?" Abby looks from me to Knight then back at me. "Did you say—"

"Come in, little sis. That's what Penny was saying, 'come in'." Knight glances sideways at me, "Isn't that right, Penny?"

Abby's gaze narrows with suspicion then, to my relief, she nods. "So, have you discussed the list of attributes of your to-be-wife with Penny yet?"

"We were getting down to it when you walked in."

"There's no getting out of this. You know that, Knight, right?" She walks over to stand next to him. "If you don't find a wife and get married in the next month, you know Dad will not hesitate to disown you."

Knight's jaw firms, a vein pops at his temple, then he jerks his chin. "A wife within a month and spawn on the way in the next year. That's what he wants. That's what he gets."

Her features soften. "I'm sorry our father doesn't seem to understand what you've been through. Any other father would be worried about you and try to give you space to recover completely. In fact, he'd have stopped you from joining the company and told you to take some time to recuperate."

"And you think I'd have listened to him?" Knight's lips curls. "Also, I debriefed before I returned to London."

"For forty-eight hours. You were a prisoner of war for six months, Knight. Six months—" She locks her fingers together. "And then, you come right back and do the one thing you were against all your life. Working for our father."

"I thought you wanted all of us to get along?" Knight tips his head.

"That was when I thought our father was changing. He met me and Cade and told me he was sorry for not doing his duty as a father. He vowed he was going to be different. And everything he's done seems to point toward that. But then, not only does he not tell you to take time off and get to grips with what you went through, but he also puts pressure on you to get married. I tried changing his mind on it, but to no avail. He's adamant that you settle down. He thinks it's going to help you process what happened to you." She shakes her head. "I wish there was more I could do to help Knight, I do."

"But you have already." He reaches out and pats her shoulder. "You suggested I get Penny to take on the role of my personal assistant. I can't tell you what a great addition she's been to my team."

"I have?" The words slip out before I can stop myself.

"Indeed." Knight nods, and looking at Abby he murmurs, "She's been indispensable when it comes to helping relieve some of the stress I've been carrying."

I bite the inside of my cheek. Did he imply what I think he did? No, there was nothing sexual about his words, was there? And he wouldn't say something so suggestive with his sister in the room… right?

"In fact, she's been indispensable when it comes to being a sounding board for my plans for mergers and acquisitions. She's the reason I've been able empty my… mind enough to focus on my job."

OMG, he paused after 'empty my.' How could he? And all that talk about mergers and acquisitions? Only he could turn business language into smutty talk. And of course, he's worded it all in such an innocent manner. If you weren't looking out for it, you wouldn't be able to find fault with his words. Abby has no reason to be suspicious of anything he says. In fact, her features light up. "Oh, I'm so pleased it's all working out." She takes his hand in hers. "I truly am, big brother. I was so worried about you, but now, I can relax a little."

"You should thank Penny for her acts of assistance," he says in a tone that is so sincere, I almost believe him. That jerkface! Acts of assistance, indeed.

"Oh, I will." Abby releases his hand and steps back, then walks over to me. "I am so grateful for what you've done, truly."

"Uh, I... I haven't done anything."

"Of course you have. You've put up with his mood-swings and grumpy tantrums, and you're able to hold a conversation with him. You're the only one in this building, other than me, who has the courage to talk to him."

Not like I have a choice. But I'm not going to tell her that. I flash her a smile. "That's me, always able to tame the lion in his cage. It takes a Barbie to subdue the wild beast, huh?"

"Are you okay?" She looks at me strangely.

"What she means is, our contrasting styles are a good foil. Together, we make a good team." He nods in my direction, then allows his lip to curl in what I assume is supposed to be a smile. It's more of a grimace, but hey, I'll take it. I made the ogre smile again. That's got to count for something, eh?

"Don't we?" He keeps his lips turned up, as if his muscles are frozen.

"Do we?" I ask with a wide, innocent gaze. *Y-e-p, two can play this game.*

His gaze narrows. For a second, his eyes flash. I see those golden sparks in their depths, the ones I convinced myself I had imagined. Apparently, not. Douchehole here, really is hiding some seriously intense emotions under that grouchy mask of his.

"Perhaps I need to remind you of your duties, Ms. Easton?" he says in a hard voice.

I toss my hair back from my face. "Perhaps I need to remind you that my responsibilities are only that of your employee and nothing more, Mr. Warren."

"O-k-a-y." Abby steps back. "You two make no sense to me. But as long as you are getting along, who am I to intervene?" She moves forward and hugs me. "I really am so happy you decided to work with Knight. I can't think of anyone better than you to find him a wife. I trust your judgement, you know."

But I don't. Especially not when I'm unsure of what to make of my attraction to her brother. Not to mention how I'm beginning to hate this effect he has on me. Not that I'm going to tell her that. Instead, I nod and smile, because that's what I'm best at, after all. I must put on a good show, for she smiles back. Her features relax. Clearly, she thinks everything is well in-hand. With a final wave at my nemesis over her shoulder, she walks out.

The door snicks shut. Silence descends. I glance across the desk to where Knight is watching me with intent. His green eyes have a hard edge to them. It's as if he's made up his mind. He reaches over, taps what must be a button on the side of his desk, and I hear an audible click. I stiffen and glance over my shoulder at the door, then back at him.

He nods. "It's locked. Neither of us is leaving until we thrash this out."

My heart jumps into my chest. My pulse rate skyrockets. I take a step back, my knees hit my chair, and I sit down.

"Good girl."

Instantly, the flush blooms across my skin. I will not be moved by his praise. Or by his dirty talking. *I will not.* I'm here to do a job, and only because he pays my salary, and for my mother to stay in the home she loves. So what, if his style of working is unconventional and he steps over the line on occasion—I wince. Yeah, typical of a situation where the boss takes advantage of his employee—only, I don't not want him to do so. Only, I enjoy it too much when he does. Only, he's going to get married soon, and then what? I'll be the sidepiece? Nope, no way. I have more pride than that. I need to preserve that part of me I've never shared with anyone. I need to hold myself in check around him. I need to… get through this list and get the hell out of here.

I grab my pen and begin to write. My fingers fly over the paper, and the words appear. I'm conscious of him tracking my movements, but I don't stop until I've filled the page. Then, I push it over to him.

He reads it, then scowls. "What's this?"

20

Knight

"Your list of qualities you're looking for in a wife?" she retorts.
   I take my time reading through the list.

1. Must be a virgin.
2. Must be ready to have sex anytime.
3. Must be meek.
4. Must be organized and able to manage the household.
5. Has no original thoughts of her own.
6. Must be good-looking—ideally, model-thin?
7. Must be ready to spawn right away.
8. Must make sure the world revolves around me.
9. Has no personality of her own.
10. Must be dumb enough to marry me.

"So, that's what you think I'm looking for, hmm?"

"I *know* that's what you're looking for." Her voice is smug.

Without looking up, I turn the sheet over and begin to write. I take my time, and the seconds stretch.

She moves around in her seat.

I ignore her.

She taps her fingers on the table. "Is this going to take long?"

"You have somewhere else to be, Ms. Easton?"

"N-no," she stutters.

I keep writing, and she continues to fidget. When I raise my gaze to hers, it's to find she's biting her nails. She flushes, then lowers her hand. "Sorry, bad habit. I do it when I'm nervous. I also talk too much when things are too quiet, but you know that."

I place my pen down on the desk, then push the paper across to her. She blinks. "What's this?"

"Why don't you read it out aloud?"

A wrinkle appears between her eyebrows, then she does as I asked.

"Number one. Must be a virgin." She huffs. "What a surprise you kept that in. Number two. Will be ready for me anytime, anyplace, especially in a public place." She freezes. "A public place?"

"Nothing like a little bit of exhibitionism to keep things fresh."

She bites down on her lower lip, and my gaze lowers to her mouth. "That arouses you, hmm?"

"What? No. Of course, not." She squirms around in the chair and my lips twitch.

Clearly, she's lying, but I'm not going to call her out on it... Yet. Also, this is the most fun I've had since... My smile fades...Since the time I hung out with Cade and Declan before I left on my mission. I've avoided them since. Fact is, I'm not ready to meet them.

Life changed for them while I was away. They're married and happy and I'd, no doubt, burst the bubble of their contentment with my unsociable mood. No, I'm not ready to hang out with my friends yet. Her though... She's different. And she's not a friend. She's... An employee? A paid lackey? A woman who keeps my interest engaged and is so entertaining to be with, I'm able to push to the back of my mind the ordeal I went through. A woman I need to keep my distance from. A woman I need to fuck and get out of my system? I stiffen. Now, that's a possibility.

She continues reading. "Number three. Will challenge me and go toe-to-toe with me—" She jerks her chin in my direction. "You want someone who can challenge you?"

"It's what keeps things interesting." I raise a shoulder. "If someone gives in too quickly, where's the excitement in that?"

She rolls her eyes. "Are you planning a business transaction or trying to find a bride?"

"The first, obviously."

"Ask a stupid question, get a stupid answer," she mumbles under her breath. I hear her anyway.

"You sassing me, Little Dove?"

"Just stating a fact."

"How could you, when you don't know me at all?"

She looks up at me for a second, her gaze contemplative, then glances back at the sheet. "Number four. Will value her family. Number five. Will follow her instinct when it comes to making decisions. Number six. Curvy, plus-size with a figure that embodies her heart— You want her to have curves?!" she bursts out.

"You should have gathered that by now." I tilt my head. "I like my woman to be soft and feminine and have the kind of hips that are perfect for childbearing."

"Of course there's a practical reason to it," she huffs.

"You didn't think it had anything to do with liking the feel of her contours under my hands—"

Her lips part.

"— or the squeeze of her pussy on my cock or—"

She inhales sharply.

"The give of her breasts when I squeeze them"—I make a crushing motion with my fingers—"the give of her butt cheeks when I knead them and hold them apart as I drive into her; the—"

"Stop," she gasps.

"Oh, that's right. You need to finish reading the list." I nod toward the piece of paper held between her trembling fingers.

"Number seven. Wants to have children. Number eight. Must be faithful."

She tosses her head. "You mean you can stray from the marital bed, but she cannot?"

"I mean, if she so much as dares to look at another man, I'll cut off his balls."

Her breath hitches. "You will?"

"Abso-fucking-lutely. I won't be seeing other women, either."

"You won't?" Her gaze widens. "You plan to stay faithful?"

"I'm old-fashioned that way." I hold up a finger. "Provided her holes are available on demand."

She winces. "No one can accuse you of being romantic."

"I'm not marrying for romance."

"Right…" She looks like she's going to say something, then shakes her head and glances down at the paper again, "Number nine. Vivacious and speaks what's on her mind. Number ten. Is smart enough to marry me." She allows the paper to float to the desk, then sets her jaw. "Number ten is debatable. What's so smart about her wanting to marry you?"

"Because she will be well compensated."

She scoffs. "For allowing you to use her body as a receptacle to grow your child?"

"Among other things."

She raises her thumb to her mouth and begins to chew on her fingernail, then thinks better of it. "I can't see any other benefits."

"For one, there will be multiple orgasms involved. I have my faults, but I'm not a selfish lover."

Her chest rises and falls. Her nipples are so hard, I can see them outlined through the blouse *and* the jacket she's wearing.

I lean forward in my seat; so does she. I drag my thumb under my lower lip, and her gaze follows my actions. "I'll make sure my wife orgasms every time I fuck her."

She tips up her gaze to mine. "You mean make love to her?"

"I mean fuck her—"

The color on her cheeks deepens.

"—Shag her. Bang her. Screw—"

She throws up her hand. "Fine, fine, I get what you're saying."

"Do you?"

"Yes, I do. No feelings. No emotions. No commitment on your side—"

"—except to my children, of course."

"Of course. Though this entire discussion seems like it's rooted in the wrong reasons."

"It's about procreation and ensuring I inherit my father's company."

"It's about love," she cries.

I take in her flushed features, her parted lips, the way she wrings her fingers together. "You really mean it."

"Of course I do."

"And you believe in rainbows and unicorns and fairies—"

"Not all of us are cynics, like you."

"Not all of us have been captured and tortured until it felt like the very skin from your body was being flayed. Not everyone was buried in a coffin-shaped hole under the ground with the rainwater seeping in and threatening to drown you alive. Not everyone was electrocuted until—" I shut my lips. *The fuck am I doing, sharing my experiences with her?* I haven't mentioned this to anyone other than Adam, and that's only because he went through something similar. He was there. He understands how it was to spend every waking moment sure you'd never last another day. Then wake up to realize you'd survived and were stuck in the same nightmare, with no end in sight. The world moved on, and I regressed.

I touched the darkness inside of me. The ache, the hurt, the sorrows which were my shadow-self became real and came to the fore. I had to draw on them. I had to become them to get through the next second, and the next, and the one after. There was no hope… No future. Nothing but that blank void I surrounded myself with. The only way to get through what was thrown at me was to disassociate my feelings from myself. It's why I remained alive. Why I'm here today, looking at her angelic face and taking in the pity in her eyes. *Pity. In. Her. Eyes.* I stab at the button which releases the lock on the doors, then jerk my chin in the direction of the exit. "Leave."

"What?" She gapes.

"Get gone, woman, we're done here."

She rises to her feet, turns to do as she's told, then stops and turns around to face me. "No."

21

Penny

His nostrils flare. His eyes burn. "Don't defy me."

"Oh no, no, no, you don't get to pretend you didn't tell me what you did. You don't get to share what happened with you and run scared again."

His gaze narrows. His shoulders bunch. His biceps flex, and I'm sure he's going to split the seams of his shirt. "You're calling me scared?"

"I'm calling you out on your posturing. You're pretending what happened to you was nothing out of the ordinary. Like you could go through what you did and rejoin the rest of us without taking the time to understand what it did to you."

He draws himself to his full height, and his gaze turns to a sheet of glass. His features smooth out, and that mask he loves to show to the world is in place again. "It's none of your business how I decide to live my life."

It feels like someone stabbed a dagger through my heart. The pain is instantaneous and excruciating. I draw in a sharp breath and grip the end of the desk until the blood flow to my fingers is cut off. "Thank you for putting me in my place, Mr. Warren." I pick up the sheet of paper and turn to leave.

"Penny, stop."

The sound of my name from his lips sends a ripple of sensations coiling up my spine. It's the first time he's called me by my name, and it feels more intimate than all the times he touched me. I pause, because of course, I would. I can't not when he's ordered me to. But I don't turn around. I can't. Not when he'll see the tell-tale sheen in my eyes and the way the blood has drained from my face. Not to mention, how pinched my features must be right now. I manage to straighten my spine and stare straight ahead.

I hear him blow out a breath, then his footsteps approach. He pauses behind me, and the hair on the nape of my neck rises. He's not standing close to me, yet I feel the heat of his presence keenly, as if he's wrapped his thick arms around me and pulled me into his chest and—I shake my head to clear it.

This… salivating after him has to stop. He's not mine. Will never be. In fact, he doesn't even think of me as anything but an employee to do his bidding. Sure, I find him sexy, and he's the most charismatic man I've ever met. He's also the most complex, and the most unreadable. If he hadn't let slip a little of what he's been through, I'd have never guessed the extent to which he was hurt during the time he was taken prisoner. And everything in me wants to do everything in my power to alleviate his pain. Which is crazy. He doesn't want it. He'd probably reject it. But my stupid, soft heart can't stop itself from empathizing with what he's gone through.

"I'm sorry," he says in a low voice. A soft voice. A voice I've never heard him use before. Oh, he's tender with his sister, but even with her, he's never revealed the frustration, the suffering, the sheer torture I can hear in his words now. "Forgive me for being a complete ass. I've forgotten what it is to live in polite society."

I shake my head. "I'd rather you be authentic than put on a veneer of politeness. Not that I'd ever expect you to censor your thoughts."

There's silence, then I sense him nod. "You're not as fragile as you look."

I half chuckle, then turn to glance at him over my shoulder. "You think?"

He searches my features, then reaches out and uses his thumb to scoop up a tear drop that I wasn't aware had slipped out from the corner of my eye. He brings it to his mouth and sucks on it, and my entire body seems to burst into flames.

"Why did you do that?" I whisper.

He looks as confused as I feel. "Fuck if I know." He holds my gaze a second longer, then reaches down and takes the sheet from between my fingers. "You were right, this list sucks."

I turn sideways, not facing him fully. "That's not what I said."

"Well, I'm saying it. It was wrong of me to expect you to draw up this list when you don't know me at all."

"Well, you are my boss, so I'm not supposed to know you... Like that," I flush as I'm saying it, and though his lips curl, he doesn't say anything to make my discomfort worse.

"But this particular assignment involves you getting to know me well enough to draw up a profile that helps you to attract the right woman for this position."

"It's not a job," I point out.

"So you keep insisting."

"You know I'm right."

He frowns, and there's genuine confusion on his features. "You can call it anything you like, but the purpose of this exercise is to attract applications from women who you will interview and then draw up a shortlist for me to choose from."

"Me?" I squeak.

He looks around the room. "Do you see anyone else I'd trust with this task?"

"Abby?"

He snorts. "She's too close to me."

"But I'm not."

"You're not," he agrees. And he's right, but it feels like a twister has suddenly emerged in my gut.

"You've seen the worst of me, and you're standing—"

Barely.

"—so, you know what to look for."

"I do?"

"Sure." He nods. "You need to find someone who's as soft as you on the outside but has a spine of steel. Someone who's adamant and obstinate enough to hold her own and knows when to give in to me."

I feel the blush sweep up my chest, my throat, right up to the roots of my hair. "Was that a compliment?"

He blinks. "I believe it was," he says slowly. There's surprise in his eyes, which he banks at once. "And to help you in this, you're going to spend time with me."

22

Knight

"So, she agreed to get to know you better so she can describe you better in order that the right kind of woman will apply for the role?" Adam takes a long drink of water from his bottle.

"That's the idea, yes." I stretch out my calves, then my thighs, trying to work out the kinks that have formed after that ten-mile-long run along the Thames. It's a perfect early autumn evening. The light is golden and slanting through the buildings along the bank of the river. It's almost nine p.m., but it's light. The days are long enough for me to complete my run and have time to return to my home office and get some work done.

"And she agreed?"

"I didn't give her a choice."

"Maybe she was happy to spend time with you?" He smirks.

"I doubt it, considering I haven't exactly been a gentleman with her." Fact is, I don't want to be a gentleman with her. I only want to be a beast—the kind who throws her down and ruts into her and sinks into her pussy. She brings out that carnal part of me. The part which wants to own her and possess her and fuck her every which way until

I've spent myself thoroughly. Until the voices in my head shut down and give me some relief from the ever-present babble between my ears.

He lowers his arm, caps his bottle and points it at me. "You, mate, are fooling yourself."

"Eh?" I straighten, then extend my other leg before dipping into it, lengthening the muscles.

"You have a thing for her."

I snort. "Sure I do. She's curvy, sexy, vivacious. She brings sunshine into any room she walks into. She smells of flowers, and her gait is like that of a dancer. Her glare is shy, her heart is sensitive, and she feels emotions in a way that I'll never be able to. She's funny, witty, and cracks me up with her errors."

"You find her mistakes amusing?"

"Of course I do."

He stares at me.

"What?"

"You're the guy who'd ask your unit to drop down and give you a hundred push-ups if we made a single mistake during our drills."

"She's not one of my team."

"No, she's something more."

I pause halfway through my cooling down exercise. "I mean, yeah, she's my employee."

Adam smirks.

"Shut up, twatface."

"I didn't say anything."

"It's what you're implying."

"And what is that?"

"That she's—" I hesitate. *What? What is she? Is it even important to give a label to whatever is there between us? No, what am I thinking? There's nothing between us. Nothing.* "Nothing." I straighten. "She means nothing to me."

"Oh?" He turns to face me. "So why did you invite her to your home for dinner?"

"So she gets to know me better?" I raise my bottle of water to my mouth.

"So, it's a date?"

I choke on the water, then spit it out. "Say what?"

"A date—when a man and a woman get to know each other, over a meal—"

"I know what a date is, this"—I gesture to my chest, then to the space in front of me—"is not a date."

"Nice of you to invite me on a date." She flashes a wide smile at me from the doorstep of my penthouse. It's the day after the conversation with Adam that left me confused and very clear that it is *not* a date. That's not why I'd invited her to my home. I've had people over— *Not since you returned from the mission—and even before, you preferred to meet Declan and Cade at the 7A Club*. Which doesn't mean anything. The only reason I asked her over is so she can get to know me better, so she can write a better profile for me, which will help attract the right kind of woman to become my wife. And I need to get this right. So, the profile needs to be spot on. And that's the only reason she's here. That is all.

This is not a date, is what I want to say. Instead, I step aside and usher her in. She brushes past me, and I lean in her wake to soak up her scent. Roses tinged with those sugary notes that make me want to bend her over my lap and dig my teeth into her fleshy thigh assails me. My cock instantly extends. If I look down, I'll see a tent at my crotch, and fuck me, but how does she have this effect on me every single time I'm in her vicinity?

On the other hand, it's proof that what they did to me did not affect that part of me... Which is reassuring. Not that I've had sex since I returned... I can't stand the thought of being with anyone else... other than her. Can't stand the idea of touching anyone else... but her. Fuck, this is crazy. This is not how I envisaged the start to this evening. I managed to avoid her all day by reaching work before her, then shutting myself in my office and asking not to be disturbed.

I skipped the coffee she normally gets me, and instead, made my own coffee and a sandwich for lunch at the kitchenette attached to my office. Then I worked all day before emerging after she'd left. It was to prove to myself that I could go an entire day without seeing her, and I had. Of course, it didn't stop me from glancing at the app on my phone that links to her computer so I could see her face focused on the screen and whatever she was working on. Still, that's not the same as seeing her in person, right?

So, I managed well on my own. Then I came home and went for a run—without Adam—returning in time to shower and freshen up. But seeing her in the flesh and in my space, watching the sway of her hips as she glides across the hallway of my penthouse and toward the living room... Placing her bag on the coffee table as she shrugs out of her jacket, giving me the full view of how the pink dress she's wearing clings to her curves... She crosses the floor toward the floor-to-ceiling windows that soar two stories high and showcase the view of London stretched out in front.

"Whoa, this is spectacular." Her voice is awed.

"It is." I take in her hourglass figure silhouetted against the sun's rays that pour in through the window.

She looks at me over her shoulder. "I was talking about the view."

"So was I."

Her cheeks redden. She looks me up and down, and her blush deepens further.

"You look good," her voice cracks and she clears her throat. "Not that you don't normally look good, but you look better. I mean —" She squeezes her eyes shut. "Why do I always come across like a nincom- poop where you're concerned?"

My lips twitch. My chest feels lighter. This... This is why I like being with her. She's a ray of sunshine that cuts through the quagmire in my head. A blazing comet that cleaves through the dark night of my soul. A shimmering, iridescent, sparkling jewel that illuminates the murky depths of my heart. I'm not aware of walking forward, but the next thing I know, I'm standing in front of her. I push a strand of her sunshine hair behind her ear, and her eyes fly open. Her gaze widens. She looks up at me, and I can see her soul in her eyes. The innocence, the hope, that optimism that comes from not having seen evil that dwells in people's souls. Not having seen the violence I have — experienced death at close quarters, held friends as they've taken their last breath in my arms, looked in the eyes of a dying man as his soul dissolves, leaving behind the shell of what he was. What I am now. A caricature, a ghost, a husk of who I once was.

I'll never go back to being that man again. The kind of man she deserves. Someone complete, someone whole, someone who can see, feel, and sense normalcy, want normal things — a life, a love, children for all the right reasons. That's not me. And I don't know who I am anymore. Don't know who I'm going to be if I continue on the path I've set myself.

She tips up her chin, rises on her toes, and I know she wants me to kiss her. To press my mouth to hers, swipe my tongue across the seam of her lips, draw from her honeyed essence, share her breath and raise her pulse rate until her knees give out from under her. That's what she wants from me, I know, which is why I step back from her and growl, "This is not a date."

23

Penny

That's what he says, but everything in the room says otherwise. Firstly, he smells delicious. He always smells wonderful, but that sea-breeze laced with pepper scent of his is especially pronounced today, like he splashed an extra dollop of cologne on after shaving. And he *has* shaved. His normal five o' clock shadow is gone, revealing that jawline which makes me swoon. On the other hand, the scruff on his jaw always makes me wonder how it would feel to have him draw that roughened skin between my thighs. My pussy clenches on cue, even as my heart feels like it's breaking. He's made it clear that the only reason I'm here is work related. Nothing else. I swallow around the ball of emotion in my throat, then paste that bright smile on my face.

"Don't do that." He frowns.

"What?"

"Don't smile when you really want to throw something at me."

My lips freeze in the curved shape they took on earlier. "I don't know what you're talking about."

"You put on a front to the world. Pretend you're happy and sunny and everything is going to be okay, when inside, you're really raging and angry."

This time, I do wipe the smile off my face. "You don't know me at all." I begin to push past him, but he grabs my wrist. Electricity shoots out from the point of contact. He must feel it, too, for his nostrils flare. He lets go of me at once, and instantly, I miss his touch. Which is crazy. How could I have let him get under my skin so quickly? Especially since I'm not sure if I like him.

"You're right, I don't."

I blink. "You agree with me?"

"Why do you sound surprised?"

"Because you haven't agreed with a single thing I've said since I came to work for you."

He seems taken aback again, likely because I've never been this upfront with him. But being away from the office has eased the atmosphere between us. It feels less formal, and he feels more approachable. It may also be because he seems a little more at ease in these surroundings.

"You're right again. I'm not easy to be with. It's not that I'm not aware of it."

"So, you just don't care?"

"Not particularly, if I'm being honest. I'm too focused on ensuring I get ownership of the company from my father."

"And that's important to you?"

"It's the most important thing in my life right now," he admits.

"Or, maybe it's a way for you to avoid facing the trauma you've been through?" The words are out before I can help myself. And... maybe that's good. Maybe, he needs to hear it from someone. Only, the way he firms his jaw and narrows his gaze on me indicates he's far from happy with what I said. It's easy to see the faults in someone else. It's much more difficult when you're on the receiving end.

"I'm sorry, I shouldn't have said that."

"No, you shouldn't have, but then, I don't expect anything from you but the unfiltered truth. It's refreshing, especially when compared to how most people prefer to be evasive about the thing that's bothering them the most."

"That's me, unfiltered." I raise a shoulder. "It's gotten me into trouble more than once."

"It shows you have a pure heart." He frowns, as if he's not happy about what he's said.

"Don't worry, I won't hold what you said against you." I allow myself a small smile.

He holds my gaze. "Going back to your earlier comment... We don't know each other that well, which is why you're here in the first place."

"I'm here to find out more about you for the profile," I correct him.

"I'd like to propose a quid-pro-quo. You get to find out things about me for the profile and I get to know things about you so we can work better together as a team."

"And if I say no to the latter?"

"Are you saying no?" The skin around his eyes creases. Clearly, he's amused by the possibility of me denying him something.

"I'm saying"—I stab my thumb over my shoulder—"I'm hungry. Aren't you going to feed me?"

"You like James Hamilton's food?"

I survey the plate of food he's placed in front of me. It holds a burger and fries, the posh version—my favorite meal. I glance up at him. "How did you know?"

He merely raises a shoulder.

"Did Abby tell you?"

He doesn't reply, and I assume that's how he found out. I'm not sure how I feel about him finding that out. On the other hand, he made the effort of asking her. He heads back inside and returns in a few seconds with his own plate. I'm seated at a table that's been set up for two on one of the terraces adjoining his penthouse. Yes, there's more than one. The one I'm on adjoins the kitchen. It has spectacular views of the city and is set up with patio heaters. I'd peeked into the kitchen to find him pulling the food from warming trays carrying the Michelin-starred chef's logo. Knight places his own plate of food opposite me, then takes his seat. "I've known James since university."

"Along with Cade and Declan?"

He nods.

"You're close to Cade and Declan, aren't you?"

"They're like brothers," he confesses.

"But you haven't been spending time with them."

He narrows his gaze. "You've been taking to Abby?"

"Guilty." I hold up a hand. "Sorry, it's none of my business."

He rubs the back of his neck. "I know my sister is worried, but you can reassure her, I'm doing fine."

I glance at the view then back through the doorway and through his kitchen to what I can see of his duplex penthouse. "You seem to be doing more than fine."

"You like the space?"

"It's gorgeous. I've never been this high in London before." Notably, there aren't any paintings or art or any other form of creative work on the walls, no pictures or anything that hints at this being his personal space. But I'm not going to tell him that.

"This is the highest penthouse in the city," he informs me.

I turn to glance at him. "It is?"

"We *are* at The Shard, the tallest building in the city, and this penthouse—more specifically the rooms on the second floor of the duplex"—he nods in the direction of the L-shaped hallway upstairs that looks down on the living room space—"are on the topmost floor."

"Right, I knew that. I mean, I knew this is the tallest building, and I did notice we came right to the top, I just didn't connect the dots fast enough in my head." Which is typical of me. I never seem to see things which are right in front of me. Like the fact that the sexy, gorgeous, complicated man sitting in front of me is definitely out of bounds. I'm helping him to find a wife, which reminds me. "I guess we should get down to work." I reach for my phone which is on the table next to me, but he beats me to it.

"Let's eat first." He picks it up and slides it into his pocket. "No phones at the dining table."

I laugh. "Is that a rule your parents imposed?"

He frowns as he walks around to take his seat. "My father was never home enough for us to eat dinner together."

"He was too busy working?"

"He was… busy." Knight reaches for the bottle of champagne and pops the cork, then pours the bubbles into my flute, before topping himself up.

"So, not a date, huh?" I allow myself a small smile.

He rewards me with a slight upturn of his own lips on one side. "It's a working dinner… And good food and drink help the creative workflow."

He raises his glass, and I clink mine with his. "To getting to know each other better." I take a sip of the sparkling wine and the flavors of citrus and peach, combined with something nutty, almost toasty, and woven through with unmistakable scent of roses teases my palate. "Oh, my god." I close my eyes and groan. "This is incredible." I make a humming sound, and when I open my eyes, I find him staring at me.

"Sorry, that was a rather un-sophisticated demonstration of how much I like it."

"You can be unsophisticated anytime," he says in low voice. My nipples bead, moisture laces the space between my legs, and I squeeze my thighs together. His eyes flare. The air between us grows heavy with unsaid words. I feel like I'm swimming through a thick syrup to get to a place I've never been before. The silence stretches. The hair on my fore-arms rises. My scalp prickles, and every cell in my body seems to light up under his single-minded attention.

I'm the first to glance away. I reach for my flute and take another sip of the bubbles. When I look up, he's busy cutting into his steak.

"Don't you want to marry for love?"

He pauses with his fork halfway to his mouth, then slowly completes the action. He chews, swallows, then reaches for the next forkful. "I'm not keen on marrying, per se, or having children. The only reason I'm doing it is because —"

"You need to protect your ownership of the company. I'm aware of that. But haven't you wanted to find the right woman and find love?"

"No." He continues eating, then takes in my features. He must see some of my shock and surprise for he shrugs. "I was focused on protecting my country and now, on growing my company. I've never had time for anything else."

"And women?"

He takes another forkful of food, then places his utensil down. "What's with all these questions?"

"Just getting to know you better, so I can draw up a more appro-priate profile. That's what this meal is about, right?"

"What does my profile have to do with my views on marriage and love."

"Because it's supposed to attract the right woman, duh!"

"One has nothing to do with the other. What you need to put down is, I make a billion dollars a year, their monthly allowance is a million dollars, with another two million for each child they push out, and another five million for every year they stay married to me."

I purse my lips. "I'm surprised you didn't specify two million for a male child and a million for a female child."

"I don't differentiate between genders."

I scoff. "You only have a traditional view when it comes to the women who work for you."

"One woman in particular, yes."

I gape at him. "You're not even denying the fact that you've treated me worse than anyone else in your employment."

"No one else has as much access to me. It makes sense that you see the unvarnished truth."

"Which is that you're scared and hurting and striking out at everyone in sight?"

We stare at each other. To my surprise, he doesn't protest. He simply looks at me with a steady gaze. "You came here to ask me questions, didn't you?"

"The list of questions are in my bag." I begin to rise from my seat, but he shakes his head.

"Sit down."

My butt hits the chair.

"Ask me your questions from memory."

"But I don't remember all of them."

"You're wasting time. Also"—he jerks his chin toward my plate —"you're not eating."

I pick up the burger and take a huge mouthful. The juiciness of the patty, the chewiness of the bread, the tanginess of the tomatoes, the fresh creamy taste of the coleslaw—all of the different flavors and textures fill my mouth. I close my eyes and moan around the mouthful of food, then take my time chewing it and swallowing it down. "It's so good." I open my eyes to find he's staring at my mouth, his jaw clenched. There's an almost angry look in his eyes.

"Sorry, I clearly have no manners when it comes to eating."

He reaches out, then drags his thumb across the corner of my lips. He scoops up some of the coleslaw that's dripped from the corner of my mouth, then brings it to his own and sucks on his digit.

The heat shimmering under my skin blazes into a forest fire. Every part of me seems to be awake, alight, more alive than I've ever been before in my life. I place the half-eaten burger on the plate, then snatch up the flute of champagne and down it. That only makes my head spin further. He places his fork down and tops up my flute.

"If I didn't know better, I'd think you were trying to get me drunk," I murmur.

"And you and I know, I don't need to get you drunk for you to allow me to do as I want with you."

I draw in a sharp breath. "I thought you said this was a working dinner?"

"And you said it was a date."

I stare at him, then chuckle. "Touché, soldier."

His own lips quirk, then he leans back in his chair. "Eat," he orders.

I focus on the food, take another bite, and another, and stop only when my plate is clean. He pours water into a glass and slides that over.

"Thanks." I take a few sips, then sit back with a sigh.

"Now ask your questions."

I resist the urge to roll my eyes and snap out a 'Yessir.' That's only going to distract the both of us, and I need to complete the job I came here to do.

"What's your favorite color?" I ask.

His forehead creases. "That's what you want to ask me?"

"Humor me."

He looks skeptical, then takes another bite of his food, before placing the fork down. "Black."

"What a surprise," I mumble under my breath.

He arches an eyebrow. "You say something?"

"No, no, of course not." I smile at him sweetly. "Do you prefer to call or text?"

"Neither."

I frown. "Indoors or outdoors."

"Either, as long as I'm on my own."

I scoff, "What do you want to do on your next vacation?"

"Climb Uluru."

I blink. It must be a coincidence he mentioned one of the must-do's from my bucket list.

"Something you've always wanted to experience?"

"Swimming with dolphins."

I gape at him, then shake my head. Another coincidence, that's all it is.

"Dark chocolate or white chocolate?"

"Bitter chocolate."

Of course, it's bitter. I stifle a snort. "Pineapple on your pizza?"

"I hate pizza."

My jaw drops. "Who hates pizzas?"

He merely gives me that 'Knight look' which says, 'hurry up and get on with it, you're wasting my time.'

"What is your hidden talent?"

The left side of his mouth curls. "Giving women orgasms."

Now, I do roll my eyes. "I walked into that one."

"You did." His smile widens, only a teensy bit. But it's enough to light up his features. He looks younger, more innocent. Is this how he looked when he was younger? Before he went into the military? Before he was taken captive?

"Do you prefer to drive or be driven—" I raise a hand. "No, don't answer that. What do you think about PDA?"

"What's that?"

"Public displays of affection?"

"If you mean sex in a public place—"

I flush. "I don't."

"But if you did, then, as you're aware, I'm all for it."

Damn, he manipulated that question to his advantage. I need to think of something that he has no choice but to answer in a straightforward manner.

"What makes you angry?"

"People who waste my time," he growls in a pointed fashion.

"What makes you laugh?"

"You."

His eyes almost twinkled when he said that. I swear they did.

"Are you a forgiver or a forgetter?"

"Neither." The creases deepen from the edges of his eyes.

Damnit, think of a trickier question. Go on, you can do this!

"What is your idea of beauty?"

"You."

I frown. "Be serious."

"I am being serious."

"So, you want your wife to look like me?'

He rubs his finger under his lip, then shrugs. "Sure, why not."

"You could be more enthusiastic, considering how this is going to change your life."

"Not as much as it's going to change her life."

I roll my eyes. "Favorite movie?"

"*Shark attack*."

"You're joking!" I accuse him.

"Nope, I like sharks."

"That's because you're like them."

"Are you talking about my pointed teeth? Or the fact that I like to circle my prey before I move in?"

Is he talking about me? Am I the prey? I push the thought aside and ask my next question, "What book are you reading these days?"

"I'm not, but if I were, it would be Harry Potter."

I swear, hearts appear in my eyes, and I blink them away. "You want to read Harry Potter?"

"Sure, time I found out what all the fuss is about, don't you think?"

"Personally, I prefer the fanfic."

"Fanfic?" A furrow appears between his eyebrows.

"Yep, especially the one featuring Dramione."

"That's a character from the story I take it?"

"Actually, it's the 'ship between two characters, Draco Malfoy and Hermione Granger."

"Ship?"

"I mean, relationship. The two are at each other's throats all the time in the Potterverse; that's the setting of the series."

"I guessed that," he says dryly. "And I take it Draco and Hermione hate each other in the series, but the fans want them to poke each other?" He touches the thumb and forefinger of his left hand and inserts the forefinger of his other hand through the gap created.

"Eww, you're such a man."

His smile widens a tad more, before he seems to remember himself, and his features straighten again. "Any more questions before I get dessert?"

"We're having dessert?"

"Yes." He rises to his feet. I rise with him. We gather our plates, and I follow him inside. I place mine in the sink and turn to find he's pulling out another dish from one of the canisters.

"Whoa, that's a chocolate brownie, my favorite." I frown. No doubt, another thing he found out from Abby.

He cuts off a slice, plates it in a dessert bowl, then adds a dollop of vanilla ice cream. He walks over to stand on the opposite side of the counter from me. He scoops up a generous portion then holds it up. "Open."

My pussy spasms on command. It's just a word. A simple order. And he made it sound like pure sex. I realize I've been staring at him when he arches an eyebrow. I part my lips, and he slides the food between them. The rich taste of chocolate, mixed with the delicate floral taste of the vanilla pods, explodes on my palate. He dips the spoon into the dessert and brings it to his mouth. I watch as he pulls the spoon back, then licks off the dregs of the treat. The fires that ignited across my skin intensify. I shudder.

"You cold?"

I shake my head. "It's getting late. I think I need to leave." I round the counter, head toward the coffee table, and pick up my handbag. I slide it over my shoulder, then turn and gasp, for he's standing right in front of me.

24

Knight

"Flying away so soon, Little Dove?"

She laughs, the sound nervous. "I, uh, have everything I need."

But I'm only getting started.

I reach out and tug her handbag down her arm, then drop it onto the couch behind her.

"What are you doing?" She sucks in her breath through her lips.

I hold out my hand. She looks down at it, then back at me. "Knight —"

"What did I ask you to call me?"

She hesitates. "Sir," she says under her breath.

"I didn't hear you."

She clears her throat. "What are you doing… Sir?"

I allow her voice to sweep away the myriad of thoughts running through my head. Allow my attention to drop back down into my chest, my arms, my legs. I push my feet into the ground and anchor my gaze on the gorgeous siren standing in front of me.

"Whatever you want me to do to you, Little Dove."

The pulse at the base of her throat drums faster.

"You're going to be married soon."

"And I'm never going to be in a relationship—not with her, not with you, not with anyone."

"So, this…" She nods toward my outstretched hand. "What's this?"

"Sex."

"A quick and dirty fling, and then we go our separate ways?" Her lips quiver, and she manages to flatten them.

"It's going to be anything but quick. And dirtier than anything you've read in your Dramione fanfic."

"How do you know, when you've never read it?"

"Why don't we put it to the test, and you can tell me, hmm?"

Color flushes up her throat. "I'm not sure that's a good idea."

I search her features, then nod. "Okay."

She seems taken aback. "That's it? You're just accepting what I said?"

"It's your choice. You can stay and be fucked on every surface in this house and in every way and in every orifice over one night, and I'll see you in the office tomorrow. Or you can leave, go home to your own bed, and I'll see you in the office tomorrow."

Her forehead furrows. She glances around the apartment then at me. "My choice, huh?"

I nod.

"You won't stop me if I leave?"

I hold up my hands. "I won't."

She picks up her coat, shrugs into it, then picks up her bag. She hooks it over her shoulder, and the tempo of my heart accelerates. It's as if wild horses have invaded my chest as I watch her head for the elevator. She presses the button to call the cage, and the doors part. Of course, they do. It's my private elevator. Only I use it, so it's always at my disposal. For the first time, I curse the benefits my money is able to buy.

I never missed it when I lived off my military salary. And didn't pay much attention to the luxury that came along with moving into this flat. I needed somewhere high enough from the ground that I wouldn't have to look at it and remember what it was like to be buried six feet deep. I wanted a place with enough light that there were no dark corners I could step into.

This penthouse delivers on all those fronts. I decided to move it because it would give me the solitude I crave. Now, I wish I hadn't been so quick to seek out the trappings that feed my desire for seclusion. A first, since I returned from my captivity.

She steps inside the car and turns. Our gazes meet, then the door slides shut. She's gone. I gave her a choice, and she took it. I could have commanded her to stay, and she would have. I could have asked her to strip, and she'd have gladly shed her clothes. I could have ordered her to bend over the chaise, and she'd have obliged.

Instead, something inside of me had wanted her to stay of her own accord, and she didn't. She left. I turn and glance about the space. The sun has set outside, and the lights of the city shine up in a cloud of iridescence. They drown out the light from the stars above, so the sky is a flattened sheet of plastic. A void into which, if I shout, not even my echo will answer me back. Like my life. My heart. My soul, which is no longer mine. I head toward the floor-to-ceiling windows, then raise my arm and crash my fist into the windowpane. There's a dull boom, then pain shudders up my arm and it feels… Cleansing.

Apparently, the only way to feel anything, other than when I'm being dominant, is by hurting myself. I stare at the fractured surface. This windowpane is not meant to crack easily. Not unless you hit it with the right pressure at the right angle and at the weakest point of the panel. All of which I seem to have accomplished. This time, luck is with me, or maybe, against me? Was it luck that had Adam come to my rescue at the right time? Was it luck that had us being captured in the first place?

The pressure presses down behind my eyeballs. My brain feels like it's pushing against my skull. Sweat beads my forehead. I need to relieve the pressure. Right this second. I throw up my arm again, intent on punching through the glass this time, when the ding of the elevator doors opening reaches me. I look into the fractured glass surface in front of me and spot her approach in the reflection.

She sweeps her gaze down my body, and halfway across the floor, she drops her bag and runs toward me. "Knight!" When she reaches me, she takes in the lacerated skin over my knuckles.

"Oh, my god!" She reaches for my hand, and I pull it away.

"Get out."

"You're hurt."

"I've been hurt before."

"You're crazy."

Not enough. I pivot and head for the bar in the corner of the room. I reach for a bottle of whiskey and uncap it with my unhurt hand. Then, I chug down the alcohol. It goes down smoothly, leaving a burn in its wake. I take another sip, then turn to find she's walking toward me.

"I told you to leave."

"I'm not going."

"You left earlier."

"I came back." She swallows.

"For what?"

She shuffles her feet. "You know what."

"No, I don't. You need to spell it out."

"I..." She glances to her left, then her right, then wraps her arms about her waist. "I want you to fuck me, okay?"

"No."

"Eh?" She jerks her chin up. "You want me. I know you do."

"So?"

"You're pissed because I didn't choose to stay. Your ego is hurt. Is that it?"

"A-n-d there you are again with your pop psychology one-oh-one. I have news for you, I've fooled hardened army shrinks. You're nothing in front of them."

"They don't know you the way I do."

"Oh?" I take another long pull from the whiskey bottle, then lower it to my side.

"You know I'm right. I see you, Knight. I know you're angry about what they did to you. I know you want revenge for what happened."

"Oh, I had my revenge." I crack my neck. "Adam and I killed those bastards before we escaped."

She pales, then seems to get hold of herself, "You may have k-killed them, but you don't seem any happier."

I tighten my fingers around the neck of the bottle. "It gave me the satisfaction of knowing I made them pay."

"And yet, you act as if you're still at war. You're on edge. You prefer to stay on your own. You avoid your friends and family. It's as if you never returned from wherever you were being held."

"Oh, I'm very aware that I returned. I made it out alive... But the rest of my team didn't." I set my jaw. "I don't deserve to be here when they aren't."

"Why can't you focus on the positive? You got out. Adam got out. There must be a reason for it."

I tilt my head. "Look at you. As usual, spouting your optimism and sunshine and hopefulness. I'd normally find it cute, but right now, you're getting on my nerves."

"You're happy I returned."

"Do I look happy to you?" I laugh, and the sound is hollow.

"You look"—she searches my features—"lonely."

"And you're the one who's going to soothe my brow and tell me I'm not."

"You're not... for tonight." She reaches for her coat and pushes it off her shoulders.

"You don't really want to do this," I growl.

She merely smiles, then bends and grabs the hem of her dress. In one swoop, she yanks it up and over her head. She flings it aside and stands clad in her bra, which barely contains her breasts, and a tiny thong, with a crotch that reveals the shadowy outline of her slit. The blood drains to my groin. I'm instantly so hard, the pain in my balls beats in tandem to the pain that pulses up from my injured knuckles.

I drag my gaze down her fleshy thighs, her shapely calves, her delicate ankles encircled by the straps of her three-inch high stilettos. By the time I raise my gaze back to her face, she's flushed. Her lips are parted. Her color is so high, her dilated blue eyes are pools of desire that beckon me to dive into them, to drown myself in them. In her. To forget, for one night, what happened to me. To remember the man I once was.

"Last chance," I snap.

She pulls down the strap of her bra over one shoulder.

"Stop."

25

Penny

"Keep them on."

"Eh?" I blink.

"I want to tear them off you before I fuck you." My pussy instantly melts. Oh, god, his filthy words are such a turn on, and I don't even understand why. I'm not a prude. Hey, I read spicy fanfiction and spicy books, but I always thought filthy-talking book boyfriends were confined to the world of fiction. I was sure I'd never meet them in real life. And definitely not in the shape of an ex-soldier who used to take on secret missions for the government and is now wounded on so many different levels. A man whose heart is so much softer than he'd like the world believe. A man who's in so much pain, he prefers to lash out rather than confront the cause for it. A man...

I want to hold in my arms and receive into my body, knowing there's no future for us. And that's what bothers and surprises me but also sets me free. I always believed in the Happily Ever After and that I'd meet a man who I'd fall for and spend the rest of my life with. Seeing the happy marriage my parents had right until the day my dad died gave me high expectations. And I know he's not the one to give me that. And in a way, that's freeing. There's no burden of having to be careful about what I do with him. There's relief in the fact that I can show the filthy side of me, the dirty things my body craves without fear of being judged.

After all, he's going to marry someone else, and I'll go back to being just his employee... for the next year. After which, I'll leave and find employment elsewhere, because the thought of seeing him with his wife is not something I can bear. Now, there's something I don't want to question too closely. Not while he's lowering the barriers he always throws up to the world and for the first time, is allowing me to see the need, the yearning, the craving in his eyes for what I can offer him. My body, my empathy, myself. He wants me, not anyone else—me. And I want him, too. More than anything else, I want him to do every single, dirty, obscene act my imagination can conjure up, and those it can't.

I lower my arm to my side and watch as he takes a step back. He looks me up and down, an assessing look in his eyes. Then he circles me slowly, so slowly, and his gaze dips into the valley between my breasts, the curve of my shoulder, the crease of my underarm, the flare of my hips, and when he stands behind me, I can feel him assess the slope of where my back meets my butt, and the crease between my ass-cheeks covered by the thin string of the thong. Why did I think it was a good idea to wear my skimpiest underwear? Did I subconsciously known I was going to sleep with him when I walked through his door today? I didn't think about it, but perhaps, something inside me knew was inevitable we reach this point: me standing in front of him in only my lingerie.

He steps forward and the heat of his body sears my back. He skims his nose up my cheek, and goosebumps pepper my skin. "You smell so good, Little Dove." My belly spasms. My heart seems to drop into the space between my legs, mirroring the pulse at my temples. He continues to stand there, his cheek pressed to mine, and heat flushes my skin. He stands there, perfectly still, the seconds ticking past.

My nerve endings stretch, the tension building in the air hot, heavy, pressing down on my shoulders, pinning me in place, until I'm unable to move. To breathe. To think. "Sir, please," I croak out the words before I'm able to stop myself, and he freezes.

He straightens, then walks around to stand in front of me. "You have no idea what you do to me," he says in a low, hard voice.

"Is that why you sound like you hate me?"

He notches his knuckles under my chin and applies enough pressure that I have to look up at him. His green eyes burn into me again. I'm a dove with a broken wing, unable to fly away. I know he's going to corrupt me tonight and I cannot... Will not... Do not want to stop him. I know he's going to change me forever and I welcome it. I welcome him.

He must see the emotions on my face because his jaw hardens. "I do hate you for being so open with me. For always baring your heart to me. For allowing me to see inside you and knowing you're everything I'm not. For knowing I shouldn't do this to you but also not being able to stop myself. If I were a better man, I'd walk away. If I were the man I was six months ago, I wouldn't have asked you here in the first place."

"If I were a better woman, I wouldn't have accepted your help in the first place. I would have returned the money you paid toward my mother's care and found another way, but I didn't. It's true, your personality is overwhelming, and you're very persuasive, and I find it very difficult to say no to you, but I'm here because I want to be. I took off my clothes because I want you to see me. And every time you touch me, I revel in how my body responds to you. I don't like you, but I know this much..." I search his eyes. "I know you're going to give me the kind of pleasure I'll remember for a lifetime."

His eyes flash, and in the next moment, he scoops me up in his arms bride style. I gasp, then wrap my arms about his neck. He turns and heads up the stairs. He reaches the landing, then heads down the hallway I glimpsed from downstairs. I briefly view a couple of doors that lead to other rooms, then he steps through the one at the far end. The moonlight pours in through the floor-to-ceiling windows that make up three walls of the room. He crosses the floor toward a super king-size bed pushed up against the only wall that's not made of glass. He sits down, then manipulates my body so I'm straddling him. I freeze. The column in his pants is thick and large and it stabs into the exact center of my core where I'm the emptiest.

"Sir," I breathe.

Color flushes his cheeks, and damn, it's something to see this big virile man reacting to the sound of my voice. I lean in until my lips are right in front of his, until I can draw in his breath without our mouths touching. "Sir," I whisper. His cock jumps. Gold flecks flare in the depths of his eyes.

"You have no idea what you're doing," he growls.

"I think I do." I slide back, then skim my fingers down the length of him and squeeze. His dick throbs and grows bigger. My mouth waters, and I swallow. My nipples are throbbing with need, hurting to feel his hands on me. "Touch me, please."

He brings one big palm up and squeezes my breast.

"Oh, god!" I throw my head back as he relinquishes his hold on my hip and cups my other breast. He kneads my flesh, and I thrust my chest forward, chasing more of his touch.

"You like that, hmm?" His gravelly voice chafes across my sensitized skin.

I open my mouth to reply, but no words emerge. He's barely begun touching me, and I'm lost in a miasma of sensations. He releases his hold on one breast, and the next second, I scream as he replaces it with his mouth. He bites down on my nipple through the thin lace of my bra. He tugs on it, and I pant. He swirls his tongue around the pulsing flesh, and my heart threatens to jump out of my chest.

"Sir, please, Sir," I whimper.

The next second, he's rising to his feet. I wrap my legs around his waist and cling to his shoulders as he carries me over to the window nearest the bed. He pushes me into the glass wall, then hooks his finger inside the strap of panties. He tugs, and it snaps. He slides a finger inside me, and I groan, "Oh, my god."

"You're so wet for me, Little Dove. Do you like what I do to you?"

I open my mouth to answer, but he begins to move his finger in and out of me, in and out. My eyes roll back in my head, and all I can do is whimper and push my hips out to meet his thrusts. It's so good. So very good.

"Open your eyes."

When did I close them? I raise my heavy-eyelids, and once more, am held captive by his powerful gaze. I'll never forget the possessiveness in his eyes as he slides a second finger inside of me and curls them. I groan and shiver as he stretches me around the girth of his thick digits. I'm so full, and he's only fucking me with his fingers. He slides out his fingers, then back in, then again. A trembling grips me. My thighs quiver and I begin to slide down the glass as only his grip on my hip holds me up. He pulls his fingers out, then pushes them between my lips.

"Suck."

I obey. The taste of my cum mixed with that of his skin makes my head spin. He watches me closely as if gauging my response, then nods. He slides his fingers under the thin material of my bra. He tugs on it, and it snaps. My breasts spill out of the restraint. A gasp spills from my lips. He glances down at my breasts and when he licks his lips, moisture bathes the space between my legs. I want him to squeeze my nipples again. I want him to stuff his fingers—no, his cock—inside my slit. I need him to drill into me right now and fill this yawning emptiness inside of me. "Fuck me, please," I beg.

He smirks. Asshole smirks. For the first time since I met him, my Sir has a twinkle in his eyes and oh, lordy, it's the most gorgeous sight ever. This is how Knight would have been if he wasn't suffering from the trauma that he went through. And I'm the one who's revealed this part of him. He might deny it, but spending time with me is doing him a world of good. It's what makes me reach up and slap him.

26

Knight

"The fuck?" I glare at her. "Why did you do that?"

"Because you were holding back."

I hardly felt that slap, but my ego insists I obtain an answer. I stiffen, then lower my eyebrows. "Tell me you didn't do that to provoke me."

"I did it to provoke you."

I chuckle. "You do not mean that."

"Oh, yes, I do." She nods.

"You're trying to get a rise out of me on purpose?"

"Because I don't want you to go soft on me."

"You wouldn't like it if I showed you what I really want to do with you."

"I thought you were done hiding from me?"

"I'm not hiding. I'm protecting you."

"And I don't want to be protected. I want you to show me who you really are."

This girl. She has no idea what she's asking of me. I peer into her features, and once more, I see her heart in her eyes. Why can't she, for once, show me she's thinking of something other than me? How can someone so generous possibly want me so much? How can someone who is so honest, so real, so everything I'm not, always show me just how wrong I am for her in every way? How can I go through with this, knowing how much I'm going to hurt her? How can I afford not to when everything in me wants to own her, possess her, make her mine... even if it's for one night only?

"You're not ready for it," I growl.

Her lips curve. "You mean, you're not ready for it, don't you?"

"Fucking hell, you're pushing me."

"Not enough because you're still talking to me and—" She gasps as I push my substantial erection into the gap between her legs.

"You ready to take all of me, baby? You ready to have my monster cock inside of you?"

She swallows. A look of uncertainty creeps into her eyes.

"That's what I thought. Let me be the judge of what is and isn't right for you."

She looks away, then back at me. "I... I know I'm inexperienced, but I want you to have my virginity."

"And I cannot understand why."

"Because... Because I know you'll be good for me."

I chuckle, but the sound is without humor. "I'm not good for anyone. Not for myself, or my family and friends, and definitely, not for you."

She raises her gaze to mine, then presses her hand to my cheek. A shudder rolls down my back. Something in my heart cracks. Before I can stop myself, I've turned my head into her palm and kissed it. Fucking hell, she's getting through to me. She's making me get in touch with the man I once was inside, and... I'm not sure I like it. I'm not ready to let go of the rage that occupies every part of me... yet. I'm not ready to let go of her, either... Not for tonight.

I lower her legs to the ground, and once I'm sure she has her balance, I step back. She looks at me with surprise, and I wrap my fingers around her wrist and walk her over to the bed. I turn her around to face me and apply pressure on her shoulder, so she sinks down onto the bed.

"Spread your legs." I infuse enough authority into my voice that she flushes. Then she parts her plump thighs, exposing the pink flesh between them. I plant myself between her legs, wrenching them apart further. She bites down on her lower lip, and a surge of satisfaction fills me. This...is what I want. To please her. To delight her. To hold her and caress her. To spank her and dominate her such that her pleasure escalates. To take her to the edge, so when I let her come, she'll remember the orgasm for the rest of her life. I sink down to my knees, and her gaze widens. I hook one arm under her thigh and throw her leg—stiletto in place—over my shoulder.

She looks at me open-mouthed. "What are you doing?" she asks in a high-pitched voice.

I merely turn my face into her leg and drag my chin up the underside of her calf. She shivers. Goosebumps pepper her skin. I toss her other ankle over my other shoulder, baring her to my gaze. I stare down at her exposed pussy, and a flush rolls up her torso.

"You're fucking beautiful, you know that?"

Her entire face goes a deep red. She tries to pull her legs back, but I hold on. I continue to take in the parted lips on either side of her clit which glisten with arousal, the nub of her clit which is engorged and swollen, though I've barely touched it. The more I look at her, the more she squirms. The trembling of her thighs turning my insides into a mass of churning need.

"I'm going to eat you out, Little Dove."

She moans.

"Lay back for me."

She stares at me with lust and need and a shyness that melts more of the ice around my heart. This princess in front of me; she deserves to be treated like a queen.

I flatten my palm onto her chest and push gently. She instantly presses her back into the bed.

I drag my hand down her belly to the weeping flesh between her legs. Then I raise my hand and spank her pussy.

She yelps, "What the—" The next sound out of her mouth is a whine when I bend my head and lick her from arsehole to clit.

"Sir, Sir. Please. Sir, Please," she bursts out.

I allow myself to curve my lips against her sopping pussy. Then I swipe my tongue up her pussy lips. She gasps, tries to wriggle away, but I hold her down. Then I go to town, licking her slit and curling my tongue around her clit, before darting my tongue inside her slit.

"Oh, Jesus, oh, my god!" she cries out.

"I'm your god, baby." I laugh, surprising myself. I haven't felt this good in I don't know how long. Not since I spent time with my friends before I left on my mission—no, before that. This feeling of tenderness, the need to dominate, combined with the yearning to share and give and drive her out of her mind with pleasure fills me, driving away the final echoes of the noise that always fills my head. A quiet descends, and I focus on the writhing woman in front of me, more specifically, the apex of her thighs which is the key to driving her out of her mind with gratification.

I thrust my tongue in and out of her, in and out. She yelps, screams, begs for mercy, and that only spurs me on. I slide my palms under her hips and squeeze her fleshy butt cheeks. She makes a noise halfway between a groan and a whine, then digs her fingers into my hair and tugs. Pinpricks of sensation roll down my back. My cock stabs into my jeans, screaming for relief. I ignore it. I continue to flick my tongue in and out of her, and glance up to find she has her eyes closed again.

I raise my head long enough to snap, "Look at me."

She cracks open her eyelids, and when her gaze meets mine, her entire body jolts. Holding her gaze, I bite down on her clit, and she yells. "Sir, please, Sir—" I slide my tongue inside her again, and she bites down on her lower lip. And when I tease the rosette between her arse cheeks with my thumb, she arches back and tugs hard on my hair at the same time.

"Oh, wow... oh, my... I'm going to come, I—"

I pull my tongue and my thumb out.

Instantly, the trembling recedes from her body. She thrusts her hips up, trying to chase the sensation of how it felt to have me fuck her with my tongue and my fingers.

"Please, I need to... I have to... I want you inside of me." She pouts at me, lust dripping from her gaze. My groin tightens, and my balls feel like they weigh a ton. Before I can stop myself, I crawl up and over her and press my lips to hers.

27

Penny

He's kissing me. Ohmigod. He brushes his lips over mine, once, twice, thrice, while his gaze holds mine. I'm drowning in his eyes. I'm falling for him. No, I *have* fallen for him. It's been a headlong rush into the cauldron of whirling emotions and tripping lust that is Knight Warren. Resistance is futile. From the moment I met him, I've known it was inevitable. A question of when, not how.

Since I saw him walk into that room all angry and beat up and frustrated—scratch that, the first time I saw him saying goodbye to Abby and thought how hot he was—I've known I wanted him. Wanted him to want me. Wanted him to fuck me and show me how good we could be together. I wanted him on a physical level. I didn't plan to fall for the man behind the growly, intense exterior. Didn't expect his kiss to be hard and sweet. Masterful and commanding and filled with an aching yearning that sinks into my heart and zips to my core, setting every part of me alight with a pining, a longing, a craving for more.

I part my lips, and he slips his tongue inside, mirroring the way he laved my core earlier. How he stabbed his tongue inside my slit, how he licked my lower lips and sucked on my clit. How he fingered that forbidden part of me—a blush envelops me.

He leans back enough, his mouth is out of reach. And when I tip up my chin and try to capture it again with mine, that left side of his mouth curls in that almost smirk that has my pussy clenching all over again.

"I want you inside me," I choke out.

"I'm not going to take your virginity, Little Dove."

"Wha-a-t?" I blink.

"If I do, you'll attach yourself to me. It's inevitable."

Wow, the ego of this man.

"I don't fuck virgins," he says slowly, as if I didn't get it the first time around.

A slow anger bleeds into my veins. "You just ate me out," I snap.

"And you liked it."

"And I want more."

"Which you're not getting."

I draw a deep breath. *Stay calm, stay calm.* "So, let me get this right." I shake my head to clear it. "You're not going to make love to me?"

"I'm not going to fuck you."

Noted. It's fucking, not making love. Thank you for the clarification, jerkface. Those sparks of anger inside me flare into tiny flames.

"You're going to tease me and taunt me, but you're not going to let me come?"

"That's not what I said."

I squeeze my eyes shut for a second, count back from ten, then lift my eyelids. "I'm not sure I'm following."

"I'm not going to fuck you. Doesn't mean I'm not going to let you come."

"Then when?" The words are out of me before I can stop myself. *Ugh, I sound so dissatisfied and so put off. Where's my self-respect? How am I allowing this man to dick me around—literally?* The flames in my blood fan higher.

"When the time is right."

"When is that?"

"When I decide."

The flames blaze into an inferno. The sadistic bastard. "Let me go." I shove at his shoulder, but I might as well be hitting a wall. Asshole may have left the army, but clearly, he's working out. "Unhand me."

"No."

"You're not going to let me come right now, you're not going to fuck me, but you're not going to release me, either?"

A considering look comes into his eyes, then he nods. "That's about right."

"You're so frustrating," I snarl.

"So are you." A look of surprise flashes across his face before that mask, once more, falls across his features.

"I'm not the one deciding not to have sex."

"It's for your own good."

I scoff, "I bet you're thinking, right now, that you're being a gentleman, but all you are is a tease."

"It's good for your character," he says with a straight face. *What the —? Is this guy for real?*

"Let me up." I begin to writhe under him. Not that he gives a millimeter. It doesn't stop me, though. I'm not going to lay here and take his decision as if I accept it. Because I don't. Not at all. I heave and wriggle and push up into him and hit that thick, hard column in the crotch. I freeze.

"It's not like this is easy for me, either, but trust me when I say, this is the best thing for us."

"Who are you to make that decision for me?"

"Someone who doesn't want to see you unhappy."

"Ha-ha!" I pretend to laugh, then firm my lips. "I've had enough of this stupid conversation. I want to leave now."

"It's late."

"I can take a cab home."

"Nope." He releases me to sit up on his knees, and I miss the feel of his body.

Not that he was leaning his body fully against me. He made sure to keep most of his weight off of me— I wish I could have felt the full heaviness of him on me. His chest against mine, his cock inside me, his breath hot on my lips. A-n-d, seriously, I need to get my head examined. How can I want to sleep with him, when he's got some stupid notion into his head about not having sex with me? Then, he unfastens first one button on his cuff, then the other, before he moves to undo the first two on his placket.

"What are you doing?"

In reply, he reaches behind him and, in that one-handed gesture that hot guys seem to have perfected without trying, he yanks off his shirt and flings it aside. The moonlight streaming in lends an ivory sheen to his skin. *H-o-l-y mother of god, this guy is ripped.* Like acres upon acres of undulating, sculpted muscles that form an eight-pack. No, I swear it's an eight-pack. I didn't think those existed, but faced with evidence to the contrary, I have to admit defeat. And what a delicious defeat it is. I take in the glorious expanse of his chest marked with scars that tell of the life he's led. The flesh is pinched in a couple of places, and I'm sure they are marks from bullets. He faced them and survived, and thank god for that, for this man is too vital to not be here and alive and on his knees in front of me. And then there's the tattoo that runs up one side of his torso:

He who blinks, dies.

I reach out to trace the heavy script, and his muscles twitch. He's so tough, the planes of his body unforgiving, and macho, and so male. It makes me want to lick up his body, then rub my pussy all over him and mark him as mine. *Mine. Mine. Mine.* Oh, shoot, I need to stop with this line of thinking. I drag my fingers down the demarcation between his pecs, down to where the shallow groove on either side of his abdomen runs from his hipbone to his groin. My pussy instantly moistens; so does my mouth. *Am I drooling? Would you blame me if I were?*

"You looking at my cum gutters?"

"Excuse me?" I withdraw my hand. "Did you say—"

"Cum? I did." His lips twitch in that almost smile that makes me want to find a way to coax a full smile from him. "Does that shock you?"

"Of course not." I've heard that particular three-letter word mentioned in my Dramione fanfiction but somehow, hearing it drawled in a British accent, and from a man who looks as hot as Sir, it's a whole different ball game. *And I'd like to play a game with his balls, too.* I flush. *I can't believe I thought that. Oh, god, what's wrong with me?* "Please, I need to leave."

"You need to sleep." He rolls onto the mattress next to me, pulls the cover over us, then turns me away and spoons me.

He *spoons* me. And every part of my body relaxes. The heat from him forms an additional security blanket that pins me to the mattress. The *thud-thud-thud* of his heart at my back is soothing. My own heart beats in tandem. Our breathing synchronizes. A drugged sensation begins to seep into my limbs.

"It's called an Adonis belt," his voice rumbles over me.

"Hmm?" I yawn.

"The cum gutters were meant to get a reaction from you." I hear the humor in his voice. "You can take a man out of the military, but you can't remove his flair for speaking filth."

"You can speak filth to me anytime, Sir." His dick twitches against the curve of my behind. Oops, guess, I shouldn't have said that, but also, his body definitely has a visceral reaction when I call him, Sir. My lips curve, I yawn again and my eyes flutter down.

A wet, swiping sensation between my legs sends a pulse of heat up my spine. I part my thighs and push up my hips, inviting the intrusion. The lapping continues between my pussy lips, then around my clit, and my heart rate accelerates. I dig my fingers into his hair, then arch my back, chasing that feeling of his tongue stabbing into my pussy, of him curling his tongue inside me and touching the melting walls of my channel. My entire body jolts. I throw one ankle, then the other, around his neck and push my thighs into either side of his face. If this were real life, I'd worry about suffocating him. Good thing this is only a dream. I can be myself and enjoy this deliciously greedy feeling as he eats me out like his favorite desert. As he squeezes my ass-cheeks and holds me up at the right angle to serve his pleasure. As he licks me from my forbidden rosette to my clit. As he swipes his tongue in long sweeps between my pussy lips and brings tears of pleasure to my eyes. I open my mouth and allow myself to cry out. I open myself up to him, but it's okay. It's all a dream. So, I can enjoy this decadent sensation of him consuming me, of him dragging his stubbled chin up that most delicate part of me and making me scream. Of the orgasm that sweeps up from my toes, up my quaking thighs, to coil deep inside me, a whirlpool of desire spiraling me and higher... And he withdraws his tongue, pulls back, and the orgasm pauses. It hovers there on the edge, showing me the light in the distance. Then, it recedes... back... further back. What I thought was a dream has become a nightmare. "No, no, no!" My pussy clenches down on the emptiness. "Come back, please."

"Shh." He crawls up my body and presses his lips to mine. I taste myself on him. I taste him. And the combination is so heady, so right, so *everything*, a tear squeezes out from between my closed eyelids. Then, I'm being pulled onto his chest, the sound of a steady thump-thump relaxing me. He throws his arm about my waist. With the other, he draws his fingers down my hair, the gesture soothing. The ball of emotion in my throat fades, and warmth once more cocoons me.

Sometime later, I wake up, alone in his bed.

28

Knight

"So, you and Penny, huh?" Adam shoots me a sideways glance. We've finished our ten-mile run and slowed down to a walk to cool down. I didn't want to leave her this morning. In fact, I confess, after the taste of her in the middle of the night when I woke up and feasted on her— when she opened herself up and allowed me to truly taste her, when her barriers were lowered enough for her to open her thighs and her heart and cry out when she was on the verge of coming without reservation— made me realize how much she held back otherwise.

Sure, I'm a bastard for taking what she gave so freely when she was sleeping and unaware of what I was doing to her. But she enjoyed it. And she curled up like a baby on my chest after that and went right back to sleep. She didn't move when I slid out from under her and placed her head on the pillow. I made sure to cover her up before leaving. And then, my steps had been slow.

I stopped in the doorway to glance at her over my shoulder. The need to go back to her and hold her in my arms, burying my face in the curve of her neck and my cock in her sure-to-be-wet pussy, is what made me turn around and leave. I cannot get addicted to her. I broke one of my rules by insisting she stay overnight. There's no way I could have let her leave last night. Not after tasting her sweetness, feeling her flesh give under my fingers, seeing the marks I left on the inside of her thighs when I dragged my whiskers across as I ate her out.

She trembled and turned to a mass of yearning need under my ministrations. I felt her climb the slope to that invisible edge of no return and backed off. She whined and protested—in her sleep—and I had to stop myself from chuckling aloud. Which is when I realized, I'd almost laughed again in her presence.

She has that effect on me. My sunshine. My Little Dove who shines light into the murky darkness of my life. And I need to make her mine. A-n-d the fact that I'd allowed myself to think that sent me scrambling into my closet to get changed. And then, I ran out. She's gotten under my skin, and I hadn't realized it. Thoughts of her, echoes of her laughter, the image of those bright blue eyes alight with mischief as she sasses me again— All of it slips through my veins like adrenaline in the middle of a gunfire.

"Knight, you hear what I said?"

"Eh?" I turn then, almost stumbling on the path. I manage to right myself then turn to find Adam smirking.

"What?"

"You've got it bad, man."

"What are you talking about?" I roll my shoulders and continue walking at a brisk pace.

"Thought we were cooling down?" He snorts.

No chance of that. Not as long as I'm thinking about her.

"Knight, man, it's okay to admit you like her."

"That is of no consequence."

"Of course, it is." He draws abreast. I ramp up my speed, but he easily keeps pace. This is what happens when you have a friend who not only saved your life on more than one occasion, but also is well-matched in strength, in power, and in the way we react to situations.

We're so similar, our team had teased us about being two pieces of a whole. We'd scoffed at that. It's true, we have similar values—we'd been drawn to a life of service—but that's where our similarities end. Where I pursue things with an intensity that's borderline obsessive, Adam is more easygoing. He's able to let go of things and move on, whereas I... I can't forgive or forget that easily. It's why, though we experienced some rough shit together, Adam has managed to move on and re-integrate back into society much faster than I have. But then, he also agreed to see a shrink from the day he returned—something I've refused to. I'm ready to open that can of worms… Yet.

"You need to stop punishing yourself for what happened." He grips my shoulder, and if it were anyone else, I'd shake it off. But because it's Adam, I allow myself to slow down.

"You were not responsible for the deaths of those men."

I scoff. Typical of Adam to put out there what any of my other friends and family have hesitated to tell me in all the time I've been back. It's why I love him and hate him.

"Fuck you, too, asshole."

"And I don't care if you hate me for saying this, but it's time you put what happened behind you and start living again."

"Have you put what happened behind you?"

He hesitates, then lowers his gaze.

"That's what I thought."

"What happened there changed us. We'll never go back to being the men we were before. The difference is, I've chosen not to let those bastards hold me back."

"And I have?"

He squeezes my shoulder. The answer is in his eyes. He releases his hold on me, only to grab the back of my neck. "I love you like a brother, man. It's why I'm all up in your business, you realize that?"

"What-fucking-ever."

He chuckles. "It's also why I see your other friends—the ones you've been avoiding all this time—jogging in our direction."

I groan. "I need to get out of here."

"Too late for that, man." He lowers his arm and steps back. "I'd wish you good luck, but since you've met the right woman, you don't need it."

I frown. "You douchecanoe, what the fuck you talking about, you—"

He merely touches the tip of his index finger to his temple, then pivots and runs off.

I draw in a breath, then turn, only to be knocked on the side of my head. "The fuck!" I reel back, more from the surprise than the force of the hit, which was just a tap. I've been through worse in training sessions before I left for a mission.

Rick throws up his fists. "Wanna go a round, man? You haven't eaten my dust in a long time."

Typical Rick, an ex-NHL player who served in the military with me, the man is one-hundred percent pure muscle. He's also the only other man I know who can hold his own against me in a fight. I crack my neck, then take a step back, but Rick steps forward and into my space so his chest slams into mine. "You're a fucking arsehole. A selfish, motherfucking, wanker of a douchecanoe who doesn't care about anything but himself."

Next to him, Cade glowers at me. "You have time to go for a run, but you don't think of reaching for the phone and calling us?"

"I've been busy." I hear the petulance in my voice and wince. Since when do I hide behind excuses? I've changed, but surely, not so much that I can't accept my fault when I'm in the wrong.

"And you're right; I'm a shit human being."

"Not to mention a tosser and a knobhead."

I roll my shoulders. "What's this, the attack of the barmy army?" I scoff.

"We're here to make sure you turn up for the get together at Abby's place," Cade growls.

I roll my shoulders, "The last thing I want is to put on a smile and pretend an enthusiasm I'm not feeling, and—" I snap my lips shut and glower back at Cade. "You know I won't say no to Abby."

"I'm aware." He smirks.

"Doesn't mean I'm doing this willingly."

"You can protest all you want, as long as you turn up tomorrow night."

I rub the back of my neck. "Abby could have asked me. I wouldn't have said no to her."

"The woman is worried about you. She doesn't like that you're spending so much time by yourself." Cade frowns.

"I've been working. I go into the office. I run. I meet my buddy, Adam—" Both men glare at me, and I realize my mistake. "Not that I don't want to meet you guys—"

"You *don't* want to meet us," Rick snaps.

"Neither of you went through what I did. Neither of you will know how it feels to be a captive and live from beating to beating and be so hungry that you have no choice but to eat your own skin."

Both men look stricken. Then, Rick throws up his fist again. I see it coming and block it. "The fuck is wrong with you?" I pant.

"The fuck is wrong with *you?*" he roars.

A couple jogging past us look at us in alarm, then pick up speed. A baby begins to cry, and a mother running with her sports-pram shoots us a nasty look as she continues by. Great, now I'm scaring little children.

"You could have picked up the phone and replied to our phone calls. You could have texted and told us you were okay. Hell, you could have told us your new address. Not even Abby knew where you had moved. We had to use a private detective to track you down, you arsewipe, you—"

A loud barking interrupts him. There's the sound of what seems to be hooves hitting the ground. Then, I hear panting and look around him to realize it's not hooves, it's paws. The paws of a massive Great Dane who's broken away from the man running in his wake. A man who looks like a very harried, Declan.

"Guys, watch out! Tiny's on a rampage," he yells.

The dog barks joyfully. Rick turns around, then steps aside in one smooth move, so when the big dog arcs his body and sails past him, he crashes into me.

Penny

"Oh, aren't you a sweetie pie?" I throw my arms around the Great Dane who pranced into the apartment as soon as the elevator doors slid open. "Where did you come from, hmm?" The dog barks. At more than three feet tall at his shoulders, all he has to do is toss his head and he's able to lick my face with a tongue as big as a dinner plate. It feels like someone dragged a soaking wet towel across my cheek. I burst out laughing, and the dog wags his tail harder. His entire body shakes with effort, and he pants loudly. I rub his neck. "You hungry, baby?"

I look past him to find a pissed-off Knight standing with his hands on his hips. His hair is standing up like he's been running his fingers through the strands. He's wearing a T-shirt that must have been white at some point, but is so threadbare, it molds to his ridiculously sculpted chest, showing off the dents between those delicious abs. He completes the ensemble with jogging shorts—that cling lovingly to his powerful thighs. Patches of sweat dampen his chest, and glisten at his temples. He looks virile and strong and like porn on two legs. Moisture bathes my pussy, the pulse between my legs speeds up. Gah, stop looking at him like you want to climb him. I nod toward the Great Dane. "Doesn't he belong to Liam and Isla?"

He nods.

"So why is he with you?"

The muscles at his jaw tick. The skin stretches across his cheekbones. He looks like he's about to snap my head off. Instead, he stalks past me and toward the kitchen, where he grabs a glass from one of the shelves and fills it with water from the tap. Then hesitates. He places his glass on the counter, bends and pulls out a serving bowl. He fills it with water, then walks over to the side of the kitchen and places it on the floor. He straightens and snaps his fingers. The dog woofs, then jumps up, licking my face for good measure, before he gambols off in the direction of the man. He reaches Knight, then parks himself on his haunches with a heavy sigh. He looks up at Knight, who glares back. The two engage in some kind of staring match, then Tiny whines.

"I think he's waiting for you to tell him it's okay to drink the water."

Knight hesitates, then stabs his finger at the bowl on the floor. "Drink up, now."

Instantly, Tiny flops down on the floor and begins to lap at the bowl noisily. I walk over to stand next to the dog. "Such a good boy."

The Great Dane slaps his tail into the ground in response.

"Is he going to stay with you?"

Knight frowns. "It would seem that way."

Tiny finishes drinking water, then places his big head between his front feet and looks up at Knight with big, soulful eyes.

"Aww, he likes you."

"So?" Knight snaps then draws in a breath. "Sorry, I'm not happy about this situation."

"Never would have guessed that," I scoff.

"It's not your fault. I shouldn't have taken my frustration out on you."

I blink in surprise. *Who* is *this man, apologizing to me?*

He drags his fingers through his hair so more of it stands on end. My fingers tingle. And oh, god, I want to jump on him, wrap my legs around his waist, and reach up and smooth out the errant strands. When he's considerate—like now-- I want to lick his face and when he's being obnoxious his appeal only increases. Watching Knight glower at the dog, I truly understand why Hermione was so attracted to Draco. It's the same reason why I can't take my gaze off this complex, wounded grumphole. It's the appeal of an unlikely pairing. It's the unabashed need to unlock his hidden qualities and help this man redeem himself—with the power of my pussy, of course. I manage not to snicker aloud.

"Liam and Isla decided to move to their island for a few months. Evidently, without my knowledge or participation, my friends decided Tiny should stay with me, for now at least, rather than make the trip with them. Cade and Abby are refurbishing their place. Declan and Solene are going to be shooting a movie in New Zealand for the next eight months. So—" He raises a shoulder.

"So, you're going to be a dog-parent?"

He points those green, unfeeling eyes at me, and my breath catches. *Damn. Is there ever going to come a time when he looks at me and it doesn't feel like I've been punched in the gut?* Even sweaty and all mussed up from his run—*especially* sweaty and mussed up—he's beautiful and solid and inflexible. And I want to lick him up like an ice-cream cone.

"You done?"

"Eh?" I blink rapidly. "What are you talking about?"

"You were ogling my body."

"Was not."

He merely arches an eyebrow, then looks me up and down. "Are you sore?"

I flush. "What's it to you?"

"Need to know if I need to stretch your hole enough to add four digits this time."

This time, I gape at him. "You do this on purpose, don't you?"

"Do what?"

"Every time you think you're coming across as too human, you say or do something to show me you're a bastard."

"And you'd do well to remember that."

"There's only one problem. I don't believe you."

He raises a shoulder. "Not my problem."

"If you were as much of an asshole as you'd like me to believe, you would've taken my virginity last night."

"And I didn't because I don't want you to catch feelings." He glances away, a bored look on his face.

"But you're going to make me come."

"Only because it entertains me to see you writhe and moan and whine and beg me to bring you to orgasm."

I know he's hitting out at me again. I know it's because he wants so hard to conform to the persona he's trying to present to the world. I know it's all a front because he's not ready to face the emotional and mental injuries he's carrying around, but it doesn't stop me from actively hating him right now. "I'd better get ready and head to the office. My boss is an unreasonable man."

I spin around and head toward the elevator doors, when he calls out, "I'll take you."

"No, thank you. Also, I need to go home and change first."

"No need."

I scowl at him over his shoulder. "I'm not going to the office looking like this." I glance down at the dress I wore last night, then back at him.

"I have a solution for that."

29

Penny

"I will not let you buy me a dress," I huff.

"Yes, you will."

I scowl through the window of the car—a Jaguar Sportbrake big enough for Tiny to park himself comfortably in the cargo space and have space left over. There was no arguing with him as he called for a quick breakfast for us—from James Hamilton's restaurant— and food for Tiny from a company specializing in deliveries for dogs. Who knew those exist? Then he called Rudy and explained the situation to him and asked for a bigger car.

He insisted I shower. I agreed on the condition that I could use one of the guest bathrooms to avoid any chance of running into him. Not that it stopped me from imagining him without his clothes. It's not as if I need an excuse for that.

We ate without exchanging a word. Then, he hooked the leash onto Tiny, and we'd headed down to find this big-ass car parked in front of the doors. Rudy waited for us with the hatch open. I assumed we were headed to the office, so imagine my surprise when the car stops in front of an exclusive boutique in St. James Park. I stare at the name of the well-known designer scrawled above the door.

KARMA WEST SOVRANO

Of course, she's Abby's friend, married to Michael Sovrano, the ex-Don of the *Cosa Nostra*, who's now the CEO of CN industries. I've met her a few times — enough to know her creations are highly sought after and priced in the five-figure range, if not higher. All the more reason not to accept this 'gift' from him.

As I contemplate my options — or rather, lack thereof — Knight slides out. Rudy rounds to the back of the car and opens the hatch. Knight hooks the leash onto Tiny, who woofs and bounds out. Together, they head for my car door, and Knight holds it open.

My gaze bounces between him and the boutique. "It's too early for them to be open."

"They're open," he says with confidence.

When I still refuse to move, he makes a low noise at the back of his throat. "Get out of the car," he orders.

I get out of the car.

I need to stop myself from jumping to obey him. As if that were possible. There's this commanding air about him, a certain arrogance when he orders me, that sparks something primal inside of me. Something that makes me want to do his bidding. It's confusing, but if I'm honest, it's also exciting. It's something new and different. A reaction I've never felt before. *And will not again, with anyone else.*

I scowl, then ignore the jerkface. Reaching over, I scratch Tiny behind his ear. The dog pants in ecstasy. Knight frowns down at him, then looks at me. He jerks his chin in the direction of the shop. *Whatever.* Best to get this over with. I march inside the door and find a dark-haired woman with flashing eyes and a wide smile waiting for us.

"Penny."

Before I can reply, she hugs me and kisses me on each cheek.

"Huh?"

"That's how we welcome friends in Sicily." She beams at me.

I knit my eyebrows. "I didn't expect to see you here in person," I say stiffly.

She laughs. "Knight called ahead and said you were on your way over, and if you're Abby's friend, you're my friend. So of course I was going to be here and make sure you were looked after."

Tiny barks. Her features light up. "Look who's here." She releases me and walks over to scratch Tiny behind his ear. He bumps his head against her, and for all his considerable strength, he's very gentle.

"Aww, you're a sweetheart." She bends slightly and hugs the Great Dane, who wags his tail with vigor.

Knight shuffles his feet.

With a final rub behind Tiny's ears, she straightens and walks over to him with her arms outstretched. His jaw hardens. He looks like he's about to protest, but Karma wraps her arms about him and hugs him. He stands immobile for a few seconds, then robotically pats her shoulder. Reluctance is written in every angle of his body, but he manages not to scowl as she steps back from him.

"I am so happy you made it," she chirps.

He manages a quirk of the left side of his mouth. "Thank you for opening the boutique for us."

"Nonsense." She waves a hand in the air. "I was so excited when you called me. After all, it's tradition."

"Tradition?" He blinks.

"When any of my girlfriends finds their man, they always come here to pick out a dress of their choice. An original Karma West Sovrano creation, which their man pays for."

"I'm not her man," he growls.

"He's not my man," I snap at the same time.

Karma steps back and looks between us. There's a smile on her face, as if she knows something I don't. "Of course not." Her tone is indulgent.

"No, you don't understand. He's my boss, and—" *I spent the night at his penthouse. And now, he's going to buy me a dress, before we head over to work together, because I didn't have anything to wear, and we were getting late—* And oh, god, this entire situation a little too domestic, a little too in the realm of the two of us knowing each other too well, a little too much for me.

She must notice the conflicting emotions on my face. Her forehead furrows. Then, she flashes me a genuine smile. "—and you need something to wear to the office today."

"And underwear," Knight interjects.

I flush, then shoot him a loaded stare; not that it makes a difference since asshole isn't even looking at me.

"And underwear." She nods.

"Also, something for my sister's get-together," he adds.

"Abby's organizing a get-together?" I burst out.

"She is." His jaw hardens further. Jeez, does he have any molars left or has he ground them all to dust already?

"My sister feels I'm not getting out enough, so she's decided to invite all of our friends to her home. I'm expected to make an appearance." He says this in a tone that implies he'd rather be swimming with the sharks instead. "You're coming with me."

"I am not."

A nerve pops at his temple. Hooray! It's sooo getting under his skin. It's becoming more exciting than watching the London Ice Kings score a goal, watching him try hard to rein in his temper.

"Yes, you are," he snaps.

"Uh, I'll get some clothes for you to choose from." Karma glides away.

I jut out my chin. "When is this get-together?"

"This weekend."

"Why don't you hurry up and choose your future wife by then? That way, you can ask her to come with you."

"I'm asking you."

"It seems you and I have a different understanding of the meaning of ask." I cross my arms across my chest. "Anyway, I don't want to."

His gaze narrows. "Remember, you're my employee. You'll do as you're told."

I curl my fingers into fists. Oh, yeah. It all comes down to money, after all. And the fact that he paid for my mother's care, and now I owe him.

Silence falls in the shop. The tension is so thick, it feels like it's squeezing in on me. Tiny plants his butt on the ground and whines.

Knight looks down at him. A strange looks comes over his face. He shakes his head, then his chest inflates. Without looking up at me he mutters, "Please."

30

Penny

"One stupid word from him, and I gave in," I mumble under my breath as I follow Karma inside the changing room. It's a spacious space with clothes hanging on a rack on one side, a mirror that covers the entire side of one wall, and a spacious chaise. We left Knight and Tiny, who strained on his leash to follow us, until Knight managed to distract him with the treat he was carrying in his pocket. And when did he slip the pack of doggy biscuits into the pockets of his perfectly cut jacket? And was that softness I spied on his features when Tiny wolfed down the first biscuit, then looked up at him with his big, melting eyes to ask for more?

Karma pulls out one of the dresses from the rack and holds it out to me. It's a wine-colored skirt and jacket ensemble with a pink sleeveless blouse... And they seem to be my size.

"How did you—?" I begin to ask, then notice the look on her face. "Knight?"

"Knight." She nods. "He messaged me your measurements, with strict recommendations of what he wanted to see you in."

"He did?" I rub the back of my neck. "This is very confusing. Not the dress—" I glance away, then back at her. "He really is only my boss, honestly."

"You don't have to convince me." She peers into my features. "You're Abby's friend, Knight is Abby's brother; I feel like I know the two of you, though I only met Knight once and I've only seen you a couple of times. So, do you mind if I say something from the perspective of my experience?" She rolls her eyes. "That came out all prissy and made me sound so old. I only meant, I've been through what you have, so I wanted to say, be patient."

"Oh,"—I begin to chew on my thumbnail—"afraid it's not one of my virtues. Also, patient with what exactly?"

"With him." She jerks her chin in the direction of the doorway leading to the waiting room. "Abby's told me what he's been through, and if he's half as hardheaded as my alphahole husband, you're going to have to give him time to come around."

"Alphahole?" I bark out a laugh.

"Yep, that's what these men are. Don't you agree? Alpha and dominant, and hot and sexy but also, obstinate and stubborn, and willful and mulish, and sometimes, simply bloody-minded."

"I call him bosshole." I stab a thumb over my shoulder.

"I heard you." Knight's voice reaches us through the open doorway.

We stare at each other, then burst out laughing. "Oh, my god, I had no idea he could hear us," I whisper. Also, did the alphahole crack a joke? Is he thawing? No doubt, it's because of Tiny. Clearly, his friends knew what they were doing when they insisted he take care of the Great Dane. Nothing like the unselfish love of a fur baby to help you get in touch with your humane side. It's also a means for him to think of something other than his past. He's going to have to be focused on Tiny's needs. Making sure the dog is fed and watered and walked and— Apparently, he means to take him to work, so he'll have to keep him entertained, too. Did he think that one through? Probably not, typical man that he is.

"Well, I'll leave you to try out these clothes." Karma gestures toward the rack. There's a mix of office wear and also gowns.

"They look amazing. I can't believe I'm going to try on a Karma West Sovrano original."

"Penny? I'm waiting!" That's the second time the alphahole has banged on the door to the dressing room. His voice is impatient, and I can all but see the nerve throbbing at his temple. Not to mention, his flared nostrils. A-n-d, I have to stop conjuring up his features when he's not in front of me.

"Penny, I won't ask again." There's a thread of steel in his voice that warns me he's not above breaking the door down and coming in.

"Oh, for hell's sake." I take one last look at myself, then slide my feet into the new three-inch high stilettos, which are real Christian Louboutin's, unlike the knockoffs I've been wearing up until now—

And how did he know that's the brand I love? You know what? I don't want to know. His level of knowledge about me is verging on being too intimate to be comfortable. And I thought he didn't pay any attention to me. Clearly, I need to be more careful around him. I glide toward the door and fling it open as he's about to knock on the door again.

His hand is raised, and his eyes widen. He rakes his gaze down my body, slowly taking in the dark red, fitted creation that dips between my breasts enough to hint at my cleavage, then proceeds to hug every curve, before dropping down in an uneven hem to below my knees. It also has a slit riding up to mid-thigh on one side. His eyes flash. Those golden sparks flicker in the depths of his mesmerizing eyes. The heat between us shoots sky-high. His nostrils flare, and he takes a step forward. So, do I.

"You are the most beautiful woman in this world." His voice is guttural. The pulse at the base of his throat kicks up. He lowers his face, and I rise up on tiptoes. That's when Tiny barks, then gallops over to shove himself between us. I stumble, and Knight grips the curve of my waist. His palm feels too big, too hot, too possessive as he spreads his fingers across the small of my back, the tips brushing against the flare of my hips.

A shiver ladders up my spine. I part my lips, and his breath brushes my mouth. I flutter my eyelids shut, and again, Tiny woofs, then bumps up against Knight. Knight stumbles, as do I. Tiny barks and tries to rise up on his hind legs. This time, he displaces Knight further. Knight leans his weight forward, and that, in turn, makes me stumble backward. I gasp as we tilt back. At the last moment, Knight manages to grab Tiny's collar and push him to the side. But the resulting momentum carries us in his direction. Knight goes down. I yelp, and he pulls me securely into his chest, making sure I land on him as he hits the floor. The resulting thud vibrates through me.

I squeeze my eyes shut, draw in a lungful of Knight's sea-breeze and pepper scent, and every part of me threatens to burst into flames. I cuddle in closer to him, dig my fingers into the front of his shirt and stay still. So does he. Tiny barks and looms over us.

Knight's hold around me tightens further. *Bam-bam-bam*, his heart gallops against his ribcage, and I feel each beat as if it were my own. His entire body vibrates. Tension leaps off of him. His chest rises and falls. I glance up to find the tendons of his throat standing out with such rigidity, it's a wonder they haven't snapped. His jaw is set, his big body a mass of seething stress. "Knight, are you okay?"

There's no reply. I try to wriggle free, but his arms are bands of steel. I manage to raise my head, glance down, and flinch. His eyes are hard chunks of blue green, his gaze blind as he stares at something in the distance. *Shit, is he recalling something that happened to him during his time in captivity?* I cup his cheek. "Knight?"

There's no answer.

Tiny, too, must realize something is wrong, for he plants his butt down and whines. I need to do something, but what? Without consciously deciding, I raise my hand and bring it down. My palm connects with his cheek. He blinks, then snaps his gaze to mine. He searches my features. "Are you okay?"

I nod. "I think you went into shock."

His features tighten. He opens his mouth to speak, but before he can say anything, Tiny lowers his head and licks his face. Knight winces. Tiny licks his face again, and this time, Knight groans. I can't stop the chuckle that spills from my lips. The tension in the air dissolves. Knight lets out a shuddering breath. His heartbeat slows. Then he pushes up to his feet, taking me with him. He scans my face again. "You're sure you're fine?"

I nod.

"Maybe we need to get you checked by a doctor?"

I roll my eyes. "You're the one who hit the floor with enough force that you were stunned. I fell on you."

"You weigh nothing."

I scoff. "Only you would say that."

He frowns, a look of confusion in his eyes. "What's that supposed to mean?"

I did not put myself down. I did not. The one thing I've promised myself is to never be ashamed of my appearance. To never be defensive that I'm curvy and I like my food. But apparently, when Knight asks me a question, he gets past my defenses and straight to the core of my insecurity. I may have hidden it from myself, but clearly, not from him.

"Look, I'm not the slimmest person in the world, so let's stop pretending."

Tiny wags his tail and looks from me to Knight. I swear, the mutt is following our conversation.

For his part, Knight releases me and steps back. He drags his heated gaze down my chest—my nipples bead—to my thighs, and I have to resist the urge to squeeze them together. Down to my fuck-me heels, and I press my feet into them to stop myself from shuffling. By the time he raises his gaze to my face again, I'm flushed.

"What?" I bite out.

"You're fucking gorgeous. And in this dress, I want to squeeze your tits and grab you by your butt and hoist you up against this door, then tear off that dress and hold you up with my cock as I make you come."

"Oh." I swallow.

"But I'm not going to."

"Because of some stupid-ass notion of not taking my virginity."

"Because—" That expressionless mask drops over his face. "Because you deserve to give it to someone who has feelings for you."

31

Knight

"You have feelings for her."

"Eh?" I glance sideways at the stranger who's walked up to me, then follow his gaze trained on the woman in the blue dress.

We're at Cade and Abby's home for her party, and I thought I'd managed to fade into the background, until this stranger singled me out. I ignore him and continue to take in the vision that is Penny, in the dress that I bought her. I also got the red one. She looked incredible in it; except, it had showed off her curves a little too much for my liking. She'd wear that one only for me. This blue one, though, has sleeves that pinch in at her wrists. It falls in an A-line to her knees and covers her to my satisfaction.

She looked at me with curiosity when I added it to the pile, then rolled her eyes when I ordered her to wear it today. She didn't object though. If she had, I'm not sure what explanation I'd have given, except that I didn't want others looking at what's mine. I mean, my employee. I'm looking after her wellbeing by buying her clothes. It contributes to the uplift of her mental health which, in turn, boosts productivity. *A-n-d what a load of bull. Not even able to come up with a plausible explanation, hmm?*

I also bought her the skirt and blouse she wore yesterday. My chest fills with something like satisfaction.

Bloody hell, I'm turning into a pussy-whipped arse around her. I rub the back of my neck. The only reason she agreed to accompany me to the event, as well as accept the clothes, is because I reminded her—again— that I paid for her mother's bill. I felt like a bastard doing it but, as they say, all's fair in love and war. If this is the only way to keep her near me, then fuck morals and ethics and all that crap I used to believe in.

I was once a regular pillar of fucking society, and look where that got me. Nope, I'm doing the right thing. Keeping her where I can track her, but also, not so close there's any danger of her misinterpreting our relationship as anything other than the boss-employee one she signed on for. In fact, for the rest of the day after our visit to Karma's shop, I didn't speak to her in the office. And today I'd managed to keep out of her way until it was time to leave for Abby and Cade's party. A prospect I've been dreading all day.

Thankfully, Tiny occupied any spare mind-space I had. That and ensuring I green-lit three mergers during the course of the day. Tiny made his presence felt on all three video-meetings, after each of which, the opposing party seemed to change their opinion of me and decide to work with me rather than oppose me. Who knew? All it took was a lovable mutt to help me further my power-grab plans. That, and the fact that Penny kept pace with me admirably.

She emailed all of the information needed for each meeting before I could ask her. She kept pace with me in a way no one else on my team was able to. The woman has an uncanny instinct when it comes to antic- ipating my needs. Too bad I'm not going to be the one to pop her cherry. I can't afford anything messy during this crucial time when I need to focus on consolidating my claim on the company. Which means, finding someone who'll agree to marry me immediately. Ergo, she should have had the list of eligible women to me before we left the office. Which she hadn't. And I was too focused on getting out of the office and taking Tiny for a walk before I met her by the car.

I'm slipping up. I need to—ask her to deliver on what she owes me… At once. I take a step forward, but the stranger grips my shoulder. "Don't do anything you're going to regret."

I shrug off his hand, then glare at him. "Who're you?"

He holds up his hands. "Didn't mean to intrude. But when I see someone committing a mistake in love, I can't help but step in."

"Love?" I scoff.

He merely looks at her, then back at me. "I'm sorry, it's more than that. You're enamored by her. So smitten, thoughts of her consume your every waking moment."

He turns his gaze to another corner of the room. His features soften. "Her voice haunts your dreams, her smile, the way her eyes flash when she laughs, how she flicks her hair when she's nervous, how she gestures with her hands when she's excited. All of the images merge and swell into a patchwork of emotions that you can't quite pull apart." He draws in a breath.

I follow his gaze to the woman he's watching. A woman who's laughing at something Abby 's telling her. A gorgeous woman with a very pregnant belly who's leaning into a tall broad-shouldered, blonde-haired man. His arm is around her and he's watching her with rapt attention. She looks up at him, they share a smile, then he leans down and kisses her forehead.

The man next to me draws in a sharp breath. "Forget what I said. I'm the last man you should take advice from." He pivots and begins to walk away.

This time I'm the one who grabs his shoulder. "Got a smoke mate?"

He hesitates, then jerks his chin in the direction of the door leading out to the garden. I follow him out. In silence, we walk down the path and past a line of trees that block the house from view. Behind it is a clearing with a bench placed under the trees. The lawn in front slopes down toward a short wall, and beyond that, the city spreads out. He walks to the wall, and leaning against it, pulls out a crumpled packet of cigarettes, with one cigarette inside.

I look at him, and he must see the question in my eyes for he shrugs. "I'm trying to give it up." He pulls out a lighter, cups his palm around the flame, and lights the cigarette. He inhales and hands it over to me. For a few seconds, we pass the cigarette back and forth, sucking on the poison stick. The nicotine suffuses my blood stream, and my head begins to swim in that pleasant way that only happens when she's near me. I swear, then dig my fingers into my hair and tug on it.

"That bad, huh?" he murmurs.

I merely twist my lips.

He stubs the cigarette on the wall, slides the butt into his pocket, then holds out his hand. "Edward."

"Knight."

We shake, then turn back to the vista of the city with the skyline in the distance.

"She the one that got away, huh?" I ask. Not that I'm interested... Okay, I *am* interested, but it's certainly not because I sense a kindred soul in this man.

This time, he's the one who curls his mouth.

"I used to have people confess to me all the time. Now, I realize how difficult it is but also how cathartic it can be to talk to a faceless man."

I glance at him, then back at the view. "You a priest or something?"

He nods. "Once upon a time, but no longer. I left the church. Then lost my girl. I've been trying to find my faith since."

I wince.

"What did you lose?" he asks, looking forward.

"My belief. My convictions." I swallow. Somehow, it's easier for me to speak to this man who I just met than to any of my friends or family... Other than Adam, that is.

It's his turn to wince. "It's fucking brutal." He curls his fingers into a fist and pushes it into the wall.

"Does it get better?" I ask slowly.

"It gets"—he pauses, then draws in a breath—"deeper, until it digs into your guts and becomes this poison that seeps into your system and corrodes your veins and eats away at your innermost emotions, until all you feel is an emptiness, a blankness, a vastness you know you'll never be able to fill."

I squeeze my eyes shut. "Hope your sermons weren't this deep, Father."

"It's Edward, and truth be told, my sermons were never the most uplifting, but they always struck a chord with the congregation, or so I'm told. People came to me to hear the truth. I took pride in being able to be honest without worrying about the consequences, until it was time for me to share my own truth. I hesitated and I lost."

"I hesitated and I lost my entire team."

This time he turns to me. "Afghanistan?"

"Russia."

"You made it out of there."

Every muscle in my body coils with tension. "So I'm told. I wish I hadn't."

"Ever ask yourself why you're here and they're not?"

I scoff. "Every fucking day. "

"Perhaps you need to ask what would have happened if you hadn't made it?"

"I'd be dead." *And even then, I wouldn't be at peace.*

"You need closure."

"No shit."

"You need to … Embrace what you feel about her."

I draw myself up to my full height. "There are no feelings where she's concerned."

He turns and props a hand on his hip. "I don't know you that well, but you're here. Meaning, not only do we have friends in common, but they trust you enough to invite you into their inner circle, so I'm going to tell you a secret."

"Not sure I want to hear it."

"Oh, trust me; you do."

"Save your breath… Father." I turn to leave, but he steps around and in front of me.

I glare at him.

He half smiles. "I wish someone had told me this when I was busy being an arse and forfeiting the chance to keep the most important thing in my life. I left when she needed me most. I was too much of a coward to face my own feelings. I wasn't ready to face my own reality. I had too many of my own issues to sort out. I didn't deserve her. I lost her."

"Sounds like a hell of tearjerker," I growl.

His smile widens. "Pride comes before a fall."

I scoff. "Thanks, but no thanks, for the free advice."

I turn to leave, only to find two men walking toward me.

"Hey, motherfucker." Rick smirks.

"Where you been hiding yourself, sunshine?" Finn nods.

"Out of my way, Rick, or I'll be forced to tell people what your real name is."

Rick groans, then slaps the back of his hand to his forehead in an exaggerated gesture that portrays angst. "Oh, no! Not again," he pretends to cry before turning serious. "I'm tired of your holding that particular piece of information over me."

I snort.

"So, Rick isn't your real name, huh?" Finn turns on him. After leaving the military, Rick went private, where he met Finn. Their love for ice hockey sealed their friendship. Rick played for the NHL in his late teens before he quit, moved back to London and joined the Royal

Marines. Finn was an NHL player until a year ago when he'd decided to move into private security.

"Is Finn your real name?" Rick drawls.

Finn sets his jaw, and Rick smirks. "That's what I thought. Also—" He stabs a finger at me. "Why you being a wallflower?"

"Because." I shrug.

Finn's grin widens. "So, you're going to exchange sweet nothings with the priest here while someone else moves in on your girl?"

32

Penny

"Here's your drink." The tall, dark and handsome man with silver at his temples, who's almost as gorgeous as Sir, but who is *not* Sir, hands me a flute of champagne.

"Thank you," I murmur, then take a sip. It's cool and crisp and nowhere as delicious as the champagne Knight served on his deck yesterday. Was it only yesterday that we had dinner and shared conversation? When I thought we were making headway in getting to know each other? Was it only last night when he'd almost made me come, then pulled me into his chest and lulled me to sleep, before waking me up in the middle of the night with his face between my legs? At least, I think he ate me out like a starving man and almost made me come again. Unless I was dreaming. No, I don't think I was dreaming. It felt too real, too intense, too good in the way that only Sir can make me feel. He's the only one who can manage to take me to the edge, and when I think I can't go any higher, he takes me there the next time around.

The anticipation licks my nerve-endings, clings to my veins, and slithers under my skin in an ever-growing pool of lava released from the volcano between my legs. My stomach flip-flops, and heat flushes my skin.

"You all right?" the man asks.

I force myself to look up at his handsome visage. "I'm sorry, what's your name again?"

He smiles. "I haven't told you yet."

"Ah." I blush a little.

"And by the looks of the man who's glaring at us from across the room, I don't think I should, either."

I suck in my breath through my lips. "Is he a tall man, with shoulders like an NFL quarterback, and a face that resembles Lucifer having a very bad day, and is he standing there with his legs slightly apart and leaning forward on the balls of his feet, with his fingers rolled into fists at his sides? And is he..." The hair on the nape of my neck rises. I swallow. "Is he rolling his shoulders and cracking his neck and giving the appearance of getting ready for a fight?"

He glances over my should, then back at me. "Seems you're familiar with the bloke." A wrinkle appears between his eyebrows. "And that was unnervingly accurate. You two married?"

"Nope—" I snort. "He's my boss."

"Hmm." His lips curl in a smirk that I should find attractive, but unfortunately, it's not the puffy lower lip and the thin, mean upper lip of the man who haunts my dreams. So, I merely register it in a desultory fashion. The kind that tells me I'm screwed, I'll never find any man as attractive, as sexy, and as appealing as the alphahole staring daggers at my back.

"Whatever his relation to you, and whatever lies he's been telling himself, it's about to change."

"Oh?" I blink.

"The fastest way to get a man to admit he wants you is to show him you find someone else attractive."

"But I don't..."

His smile broadens, and really, though he's older than me—or perhaps, *because* he's older than me—he has that entire forbidden thing going for him. Which, I have to admit, is hot. A-n-d the penny drops. "You think if I were to pretend to be interested in you, it'd make him do something out of character?"

"Smart girl." He laughs, showing white, even teeth, which set off his tan. He has that Pedro Pascal 'Daddy' vibe going for him, that honestly, should have made my panties moist by now, but newsflash, my pussy only weeps for one man. And he's the meanest, growliest, most wounded man ever, who prefers to pretend he has no more feelings left for anyone.

"I'm Penny Easton." I hold out my hand.

"Philippe Beauchamp." He takes my hand in his, then raises it to his lips and kisses my knuckles.

I swear I can hear a growl roll my way from somewhere on the other side of the room. I suppress a smirk of my own.

"You're beautiful, Penny, and you're young enough to be my daughter, so you should know I'm not coming on to you at all—" He releases my hand. "However, thanks to my age and experience, I'm able to see when a couple is about to make a mistake they might regret for the rest of their lives. And then, my conscience tells me if I don't step in, I'll never forgive myself."

I laugh. "You always this generous with your interventions?"

"Only when it's too easy to push the wankhead involved into making a move."

"You know Knight, I take it?"

His smile fades a little. "I know of him. My son, Declan, is his friend. I happened to be in town for work, so Abby insisted I come. She thought it wouldn't hurt to have a few newish faces around; though now, I wonder if she asked me precisely so I'd do something to make the proceedings more interesting."

"You're wrong about that. Knight might be a little pissed off at the fact I'm talking to you, but he's not going to make a move."

"You sure?"

I nod. "He told me he isn't interested in pursuing a relationship."

Philippe laughs. "There's a difference between saying something and then being put in a situation where you have to act on your instincts. And given how your *boss* hasn't taken his gaze off of us, I do believe it's not long now before he does."

I draw in a breath. I think he's mistaken. I think it's possible Knight might feel a little jealous, but he'll probably brush it off and go about his business. Still, if I can have some fun at his expense, then sure. Anything to get His Snarliness a little hot under the collar. I reach up and put my hand on Philippe's collar. Then, for extra effect, I tip up my chin and flutter my eyelashes. I have the satisfaction of seeing the older man's eyes glaze. I lean in enough to draw in his spicy, citrusy scent—

nowhere as much of a turn on as Sir's sea-breeze and pepper one, but it's not unpleasant, at all.

One side of his lips curl. "I hope he realizes he may have met his match."

I blush again. "You're too kind."

He smirks. "And he's underestimating you. You're going to be running circles around him, girl. He's not going to know what hit him."

I laugh. "Not likely."

He winks. "Shall we test the theory?"

33

Knight

"Who the fuck is that?" I grab the drink Rick offers me and toss it back.

"That, is Declan's father."

"Huh, fucker's old enough to be *her* father."

"He's in his late forties, not that old."

I scowl as he takes her hand in his, and then the bastard kisses her knuckles. He. Kisses. Her. Knuckles. A growl rumbles up my chest. I take a step forward, but Rick squeezes my shoulder. "Easy, ol' chap."

I try to shake him off, but someone grips my other arm. "You sure you're ready for this?" Edward shoots me a sideways glance. "Once you go down this path, your future as you know it is going to change."

I hesitate.

That's when Philippe turns and gestures to her. She steps forward, and he cups her elbow and leads her toward the door that leads out onto the opposite side of the garden.

The fuck? My vision tunnels. That anger simmering in the background of my mind begins to bubble. All of my senses focus. I can't see my future, so anything would be better than the dark quicksand that spreads out in front of me. The only patch of light is her. And I'll be damned if I'm letting go of her that easily. I shake off the restraining hands, then stalk through the room.

Cade steps forward, looks at my face and freezes. "Are you okay?" He frowns.

Without bothering to reply, I brush past him and out the door, catching a glimpse of them as they disappear around a curve in the garden path. I take the steps two at a time, then quicken my pace. I jog up the path around the curve, past a few flower beds, until I burst into a clearing. This one has a fountain in the center. I walk around it and freeze. They're sitting on a bench, heads bent toward each other. They're not touching, but that doesn't mean anything.

She looks up at something he says and smiles. Her features are soft, her hair flowing about her shoulders. The neckline of her dress dips in the front, showing her cleavage. I tighten my fists at my side. The wind blows her hair back from her face. She shivers. I'm too far away, but I swear, I can feel the goosebumps arise on her skin. And then Philippe pulls off his jacket.

He places it around her shoulders, and something inside me snaps. My feet don't seem to touch the ground as I stalk over. They're so engrossed in each other, they don't hear me approach. It's only when I'm standing in front of them that she glances up.

"Oh, it's you?" She scowls.

Without replying, I yank the jacket from around her shoulders and fling it aside. Then I shrug off my own jacket and plant it over her shoulders. For good measure, I button it over her chest. My fingers brush the skin above her cleavage, and she shudders. Good. She isn't as impervious as she'd like me to believe. Of course, I *know* that, but the additional confirmation soothes something inside of me.

"We're leaving," I snap.

"Okay, bye." She turns to Philippe. "You were saying, Phil."

"Phil?" I growl. "You called him Phil?"

"That's his name; isn't it, Philly?" She smiles at him sweetly.

Philippe smirks. "As I was telling Pen here—"

"Don't fucking call her that."

"And you are—?" He tilts his head.

"Her boss," I growl.

"Well, I'm the man who's going to take her out on a date, so—"

The anger in my gut roars forward. I grab his collar and haul him to his feet. "Get the fuck away from her."

Philippe merely raises an eyebrow. "You establishing a claim here?"

I growl.

"Are you?"

He looks between my eyes. I tighten my fingers on his collar and... *Fuck, fuck, fuck, am I really going to do this? Am I going to say aloud what's been bouncing around in my mind, in my heart, in the corners of my gut, in my every pore? I want her. I need her. I cannot do without her... for one more night.* And this time I'm going to take what she offered. Fuck propriety.

"Yes," I snap.

Philippe seems taken aback.

Penny gasps.

Then, the wanker slowly smiles. "So, you're saying—"

I shove him to the side. "Get away from her and keep away. If I find you sniffing around again, I'll shoot you."

Philippe straightens his collar, then winks at Penny. *Motherfucking twatface.* I throw up my fists and take a step forward, and he holds up his hands. "I'm leaving, just going to"—he bends and picks up his jacket and dusts it off—"get what's mine."

"You stay away from what's mine, you hear me?" I snap.

Philippe touches two fingers to his forehead in mock salute, then walks off whistling. I scowl after him, then turn on my woman—not my woman, my assistant. Yep, that's what she is. I paid her bills. I own her. She's *mine.* Until I decree otherwise.

"Get up." I jerk my chin.

She sets her jaw and folds her arms across her chest, or tries to, since my jacket is buttoned over her arms.

"This is bullshit." She tries to undo the buttons, and I make a growling noise at the back of my throat.

"What?" She frowns.

"You're forgetting your position."

"You mean as your employee?" She jumps up to her feet. "Well, I have news for you. I quit." She turns to leave, and I step in her path.

"You can't."

She stares. "What do you mean?"

I click my tongue. "You didn't read the fine print on your employee contract, I take it."

She pales a little. "It was, uh, a standard employee thingy. The HR woman gave it to me and—"

"—you signed on the dotted line like a little lamb. Ergo"—I raise a finger—"you're trapped."

"Wh-what do you mean?"

"You're my employee until I decide otherwise."

She scoffs. "That's stupid. I have a choice in this."

"Do you?"

"I'm quitting your job, and I'm going to take a loan and pay back what I owe you for covering my mother's bills at the home."

I rub my nails down the front of my shirt. "Nope."

"What do you mean, nope?"

"Just that. It's too late to fly away. You're well and truly caged."

"No, I'm not."

I yawn.

It has the intended effect, for splotches of color pop on her cheeks. She manages to free her arms from under my jacket and begins to unbutton it from around her shoulder.

"Don't you dare," I warn.

She huffs. "What're you gonna do, huh?"

"Don't test me, Penny."

She makes a rude noise. Then shoves the jacket off her shoulders. It begins to slide off, when I close the distance to her, then pick her up, along with the jacket, and throw them both over my shoulder.

She freezes then yells, "Let me go, you neanderthal."

34

Penny

He chuckles. The bastard chuckles like it's all a big joke. I bring my fists down on his back, but he doesn't feel it. He merely turns and strides up the garden path. My cheeks flush. I wriggle and swear, then yell out because he's spanked my ass. "Let go of me, you oaf. You uncouth knucklehead. You dumb block of—"

He clicks his tongue. "I'd be very careful what you say next."

I draw in a breath. My heart begins to race. He sounds like he's nearing the end of his patience. Well, so am I. If he thinks he can handle me like I'm his fuck toy, he has another think coming.

But would it be so bad if he did treat me like his fuck toy? No, no, no. Stop that line of thought. Have you no pride? When it comes to this alphahole, apparently not. Aargh!

I cannot stay here without putting up a token resistance, at least. I can't accept that he's going to drag me off to his cave and have his way with me and—my pussy clenches. I squeeze my thighs together. He has his arm banded below my hips, so of course he feels it.

"You turned on, Little Dove?" he asks in a voice that has a hard edge but also a certain confidence inherent in it that is so, so arousing.

I swallow down the small moan that rises up my throat and scoff, "Of course not."

He laughs. And the sound is dark and deep and promises all kinds of evil things that he plans to do with me, and this time, a jolt runs up my spine. Goddamn this man for the effect he has on me. It's almost as if our every encounter has been planned so I can't win. Not only is he in a position of power over me, but he holds all the cards. And that's so unfair. *And what are you going to do about it, hmm?*

I begin to writhe in earnest, and that's when he comes to a stop. Before I can get another word out, he lowers me by my hips so I'm at eye level with him, feet dangling in midair like I'm a child. But he locks his mouth over mine and kisses me with such intensity, it's clear he sees me as anything but. I part my lips, and he sucks on my tongue as if he wants to draw my very essence into him.

My head spins, my breasts hurt, and my knees turn to jelly. I wrap my arms about his shoulders and my legs around his lean waist and hold on as he continues to drink from me and share my breath, until I'm sure I'm going to explode into a million little pieces, each of which is going to scream one thing. *"Fuck me, Sir. Please."*

He must hear my silent plea, for he tears his mouth from mine. His chest heaves. Color smears his cheeks. Gold and silver sparks flash in his eyes. There's an expression on his face I've never seen before—one of helplessness and anger and need, and so much need that I lean in closer and rub my nose against his. He jerks, then wraps one thick arm around my butt to fit me more firmly over the thick column at his crotch. I swallow and gaze up into his face. He presses a hard kiss to my lips, then begins to walk. He skirts the room where his friends and mine are—thank god. I'm not sure how I would have lived it down if he'd carried me through their midst. On the other hand, I probably wouldn't have cared. I bury my nose in the hollow at the base of his throat and keep it there as he carries me out to the car.

There's a woof, then I sense Tiny prancing about us. There's a low rumble of voices—Rudy's, who took Tiny for a walk earlier. Then Sir lowers me into the backseat of the vehicle. I scoot over, and he slides in next to me. Instantly, I straddle him. He wraps his arm about me and moves further inside. Tiny bounds in and occupies most of the seat.

"Ah, sorry, Knight." Rudy reaches for Tiny's leash to coax him into the cargo area, but Knight shakes his head.

"It's fine."

He pulls me into his chest. With the other, he scratches Tiny behind his ear. Tiny makes a sound that's almost like purring.

I giggle. "Now, that's what I feel like doing."

"That's what your pussy will be doing very soon," he promises.

"Knight!" I blush and glance over my shoulder at Rudy. He's focused ahead as he eases the car out onto the road.

"He won't say a word," Knight assures me.

"But he can hear us," I whisper.

"You shy?"

I look up at him from under my eyelashes. "Only if it's someone I know who's watching us."

"But if it were someone you didn't know?"

I bite the inside of my cheek. "Would you think less of me if I said it's something that intrigues me?"

He notches his knuckles under my chin so I can't look away. "I'd never think less of you. You should know that by now."

"Only, you don't want to have a relationship with me."

He sets his jaw. "I can't. But"—he tucks a strand of hair behind my ear—"I promise, by the time I'm done with you, I'll have fulfilled every fantasy of yours."

What if my fantasy is to keep him for myself? But clearly, there's an expiration date on this—whatever it is between us. And am I going to sleep with him? Am I going to go into this fuckfest—which, given the size of the thickness the stabs into my core, promises to be epic—with no expectation of anything more from him?

"Was seeing me with another man so painful that you decided you were going to fuck me?"

A nerve pops at his temple. Then he leans over and slaps the button that raises the screen in front of us. Guess there are some conversations he doesn't want Rudy to hear, after all.

He plants his big hands on my hips, then proceeds to fit me over the tent in his crotch.

My entire body shudders. I dig my fingers into the front of his shirt and arch my back. "Not fair," I gasp.

"Don't care," he replies.

He continues to move me back and forth, back and forth over the thickness between his legs, and my eyes roll back in my head. "Ohmygod, ohmygod, I'm going to—"

He pauses, then locks his fingers around the nape of my neck. "Open your eyes."

I slowly peel open my eyelids. And instantly, his gaze locks with mine.

"The first time you're going to fall apart will be on my cock, in my bed, with my fingers around your throat and my thumb testing the rosette between your arse cheeks, you feel me?"

35

Knight

I carry her inside my private elevator, her arms and legs wrapped around me. She has her face buried in my throat, and I know it's because she's too embarrassed to meet Rudy's gaze. She has nothing to be ashamed about.

Rudy served in the military. I met him at an event for veterans I attended before I left on my mission. We hit it off at once.

When I returned from my recent misadventure, I found out he was looking for a job. He's a good man. I immediately contacted him to offer him the position of my chauffeur. It's a far cry from the tanks he used to drive on the front-line, but there's no one else I'd trust with my life more than him.

I wanted Adam to come work for me, but that was a no-go. He's not going to set foot inside an office, if he can help it. He much prefers to work outdoors. He wants to use his hands. Wants to feel the roughness of sand between his palms, of grit under his fingernails as he labors under the sun and in the cold. He wants the satisfaction of building something from the ground up, he said.

He also wants to spend time with his wife and daughter. He's fond of reminding me that tomorrow is never promised. After being away so long, he doesn't want to waste time. They need him and he wants to be there for them. In a sense, I don't blame him.

In fact, I envy him. The man has a family he cares for, a wife and daughter he loves for whom he'd do anything. Also, he doesn't have the weight of his father's company hanging around his neck. He doesn't have this driving need to prove something to the world. He isn't driven by revenge or the pull to self-destruct. He hasn't yet made his peace with what happened, but he doesn't let it rule his present. He's following his instincts and doing what he feels he needs to do to heal himself and his family.

And me? I don't want to heal. I want to keep the frustration from what happened fresh so it can fuel this intense rage inside me. The only time I feel calm, the only time I allow myself to feel peace, is when I'm with her. It's why I brought her back home.

I carry her inside the kitchen and place her on the island. When I pull back, she refuses to let go. I kiss her nose, her eyelids, each of her cheeks, then brush my mouth over hers. Tiny bumps against me, pushing me deeper into the space between her legs. My swollen shaft stabs through the crotch of my pants and into her core, and she moans. I swallow down the sound, then drag my tongue across the seam of her lips. She tilts her head up, and I deepen the kiss. I stab my tongue inside her mouth, wrap my arms about her, and pull her in until her breasts are flattened against my chest.

Tiny shuffles against me, then whines.

I manage to release her mouth and push my forehead into hers. "I need to feed him."

"You do," she murmurs.

"You need to release me."

"I don't wanna."

I smile; so does she. We look into each other's eyes, and a warmth invades my chest. For the first time since I returned from being held captive, I feel alive.

Then Tiny plants his butt down on the floor and barks. She looks at him. "Poor baby, he really is hungry."

I frown. *Am I really going to be envious about the tenderness in her eyes when she talks about the mutt?*

She notices me glaring at her and widens her gaze. "What?"

I shake my head, then step back so she has no choice but to release her hold on me. I miss her instantly, and fuck me, but this is not something I counted on. I brought her home because... No way, was I going to allow her to be anywhere else today. And now that she's here, it's clear she belongs here at my side, and it's evoking emotions I'm not sure how I feel about.

I stab my finger at her. "Stay." Then pivot and head for the shelf where I stock the dog food. I top up Tiny's bowls with the chow and water and can't resist scratching him behind his ear before I turn and stalk back to her. She's looking at me with a slight smile on her face, and there's this look in her eyes, something that makes the back of my neck heat. "What?" I growl.

She shakes her head.

I prowl up to her, then plant my hands on either side of her thighs on the counter. "Something you want to tell me?"

"If I do, you won't like it."

"Try me."

She places her hand over my heart, and my breathing grows shallow. My balls tighten, and fuck me, never has anyone's touch affected me like this. "You're a good man, Sir. A tough man. A man who's been through a lot and who's still standing and taking life one day at a time. Your strength, your protective instincts, and your need to do the right thing is the sexiest thing about you."

Jesus, this woman. Her words cut me to the bone like a laser saw. I straighten, then laugh without humor. "You have no idea what you're talking about. You don't know me. If you think I'm intent on doing the right thing, you're mistaken."

"I'm not. However much you insist otherwise, I know the truth. I see you, Sir. I see you more clearly than I see myself and that's"—she looks to the side, then back at me—"that's scary as hell."

Me, too, Little Dove. I'm fucking scared about what this feeling is that grows between the two of us only, I'm too scared to say it aloud. Instead, I cup her cheek and drag my thumb over her lower lip. "Not as scary as the things I'm going to do to your body."

She flushes, and her pupils dilate. The pulse at the base of her throat speeds up, and everything within me insists I throw her down on the ground, part her thighs, and bury myself inside her hot, tight cunt. Instead, I hook my fingers into the neckline of her camisole and tug.

36

Penny

The cloth tears down the middle, and I yelp. He doesn't stop there. He reaches into a drawer and pulls out a knife, then slides it under the center of my bra. He twists his wrist, and the lace snaps. My tits spill out. I suck in a breath from between my lips, and my chest heaves. He stares at my breasts for a second, another. Goosebumps flare across my skin. My core weeps. I squeeze my thighs together, and he drops his gaze there.

As if I reminded him of what he wanted to do next, he slips the blade under the waistband of my skirt and snips—the material splits down the middle. He places the knife aside, then grips the two ends of the skirt, and in one swoop, tears it down the center.

I cry out; I can't stop myself. This man is so strong, the brute force trapped in his body has never been more evident than it is today. My pulse rate speeds up. My throat dries. All that manliness, all that alpha-holeness concentrated under his skin, and I'm going to be at the receiving end of it.

Will I survive this encounter? Does it matter if I don't?

To feel his body on mine, his palm-prints on my skin, his breath on my cheek, the rough hair of his thighs scraping against mine, his fingers inside me, his cock, his tongue, his eyelashes tangled with mine... To be his would be heaven and hell and everything in between, and I want it more than I can say.

He reaches for the waistband of my panties and tugs. The fabric gives way so quickly, it's easy to forget it's because of the power locked in his muscles, his tendons, his flesh—that I want to mark as thoroughly as he will mine. I raise my hand to cup his cheek, but he catches my wrist and twists my hand behind my back. Then the other. He drags his gaze down my naked breasts to the triangle between my legs. "You're so beautiful, I want to eat you up."

I swallow.

"I want to lick your pussy and suck on your clit, then stab my tongue inside your slit. I want to stuff my fingers inside you and ensure you're stretched enough to receive my cock. I want to suckle on your tits and twist your nipples and violate the hole between your ass cheeks."

My stomach flutters, and my toes curl. My skin feels so sensitive that if he touches me now, I'm going to burst into a million tiny sparks.

"I want to wrap my fingers around your throat"—he drags his fingers around my neckline, and I shiver—"and squeeze so you get enough oxygen to fuel the building orgasm in you... slowly... slowly"— he cups the nape of my neck—"to the edge, so when I bury myself inside of you, you'll beg to come. But I won't let you."

"You won't?" I gasp.

"Not until I've teased you and taunted you and built up the anticipation, the expectation, the need that builds inside you, layer upon layer, until it consumes you and eats at you from the inside to get out, and then—"

"Then?" I breathe.

"Then, nothing." He releases me, steps back, turns and begins to walk away.

I blink. "What are you doing?"

"Going to bed, of course."

I gape, then anger crashes over me. I jump down from the island, and my cut-up clothes slither to the ground, leaving me without a stitch on. I ignore it, race forward, and launch myself at him. Of course, he hears me coming, so he turns and catches me. I raise my hand, intent on slapping him, but he throws me over his shoulder. Again.

"The hell? What are you doing?"

"Your anger is the most cleansing thing in the world, Little Dove."

"I'm not your Dove. And I'll give you anger, you bosshole." I begin to rain blows on his back, his side, wherever I can reach. It makes no difference. He passes by Tiny, who raises his head and looks at us, then goes back to slurping from his water bowl. Argh! Not that he'd be able to help me. No one's going to stop what's going to happen—this man is going to ravish me tonight, and I'm going to love every bit of it.

More moisture slides down my inner thigh. His shoulder muscles ripple. Without breaking stride, he runs his fingers between my legs and brushes my throbbing clit. He doesn't say a word, but he increases his pace until he's almost jogging. My cheeks turn fiery. He's noticed how turned on I am. And he can't wait to claim me. I squeeze my eyes shut. And I find that so very sexy. So erotic. Oh god, oh, god, oh— He bursts into his room and kicks the door shut behind him. Then turns and locks it.

"What are you doing?" I squeak.

Without replying, he stalks toward the massive bed and throws me down on it. I bounce once, my arms and legs akimbo. My hair falls over my face, and I blow it out of the way. I jump up—my stilettos sink into the bed, but I don't care—and throw up my fists.

He unbuttons the first button of his shirt, then another. Then, in that one-handed move that makes my insides squeeze together, he reaches behind himself and yanks off his shirt. He toes off his shoes, then shoves down his pants, his boxers and his socks in one sweep. When he straightens, I freeze. H-o-l-y hell. You've seen that scene where Daniel Craig emerges from the sea in that James Bond movie whose name I can't recall, or a young, bare-chested Tom Cruise in Top Gun, or Channing Tatum in Magic Mike. Hell, pick any shirtless, hot man chest from any film and multiply that by a hundred—no, a thousand—and it wouldn't compare to seeing Sir in the flesh. His shoulders are bunched, his chest tattooed and ripped, his abs a work of art, which should be cast in a mold and preserved for eternity. I gaze dreamily at his concave stomach, trim waist, and those powerful thighs—between which, his monster cock points straight at me. I gulp. The blood drains from my face. "Th-that... thing—"

"You mean my *thang*?"

I glance up in time to see his lips twitch.

"Did you crack a joke?" I whisper.

"I'm getting ready to crack *you* in half, baby."

His biceps flex, and I follow the rippling muscles of his forearm down to where he squeezes the base of his cock. The veins on the back of his palm stand out in relief as he strangles his cock from base to swollen head. Little drops of liquid ooze from the slit. My mouth waters. My breathing grows patchy. My breasts grow heavier, and a thick, liquid pulse slides down to coil behind my clit.

I should look away, I should, but that *thang* he's holding in his fist is massive and ugly and beautiful and within its every ridge, it holds a promise that he can bring me to orgasm with a thrust. Also, it's big. Too big. Way too big to fit into my tiny little hole. I swallow and take a step back. And his eyes flash. His lips thin, and a mean look comes into his eyes. And that's scary and also, arousing. More moisture slides down from between my pussy lips. His nostrils flare. He takes a step forward. I skitter back. And it must please him, for his lips curl. The man's stingy with his smirks. Good thing, too. I don't think I have enough panties to change out of the ones that would melt every time he did it.

He tilts his head. "You going to run, Little Dove?" he growls.

I shiver and take another step back.

"You going to try to escape me?"

I nod, the motion jerky.

"Fine, then." He moves to the side. One hand fists his cock, the other he waves in the direction of the door.

I look at it, then back at him. "This is all a game to you, isn't it?"

He merely stares back. The mask is back on his face, and I can't read his expression. So annoying. I take a step forward, then another. And when he doesn't move, a third one. I reach the end of the bed, then step down. I sit on the edge, reach for my stilettos, and he snaps, "Leave them on."

"What?"

"I want you to dig those heels into my back when I fuck you."

Oh, my god, I almost combust. Almost lie back and spread my legs and ask him to impale me right there. But that would be giving in too easily. Besides, some hidden part of me knows he wants me to run. He wants the thrill of the chase. The illusion that he allowed me a chance to escape, though we both know it's just that. An illusion. No way, is he going to let me out of here with my virginity intact.

I swallow around the ball of anticipation in my throat. Then rise up.

My legs are shaky, but they support me. I glance at him. He jerks his chin toward the door. With the other, he continues to stroke his dick, which has definitely grown thicker and fatter in the last few seconds. I gulp. Resist the urge to sink to my knees and worship at the altar of his cock. Then I take off toward the door.

37

Knight

Her butt twitches, and her thighs quiver. I take in the glorious sight of my Little Dove trying to flee as every curve, every jiggle, every inch of her flesh calls out for my touch. Squeeze her hip, pinch her nipple, flick her clit. Then bite down on the curve of her neck as I take her from behind like the rutting animal I am. Soon. I snatch up a pillow from the bed and prowl forward.

She reaches the door, jiggles the lock, and begins to slide it back. Her hand slips, and she swears aloud. Grabs at it, misses. "Come on, come on." She pants, snatches at it, paws at it, as I come to a stop behind her. Her entire body shudders. Her movements grow sluggish. I bend down, then lean in toward her, close enough that my next breath raises the hair on her head. She moans. Then pushes her forehead into the wood of the door.

"You wanna walk out?"

She shakes her head. Thank fuck. If she'd said yes, I might have let her. Or not. Good thing I don't have to find out.

"Turn around," I order.

She instantly complies. And keeps her gaze lowered, arms at her side, her pose so yielding, I could take her right now. *Hold. Slow down. Savor this moment. And the ones after. After tonight, you're never going to touch her again. You can't afford to touch her. Not if you want to keep your sanity intact —your focus clearly on the goals you've set out to achieve.* I drop the pillow in front of her. "On your knees, Little Dove."

She sinks down and folds her palms over the juicy flesh at her core. Then lowers her chin so her thick luscious hair falls forward.

"Do you want to suck my cock to help you calm down?"

She nods at once, and that softening in my chest spills over to my guts. For the first time since my return, the churning in my stomach recedes.

"Tip your head back; open your mouth wide."

She does. I guide my cock between her lips, and she blinks up at me. "Lick me off."

She swirls her tongue around the head of my shaft, and a groan rumbles up my throat. My knees threaten to give out. I slap my hand into the door; the other I slide into her hair. I tug, she arches her neck, and I slide in until I hit the back of her throat. She gags; her gaze widens. Her blue eyes are limpid pools, still clear. I could dive into them and never come out. I want to bathe in them until every single stain on my soul dissolves. Tears slide down her cheeks, leaving tracks of mascara. Saliva pools at the edges of her mouth, and I haven't ever seen a more glorious sight. I pull back until I'm poised again on the rim of her lips. "Breathe through your nose, baby."

She draws in a breath, another, and a third. When her eyes clear, I push forward and down her throat. She gasps, the sucking sensation a vice around my shaft that threatens to draw every last drop from my balls. But not yet. Not until she's ready for me. Absolutely. Completely. Drenched and wet and open for my intrusion. I pull back, then propel forward. Her entire body jerks. She grips my thighs, while she holds my gaze as I violate her mouth. Again and again and again.

"Touch yourself."

She blinks, then slowly lowers her hand between her legs. A moan swells up her throat, the vibrations traveling up my shaft to embrace my balls. I release my hold on her hair, only to wrap my fingers about her throat. I tilt my hips and sink my cock down her throat. She swallows, and I feel my dick grow thicker, constrained only by the circumference of her gullet. "Pinch your clit, Little Dove."

She does, and her eyes roll back in her head.

"Don't stop, keep going."

Her shoulders shudder, her body jerks, and I know she's close. I pull out of her, and when her gaze clears, I ask, "Better?"

She nods.

I haul her to her feet and push her into the wall then, holding her up with my grip around her throat, I drag the fingers of my other hand down her cleavage, her stomach, to her pussy. I slide three fingers inside of her, and she gasps. "You're so wet, your cum is dripping down my arm."

She moans.

"Open your mouth, Little Dove."

When she does, I spit onto her tongue. "Swallow."

She does, and her eyes shine with need, and a trust that almost fells me. I place my lips on hers and breathe from her. Then, holding her gaze, I curl my fingers inside her. Instantly, she orgasms. The climax shudders up her spine. Her back arches, a whimper travels up her chest. Her blue eyes dilate, and she digs her nails into my arms.

I move my fingers in and out. Her trembling subsides, and I pull my fingers out and slide them inside her mouth. She licks my fingertips, and my balls draw up. I scoop her up in my arms and turn to stride to the bed. I place her on the mattress and crawl between her legs. Urging her to lock her ankles around my back, I fit my cock to her opening. She whines, pushes up her breasts, and I bend and lock my teeth around one of her nipples. I tug, she whimpers, and the sound sinks into my bones. "Eyes on me, Little Dove."

She raises her heavy eyelids, and I hold her gaze, then sink inside her. Her pussy clamps down on my shaft. Sensations shudder out from where we are connected. My entire body convulses. I am not even fully inside her, and I know everything is going to change forever.

I stay where I am, unable to move. Unable to comprehend why it feels like it's not only her first time, but also mine. Why every cell in my body is open and alive and focused on making this good for her. I grit my teeth and wait... Wait as she adjusts to my size. Her chest rises and falls. She wraps her fingers around my arms that I've planted on either side of her head, careful to hold my weight off of her, while allowing her to feel the full impact of my cock. I pull out slightly, then thrust forward, and it's like coming home.

38

Penny

He pushes inside and a sharp pain ladders out to my extremities. I cry out, and he pauses. Sweat beads his forehead. His shoulder muscles bunch. Under my fingers, the muscles of his forearms vibrate. He's holding himself back. His chest muscles seem to have turned into stone. The veins in his throat stand out, and the nerves at his temple pop. His jaw is so hard, I imagine he could cut a diamond with the edge. This big, strong, powerful man, who's more wounded inside than anyone else I know, is trying not to hurt me.

Little does he know, he's shattered every single wall I've tried to put up in front of him. I'm here knowing I won't walk away unscathed. That I want him to leave his mark on me because it's the one thing I can hold onto for the rest of my life. I know, I'll never have him, but at least, I can savor these memories. I dig the heels of my stiletto into his back then push up. He sinks in further. A groan rumbles up his chest. I answer with a whine. Our bodies communicate with each other without words, and it's so instinctive. So real. So everything. A tear crawls out of the corner of my eye.

He bends and licks it up. "Did I hurt you?"

"Not enough."

He freezes.

"Don't hold back. I want you to show me how much you want me. I want you to need me as much as I have craved you. I need you to let me feel everything you're experiencing. Open yourself up to me and let me see who you are."

If I thought he was rigid before, it's nothing compared to how he goes completely still. He could be the trunk of a redwood, tall and strong and utterly grounded, despite the storm raging around it. Only his eyes are sharp and alert. There's a wealth of unsaid meaning in their depths that I'm not sure I want to probe... Yet. Right now, I want to bask in being the focus of attention of this very virile male.

"You don't know what you're asking for," he says in a low voice. "You don't know who I am."

"You're Sir. You're Knight. You're my best friend's brother. The man who came back from war wounded. The man who gave up any semblance of living a normal life so others could sleep in peace at night. You're you and I want all of you. Your pain. Your hurt. Your strength. Your charisma. Your personality. Your force of will. Give me all of it."

His lips firm. His jaw tics. He glares at me with such anger, such torment, my heart flips in my chest. He's not happy. And I so very much want to do what he wants...but on this... This, I claim. On this, I will make him bend. He must sense some of my thoughts, for his gaze narrows. He lowers his chin until his nose bumps mine.

"I'm not the hero you're making me out to be. I'm not the leading man of your story. I'm a villain in disguise. Scratch the surface, and you'll see I don't care about anyone other than myself. It's why I'm taking your virginity —" He pumps his hips forward with such force the entire bed jolts. The headboard slaps again the wall, and the windows shudder. "I'm not the kind of person you want to get to know better. I'm not the man you want to introduce to your mother." He pulls out, then digs his knees into the mattress and pumps into me again. This time he slides in further.

His dick pulses inside me, and I swear, I can feel every ridge, every vein, throbbing against my inner walls. He seems to expand inside me, filling my channel, pushing against the constraints of my pussy, stretching me around him, so I all can do is lay there and gasp as he pins me to the mattress with his cock. "Sir, please," I gasp.

"You asked to see me, baby. Now, you're going to get all of me."

He drills into me further and my thigh muscles quiver. My scalp tingles. I swear, I can feel him in my throat. "Enough," I gasp. "I can't take more."

"I'm only halfway in, Little Dove."

"What? No." I chuckle, and the sound comes out broken. "You're joking."

In reply, he pulls out and slams into me with such force, I huff. I try to wriggle away, but he leans some of his weight on me. I pant and sweat pools under my armpits. "If you're trying to scare me, you're—" I cry out, as he pulls out and pistons his hips forward and plunges into me. His balls hit the curve of my butt cheeks, his cock brushes up against a secret spot inside that unfurls sensations I never imagined I could feel. My nerve-endings crackle. And I climax.

The orgasm crashes over me. I open my mouth to scream, but he closes his mouth over mine and swallows the sound. Then, he thrusts his tongue over mine, and begins to fuck me in earnest. The aftershocks course through me, and with each wave, he slams into me, over and over and over again. He balances himself on one arm and slides his big palm under my butt cheek. He squeezes down, then stuffs his thumb inside my forbidden hole, and the trembling gathers again at the base of my spine.

No, no. I cannot orgasm again. I can't. I try to tell him, but he swipes his tongue over my teeth, and pleasure centers I didn't know existed light up in my brain. I've turned into a mewling, whirling, mass of need. I strain against him. I throw my arms about his shoulders and hold as he pumps into me. Sweat clings to his skin. My body braces as my mind, my soul, climb higher and higher, reaching for that horizon in the distance. Then, he tilts my torso at just the right angle so his pelvis hits my clit when he penetrates me next.

I instantly climax. Moisture bathes the space between my legs. I soar through the air, a dove set free. Higher and higher, until everything disappears. As I float down to earth, I hear his hoarse cry, feel his big body shudder, and he shoots his load inside me.

I black out, and when I come to, he's watching my features closely. There's a wrinkle between his eyebrows. I reach up and smooth it out.

"You're okay?"

I nod, not trusting myself to speak.

He searches my eyes, then nods. He begins to withdraw, but I squeeze my arms and legs about him, refusing to let him go. He hesitates, then slowly sinks down and nestles his face into the hollow of my throat. I run my fingers through his hair, and he sighs. Still inside me, he turns his cheek and nuzzles me. I tighten my arms about him, and bit by bit, the tension drains from him. I close my eyes and drift off to sleep. When I wake up it's dark.

Now, he's on his back, and I'm cuddled into his chest. His body twitches. He mutters something under his breath, but when I glance at him, his eyes are closed.

"No, stop," he cries out, the sound guttural. He throws his arm up as if trying to protect himself, then lowers his arm to his side. He grips the bedclothes, thrashes his head from side to side. Sweat clings to his chest, but he's pale below his tan. He's definitely dreaming, for he cries out again. "No, don't. I can't take it. Kill me. But spare them. Please."

My heart somersaults into my mouth. My throat closes. I sit up, wondering what to do, when he cries out again. The sound is so full of pain and sorrow and helplessness, my stomach twists on itself. I feel like I'm going to be sick. "Sir. Knight. You're dreaming." I touch his shoulder, and in the next second, I'm thrown on my back, and he's straddling me. He has his fingers around my throat. His eyes are open, but his gaze is unseeing. His mouth twists, and his grasp tightens. I claw at his wrists, to no avail. The oxygen cuts out. My heartbeat slows. Flickers of black dot my vision, and just before I surrender to it, I slap him across the face.

Suddenly, I draw in a breath. My lungs inflate. Flashes of white cross my vision, and when they clear, Knight's face fills my line of sight. He holds up his hands, glances from my face to them, and a look of utter horror comes over his features. He scrambles back, until he's on his haunches at the very edge of the mattress. At once, I sit up and pull my knees into my chest. We stare at each other across the length of the bed.

His bare chest heaves, and his nostrils flare. Sweat glistens on his forehead, and his hair is stuck to it. His throat moves as he swallows. He squeezes his eyes shut and pulls on his hair. "Fuck," he growls, sounding like a wounded animal. "Fuck. Fuck. Fuck."

His features twist into a look of such revulsion, I know I have to do something. "Knight, it's okay," I say softly.

He shakes his head. "It's not." He snaps his eyes open, and the look in them is so bleak, I flinch. And that only hardens his jaw further. He balls his fists at his sides. The muscles of his body are wound tighter than I've ever seen them before. His shoulders flex, and he seems frozen with indecision, and that's a first.

I've never seen this man look anything less than self-assured. Of course, I knew he carried a wound inside from what happened to him, but that seemed to have made him even more confident about facing challenges head-on. I realize now, it was all a front. I realize now, my instincts were correct. The Knight inside is tormented, anguished and suffering. He's in such agony, carrying so much trauma from what happened to him, that my breath catches. My throat closes. The frustration and helplessness that vibrate off this man twist my gusts. Tears stab the backs of my eyes, and I blink them away. I lean forward, and he stiffens further. The veins on his arms stand out in relief. The tendons of his throat are so prominent, I'm sure they're going to snap.

I inch forward, and though he watches me with a wary gaze, to my relief, he doesn't push off the bed. With that haunted look on his features, and tension radiating off of his body, he resembles a caged predator. One who'll lash out at me, or worse, break through the bars and run so I'll never see him again. Somehow, I think it's the latter and I definitely don't want that. I don't want to lose him. I can't lose him. Not when I'm beginning to understand the many layers of this complex man. When I reach him, I cup his cheek, and he winces.

"I could have... killed you," he says in a voice that cracks.

39

Knight

"But you didn't."

Her voice is soft, her gaze softer, and her touch? Her touch is so gentle, it slices me to the core. I've shot at men and killed them. I've withstood torture. I've seen my fellow teammates die. But nothing has affected me as much as the whisper of her fingers as she trails them down my cheek. I want to turn my face into her touch. To press my lips into her palm, absorb the comfort she's offering me. I want to... Push her on her hands and knees, grab her hair, and tug on it as I take her from behind. *What does it say about me that she tries to console me, and I want to fuck her, and in the most animalistic way possible? Why do I feel incapable of giving her the tenderness she obviously deserves? Why is it that I want to channel all of the violence, all of the hate inside me, into what should be an act of affection? Why do I want to rut her like the animal I have become instead of make love to her like the man I wish I could be for her.*

I pull away from her, and her face falls. A piercing pain fills my heart. I tamp down on it, then swing my legs over the side of the bed and rise to my feet. I struggle against my desire to see her one last time, and I lose the fight. Turning, I see her crawling toward me, and fuck, if the sight of her in such a subservient pose doesn't make my balls ache. The blood drains to my groin. I try to move back, but my feet seem anchored to the floor. She pauses in front of me, her breasts swaying, her back curved to meet the flare of her hips. Then she sits back on her heels, and I can't look away from the triangle of skin between her thighs.

"You didn't hurt me, Sir."

I draw in a sharp breath because, fucking hell, when she calls me Sir, I forget about that heaviness in my soul, the emptiness in my heart, that grief for what I've lost that haunts my every waking moment. The echoes of cries, of pain, of the despair that laces my dreams... All I become then, is hers. And she's the only one, the only thing that will stop me from losing my mind to the cavernous darkness that stretches in front of me.

She tilts up her chin and meets my gaze. "You can never hurt me. You would never allow yourself to do so. Surely, you realize that?"

"I woke up with my fingers around your throat. You could have died. You realize that?"

"You stopped before you cut off my breath. Besides..." She brings her finger to her mouth and chews on her fingernail. "Besides, isn't erotic asphi...asphiation a thing?"

"You mean erotic asphyxiation?" I narrow my gaze.

"Yes, exactly."

"How do you know about erotic asphyxiation?"

She rolls her eyes. "I might have been a virgin, but remember, I was also an actress. And when I realized I had no roles lined up, not even auditions, I contemplated taking part in an, uh, art film."

An unknown emotion—anger, combined with possessiveness?— twists my guts. "You acted in a porn movie?"

She rolls her eyes, then holds up a finger. "Wait a minute. I didn't act in it; I only contemplated it. Almost went for an audition, too—"

"You auditioned for a skin flick?" I growl.

She blinks. "Aren't you hearing what I'm saying? I *almost* audi-tioned. Except, I got cold feet at the last minute. Doesn't mean I didn't do my research."

I slowly uncurl my fingers at my sides. Some of the tension leaves my muscles. I take in the glint in her eyes and realize—"You didn't almost audition for an adult movie, did you?"

She looks guilty for a second, then shakes her head.

"You said that to distract me?"

She hitches a shoulder. "It worked, didn't it?"

"Hmm…" I cross my arms across my chest. "You knew I'd be pissed to find out you contemplated taking part in one of them."

"I wasn't sure, but I thought it was worth a try." She searches my features, and whatever she sees there makes her swallow. "I don't regret saying it. I wanted to take your mind off whatever you were thinking, and I believe I succeeded."

"Maybe too well."

This time she pales. I expect her to put distance between us, but instead, she tilts up her chin. "Are you going to punish me for almost fibbing, Sir?"

I hold her gaze for a second, then another, and let the silence stretch until she wriggles in place.

"Do *you* think I should punish you?" I purr.

Her breath hitches. Pink crawls up her throat and streaks her cheeks.

"Should I, Little Dove?"

She lowers her chin.

"I didn't hear you."

"I think you should punish me," she replies at once.

"And how do you propose I do that?"

She peers up at me from under her eyelashes. "By doing anything you want with me."

My pulse rate instantly shoots up. My blood thunders in my veins. *How is it that she knows exactly what to say? How can she be so absolutely perfect? How can she be precisely what I need right now?* "You don't know what you're saying."

She merely smiles. A sweet, shy and very confident smile that makes my heart bang against my ribcage, my dick extends, and my balls grow so tight, I'm sure I'm going to come right then. And I can't do that. Not until I've shown her the kind of pleasure she's never experienced in her life, and never will again with anyone else. She can't be mine. Doesn't mean I'm not going to ensure she's so high on endorphins that she'll have a satisfied look on her face and an ache between her legs for the next week. So every time she moves, she'll remember who fucked her.

"*You* don't know what *I'm* saying." She rises to her feet then launches herself at me.

40

Penny

He catches me with his big hands under my butt, and I wrap my legs about his waist. I saw the emotions flit across his features. The nightmare he had earlier must have lowered his barriers because I've never seen him this open, this vulnerable. This real. And I can't lose this opportunity to get close to him. Physically. Emotionally. This is my chance to get him to reveal the person he truly is—to the extent he's willing to share, that is. And maybe I'm making use of the fact that his defenses are down, but that's okay. A girl's gotta play with the cards she's dealt. And the one thing I know is that, regardless of how grumpy and growly he comes across in my presence, he's affected by my body. If that's what I have to work with, then so be it. I'm going to use every advantage I've been afforded to ensure he never forgets what it feels like to be with me. I twine my hands around his neck and hold on.

His nostrils flare. "You shouldn't have done that, Little Dove."

"And you're still talking, Sir, you—" I gasp as he plucks me off his body with seemingly no effort, then throws me over his shoulder. My heart flutters like a trapped butterfly. My hair flows down my face, hiding my line of sight, but I sense him moving. I manage to push back the strands from over my eyes as he turns and marches off toward the closet.

"Where are you going?" I huff when he brings his big palm down on my backside. The pain shivers over my nerve-endings and my scalp tingles. All the pores in my body seem to wake up. He walks across the floor of the closet—in between empty shelves built into the walls. Huh? I tilt my head and spot a couple of pairs of shoes, and a row of suits—all black—as well as a few pairs of jeans and sweatshirts folded on a shelf. There's nothing else in the space.

He may have decided to embrace this mean billionaire persona, but deep down, he's the Spartan soldier who went on a mission to defend his country. He might try to deny it, but I know he hasn't changed as much as he'd like me to believe. He pushes against the paneling on the far side of the closet, and a door—one which is hidden until you push on the panel— opens. He walks in, touches a button, and the door swings closed behind us. Then, he hits a light switch, and a golden glow illuminates the space. His bare feet make a thudding sound as he prowls forward, then lowers me onto my back on a bed. The mattress is so thin, I can feel the hardness of the wood through it. I sit up and glance around the space.

The single bed has a thin pillow and a threadbare sheet which is mussed up. The room itself, is only about sixty square feet, if that, and it has no windows. On a table pushed up against one wall are a few pairs of jeans and folded sweatshirts. Below it, is a pair of boots, another pair of formal shoes and a pair of sneakers. There's a table—with a few books—and chair pushed up against the opposite wall. In between the table and the bed is a nightstand, with a lamp, a phone charger, and some coins. There's also a coil of rope on it. Huh? The space feels claustrophobic. It's also more lived in than the rest of the house. *Is this the only space he feels at home? Does it feel safe to him because it's hidden from the outside world?*

He walks over to the nightstand and snatches up the rope. He turns to me "Hold out your hands."

"What is this space?"

"Lay back on the bed," he orders.

"B-b-but—"

"You will do as I say." He glares at me, and my heart seems to slide down to the space between my legs. A dull throbbing springs to life there. I draw in a breath—suffused with his scent, which is so much more concentrated in this space—and my head spins. He holds my gaze. Those green eyes of his are, once again, emerald chips, and I know then, he's close to breaking. A crack in the ice that'll show me the turmoil he holds within himself. The rest of the room recedes. All I see is his features, his lips, his jaw, his cheekbones, and his scowl, which hold me captive. As if in a dream, I lay back and hold out my hands.

"Good girl."

I flush, and my pussy clenches.

He looks down between my legs with interest. "That turns you on, hmm?"

Without waiting for an answer, he transfers the rope to one hand and swipes the fingers of his free hand up my slit. He brings them to his lips and sucks on them. "Caramel and honey," he says around a groan, and a whimper spills from my lips. It seems to galvanize him into action, for he brings my wrists together, then wraps the rope around them.

When he knots the restraint, the soft material whispers across my skin, making goosebumps burst all over. My nipples tighten, and I don't need to look down to know they're saluting him right now. He twists my arms up and over my head. I draw in a sharp breath. I glance up to find he's looped the rope through the headboard. He tugs, forcing me to straighten out my arms. I'm forced to flatten my back onto the bed as he secures me. Then he walks to the bottom of the bed, ties each of my ankles to the footboard, so I'm spread-eagled. As he straightens, he drags his fingers over the underside of my foot, and I shiver. "Ticklish, hmm?"

"Isn't everyone?"

His eyes flash, then he lowers himself to his knees on the floor. He wraps his thick fingers around the sole of my foot, then bends and sucks on my big toe. I feel the suction in my core, I swear. My pussy clenches down and comes up empty, and it's almost painful. I try to pull my foot away, but of course, I can't because I'm tied down. He looks at me from under his heavy eyelashes, then flicks out his tongue into the space between my toes.

My scalp tingles. My leg muscles spasm. More moisture slides out from between my pussy lips. His nostrils flare. His gaze lowers to my core, and he stares at my throbbing center. The more he looks at it, the wetter I grow. I'm sure the bedspread below bears a wet spot from my cum.

"You're so pink, so pretty. Your cunt can't wait to welcome me inside you, baby."

"So, what are you waiting for?" I cry out.

His lips quirk. Asshole chooses to smile at my discomfort. He moves to my other foot, and before I can protest, he's sucked on my big toe again.

OMG, it's sooo arousing. My back arches. I can feel the sucking motion in my center, on my nipples, even on my tongue. It's as if all my erogenous centers are connected to where he flicks his tongue out and licks down the outline of my foot. "So, you have a foot fetish?"

"Only if it's *your* foot." He straightens to his full height, and instantly, my gaze is captured by his thick cock that juts out from between his massive thighs. It seems bigger and thicker than the last time. A vein stands out in relief on the underside, and precum drools from the crown. He squeezes the base, and I shudder, then lick my lips.

"Do you want me to feed you my cock, Little Dove?"

I instantly nod.

"That's too bad."

"Eh?"

"You haven't earned it yet."

"What do you mean? What do I have to do?" I pant.

He walks, once more, to the bedside table. This time he pulls out the drawer, snatches something up, then throws his leg over my thighs to kneel over me on the bed.

When he holds out his open palm, my gaze widens. "What are you going to use that for?"

41

Knight

"What do you think?" I pluck one of the clothes pins from my palm and squeeze it open, then allow it to close.

She pales a little, and the scent of her arousal is laced with fear, and... Fuck, if that doesn't turn me on further. Something about my Little Dove panting for my cock, while also dreading what she'll have to do to get it, brings out the sadist in me. It satisfies that craving inside me, fills the emptiness inside me.

Everything about this woman was made to satisfy me. Why didn't I realize that earlier? Now, with her sprawled out, with her cunt on display, and her pussy lips swollen and begging for my touch, I'm filled with the need to stuff her holes and ensure she feels so good, she'll never want to be with anyone else. Which is wrong because I don't intend to stay with her, but... Something within me insists I show her the heights to which I can take her. Yes, I'm selfish, and I'm going to hell for this — Oh, wait, I've already been there, so chalk this up to another of my unpardonable sins.

I lower the peg. She gasps, then cries out, for I've fastened it around one of her pussy lips. "It stings," she cries out.

"Does it hurt?"

She bites on her inner lip, then slowly shakes her head.

"Good girl."

Her throat moves as she swallows, and red creeps up her chest. I lock the second peg around her other pussy lip, and she moans.

I sit back on my haunches, take in her features. "How does it feel?"

Her chest rises and falls, then she tips up her chin. "Different. It feels like I'm being pulled apart and offered up for your enjoyment."

"And?"

She looks away, considering my question, then back at me. "And all of my attention is focused on where the pins pick my skin. The area feels tight and very sensitive."

"And it's going to feel more even sensitized when I remove them."

"Oh." She swallows.

"Indeed." I plant my hands on either side of her torso and lean in until my breath mingles with her. "That focused sensation will slowly grow and build, until it fills your mind and all you can think of is how, when I remove them, one by one, the blood is going to rush in and fill the space and turn it into throbbing sparks of desire that are going to spread and engulf you and light you on fire."

"Like when your foot goes to sleep, and when you move it, the blood pours through your veins and you feel numb and then tingly?" she chokes out.

"Only much number, and then"—I drag my nose up her jaw toward her ear—"much, much more tingly." I suck on her ear lobe, and a whimper escapes her.

I lean back and peer into her eyes. "Do you realize how turned on I am to see you in pain?"

She swallows.

"It gives me fierce satisfaction to see you squirm from the discomfort I've inflicted on you."

"Oh." Her mouth opens, and all I can think is that it's the perfect shape to receive my cock.

"I'm going to fuck your face, baby."

Color sweeps over her features.

"Think you can take that?"

She jerks her chin.

"Blink twice in quick succession if you want me to stop. Now, show me what you'll do… but only if you want me to stop."

She demonstrates, and I can't stop my smile from widening. "That's my good girl."

She draws in a sharp breath, then sinks her teeth into her lower lip. I gently release it. "Only I get to hurt you, baby, no one else."

She squeezes her eyelids shut before piercing me with an imploring look. "Why do I like it when you say that? Why do I like these strange, torturous things you're doing to my body? Why do I get so aroused when you treat me with such contempt? Why do I want you to use my body for your pleasure, and only your pleasure?"

Because you're mine.

Only I'm never going to accept it. I might ravish you. I might ravage your pussy, and your arse, and your mouth, and imprint my touch in every cell of your body, but then… I'm going to let you go. I have to.

She continues to gaze at me, and the sight of her dilated pupils fills me with an urgency I cannot deny anymore. I slide up her body until I'm poised below her tits. I squeeze them together, then slide my cock in the valley between her breasts. My entire body grows rigid. I thrust forward so my cock slides up her cleavage and bumps into her lips. She opens her mouth, licks the crown, and a growl rumbles up my chest. I begin to thrust forward faster, quicker. Each time I push in, I squeeze her breasts so they push down on my shaft, then I penetrate the hot, moist hole of her mouth. She sucks down, then releases, and I pull back. Again and again and again. Sweat sides down my back. My balls hurt. My thighs threaten to cramp, but I don't stop. Not until her body shudders, and I know she's close. When she curves her back, squeezes her eyes shut and elongates her neck, I know she's going to come. That's when I pull back. I release her tits, grab the two clothing pins I hid from her view, and fasten them to each of her nipples.

She gasps, and her eyelids fly open. She looks down, and the pulse at the base of her throat beats double time. "Y-you…"

"Clamped your nipples with clothes pins."

She pants, then raises her gaze to mine. "Sir, please, Sir," she whimpers.

"How does it feel, Little Dove?"

"It feels like I'm on the edge, like I'm poised at the end of a wave that's going to crash any moment. Like I'm about to jump off a steep mountain and glide on air currents, circling and soaring until I float to the ground… Sir."

I ease down her body until I'm between her legs. I stare down at her pussy lips spread for me, and her thigh muscles tremble. "You don't have to be shy in front of me, sweet thing. I've never seen anything more delicious, more beautiful than your cunt weeping and calling out for my attention. Do you want me to lick up your slit, Little Dove? Do you want me to stab my tongue inside your pussy and suck your life through your hole? Would you like me to slurp at your rosette while I'm at it? Maybe stuff my huge cock inside your tight little back hole and show you a forbidden pleasure you'd have never imagined otherwise."

"Oh, god," she wheezes.

"The only name that should emerge from your lips is mine, you feel me, baby?"

She nods. "Oh, Sir, please, Sir. I want it, Sir."

I cup my palm outside my ear. "What's that?"

"I want you to fuck me, Sir!" The words burst out of her.

I bare my teeth. "Where do you want me to put my cock, Little Dove?"

"Wherever you please, Sir."

A-n-d, that's when the remnants of my control dissolve. I pull on the pegs that clamp her nipples. She hisses. I twist them, and she pants. "Sir, oh my goodness. Sir, it's too much."

I whisper my fingers over the roll of her stomach. She writhes under me. I toy with her belly button and she arches her back further. I drag my fingers down to her clit. I pinch it, and she cries out. Her eyes roll back in her head. That's when I pull off the pegs on both her nipples, then her pussy lips.

A full body shudder grips her. I rise up and position my dick at her entrance.

42

Penny

His thick, blunt head teases my slit, and a thousand glow-worms seem to stir to life under my skin. The blood rushes to my nipples, fills in the grooves left by the clothespin on my pussy lips. My scalp tightens, and my toes curl. Every part of my body has become extra sensitive. The glow worms under my skin threaten to break through, sending zaps of sensation streaking out to my extremities. I moan and writhe, reduced to making noises that don't mean anything. Yet, they mean something to him, for he plants one broad palm next to my head, then holding my gaze, he thrusts forward and impales me. The combination of the blood pouring into my throbbing pussy lips, of sensations leaking out from my nipples, and the fullness of his shaft stuffed inside my pussy... It's too much. The climax shudders out from where he's joined to me.

He pulls out, and it recedes. I push my pelvis up, chasing that feeling of fullness, of him pulsing against the walls of my channel, of him pushing himself inside me. He slides a hand under my butt and squeezes. When I gasp, he pushes the thumb of his free hand inside my mouth. I suck on his digit, and his green eyes flare. He toys with the rosette between my cheeks. I moan. He leans in close enough for his breath to sear my face, for his eyelashes to fan against mine. He holds my gaze, then kicks his hips forward and impales me. I bite down on his finger between my teeth, and he growls, "You're going to be the death of me."

I shake my head. *I don't want you to die, Sir. I want you to sink into me. To melt into me. To fuse our skin until we become one entity.* My heart swells in my chest, growing until it seems big enough to fill my entire body. I strain against my bindings, wanting to get closer.

He seems to understand what I'm saying, for he reaches up and unties the rope. Instantly, I throw my arms about his neck. He continues to fuck me, in-out-in, and I hold onto him. Sweat pours down my chest, so each time his body touches mine and leaves, a sucking sound fills the air. It adds to the erotically charged air that thickens and pulses and pushes down on me. With his next thrust, he brushes up against that secret space deep inside me, and when he curls his thumb in my forbidden hole and looks deep into my eyes and commands, "Come," I shatter at once.

I ride the wave down, down, down. All of my senses vibrate and come alive, and I can feel every last sensation until I crash down. I'm aware of my body pulsing as he thrusts into me one last time and groans as he empties himself. My limbs tremble, I can't hold onto him anymore. My body slumps. I close my eyes and float.

He stays inside me for a few seconds, his heart thudding strong-hard-fast, while his cock mirrors the pulsing between my inner walls. There's a soft touch on my forehead, then on one closed eyed, the other, my nose. Then he pulls out. I begin to protest, but he presses a kiss on one corner of my lips. "Let me take care of you." My last recollection is of him untying the ropes around my ankles and carrying me out of his secret room.

When I come to, I'm in his bed in the main bedroom and, swaddled so tightly by his sheets, I know he tucked them around me. Light pours in through the windows. I wriggle my toes and realize I'm no longer wearing my stilettos, and when I stretch, the flesh between my legs protests. My pussy feels sore, my nipples are so sensitive, a shock of sensations floor me when the sheet rubs against them.

"Oh," I gasp and lay back against the pillows. I turn and find the space next to mine is empty. I inch my arm out from under the sheets and touch the pillow. It's cold. *When did he wake up? Did he come to bed after we —fucked? Yeah, it was fucking... And more. What that more is, I'm not sure. I don't think I can give it a name. I can only say it was something a whole lot more than meaningless sex... For me. And for him. I'm sure of it. Only he's not going to admit it. He —* There's a buzzing sound. I glance to my other side to find my phone on the nightstand. I snatch it up, look at the text message.

Bosshole: You're late, Ms. Easton. I expect you to be at the staff meeting within the next hour.

I burst into the conference room in the office, and every single face turns to look at me. I flush to the roots of my hair but hold my head high as I stomp to the only remaining chair in the room, which happens to be the closest to his. At least, I'm not wearing the same dress I wore when I went to the bosshole's place. I can't because it's shredded. Also, he left me a skirt suit and blouse draped over the chair near the bed, along with fresh underwear. The label shows it's from Karma's boutique. Did he have more clothes in my size delivered to his place? He must have. Did he anticipate me spending the night with him? Did he plan it all? I don't think so, and even if he did, it doesn't matter. The Sir who can make my body sizzle with his ministrations, who is a demanding, dominant lover who can make my bones melt with one glare is gone; in his place, the jerkosaurus is back and gauging by the disapproving look on his face, he's not happy.

I stomp over to the chair and throw myself into it, then wince when my butt and my pussy protest. Jeez, but I can feel his palm-print on my backside and his dick-print inside me.

A look of satisfaction comes into his eyes, but he banks it. "Glad you could join us Ms. Easton," he drawls.

"Wouldn't dream of missing this important announcement," I reply sweetly.

"You're only twenty minutes late." He makes a show of looking at his watch, a black-colored Casio G-Shock, which is not only cheap but also durable. The kind I'd have expected the former Knight who was a soldier on a mission to wear. Another clue that the man I'd love to know is in there somewhere.

But that man wouldn't have fucked me, then left me in his bed while he made it to office on time. That man would have woken me up with a kiss, then fucked me in the shower and cooked me breakfast, before giving me a ride to the office.

Ugh, and I was visualizing a future with this... This emotionless bastard. Only he's not. I've seen glimpses of the man he is inside. The man I want to get to know. The man I know is right for me. The man I want to spend the rest of my life with. And, no, no, I cannot go thinking like that. I need to —

"Ms. Easton, did you hear what I said?"

I blink, then scowl up at him. "Of course I did."

"Care to repeat it?" One side of his lips curls, and I can't stop looking at it. He definitely didn't smirk so much earlier, so this has to be an improvement to his personality, right? One of the other girls in the room titters. I shoot her a sideways glance.

"Ms. Easton, clearly, you're not focused on the matter at hand. Do I need to remind you how important it is for you to do your job properly?"

I snap my teeth together, then slowly shake my head.

"Can you tell me what we were discussing earlier?"

"The new marketing tie-in with CN Enterprises."

He jerks his chin, then turns his attention to others in the room. "The next time anyone is late to a meeting, you'll all need to stay late to compensate for it."

There's a murmur around the room. Some of the people — not all of whom I know — glower at me. Nice. If this was a way to make me the focus of ire with my new colleagues, then he's succeeded. I place my hands in my lap, stare at a point past the handsome visage of the man I want to punch — and jump, and slap, and kiss, and push my nose into his throat and draw in his heady smell, all at once. A flush steals up my cheeks, and I make sure I don't look at his face.

He continues speaking, and I let his words rumble over me. And of course, the timbre of his tone causes my pussy to clench and my nipples to bead. I squeeze my thighs together and manage not to wriggle in my seat. If I did, I'm sure the bosshole would know what the source of my discomfort is. At some point, he stops speaking. And when the rest of the people rise to their feet, I jump up too. They begin to stream out, and I turn and begin to follow them, when he calls out, "Ms. Easton, a word?"

43

Penny's bucket list

- ~~Type at 250 words a minute (done!)~~
- Have 5 O's in the course of 1 night (I'll settle for 1 tbh) => Almost made this one last night when he gave 4 orgasms. OMG 4 freakin' orgasms!!
- ~~Learn to cook a gourmet meal. => I wasn't very good at it, but it's the spirit that counts, right?~~
- ~~Act in a movie or a play — I'll take a street act => It didn't go down that well. :(~~
- See the London Ice Kings play a game.
- Swim with dolphins.
- See the Northern Lights.
- Climb Uluru in Australia.
- Eat a chocolate croissant in a sidewalk café in Paris.
- ~~Be dominated. (Uh, maybe this should go up to the top?)~~
- Find a man who cares for my mother as much as I do.
- Be proposed to by the man I love.
- Explore anal. (I'm chicken so this is right at the bottom — pun intended. Hahahaha!)

44

Knight

Yes, that was an asshole move on my part. Heading to the office without her and messaging her, knowing she was going to be late. And knowing I was going to tell her off when she came in, and that I'd see the anger on her face when I did. And I wanted to see her eyes flash and her cheeks redden. I was sure she'd slink into the room, but she marched in like she owned the place and took her seat like she didn't have a care in the world. And I didn't miss the way she winced when her bottom hit the chair. Nor did I miss the way she kept raising her hand to her mouth as if she wanted to bite her fingernails, only to stop herself and clasp her fingers in her lap, which told me she wasn't anywhere as composed as she was pretending to be.

For the record, it took everything in me to tear myself away from her to head to the office. I skipped my morning run with Adam, who'd only have had a knowing look on his face if I'd turned up with the sated look on my face — so I was only too happy to pass that up.

I watched her sleep in my bed and recorded it in my mind before I left. Because it's not going to happen again. I'm not going to slip up. Won't allow myself to get lost in her pussy, her skin, the touch of her fingertips on my scars, her nails digging into my shoulders, her heels into my back as she took all of me like the good girl she is.

Now, her shoulders rise and fall as she draws in a breath to compose herself, no doubt, before she turns and tips up her chin at me. "You needed something, Mr. Warren?"

I need everything you can give me and that you can't give me, too, and that's why I'm going to have to let you go.

"Do you have the list of women from which I can choose a wife?" I snap.

The color fades from her cheeks. "Y-you're going through with that?"

"Of course, I am. In fact, I've decided I should marry within the next week."

Her gaze widens. "The next week?"

"Enough of this faffing around, it's time to get on with my plan."

"But—" She swallows. "But I thought that—"

"Because I fucked you, I'm not going to marry someone else?"

She winces.

"You weren't bad, especially for someone who's so inexperienced, but your pussy isn't made of magic that it's going to hold me captive."

She firms her lips. "You took my virginity, you bastard."

"Do you expect me to write a poem about it?"

"I expect you to—" She shakes her head. "I don't know what I expected, but it wasn't this."

"It's good to be surprised. It keeps you on your toes. Keeps you alert and aware. Makes you a good employee."

She draws herself up to her full height. "If I had a choice, I wouldn't be working for you."

"If I had had a choice, I wouldn't have employed you, but here we are."

She searches my features. "I don't understand why you paid for my mother to stay in her home."

"Because I could?" I raise a shoulder. "Don't go reading anything into it. It was a way of buying your loyalty."

"You mean using it to blackmail me, don't you?"

"What-fucking-ever." I stifle a fake yawn. "We done? I have an important meeting to go to."

She visibly reddens, then turns and begins to stomp out. "Don't forget to email me the list of potential candidates, Ms. Easton."

"Black is my favorite color." The thin woman with the scrunched-up face and lips so big they are, clearly, botoxed looks at me with a glint in her eyes.

I finish the last piece of my steak, then lean back with a sigh. "Are you sure you don't want to eat your"—I gesture to her plate with the pile of greens on it, without dressing, as she'd requested—"uh, whatever that is."

"Oh, no, I'm not hungry." She glances down at the remnants of the meal on my plate then back at my face. "Not at all."

"And why do you want to marry me?"

"Uh, I have the bloodline. My fifth cousin is a distant relation to the Prince of Wales. Also, I know how to throw a party for a thousand people, and how to command a retinue of servants and—"

"Get gone."

"Excuse me."

I jerk my chin in the direction of the door.

Her jaw drops. "You're joking?"

I merely stare at her. She swallows, then rises to her feet and stomps off.

"Which one was that?" Adam drawls as he slips into the vacated seat.

"Does it matter?" I growl.

"I'll tell you; that was the last candidate on your shortlist."

"You trying to run my life for me?"

He raises a shoulder. "You trying to run from the reality that's been staring you in the face all this time?"

"What's that?"

"That you have the perfect nominee for the role, but you refuse to acknowledge it."

"Huh?" I narrow my gaze on him. "What are you talking about?"

"The woman who could be pregnant with your child as we speak," he murmurs.

"Hold on. The only woman I've slept with since I returned is—" my voice trails off.

"Exactly." He tilts his head. "Did you use protection?"

Realization sinks into my bones. I sit back in my seat. "Fuck."

"You did not, and you have to pay the consequences, my friend."

"She was a virgin," I say slowly. And I didn't ask her if she was on birth control. Of course, she might be, but I didn't check. And who was I to assume she wanted unprotected sex? I didn't even think of using a condom. How could I be this careless? It didn't cross my mind until Adam bought it up, which shows how distracted I've been by her. All the more reason to keep my distance from her. Except—if she is pregnant with my child, then—

"Looks like you got ahead of the game. After all, the deal with your father was for you to marry in the next month and produce an heir in the next year, so things are going according to plan." Adam reaches for the bottle of water on the table and takes a swig. Asshole's sworn off alcohol. Good for him. Wish I had the same restraint. But the booze is the one thing helping me forget—other than when I'm deep inside her and the noises in my head recede. And now, I have to find out if I'm paying the price for being addicted to her.

Adam places the bottle back on the table, then wipes the back of his hand over his mouth. "So, what are you going to do about it, hmm?"

Penny

"I'm coming! Jesus, if you bang on the door anymore, it's going to break, you—" I throw open the door to the apartment I share with Mira, and freeze. There, framed in the doorway, with his shoulders filling the breadth of the entrance, wearing a suit, with his tie half-done and hair disheveled, is a very pissed off looking Sir.

He glowers at me. I shiver, then force myself to not do the obvious and drop to my knees, even though everything in me wants to when he glares at me with that look in his eyes that's so damn sexy and dominant and hot. *Why is he so hot?*

"The lock on the front door is broken," he snaps.

"The landlord hasn't gotten around to fixing it yet," I admit.

"And you opened the door without checking who it was."

"It's you, so—" I raise a shoulder.

"It could have been someone else, someone who you didn't know, someone who—"

"Was out to hurt me? Well, you hurt me, so it's best you stay out then." I try to close the door, but he plants his foot in the doorway. I blow out a breath. "What do you want, Mr. Warren?"

"We need to speak."

"I don't want to talk to you."

"You're my employee—"

"In the office. Here, I'm not."

"Your contract requires you to work for me around the clock."

"Eh?" I blink.

He shakes his head. "That pesky fine print again, huh? Should have read it all before you signed it." He steps forward.

I release the door, and he brushes past me, leaving that sea-breeze and pepper scent in his wake. My stupid nipples perk up, and my pussy —well, I confess, I've been wet since I opened the door and saw him. He prowls into the living room, which seems to shrink with him in the space. He's drawn in all the oxygen, leaving me gasping for air. He glances around, then back at me. "Are you pregnant?"

"What?" My jaw drops.

He shuffles his feet. "We, uh… I didn't use a condom."

I shut the door and lean against it for support. *Shit, shit, shit.* He's right. And he came inside me. And I loved it and— "Oh, god." I press my knuckles to my mouth.

His jaw tightens. "I take it you aren't on birth control?"

I shake my head. "Never needed to use it before."

His chest rises and falls, then he draws himself up to his full height. "Pack a bag. You're moving in with me."

"Excuse me?" I gape at him.

"You heard me. Not going to repeat myself."

"You're crazy," I burst out.

"And you might be carrying my child."

Any remaining blood drains from my features. He's right though. I could be pregnant. Right now. With Sir's child. I place my hand on my belly. His gaze drops there, and a nerve pops at his temple. "We're getting married."

"What?" I gasp.

"Not for real, of course. I need a wife and an heir. And if you're pregnant, you deliver on the second, pun intended. As for the first, you merely have to pretend for the next year."

"A year?"

"Long enough for the union to be seen as legitimate by my father. Long enough for him to have signed over the company to me."

"And if I'm not pregnant?"

He blinks as if that possibility didn't occur to him. "Well, then, I can simply pump you full of my cum until you are."

I wince. "Must you be so crude?"

"Just stating a fact." He looks around, then heads inside.

"What are you doing?"

"Since you don't seem inclined to pack, thought I might do it for you."

He steps into the hallway, looks around, then heads in the direction of my bedroom.

"Wait, how did you know which room was mine?" I burst out.

In reply, he wrenches open the door and steps inside. I rush behind him, and when I enter the room, it's to find him picking up my bottle of perfume from the dressing table and sniffing it. "Roses, with notes of caramel; all I had to do was follow the scent."

"Give that back." I go to snatch it, but he holds it out of reach. "Unusual combination."

"I'm an unusual woman."

"I'll give this back if you hold out your left hand."

"Wh-a-a-t?" I manage to keep my jaw from dropping. "I'm not doing any such thing."

"In which case..." he begins to pocket the bottle and I almost stomp my feet. This man has the power to piss me off like no one else.

"Give me back my perfume," I hiss.

"Hold out your left hand first," he growls.

I hesitate.

His glare deepens. "I could order you to do it and we both know you'll obey me. So, can we both stop pretending you're not going to do what I want?"

I stiffen, attempt to hold his gaze for a few seconds more, then huff. I hold up my left hand, palm outstretched. He places the bottle back on the dressing table, then slides his hand into his pocket and pulls out a ring. A ring? What the—? I begin to pull back my hand, but he's caught it in his. He turns my palm over and slips the ring onto my finger.

"Oh, my god!" There's a gasp from the doorway. I turn to find Mira staring.

"It's not what it seems." I attempt to pull back my hand, but he tugs on my arm. I fall into him.

He wraps his arm about my waist, then turns to face her. "It's exactly what it seems."

"Are the two of you engaged?" Mira cries.

"No, we're not," I protest.

"Yes, we are," he says at the same time.

I scowl up at him. He looks down at me with a bland expression on his features. "The wedding will be five days."

"Five days?" I exclaim in horror.

"Five days?" Mira scoffs. "Who gets married so quickly after the engagement?"

The Bosshole does, apparently. Only, I'm not having it. I try to wriggle away, but his hold around me tightens. I'm hauled against him so I can feel every hard plane of his body dig into my side. "What are you doing?" I hiss.

"Following the plan I devised to gain control of my father's company —which will soon be mine."

"I want nothing to do with it," I lower my voice, so Mira can't hear the conversation.

"You've been pivotal in executing the plan since you became my employee. And now, *you're* the plan, it seems." He looks at me strangely.

"What?"

"If you don't agree and come home with me, I'll withdraw the funds I deposited for your mother's stay in the home."

"You can't do that." I swallow.

"Try me." He holds my gaze, and in his, I see the utter conviction that he's willing to follow through with his threat.

"I hate you," I saw in a low voice.

"So do I," he agrees.

Wait, did he say he hates himself? "Wha—"

He places a finger over my mouth. "Hush now. I know how excited you are, but perhaps we should head to my place where we can talk more without disturbing your roommate?"

"Oh, no, now—" Mira shakes her head. "I'm in no hurry for you to leave. In fact, I'm finding this entire proceeding rather entertaining—" She coughs. "I mean, it's enlightening. I mean… uh, it's so romantic that the two of you only met and now you're getting married. And I stopped believing in love at first sight, too."

"It was more like hate at first sight," I snarl.

"First hate, then love. All that chemistry that swirls between the two of you—" Mira fans herself with the palm of her hand. "I knew I sensed it, but I thought it was all in my head."

"It was." I nod.

"It was all true." He nods.

My eyes shoot daggers at him, and he cups my cheek. Douchebag cups my cheek and stares soulfully into my eyes. "You know what I thought the first time I saw you?"

"What?" I narrow my gaze on him.

"That you were the most striking, most beautiful, most sensuous woman I'd ever met ,and that no one else could ever compare to you."

I hear Mira sigh.

"And when you looked at me, it was the first time—the only time—in my life I felt nervous."

"You felt—nervous?" I blink.

"I knew my life would never be the same again. I knew everything as I knew it was going to change. I knew my future had arrived and that I had to find the courage to reach out and grab it. I knew if I didn't hold onto you, I'd never forgive myself."

"You did?" I ask, unable to keep the suspicion from my voice.

He snatches up my left hand and brings it to his mouth, then kisses the ring.

Mira makes an "awwww" noise.

I ignore her and focus on the conniving man in front of me. He doesn't play fair. He was willing to pay millions to the woman who agree to play the role of his wife and bear him a child, and all to ensure his plan of taking over his father's company comes to fruition. He'll never let anything get in his way. That's why he threatened to rescind the funding of my mother's care unless I worked for him. *He doesn't mean anything he says. He doesn't.* And yet, when I search his features, I only see sincerity in his eyes. *Huh?*

He twines his fingers through mine, then takes my other hand in his and holds both of my palms between his. The warmth from his touch seeps into my blood. My heart skitters, and my stomach flutters. A shivery feeling coils in my belly. He's playing a part. That's all it is. I may have gone to drama school, but he's the consummate actor here.

Then he goes down on one knee. "Penelope Mary Easton, will you be my wife?"

45

Knight

"You did it, huh?" Adam jogs up until he's abreast with me.

I increase my pace, but so does he. We run in silence for a few seconds, then he chuckles.

"What?" I growl.

"Nothing."

I hear the smirk in his voice. "You may as well spit it out," I say through gritted teeth.

This time, he chuckles, I come to a stop, then turn on him. "Okay, that's it. Either say what's on your mind or get out of here."

"Whoa, whoa, is that a crack in the Iceman's facade I detect?"

"You done?" I cross my arms across my chest.

"No need to be defensive; it happens to the best of us."

"The fuck you talking about, man?"

"It's love, baby," he sings out. " Penny and Knight sitting in a tree, k-i-s-s-i-n-g." He smirks.

"What are you, five?"

He looks me up and down. "What are you? Still denying your true emotions for her?"

"I have no feelings toward her." I set my jaw.

"That's why you asked her to marry you?"

"I asked her to be my wife because one"—I hold up a finger—"I need a wife to consolidate my claim on my company, and two"—I lower the first finger and hold up the middle finger—"you're the one who pointed out she might be pregnant with my child so—" I shrug.

"So, are you telling me this to justify yourself, or because you're trying to talk yourself into believing your own bullshit?"

"What's bullshit is that I'm standing here talking to you when I should be—"

"Running back to your little fiancée?" He laughs. "Aww, you're so in love, it's cute. And the way you're trying to deny yourself would give the rest of the unit a real hard-on." The moment the words are out of his mouth his face falls.

I hunch my shoulders. "If only they were alive to rag me about the situation I've gotten myself into..."

"Fuck, I'm sorry I brought them up, man." Adam rubs the back of his neck. "Old habits—" He sets his jaw.

"Do you ever wonder why it is that you and I were the only two to get out alive?"

"Only all the time." His lips tip up, but the smile is sad. "But I do believe I've been spared for a reason."

"You mean, to make my life miserable?"

He scoffs. "That, too. But I've been given a second chance. I'm not going to waste it."

"You mean, I am?"

He shrugs.

"So, you do think I'm wasting the opportunity I've been given."

"Any one of the rest of the group sent in with us would give anything to stand here. But they're not, and you and I are."

"Your point being?"

"Don't faff around. Pull your finger out of your arse and tell her how you really feel." He reaches up to grip my shoulder, but I pull away.

"You don't know what you're talking about. You weren't conscious to see what they did to my men."

"My men, too."

"You didn't lead them."

"And you're being too hard on yourself."

"Am I?" I search his features and glimpse the pity, and also, the anger in them. "So, you do hold me responsible for what happened."

He holds up his hands. "I didn't say that."

"You don't need to. The look on your face is enough."

"You're mistaken."

"Am I?" I glare at him.

He holds my gaze, his own steady. "That's your guilt speaking, Lieutenant," he murmurs.

Anger punches my chest with such force I can barely breathe. "Fuck you, too, arsehole." I turn and jog away, my ribcage so tight, each breath feels like I'm drawing knives down my throat. I increase my pace, my feet pounding into the footpath by the Thames. I could throw myself off and into the depths of the river—oh wait, I'm a fucking good swimmer, the curse of being a Green Beret. We're put through our paces and need to be excellent swimmers. After all we marines are part of the navy. So, that won't work. I could shoot myself, but that would be too messy for the person who finds me —besides, I can't put my family through that. I'm not that cruel, am I? Not after what I went through. Seeing the people you care for die is worse than facing death yourself. It's worse than having the skin peeled off you when you're alive, worse than the abuse you're subjected to when you're—

"Hey, motherfucker!" A new voice calls out to me. Footsteps pound behind me, then Rick pulls up on my left.

I groan, pretending not to notice him.

"Aww, you upset with me, darling?" He makes kissing noises, and I resist the urge to roll my eyes.

"I do believe the boy is pouting." Finn's Texas drawl reaches me first, then the dickface, himself, pulls up to my right. With the two men bracketing me, I continue to jog, and the two fall in step with me. Our pace aligns, and the three of us mirror each other's speed. Soon we're running in tandem. It's almost like being back in that frozen jungle with my men running single file behind me.

The silence of the space wraps its arms about me, our footsteps muffled by the snow, each branch of each tree shorn of any leaves, the bark glistening in the morning sun rays. Tiredness catches up with me. Three days of running with short pauses for eating and a few hours for sleep has dulled my attention span. Or perhaps, the beauty of nature has lulled me into a sense of false safety. I find my steps slowing down to a walk as I take in the quiet, allowing it to soothe my nerves, follow a rabbit that darts out of the undergrowth and crosses my path. The hairs on the back of my neck stand up. I tighten my fingers around the trigger of my gun as the first shot is fired. A scream splits the air and I stumble on a piece of ice in my path and—

"You alright?" Rick grips my elbow.

I shrug him off, straighten myself, and continue running.

He exchanges a glance with Finn, who scans my features with a worried frown.

"Stop looking at me like I'm going to self-destruct any moment," I snap.

"Stop holding back. It's okay to rely on your friends."

"My friends are dead," I say through gritted teeth.

Finn scoffs. "Poor ol' Knight, mourning those he lost. Sinking in self-despair. Lonely and sad in his penthouse, succumbing to hopelessness, and waging a war against destiny for the blow it has dealt him, and—" He reels back when I plant my fist in his face. Blood spurts from his nose, and he stumbles back laughing.

I scowl. "You got a death-wish man?"

"At least that got a rise out of you." He coughs.

I shake out my hand. "Your face might be pretty, but it's harder than I gave it credit for."

"So are you, my man. You don't give yourself enough credit for how far you've come." He snatches up the bandanna Rick's tossed him, then balls it and pushes it into his smashed nose.

"Jesus, you have a mean strike." Finn coughs.

"Comes for years of conditioning. Every morning, for two hours at the naval base, right until the day I—" I firm my lips.

"The day you left on the mission?" Rick widens his stance. "Time you spoke about what happened there with someone."

"I'm talking to the two of you."

"I mean with someone who has the professional background to listen to you and steer you through the emotional minefields."

"Now you're talking like her."

"She's right," Finn pipes up. His voice sounds muffled, thanks to the cloth he's holding against his nose. "You should see a shrink."

"I talk to Adam—often."

"Considering he was there with you through the ordeal, I'm not sure how beneficial that's going to be for either of you."

"Oh, it's beneficial," I laugh, my tone bitter. "More than you can imagine."

Finn and Rick exchange another glance.

"Now what?" I glance between them. "It's bad enough my employees pussy-foot around me in the office—"

"And who's fault is that?" Rick scoffs.

"Not her though, I assume?" Finn smirks, then groans. And honestly, any remorse I may have had for how I hit him fades at that.

"You mean my fiancée?"

"Fiancée?" He blinks.

"Finally, fuck." Rick beams.

"Don't get your panties in a twist. It's a marriage of convenience. That's all it is."

46

Penny

"He sure seems nervous," Mira peeks out through the door of the dressing room adjoining the main ceremony room where I'm standing at the town hall in Islington.

Sir and nervous? I snort. "He's probably devising new ways to make my life miserable, is all."

Mira shoots me a curious glance. "Is that code for —" she stabs her forefinger through the hole created by bringing her forefinger and thumb of her other hand together.

I roll my eyes. It's been four days since he proposed. Four days since he went down on bended knee and proposed with words that sounded so heartfelt, it's no wonder Mira has stars in her eyes. I, too, would have been taken in by it. I confess, I *was* taken in by what he said. Only, before I could ask him about it, he hustled me out into the car, then become immersed in his phone so I couldn't really ask him for clarification.

When we reached his penthouse, he guided me to one of the guest rooms on the opposite side of the corridor from his room. Tiny bounded in after me. Knight hesitated, then glared at the dog, who panted and happily parked himself at my feet. I gripped Tiny's collar and stared back at Knight. He firmed his lips, then nodded, as if coming to a decision.

He told me the kitchen was stocked and I could order anything I wanted to eat from the app on my phone. He also said that he'd arrange to pay for the food. Then, he thrust something into my hands, which turned out to be his platinum credit card, before he stepped back and left. I haven't seen him since. Not when Abby threw me an impromptu bridal shower at her place, not when I came into the office to continue with my job—he didn't tell me not to work, and if I didn't have a place to go to each day, I'd go crazy twiddling my thumbs—not when I lingered around at lunch time—which he now allows me to take as a break because I might be pregnant—and after work, trying to catch a glimpse of him on the floor. That is, until the receptionist sweetly informed me that Mr. Warren is away on a business trip for the next four days.

That bastard! I am his assistant. I'm the first person he should inform about his plans, but he didn't bother to update me. Not a text message. Nothing! *Nada*. Argh! He didn't ask me to cancel his meetings for the week—no, he did it himself. He went to the extreme to cease all communication with me.

At first, it made me a little mad, then a little sad to realize I wouldn't be able to talk to him before the wedding. That is, until the wives and girlfriends of the Seven and the Sovranos and their friends descended on me.

Karma came, weighted down with dresses for me to try on. Summer brought along Rachel—a wedding planner who's worked with Isla—to help me with organizing the event. Mira commandeered Knight's black Amex and ordered enough food for us and Tiny, along with enough champagne to make us all very happy. Yep, the bosshole left his credit card, with instructions for me to use it as needed. I balked at that, but Mira had no such compunctions.

Then there was Abby, who beamed from ear to ear and refused to listen when I told her the wedding was fake.

Apparently, my closest friends, too, want to buy into the notion that we are in love and getting married, so much so, that a part of me began to believe in the story. Especially when I stood in front of the mirror in my bedroom and saw the gorgeous creation Karma had made for me.

Now, I glance down at the gorgeous champagne-pink colored gown that clings to my curves with a fishtail train that spreads out behind me. Not as elaborate as the train on the Princess of Wales' wedding dress, but also, not too short as to be insignificant.

The dress has a high neckline and long, sheer sleeves, but it's the second skin effect with the nude underlay that I love. When I move it gives the impression that I'm not wearing anything underneath the lace, and the back? Well, there is no back. The neckline plunges all the way to the cleavage between my ass-cheeks. It stops short of being obscene. Barely. Also, she carefully stitched in some of the lace I'd carefully cut from my mother's bridal gown, so it made me feel close to her.

I'd wanted my mother to attend, but when I went to tell her about my upcoming nuptials, I found her in a state of agitation. That's what I get for visiting her after dinner. She became very upset upon seeing me and burst into tears. When I tried to calm her, she pushed me away and started yelling. Eventually, Sunita stepped in and, by calmly talking to her, managed to assuage her agitation. Once my mother was otherwise occupied, Sunita indicated I should leave while she was distracted.

I haven't had the courage to go back to the nursing home. It's not that I worry about her being angry with me. I just hate to see her that way. The fact that she probably forgot all about me as soon I left is what hurts the most. Can you blame me for throwing myself into the day-to-day work of the office? Which was much easier, since the bosshole wasn't around, but also a little boring, if I'm being honest. As since I'm being honest, I must admit I've been dying for a glimpse of my bride-groom. I know he didn't have any kind of bachelor party, and in fact, only flew in this morning. Abby told me he was coming to his wedding straight from the airport.

I also know he's in the ceremony room up ahead—because I've had these little tingles pulsing under my skin, which only happens when he's nearby. A-n-d that's the sad thing. I hate this man, but I'm so attracted to him. I may have slept with him, but instead of getting him out of my system, it's only primed me, so I want more of him. Which makes sense, in a way. I was foolish to think I could get him out of my system by sleeping with him. He was my first, and I was bound to develop feelings for him. But I didn't anticipate that the physical draw to him would continue to grow.

And the enforced absence of the past week has made me so mad at him, and that has only fueled my desire. Bet it's all part of some evil plan to make me desire him further. Bet he's trying to show me I'll never be rid of thoughts of him, the images of how he fucked me, how I wanted him to destroy my pussy again, how—I love to hate him. My core clenches, and my thighs tremble. I shuffle my feet to try to release the pressure between my legs.

"You okay?" Mira murmurs. She's wearing a pantsuit, also pink, that shows off her figure. That was my only criteria for her and Abby and Solene. They could wear anything, as long as it was pink. Abby's wearing a dress with a sweet-heart neckline, and Solene's wearing a pink, leather mini-dress with berry-red, over-the-knees boots with seven-inch high heels, which confirm she's a world-famous popstar.

Between Solene and Declan, they created quite a stir when they walked up the steps of the Town Hall. Of course, this being London, people were too polite to approach them, but there were enough girls holding up their phones to record their entry, albeit from a distance. Now, Abby turns to me and says, "You ready?"

I shake my head.

Her gaze softens, she closes the distance, and takes my hand in hers. "Can I confess something? When I asked you to find Knight a wife, I secretly hoped he'd come to his senses and realize you were the woman he's been looking for."

"You did?" I gape.

"The only person I mentioned my plan to was Cade. No secrets from my husband." She chuckles. "And the one person I couldn't breathe a word to was Knight. If he'd found out, he'd have made things very difficult. I knew I was being wishful. I wanted us to be sisters, but I didn't want to get my hopes up. So, when you told me Knight had asked you to marry him, imagine how floored I was."

"Me, too," I murmur.

She searches my features. "I'm aware the circumstances of him asking you to be his wife aren't ideal. I know he probably did it because he's under a deadline—"

I wince.

She tightens her grip on my hands, "—but trust me when I say, you are the best thing that's ever happened to him."

"And me? What about me?"

"He's not easy to get along with—I'll be the first to admit that—but he's a man of his word. If he's marrying you, it's for keeps. If he's taking his vows, he'll do everything in his power to abide by them. Also—" She glances away, then back at me. "Also, he has feelings for you."

"Yeah, we both want to murder each other," I say dryly.

She laughs. "Relationships have been built on less. Look at me and Cade. He wanted revenge for what I did to him when we were younger. I swear, that man made my life miserable, but when I needed help, he was the only one I could turn to, and then—"

"Oh, they're ready for you," Mira exclaims.

"This is it, babe." Solene grins at me.

My heart seems to stop, then starts up at such a heightened pace, my breath catches. The blood drains from my face and I sway.

"Hey, hey." Abby wraps her arm around me; so does Mira. Bracketed between two of my friends, I grip the bouquet of blue feathers I opted for instead of a traditional bridal bouquet. Blue because I needed something blue.

"Deep breaths," a new voice commands.

I glance up to find a gorgeous woman wearing a dress that clings to her every curve, with a matching jacket, hair piled on top of her head, and pencil-thin stilettos marching into the room. "I'm Giorgina, and I came to find out what the hold-up is about."

"Hey, Gio." Solene tips up her chin. Her tone is cautious. The two women—who could not be more opposite in the way they're dressed— eye each other up.

"Nice get up; goes with the image," Gio offers.

"Nice dress; a step up from your usual Barbie Doll outfit." Solene smirks.

The two chuckle, then move toward each other and embrace. Solene steps back. "Gio, meet the bride, Penny, one of my closest friends." Solene dips her chin in my direction. "Penny, Giorgina used to be Declan's manager in LA, but she's moving to London."

Gio turns to me and her features soften. "I realize we don't know each other but I'm privileged to be here on your special day."

"I can do with all the support I can get." I curve my lips and paste on my trademark smile. My fake smile. The one which convinces everyone that everything is fine with me. Everyone but me... And Knight. He's the only one who can look through my false cheer. The only one who demands I be honest with him, when he himself never is. The only man who knows the real me asked me to marry him. In a way, this should be a perfect match; only, it isn't. Because it's all fake. His proposal, his reason for asking me to be his wife. All of it is as fake as my smile. I straighten my lips. Perhaps if I hadn't pretended everything was fine things wouldn't have come to this stage?

"Good thing Rachel booked the largest room in city hall to accommodate everyone," Mira chirps.

"Eh?" I blink.

"This is the only room in the place which can accommodate up to fifty people, it was smart thinking on Rachel's part to have booked it given the number of people attending your wedding has increased," she explains.

Solene turns to Giorgina. "When did you get in from LA?"

"This morning. I flew in with Knight."

"You did?" I frown.

She tilts her head. "It was coincidence that we were leaving around the same time. Also, I can't say no to flying private. Beats commercial, any day," she sniffs.

I narrow my gaze. "You and Knight—"

"—have never met before. I'm here because I lost a bet to Rick, who insisted I accompany him to your wedding. Not that I have anything against *you*."

"You're against weddings?"

She looks at me with respect. "You catch on fast."

Except when it comes to Sir Bosshole, apparently. I should have cut my losses and found a way to pay off the money I owe him. Instead, I seem to be caught deeper in the web he's spun around me. It's almost like he's trying every way possible to bind me to him and make it difficult for me to escape him. Including not using a condom when he fucked me. Did he do that on purpose? I blink. Nah, not possible. He wouldn't have, would he? On the other hand, what if he did it subconsciously? What if he really does care about me but can't admit it, even to himself?

"Oh, hold on, I have something for you." Giorgina dips into her handbag, then comes up with a brooch. "It belonged to my grandmother, who had a very happy marriage—unlike my own mother. And since I'm never going to get married, I thought you should have it." She nods in the direction of my dress. "May I?"

I nod. She pins it to the front of my dress.

"Oh, it's beautiful." I touch the piece, which is in the shape of a feather—and studded with tiny blue stones.

"It goes with your bouquet." She nods toward the bunch I'm clutching.

"It does!" I exclaim.

"It was meant to be," she says in a pleased tone, "and — "

"Ladies, we're very late." A harried woman in an emerald-green dress hustles in. Rachel's been a godsend. She worked with Isla on the weddings of the Seven, and the experience shows. She made sure to consult me at every turn, putting together the wedding ceremony and the reception afterward. I told her to do as she pleased, but she insisted on having my input. And now, I'm grateful for it. *What if the only wedding in my life is this fake wedding? What if I never find the man who's supposed to be the one? What if Sir is the one?* The band around my chest begins to tighten again, and my head spins. This time, it's Gio who grips my shoulders. "Woman, you need to go out there and show him he can't get the better of you."

I swallow.

"You can't let these men overpower you. You need to show him you have the firepower in you to stand toe-to-toe with him. You need to hold your own and make him respect you. You need to draw the line — here, now, this moment — and show him he's underestimated you."

I glance between her eyes. Apparently, it took a stranger to read between the lines and realize not everything is as it seems on the surface. It took someone who doesn't know me to call me on my bluff and tell me I need to stand my ground. To find the courage to go through with this without losing face. To believe in myself. I draw in a shuddering breath, then nod.

"Good." Her features light up. "Ready to make this wedding your bitch?"

47

Knight

"You're a bitch," Rick glares at me.

I raise my glass at him then toss back the contents. The whiskey slides down my throat and hits my stomach, leaving a trail of heat in its wake. I slap the empty glass onto the counter of the bar at the 7A Club. It's midnight, but inside the club, it's buzzing, men seated in comfortable armchairs with snifters of whiskey in front of them, and half-smoked cigars building ash in between their fingers. The air is thick with the scent of tobacco smoke. No, you're not allowed to smoke inside, but the douchebag billionaires around me have found a way around the rules. I grab the bottle of whiskey that the bartender helpfully left me and top myself up.

"So you're getting drunk on your wedding night, is that it?"

"Nope." I shake my head. "I am *already* drunk." I lie. I'm halfway there, but semantics. I toss back the contents of the glass, this time barely feeling the warmth. I reach for the bottle, but Rick snatches it away. "Gimme that," I growl.

"Not until you tell me why you're not with your wife on your wedding night."

"Or better still, on your honeymoon," Finn interjects from my other side, and I groan. "The two of you come as a package deal, is that it? Befriend one motherfucker, get two for free, is it?"

"You're not going to drive us away with your infantile attempts at vexing us," Rick snaps.

"Oh?" I reach for the bottle of whiskey, but he slides it across the counter and to the other side.

"Talk, arsehole, or I'll rip you another."

"You want me to talk? Fine." I snicker. "How about this? There once was a virile young Viking, whose sexual prowess was striking…"

Finn picks up the thread of my limerick. "He would plunder the asses, of hot Viking lasses…"

I interject with, "Each time he found one to his liking."

He holds up his palm, and I slap it.

Rick glowers at us. "And I thought you were here to knock some sense into his thick skull."

"If you can't beat 'em." Finn shrugs. "Also, I have a softness—or is that a hardness—for filthy limericks." His grin widens. "How's this? There once was a maiden from Ealing, who claimed to lack sexual feeling…"

"'til a fellow named Norris…" I mutter.

"First found her clitoris…" he adds.

The two of us look at Rick with expectation. I'm sure he's going to snap our heads off then, he blows out a breath. "And she had to be scraped off the ceiling," he says in a droll voice.

Finn barks out a laugh.

I can feel my lips stretch in a smile. I reach across and under the counter to feel around. My fingers brush a bottle. I pull it out. "Vodka, huh?" I uncap it, then swig a gulp straight from the bottle. The alcohol content of this liquor is much stronger. It tastes close to turpentine—expensive turpentine, but turpentine, nevertheless. I swallow, and this time, when the liquid hits my stomach, a ball of heat seems to detonate in my belly. My fingers and toes begin to tingle. Fucking finally.

"There once was a man from Nantucket…" Finn grins.

"Whose dick was so long he could suck it…" I mumble.

Rick reaches for the bottle of vodka I'm holding. I take a sip, then pass it to him. He takes a sip, winces, then rolls his shoulders, before continuing, "He said with a grin, as he licked off his chin, if my—" He hesitates. "Ugh." He frowns. "If my—" His forehead smoothens. "If my ear was a cunt, I would fuck it."

Finn smirks, "Did you forget the ending, old man?"

He narrows his gaze on Finn. "I'm only ten years older than you."

"Descended from the Jurassic age, this one." Finn nods in Rick's direction.

"That sounds like something she would say," I murmur, then stiffen when I hear my own words. Silence falls between us, then Finn reaches over and grabs the bottle from Rick. He takes a swig, coughs, then thumps his chest.

Rick snorts, "Too strong for you, knobhead?"

Finn wipes the back of his hand across his mouth. "There once was a man from Leeds, who swallowed a packet of seeds..."

"Within half an hour, his dick was a flower..." I add.

"And his balls were all covered with weeds." Rick laughs, then snatches up the bottle of vodka Finn tosses across. He takes a swig, then says in a droll voice. "You may think these limericks are crass and throw me a comment to sass."

"But I will agree, to some degree," I counter.

"And I'll show you the crack of my ass." Finn jumps off the barstool and does a mock bow. "Thank you. Thank you. Don't all of you applaud at once."

Rick scoffs. I take the bottle of vodka from him, take a long drink from it, and another, and another. By the time I plant the bottle on the countertop, my entire body is numb. Everything except my heart, that is. The fucker's been in a state since I slipped a ring onto her finger, then signed the paperwork at Town Hall, before turning away without a kiss.

Y-e-p, not only did I not kiss her, but I also haven't spoken a word with her since the event. Not when our friends crowded around us and congratulated us. Not when Abby glared at me and hissed that she'd kill me if I didn't treat her friend the way she deserved. Not when Cade gave me a funny look, or when Phillipe and JJ paused their conversation long enough to glare at me at lunch. Not when Sinclair pulled me aside and told me I'd better not fuck this up. Not when I went to the gents, and Michael hauled me forward before I finished pissing and threatened me with a fate worse than death if I didn't get my shit together. I merely zipped myself up, pulled away, and walked out of there. I didn't return to the lunch organized in honor of our wedding. I headed to the 7A Club and wasn't surprised when Rick and Finn showed up shortly after. They told me the only reason the other men hadn't come was because they'd managed to persuade them that the two of them would be enough to knock some sense into me.

Ha. Little do they know, that ship has sailed—since they tortured and killed my teammates, then abused me and left me to die, buried under six feet of mud and snow in the Tundra. If it hadn't been for Adam, I'd never have made it out alive.

If it hadn't been for Adam, I wouldn't have married her, either.

Fucking Adam, who said he couldn't attend the wedding of his best mate because he was too busy helping another veteran deal with the aftermath of a mission gone wrong. Fucking do-gooder, couldn't put a step wrong if he tried. And now, when I need him most, where the fuck is he? I slide off the bar stool and sway.

"Whoa, ol' chap." Rick grips my shoulder.

I shake him off. "I'm good." The words come out sounding like *Ihhhmm goose.*

"And I'm the gander." Finn grabs my arm.

I try to push him away, but motherfucker is one strong son of a bitch. He hooks his shoulder under my armpit, then nods in Rick's direction. "Got him?"

48

Penny

"Good thing we got him before he got completely sozzled," Rick murmurs. He has an apologetic look on his face as he and Finn half-carry half-drag my husband—my very drunk, barely conscious husband, who mutters under his breath as they heave him up the steps and toward his bedroom. Yes, it's *his* bedroom because the wankhole fucked off halfway through our lunch and left me alone with the expressions of concern on his sister's and my friends' faces. Not to mention, the angry looks his mates sported as they'd conferred with each other before Finn and Rick headed off in his wake.

To the credit of those left behind, they banded around me with Abby apologizing on Sir's behalf—and why am I calling him Sir?—he's not my Sir anymore. If he were, he wouldn't have left me on my own, a scant half an hour after our wedding. He didn't looked at me as we exchanged vows. Not when he slid the band on my finger next to my engagement ring. Not when he sat next to me at lunch. He didn't kiss me, didn't touch me. It was as if I were an object—a possession he lost interest in the moment he had me.

He had more affection for Tiny, who'd been our ring-bearer. Something I'd trained him for in the last week—the canine was so much smarter than his temporary master. And honestly, it's good that Knight is only dog-sitting because Tiny deserves better. I deserve better. The only time Knight seemed to show any emotions was when Tiny made a dash for the champagne. At which point, he pulled on the leash and snapped at Tiny to 'sit.' The dog obeyed—reluctantly.

And I, who was standing, planted my butt in the seat—much to my mortification. I glanced about, but no one seemed to notice. Thank god. Although, of course, they'd have attributed my flushed features to the excitement from the wedding. I wish I could tell Mira the entire ceremony was make-believe, but given she can be as filterless as me, I'm not sure that's wise.

And so what, if this entire sham of a wedding was fake? I've seen whores in movies treated better than the way my husband behaved toward me. I was so pissed off with him, enough to want to throw my champagne in his face instead of drink it—which would have been a pity. They were good bubbles. So instead, after the staff at the restaurant where the reception lunch was held had poured it, and after Rick and Mira each made their speeches, when it came time for the groom to say a few words, and after my husband declined to do so, I brought the flute to my lips and began to drink, when he stopped me.

His touch had sent a shudder through me, and the glass slipped from my hand. He caught it—his reflexes weren't affected by whatever ordeal he went through, apparently. He caught the glass, placed it on the table, then pushed the glass of water in my direction. Good thing no one saw it because it could have raised speculation. I scowled at him, but he turned away to talk with Rick.

I reached for the flute of champagne again and hesitated. I don't think I'm pregnant. But then, I don't know how it feels to be pregnant. So, I touched the glass of bubbles, then reached for the glass of water, instead. I glanced sideways in time to see his shoulders relax. So, he wasn't completely impervious to my presence. Which only made it worse.

He must have known how horrible I was feeling right then. He must have realized what a humiliating position he was placing me in. After that embarrassing silence, when he'd refused to say anything, the food was served. And though Mira and Abby watched me with concern, and Giorgina glared at my husband, the rest of the meal proceeded without incident—that is, until he left. He left me, his *bride*, at our wedding luncheon, oh, god, I'll never live this down.

Abby, Mira, and Solene insisted on accompanying me home. And when Giorgina invited herself and Rachel along, I didn't have the energy to say no. In a way, it's good the girls came over. They took my mind off the shitty behavior of my husband. I'll bet, if it had been a working day, he'd have headed to the office after. And I'd have gone along with him and taken my place at my desk as his assistant, and gotten on with my day because, clearly, I've totally lost my spine.

Why is it that he seems to hold all the cards here? Why is it that, because he has the money, he can do as he pleases and control my future? But if I'm being honest, it's not the money. I don't care about that. On the other hand, his magic cock, and his fingers, and his tongue have a way with my body. The pleasure he elicited from me makes my body quiver. He controls my body's responses, and I hate him for that as much as for making me so dependent on him.

I managed to keep a leash on my thoughts for as long as the women stayed. Mira wanted to spend the night, but I wouldn't listen to that. I was grateful for their company, but it's my wedding night, and I'll be damned if I'm going to spend it with my friends. I stayed off the alcohol, too, by nursing the same glass of wine throughout the evening. If my friend's noticed, and I know at least Mira and Giorgina did, they didn't give me grief about it. The result was, by the time I shooed Mira out the door, I was stone cold sober.

I didn't change out of my wedding dress, either, so now, as I follow Rick and Finn as they carry Knight into the bedroom, I have to hold the skirt out of the way. They ease him onto the bed, and Rick goes so far as to slip off his shoes. Finn throws the cover over him. They straighten and turn to me, and then, to my surprise, Finn comes up and hugs me.

He wraps his muscled hockey-player's arms about me and tucks my head under his chin. "I'm so sorry, beautiful. This man doesn't deserve you."

"He bloody well doesn't," Rick growls, then pats my back.

It's like being wrapped in comfort. I don't have brothers, but if I did, I imagine it'd feel like this. Safe, secure, and for a second, my worries recede. I sniffle, and Finn strokes my hair. "There, there, it'll all be okay, I promise."

I half laugh. "You sound very confident."

"Your husband's an asshole, but sadly, he's *our* asshole, and while I'm not sure if he'll sort out whatever it is that's bothering him in the short term, I know it's only a matter of time before he puts things in order and makes it up to you," he murmurs.

I pull back, and he releases me.

"Somehow, I'm not so sure."

"Be sure." Rick takes my hand in between his big paws. "We'll be on-hand to tap sense into his thick skull."

I look toward the sleeping man, as do the two of them. Lying there with his eyelids closed and his eyelashes fanning over his cheekbones, he seems at peace. But I know better. There's so much tearing him apart from the inside, and if he doesn't deal with it, it's going to spill over — and oh, god, I'm not sure what's going to happen then. Will he hurt himself? I know he won't hurt me. That much I know about this man. At his core, he's a man who knows good from bad, but his values have been tested, given what he's been through, and he's yet to find a balance.

"Don't forgive him too easily." Finn arches an eyebrow in my direction.

"Make him pay for it," Rick agrees, then releases my hand. "But I'm sure we don't need to tell you that, do we?" He nods toward his friend, and with a last glance at my husband, followed by a with a kiss on the cheek from each of them, they turn and leave. I stare at Knight for a few seconds more, then hold up my dress and make my way back to my room.

I slide into bed, and reaching for my feather bouquet, I press it into my chest. The next time I open my eyes, I'm clutching the bouquet. It's dark outside. I glance at my phone on the nightstand and realize it's four a.m. Dawn is a few hours off.

I sit up, and holding the bouquet, swing my legs over. I rise to my feet and stretch, holding the bunch of feathers over my head. Something makes me glance toward the corner of the room, and I gasp, "What are you doing here?"

49

Knight

The bouquet begins to slip from her fingers. I jump up from the chair and close the distance to her in time to catch it before it touches the floor. I straighten, then look from it to her. "It's customary for the bride to toss the bouquet over her shoulder to a group of single women."

"It's customary for the groom to accept a ring from his bride at the wedding," she retorts.

"I hate any kind of metal next to my body." I frown.

"Is that why you don't wear your dog tags?"

I stiffen; every muscle in my body tenses. She notices my reaction and holds up her hand. "Sorry I asked."

She goes to brush past me, but I step in her way. "It's also customary for a bride to carry a bouquet of flowers." I glance pointedly at the bunch of blue feathers.

"Like it is for the groom to stay with his bride through the reception. And to cut a cake and have a first dance, and to kiss the bride after the vows are exchanged."

"Lay back down," I snap.

"Excuse me?"

"On the bed, my new blushing bride."

"So you can consummate the marriage? No, thank you."

She tries to push past me, but I don't budge.

"What do you want, Knight?" she asks in a tired voice. "Isn't it enough you diminished me in my own eyes? Do you want to rub in the fact that you own me and my time and my choices? Is that what this is about?"

A strange sensation squeezes my chest. I don't dare examine it too closely. If I did, I might have to call it remorse. And that's something I haven't experienced in a while... Not in a situation not connected to my team and what I let happen to them. And—

Goddamn it, but I was in the wrong. She's still wearing her wedding dress as if to remind me. And I need to make it up to her in the one way I know I can. The one way I know will make her forget everything that happened yesterday. The only way in which I can communicate to her without fear of hurting her—except in the way she yearns for, only she doesn't know it yet.

"You wanted a kiss. I'm giving you a kiss."

"I changed my mind."

"Too late."

She huffs. "I'm a woman. I'm allowed to change my mind."

"Not this time."

She firms her jaw, and that look of defiance on her features is such a fucking turn on. Everything about her makes me want to find a way to subdue her, to handle her body and mark her skin and squeeze her curves and imprint my dick inside her pussy all over again.

"Lay. Back. Little Dove,"—I draw in a breath—"please."

She blinks, then complies. Is it because I used my Dom tone or because I said please? Doesn't matter. What's important is that she sits down on the bed and slides back a little, then eases herself back.

I flip the hem of her wedding dress up and around her waist, then groan when I spot the garter on her thigh. She wore it for me. Of course, she did. And now, I'm going to use it.

"Wh-what are you doing?" she squeaks.

"You wanted a kiss; I'm giving you a kiss."

I step between her thighs, forcing them further apart, and this time, a shudder runs up her body. "M-my lips are up here."

"Not the only lips on your body." I bend, then tear off her panties, and she yelps. She tries to squeeze her legs together, but I'm in the way.

And fuck, if I don't pat myself on the back mentally. I pinch a feather from her bouquet, then toss it to the side. I plant a hand next to her head and fold over her, making sure not to touch her anywhere. In this position, my face is above hers, my breath raising the hair on her temples. I place the tip of the feather in between her eyebrows, and she swallows. I drag it down her nose, her trembling mouth, over the pulse that beats at the base of her throat, across the sheer lace between her gorgeous breasts and a moan spills from her lips.

I trail the feather over the lace-covered fabric that's bunched around her hips, then pause at the soft flesh above her melting lower lips. Her thigh muscles twitch, and I draw the feather over her pussy. She gasps. I ease the garter down her leg, and when I lean over her, she stares up with dilated pupils. "Open your mouth."

She instantly complies, and I stuff her garter between her lips. Her gaze widens, and the pulse at the base of her neck speeds up until its beat echoes the drumming of my heart.

I slide back down and kneel between her thighs.

"Place your feet on the edge of the bed," I order. Once more, she does as she's told without hesitation. The result? I'm presented with a tastefully presented pussy framed by her gorgeous, fleshy thighs. "You're fucking beautiful, you know that?"

She moans, or I assume she does, for the sound is stifled.

"Such a pretty cunt you have. When I'm done with it, you won't be able to pee without feeling me inside of you for the next week."

Her back arches, and her hips twitch.

"You like it when I talk dirty to you, don't you, baby? Such a willing little slut you are. Can't wait to feel my dick stuffed inside your little hole, hmm?"

She writhes under my scrutiny. A fat drop of cum slides out from between her pussy lips. I bend and lick it up. Instantly, she pushes her pelvis up, chasing the feel of my tongue. I laugh. The sound is mean, and she trembles.

And when I trace the feather over her swollen clit, she digs her fingers into the sheets on either side of her and pants so loudly, I can hear her, despite the gag stuffed in her mouth. I continue to whisper the feather down her leg, around her ankle, and across her soles. Her toes curl, she tries to wriggle away, and I grip her other thigh with my free hand to hold her in place.

"You ticklish, Little Dove?"

I glance up in time to see her shake her head vigorously.

"You lying to me, hmm?"

She swallows, then shakes her head again.

"Let's test that theory, shall we." I transfer the feather to my other hand, and once more, drag it down the sole of her foot. She tries to pull her leg back, but I curl my fingers around her ankle. I draw the feather over her toes, then across the ball of her foot. She makes a choked sound and tries to writhe away, but I hold her in place. I continue to glide the feather across the arch of her foot, and she brings up her other foot and places it on my shoulder. I look up at her, and her big, wide eyes have a beseeching expression in them.

"Want me to make it stop?"

She nods.

"Want me to make you come?"

She nods again.

"Want me to fuck your ass?"

She begins to nod, then frowns.

"Maybe not today, hmm?"

Her frown deepens.

I release her foot, only to lock my hand under her knee and push her leg up so she's exposed more to my gaze. I stroke the feather down the valley between her lips, down her slit, to the rosette between her arse-cheeks.

Blood rushes to her cheeks; splotches of pink cling to her chest. The look in her eyes turns desperate. Her hips jerk, a single bead of sweat slides down her cleavage. That's when I toss the feather aside and lower my head between her legs.

50

Penny

He sucks on my clit, stuffs three fingers inside my melting pussy, then slides the thumb of his other hand inside my back hole, all at once, and I detonate. All the sensations in my body coalesce in the triangle between my legs. My eyes roll back in my head. I cry out, hear the muffled sound I make through the garter stuffed inside my mouth, smell the sugary scent of my arousal, feel him bite my clit, then lick the swollen flesh while he curls his digits inside me, pressing down on that spot deep inside me that only he's ever touched, and the orgasm ratchets up. It hammers through me and bursts behind my eyes. The sparks detonate, and I fly over the edge.

As I slowly come back into myself, I'm aware of him licking my inner thighs, then the throbbing flesh of my pussy, before he plants his hand next to my face. He pulls the garter from my mouth, only to replace it with his tongue. The taste of me fills my palate, and I moan as he bites down on my lower lip. He slides his hand between us. I hear the hiss of a zipper being lowered, then something thick and blunt nudges my opening. He holds my gaze, and in one smooth move, impales me. I gasp. He swallows the sound and stays where he is, stretching me around his cock and giving me time to adjust to his girth.

He's been inside me before, but it may as well be the first time for how massive he feels. He releases my lips, but stays with his face above mine, his eyelashes brushing mine, his breath blending with mine. He pulls back until his cock is balanced on the rim of my slit, then pistons forward and into me again with such force that the entire bed moves. I open my mouth, wanting to cry out, but I'm so full, no words emerge. Once again, he stays immobile, except for his dick, which pushes against my inner walls. And the fact that he's looking deeply into my eyes while he's fucking me makes it so intense. My chest hurts, and my throat closes. Stupid tears knock against the backs of my eyes. He seems to understand something of what I'm feeling, for he lowers his forehead to mine. The next time he thrusts into me I cry out, convinced I can feel him all the way in my throat.

"It's too much," I gasp.

"It's not enough," he growls.

"I can't take this."

"You'll take this, and everything I give you."

I look into his eyes, feel his conviction, his belief in me, and it's so hot. It's insane, the unspoken message he's communicating to me. That I can do this. I can take it. That I'm... *His*. His gaze widens, and the muscles of his back seem to vibrate with everything he's not saying aloud. The air between us hums. The very atmosphere seems to push down and envelop us in a cocoon that leaves no room for anything else. The world recedes, and it's only me and him and the heat of his body reflecting off of me. And his cock throbbing inside me. It's so intense, my nerve-endings screech in protest. "Sir, I love you," I burst out.

His green eyes flash, then turn into blocks of ice with such alacrity, I gasp. He begins to pull away and—

No, no, no, no way, am I going to let him leave. I throw my arms about his shoulders and lock my ankles about his waist. "Does that scare you? Is that why you're going to leave your wife the morning after your wedding and run away? You going to hide and pretend I never said that, you—" I cry out when he pulls out of me. He rises up on his knees on the bed and grasps my waist. He flips me around and onto my knees, as if I weigh nothing.

"What are you doing?" I huff.

He applies pressure between my shoulders, so I'm forced to drop down on my hands. Before I can say anything more, he fits his cock at the opening of my slit and pushes into me. And then there's no respite. He begins to fuck me in earnest. He grabs my hips and plunges in and out of me. Each time he impales me, his balls slap against my clit and he brushes up against that spot deep inside me with such unerring accuracy, tears spring anew in my eyes. I groan, gasp, plead with him—not sure what I'm saying, only aware he's angry with me and fucking me with an unrelenting focus aimed at punishing me. And I should hate it, but god help me, it only turns me on more.

And I'm not going to back down. I'm not going to let myself feel bad for blurting out those three words. And I'm not going to take it back. It's what I am. I say what's on my mind, and if he doesn't like it, too bad. If it scares him, good. I push up my hips and meet him thrust for thrust. Open myself up and receive him. He picks up his pace, and slams into me with such force, the bed creaks. His balls continue to slap against my clit. Goosebumps flare on my skin, and I know I'm close.

And that's when he wraps his fingers around my throat. He bends over me, so his massive chest pushes into my back. "You love me, huh?"

I manage to nod.

"Let's see how much you love me after this."

He squeezes, and the oxygen supply to my lungs begins to diminish. My nipples harden into peaks of hurt and desire as I strain to draw a breath again and fail. And still, he continues to fuck me. His body has transmogrified into a weapon with which he's intent on making me pay for what I said. I start to feel lightheaded, then flashes of dark dance in front of me. The black deepens and, unable to hold myself up, I begin to slump. Then gasp as he releases his hold on my throat. The oxygen fills my lungs, and that's when he reaches around and pinches my clit as he slams into me one last time.

"Shatter for me," he growls in my ear. And I scream as I come. The orgasm seems to go on and on, and he continues to fuck me through it. When I begin to slump again, he props me up with a firm grip on my hip. He reaches up, pinches my nipple, and my pussy clamps down on his cock again. He rubs on my clit, and the sensations that slice through me are like electric shocks. His dick seems to thicken inside of me as he licks up the side of my cheek. "You're going to come for me again." His voice is so cold, so distant, I shiver, then shake my head.

"Is that a no?" he says in a low, hard voice, and instantly, I'm turned on again. Moisture gathers in my core, my scalp tingles, and every pore in my body seems to pop. I know then, my body is simply an instrument for him to play. To draw the kind of music from it that I wouldn't have thought possible. Soaring notes, operatic highs and the kind of lows I may never recover from.

"Is it, Little Dove?" he asks again.

I shake my head this time.

"Such a good girl. Your cunt was made to be destroyed by me."

I flush, and my heart swells in my chest as a sob wells up. That's when he slows down. He pulls out, then sinks his cock inside of me inch by inch, so I can feel every throbbing ridge of his shaft. He does so again and again. I feel his heartbeat pick up, his body shudder, then he whispers, "Come for me, sweet girl."

That tenderness, that softness I've never heard in his tone is all it takes. This time, the climax ripples through me like rain washing away the dirt of a long, hard summer. I slide over the edge, then cry out when he buries his teeth at the curve of my shoulder. My pussy squeezes his dick, milking him, and I feel him shoot his release inside me. As my eyes flutter down, the last thing I sense is his big body slumping down with me. When I wake, it's to find I'm on my back, and he's leaning over me, a bleak look in his eyes.

51

Knight

"I can't love you. It's not in me to love you." I begin to straighten, but she throws her arms about my shoulders and pulls me in. "I don't believe you, Sir."

My heart stutters. She called me Sir. So, she hasn't completely turned her back on me, yet.

"What happened to me when I was captured changed me. I'm not the man I was. I can't feel. Can't behave like other men do. I can't return to everyday life and set up a home with a wife and kids. Those things are not for me."

"So, tell me what happened to you."

"You don't know what you're asking for."

She cups my cheek, and her touch slices through every single barrier I've erected since the day I was buried alive. The day I was made to feel like it was the end of the road for me. Like I was losing the very core of what I was. The day I lost my mind. The day I almost gave up hope of making it out of there alive. The day Adam came for me.

"And you're making excuses. You're running from your fears, Sir, like you're running from the truth."

"Which is?"

"That whatever you do to me, I cannot stop loving you. No more than I can stop breathing or living. The day I saw you swagger in to meet Abby before you shipped out on your mission? That's the day I knew you were it for me.

"Swagger ,huh?" Despite telling myself it doesn't mean anything, I'm male enough to be pleased she used that adjective for me.

"Is that all you heard?" she scoffs.

"I also heard that you saw the person I was before I was broken."

"And I can make you whole"—she looks between my eyes—"if you'll let me."

I chuckle, and the sound is brittle. "So, you're the woman who's going to fill the wound I carry around, hmm? The one who's going to tame the bad boy, the one who's going to redeem me and—"

"Show you what it is to live again."

"And what if I don't want that? What if I prefer to stay in the darkness?"

"Then you're not the Sir I dream about—the man who's larger-than-life. The bosshole who can reduce an entire meeting room to their very basic fears. The brother who loves his sister enough to come to a party she's thrown in his honor, even though you hated every moment you were there."

I blink. "Didn't think I was that obvious."

"To me, you were."

"So, you can read the expression on my face. Most likely, you can interpret my gestures and read between the lines of my unspoken words, as a good employee should."

She gapes. "So that's all I am to you? An employee?"

"And my wife—by contract. You sure do give new meaning to working for me around the clock."

She pales, then shoves at my shoulder. "Get off me."

"Thought you loved me? Thought you could put up with anything I said or did?"

"That doesn't mean you can say anything that comes to your mind. That you can insult me, and treat me like—"

"My personal fuck-toy?"

She swallows, and her breathing grows shallow.

"That turns you on, doesn't it? Under that wide-eyed, pink-color-loving, sunshine and rainbows and butterflies persona you love to project, you're a submissive. A dirty girl who wants to be dominated, and handled roughly, and told what to do, and fucked to within an inch of her life."

A low gasp spills from her lips, then she tips up her chin. "Yes, I love sex with you. I love how you make me orgasm. How you handle my body, how when you look at me, it's to the exclusion of anything else in the world. I lost my father early, missed a male presence in my life, one which you are, clearly, fulfilling."

I chuckle, then lower myself within her thighs enough that the evidence of my arousal stabs into her core. "Does that look like I'm fulfilling the role of a father figure in your life?"

She swallows. "You know what I mean. You're not that much older than me, but you have the kind of solid presence that makes me want to lean on you. Physically, you're much bigger than me, and you have that unshakeable core in you which makes me feel secure. You treat me like I'm your possession, like you own me, and I should hate it, but it only seems to turn me on more. I hate myself for it—"

"But you love me."

"And I hate myself for loving you, too."

"Sounds like a B-grade pop song." I laugh.

"That's all my feelings mean to you?"

I blow out a breath. "I warned you not to fall in love with me."

"And I told you, you would with me—" The light fades from her eyes, and she mumbles, "Guess I failed."

"But what neither of us can dispute is this." I position my cock between her lower lips and slam into her.

Her breath hitches, and her body trembles. Her moist walls embrace my dick like they've been waiting for it to penetrate her. Her channel flutters around me, and my heartbeat instantly shoots up.

"There it is—the language we both understand. There are no misconceptions, no possibility of mistakes, nothing lost in translation." I lower my chest into hers and bracket her between my arms. "This, when I'm inside you, and your pussy squeezes down on my cock, and your nipples are so hard they all but tear into my skin when I push my body into yours, when your eyes are so dilated I can see myself in them, and your essence bathes my shaft, and your scent intensifies until I can smell myself on you, in you, around you, imprinting in your skin, then neither of us can lie. Then neither of us needs to say a word. We can let our bodies talk, and that's when we don't need to worry about tomorrow or the past. That's when we can give ourselves up to the sheer enjoyment of each other." I pull out and stay poised on the rim of her entrance. She wraps her legs around me, digs her heels into my back, and tries to urge me closer.

"What neither of us can deny is that you need me."

I push into her, and she moans, "And you need me."

We hold each other's gaze and I nod. "I do, but only in the carnal sense."

"And I do, in every sense," she says without hesitation. Something weird squeezes my chest; I dare not dwell on it. Instead, I tilt my hips and press in, so my pelvis rubs up against her clit. "I told you, I can't give you what you want."

She sinks her fingers into the hair at the nape of my neck and tugs. My cock twitches inside her. She allows herself a small smile. "And I'm telling you, it's my choice to share myself with you."

My chest hurts, and my pulse booms at my temples. *It's a trap. A trap.* "You're setting yourself up for a fall."

52

Penny

"That's my choice, isn't it?" I hold his gaze, even though everything in me wants to punch him and tell him to wake up and recognize what we have here. I may not have been with any other man, but I'm worldly wise enough to know that if the sex is this explosive, and if the chemistry between us is such a tangible force that I can sense him anytime he's in the vicinity, and that, despite the fact that he comes across as such an asshole, I can look past his persona to the man he really is inside, then—whatever is between us is worth fighting for. It's worth trying to convince him that he loves me, too, even if he doesn't want to admit it.

He pulls out of me, then stays poised at my entrance in a way that builds anticipation and makes every part of me tingle and my nerves scream with expectation. *Gah, why does he have to tease me like this?* I push up my pelvis and try to take him in me, but he clicks his tongue. "You can't top from the bottom, Little Dove."

"What?"

He glares at me, and my insides clench in anticipation. He looks a little mad and frustrated and as if he's reaching the end of his tether, which means he's going to do something I don't like—but also like. A lot.

"You know what I mean," he growls.

"I have no idea what you're talking about." I widen my gaze, trying to portray a picture of innocence.

His eyebrows draw down. "Do you know what happens to bratty girls who don't know their place?"

"No, Sir," I say in a coy voice.

Instantly, his dick pulses, and this time, when I push up, the crown breaches me. I groan; so does he.

"It feels so good, I want more. Please, Sir. Please."

"You beg so beautifully. This time, I'm going to take you against my better judgement, but you're going to pay for this, you feel me?" He lowers his head until his lips are, once more, so close I can feel his breath on my mouth. I lick my lips, and his shaft pulses.

"I feel you, I—" I cry out as he kicks his hips forward and slams into me. My entire body moves up the mattress. He cups the top of my head, so I don't slam into the headboard, then he begins to pound me.

"Such a tight cunt you have, Little Dove."

Thrust.

"You take my cock so beautifully."

Thrust.

"Such a perfect little receptacle for my cum."

T-h-r-u-s-t.

"Such a willing, obedient hole for me to take whenever I want."

He begins to slow down, and I pant. No, he's not slowing down. He's merely changed his rhythm to long, deep strokes, so each time he enters me, it's like he's sliding all the way up to my throat.

"Sir," I moan. "Sir."

"You look so good when you plead. You'll look better wearing my cum." With that, he pulls out, grips the base of his dick, then straddles my chest and plants his massive thighs on each side of my face.

"Open your mouth."

I do.

"I'm going to come down your throat, and you're going to take every single drop."

Before I can nod, he pushes his dick into my mouth. He hits the back of my throat, and I gag. A groan rips out of him. Beads of sweat stand out on his forehead.

"Fuck." His nostrils flare, his cock pulses, and on instinct, I reach up and squeeze his balls. With a low growl, he shoots his cum. Some of it spills over the corners of my lips. There's an expression of pain—or maybe, ecstasy— on his features as he squeezes his big hand around his shaft and drains every last drop. Then he pulls out.

"Show me," he orders.

I open my mouth. He scoops up the overflow and slides it onto my tongue.

"Swallow," he growls, then, wraps his fingers around my throat, feeling the liquid slip down my gullet.

He shifts down my body until, once more, he's planked over me, and as if he can't stop himself, he presses his lips into mine. Without breaking stride, he rolls on his back, pulling me onto him as he continues to ravage my mouth. My eyelids shut, and I fall asleep with his tongue sliding over mine.

I wake up briefly to find he's carrying me into the ensuite bathroom. "What are you doing?" I yawn.

"Shh, go back to sleep," he whispers.

I do. I float in and out of consciousness, barely aware he's holding me up in the bath as he slides the washcloth down my body and between my legs. When I moan, he hushes me. His touch is so gentle, the thud-thud-thud of his heart at my back so comforting, the sound of his breathing is a lullaby. Once again, I fall asleep.

This time, when I wake up, I'm alone in my bed. Light pours in through the window, and I feel light, myself. I sit up and stretch. I'm a little sore, but I feel refreshed. When I throw off the covers, I find I'm dressed in a sweat-shirt—which is not mine. I raise the cloth to my nose and sniff. Sea-breeze and pepper overlaid with the scent of fabric conditioner. It's his sweatshirt. He rolled up the sleeves, and when I stand, it falls to mid-thigh. I take a step forward and wince—okay, strike that, I'm very sore, but only in between my legs. I walk over to the ensuite, pee, and the water sliding past my abraded labia sends a not-unpleasant shiver up my spine.

Good god, now I'm aroused by peeing? Is it because he suggested I would feel the imprint of his cock while I did or is it because I actually do? A-n-d I'm not going to dwell on it. I jump up from the toilet, flush, wash my hands, brush my teeth, then head into the bedroom and come to a stop when I see him. He's standing in front of the bed, dressed in a fitted suit that makes him look like he's walked out of the pages of GQ. He lifts his wrist, glances pointedly at his watch, then at me. "You have ten minutes to get dressed."

"You could have stopped me from oversleeping," I huff as I race after him to the car. I managed to stretch the ten minutes to twenty, okay twelve... But I wrangled two minutes more from the bosshole. That has to count for something.

"I went running. Adam was waiting for me, so I didn't have the time to wake you up before I left." He picks up his speed, and by the time I reach the car door he's held open for me, I'm panting. I scowl at him, but he merely nods toward the back seat. I slide in, he follows me, slams the door shut, and we're off.

Of course, he buries his nose in his phone. The early morning sun slants through the window and bounces off the emerald set in my wedding ring. I raise my hand, take in both the engagement and the wedding rings. Whoa, I'm married. Not for real—he'd like to claim— but last night sure felt real. Also, he waited for me, and we're driving to work together—like a married couple. Another point in my favor, I think. We travel in silence for another twenty minutes until my stomach rumbles loudly. I freeze and pretend I didn't hear it. Only Sir Grumphole, aka my new husband, of course, hears it.

Without looking up from his phone he says, "Rudy, take a right up ahead."

"Where are we going?" I turn to him, but he's, once more, lost in whatever he's reading on his phone.

Rudy brings the car to a halt in front of a bakery, but it's not just any bakery. It's the one near the office. The one where I buy the coffee and the croissants and my cupcakes.

I shoot him a suspicious glance, but he's getting out of the car. I trail him inside and slide into the seat opposite him at a table by one of the windows.

"You're going to be late," I murmur.

"No, we're not."

I roll my eyes. "The food and coffee here are excellent, but the service is slow and—"

"Here you go Mr. Warren." A waitress places a croissant, another plate with two cupcakes—one with sprinkles and the other with chocolate chips on the frosting—a third plate with a cinnamon roll, followed by a fourth which is heaped with eggs and toast, along with fresh orange juice and a cup of frothy coffee, in front of me.

She slides a plate of eggs and toast, then a cup of coffee—black, of course—in front of him, followed by a copy of the Wall Street Journal. Oh, she also slips a piece of paper with her number scrawled on it under his plate.

"Anything else you'd like, Mr. Warren?" she asks sweetly.

A burning sensation cuts a hole through my stomach. I grip the edge of the table with my fingers. *Don't say it, don't say it.* "Darling, we forgot the condom again last night. At this rate, I'll be pregnant before the month is out. Your father is going to be over the moon, don't you think? Have you thought about a name for the little one? I have some thoughts, if you'd care to hear."

The waitress flinches and shoots me a venomous look. I wave my hand—my left hand with the wedding ring—in the air. "Shoo now."

She turns and walks off. I reach for the paper with her number on it, but he picks it up first. He holds it in between us. My breath catches in my chest. Then he crumples it and tosses it on the table, and I cough.

"Your coffee's getting cold, *Darling*," he murmurs.

The last word is heavy with sarcasm, but I ignore it. I reach for the coffee, take a sip, then freeze. "This has cinnamon flavoring and a dollop of cream," I say slowly.

"Indeed." He reaches for his fork and scoops up some of the eggs. He brings it to his mouth, and I can't take my gaze off of how he wraps his lips around the morsel and licks the tines clean. My pussy clenches, and my panties are wet—again. Jesus, I might as well start wearing diapers, at this rate.

He places his fork on the table and glances at me.

I flush, knowing I've been caught staring. "What?" I scowl.

"You're not eating."

"Eh?" I take another sip of the coffee and the bitter-sweet taste of cinnamon fills my senses. "How did you know how I take my coffee?"

"I told the coffeeshop to get you your regular drink."

"And how did you get such quick service?"

"I messaged them ahead to let them know our order."

"Ah." I blink.

He nods toward my food. "Now, will you eat?"

"You ordered me cupcakes?" I ask, unwilling to let go of the topic. There's something here that's important, something I'm missing.

"And chocolate croissants and the cinnamon roll."

"All my favorites." I narrow my gaze on him.

"I told them to bring a selection of their best breakfast pastries along with the eggs and toast." He shrugs.

"Right, of course." I deflate a little. Guess it was wishful thinking to hope that he noticed what I liked to eat. I reach for the chocolate chip cupcake and take a big bite. The bitter taste of the chocolate and the silky softness of the frosting melts on my tongue. I close my eyes, focus on the tastes, and moan as I swallow. When I open my eyes, he's glaring at me.

"Now what?" I mutter.

"You have something at the corner of your mouth." Before I can react, he reaches forward and scoops up the frosting.

"Open," he commands in a husky voice.

I do, at once. I part my lips, and he slides his finger inside. I lick his digit, and his nostrils flare. And when I bite down on his fingertip, his big shoulders flex. The air between us sizzles with so much chemistry, beads of sweat pop on my upper lip. He leans forward; so do I. Closer. Closer. Oh, my god, he's going to kiss me. His gaze slides to my mouth.

That's when the waitress places a jug of water on the table with two glasses. "How's everything?"

Bitch.

"What a bitch," Mira huffs up at me from the phone screen.

"Right?" I toss my head. "I wanted to claw her eyes out. She knew we were married, but that didn't stop her from all but falling into his lap."

I'm in the ladies' room where I managed to peel off during a lull in the emails that have been steadily pouring in all morning. I skipped lunch—not that I needed any after the massive cupcake I inhaled. Despite the interrupted breakfast, he insisted we stay until I finish my food. But the cupcake had been so rich, I pleaded off the rest of the food. He had it boxed so I could carry it back with me. I told him I didn't want to, because if I did, I'd eat it all. He looked at me, bewildered, and said that's what one does with food. You eat it. I stopped trying to convince him otherwise and carried the decadent treats back with me. Then, I slid it to a corner of my desk and stared at it all morning. I am not going to sneak another of the pastries. I'm not, and so far, I've been good.

Then, when the temptation got to be too much, I snuck off to the restroom, where I called Mira and told her the entire saga… Leaving out the details of what happened last night, that is.

"He did crumple the piece of paper with her phone number on it," she points out.

"For a minute there, I thought he wasn't going to," I huff.

"He's married. Of course he would," she says with complete confidence.

Not that it needs to stop him, considering our vows aren't for real. Not that I've told any of my friends, or even Abby, about the fact it's an alliance of convenience—on his part, at least. Funny, how it didn't trigger suspicions. Of course, they don't know that he made me sign a contract stating that the marriage would last for not less than a year, during which time I'm contracted to stay with him. In return, he'll pay all of the expenses for my mother's treatment and stay at the home for the rest of her life. Of course, my monthly allowance is a million dollars. And if I get pregnant within the year, it's another million. With another two million deposited in my account when the child is born. And then, for each year I stay married to him, I get a million, and for each child I push out, add on another two.

My head spins with all the zeroes that means. I've stopped trying to keep track of it. Also, I refuse to check my bank account because I'm not going to touch a penny of what he's giving me. The only money I'm going to use is that which my salary as his assistant gets me. One I insisted I draw and which I'm using to pay fifty percent of the rent on Mira's apartment. This way, I can keep my room there and have somewhere of my own I can go to… If needed.

"Penny, you listening to me?" she asks.

"Of course I am."

"Don't blame you if you are a little distracted. I would be, too, if I'd spent the first night of my marriage with that irresistible masculine deity."

I laugh. "Haven't heard that one before."

"That's because I invented it."

"You did, huh?"

"I'm having my go at writing my own smutty fanfic."

"Ooh, is it Dramione?"

"What else?" she asks with an expression that implies it couldn't it be anything else but.

"I'm so envious you found your Draco. Now, if only I could find mine."

The door opens then, and Giorgina glides in on her six-inch, spiky heels. I glance down at my wedges. Damn. Why is it that I always feel so underdressed in comparison? I cup my palm around my mouth and lower my voice, "Uh gotta go, Bellatrix Lestrange walked in."

"Wh-a-t?" Mira chokes out a laugh. "Do you mean —"

"Yes, can't talk, bye." I hang up, slide the phone into the pocket of my trusty pink jeans — because yeah, skinny jeans may be passé, but you'll have to tear mine from my body when I die. Also, I'd paired it with a blazer, so the effect is very much Gen-Z. I wash my hands under the tap, then dry them. When I toss the paper towel into the wastebasket, I turn to Gio. "Hey, what are you doing here?"

"Had a meeting with that prick, Rick." She caps her lipstick and drops it into her handbag, then pauses. "Prick Rick has a certain ring to it, no? Maybe I should call him Prick, instead of Rick."

I chuckle. "Not sure he'll like that."

"Exactly." Her eyes gleam.

"You don't like him much?"

"That's an understatement. I'd have preferred not to have anything to do with him, but I couldn't get out of this meeting with him and your husband."

"My husband?" The words are out before I can stop myself.

She glances at my left hand and raises a brow. "Difficult to think of him as that when you're not sure if he was serious about his vows. Not to mention, it's the day after your marriage and not only are you back at work, but also you're in the ladies' room when, instead, you should be bent over his desk and —"

"Stop right there." I hold my hand up. "What gives you the right to pass judgment on my life?"

"No judgment. But considering your friends can't see past the assumption that he has feelings for you — which he probably does, but I reserve judgment on that — fact is, you deserve better than how he's treating you, girlfriend."

My gusts twist, and anger slams into my chest with such force, I gasp. I open my mouth to tell her off, then snap it shut. She's right. I know she's right. And only she has the sense to see through the rose-tinted glasses my friends seem to have pulled on. I lean against the counter and stare at my rings.

She blows out a breath. "I'm a bitch; ignore me. I'm also a little emotionally off-kilter, which is no excuse for taking it out on you. It's me. I'm not good at sugar-coating the truth. And unfortunately, I can see through all the bullshit and cut to the chase and—"

"No, you're good," I murmur.

She seems taken aback, then nods. "Sorry again, don't mean to hurt your feelings."

"You didn't. It's good to hear someone else say something that everyone else is afraid to say. Or maybe, they just can't see it." I lower my hands to my sides. "What would you do if you were in my shoes?"

She tilts her head, a thoughtful expression on her face. "I'd march in there and demand he take me on a proper honeymoon, to begin with."

53

Knight

Rick is the first to rise to his feet. "Hey Penny, this asshat treating you okay?" He stabs his thumb in my direction.

Across from him, Finn cackles. When I glare at him, he mimes zipping up his lips.

"Hey, Rick, thanks for bringing him home the other day." She turns to the other man. "You, too, Finn."

"Any time." Rick jerks his chin.

"You bet." Finn flashes her a wide smile.

She smiles back.

A slow burn creeps under my skin. *Hold on, are you jealous because she smiled at another man?*

"I need to talk to my husband, and I'd appreciate it if you gentlemen would—" She gestures toward the door.

It's Finn who jumps to his feet now, "Of course. No problem." He walks over to my wife. " Just a reminder, he doesn't deserve you." He grabs her by her shoulders and kisses her on each cheek.

Something funny twists my stomach. Anger stabs my chest. I spring to my feet so quickly, my chair hits the floor. Rick gapes at me as I rush past him. I reach Finn, grab his arm and yank him away from her. "Hands off her," I growl.

He seems taken aback, then a sly smile curves his lips. "Getting all jealous and possessive, huh? That's good." He closes one eye in the direction of my wife. "Maybe you'll get that honeymoon after all."

"Did you wink at her?" I snap.

"Moi?" He holds up his hands an innocent look on his face. "Just something in my eye, dude."

"Get out of here or you'll get something in your eye, all right," I wave my fist in front of his eyes.

Finn's grin widens. "Whatever you say." He steps back, and with a last bow in her direction, he heads for the door.

Rick walks over. "I'll let you know once I finalize the details of the sports-management company." He holds out his hand.

I shake.

With a tilt of his head toward her, he leaves. The door snicks shut.

She turns on me. "What was that?"

"What was what?"

"You going all caveman and pretending to be all territorial."

"I have no idea what you're talking about." I head toward my desk.

"You got jealous when Finn kissed me on my cheek."

"You must be mistaken." I pull up a document on my computer. The words blur in front of my eyes. I'm too aware of her scent, her presence, the way she walks toward me with that sensuous sway of her hips. She drips sex-appeal, and she has no idea about it. Her innocence— Despite everything I've done to her body, she has that innocence about her eyes that draws me in and threatens to engulf me.

It's why I need to stay focused on this merger. It's important to keep my eyes on the prize. The ownership of this company. That's what matters. I manage to bring my attention back to the job at hand when she walks around the table and leans a hip against it.

"You're going into business with Rick and Finn?"

"It would seem that way, yes."

"As your assistant and your wife, it would be helpful to know what you're planning."

I hesitate, then nod. "You're right."

"I am?"

I turn toward her. "It will help you do your job better if you have some idea of what was coming down the line, yes."

She frowns. "Being your wife is not a job."

"But being my fake wife is."

Her frown deepens. "Last night didn't feel fake to me."

"You mean the passion, and the spontaneous combustion when we come together? Sure, there's a thread of truth running through it. But that means nothing. You signed a deal. That's all that exists between us. We're an arrangement, and don't forget that."

The light in her eyes fades, and I instantly feel like I'm lower than an earthworm in the food chain, fuck. Then she squares her shoulders, and says, "You haven't told me about this sports management venture with Rick and Finn."

I search her eyes, but other than the slight dullness, she seems to have gotten a hold of her emotions. Apparently, I'm not the only one who can present a mask to the world.

"I'm buying an ice hockey team."

She blinks. "There's no ice hockey in England."

"Sure there is. You Americans don't know, is all. Britain's men's national ice hockey team won gold at the Olympics and medals at the World Championships in the 1930s." I turn back to my computer screen and pull up a new page. "Take a look."

She walks toward me to peer over my shoulder. "The London Ice Kings?"

"That's the team I'm buying."

"And the national league is called the Elite Ice Hockey League?"

"Yep, it's growing in size every year. There's global interest in sponsoring teams."

"And you plan to get in on the action early?"

"Very good." *Of course, my wife is clever and bright, and if she'd had the opportunities I've had, she'd have thrived in the corporate world. It's not too late. She can be your partner, in more ways than one. An asset. Someone in your corner, with your best interests at heart. The only other person I've trusted like this is Adam. Is my Little Dove someone who will not be revolted by what happened to me when I was taken captive?*

"But how is Rick connected to this?"

I push away the laptop then pat the desk in front of me. "Come sit, I'll tell you."

She frowns. "You're not going to try any hanky-panky are you?"

I hold up my hands. "In the office, I'm your boss. You're my assistant. I promise to keep our relationship strictly professional."

"Hmm."

When she doesn't sit, I glance down at her feet. "Those may not be very high heels, but I bet you'll be more comfortable if you take the weight off your feet."

She searches my features, and whatever she sees there, must reassure her because she slides onto the desk.

"Here, let me help you." I rise to my feet then boost her further onto the desk. Without taking my hands off her curvy hips, I murmur, "I'm trying to coerce Rick—who's an ex-NHL player—to come out of retirement and be the captain. Finn, who's also ex-NHL, has agreed to be the goalie. Your friend Georgina will be perfect for the role of the PR manager."

"I do like Gio." She purses her lips. "Though she can be outspoken."

"How so?"

"She's the only one who suspects our relationship isn't what it should be, and she hasn't held back from mentioning it to me, either."

"Is that right?'

She nods. "It's thanks to her, I realized I want to go on a honeymoon."

I slide my hands down until I'm gripping the outside of each of her thighs. When I tug, she parts her legs. I step between them, and she's forced to widen her stance. I lean in, and the tent at my crotch pushes into her core.

"I hope you're taking notes of the highlights of our meeting, like a good assistant." I palm the back of her butt and smoothly slide her forward so her pussy is snug around my dick—through the barriers of what we're wearing, I know I'm big and aroused enough that she can feel every throb of the blood draining to my cock.

"I—" she gasps. "I—"

I pinch her nipple through her jacket and the camisole she's wearing inside, and she moans. I cup her tit, and she pushes her chest forward so her breast is enveloped by my palm.

"Do you have any more questions?"

She shakes her head.

"Well, I have one, Little Dove. Is a honeymoon where I fuck you day and night enough, or would you rather we do it my way?"

"Wha—" She swallows. "What is your way?"

I urge her to tip up her chin so I can peer into her eyes. "One in which I stay buried inside you for the entire time."

54

Penny

Oh, my god, I detonate into a ball of fire. Just when I think he couldn't turn me on further, he has to go and talk filthy to me in that rough voice that's sure to send me over the edge.

"Well?" He glowers down. "What's your preference? Not that I'm giving you one right now, but theoretically, if I were to, which would you choose?"

The force of his personality presses down on my chest. I peer into those green eyes, now flashing with a mix of possessiveness and need and lust and... I swallow. "Is that a trick question?"

"I take that as an assent to whatever I have in mind?"

"What do you have in mind?"

He ghosts his lips up to my temple, and I shiver. He licks the shell of my ear, and I all but climax right then.

"Sir," I gasp out. "Please."

"You beg so beautifully, my Little Dove, it makes me want to throw you down and fuck you until you can't think straight."

"Do it." I turn my face so I can meet his lips, but he clicks his tongue.

"Not so soon, sweet girl."

"But I wanna," I whine.

His lips twitch. "So impatient to have my cock inside you, hmm?"

"Very impatient." I reach down to grip the tent in his crotch, but he grabs my wrist and twists it behind my back.

In this position, my breasts are thrust out. He bends and nuzzles my nipple and I moan. My pussy spasms, I try to close my thighs but can't because he's standing between them. Every part of my body seems to light up at his proximity. I strain against his hold, trying to shove myself closer to him. I want to push my breasts into that hard wall of his chest and feel his unyielding muscles dig into me. He steps back a little, and I look up into his face.

"I need you, please. If you don't fuck me right now, I'm going to—" I gasp. He grabs the front of my jacket and tugs. The buttons scatter. Before I can react, he grips my camisole. He yanks on it, and it tears down the front. I cry out. He shoves my bra-straps down so my breasts are lifted up. Then, he reaches for my jeans. He unhooks the button and draws down the zipper. He reaches around me and makes a sweeping gesture. I turn in time to see papers go flying, while a pen and some pencils clatter to the floor. Then, before I can get a word out, he plants his palm on the front of my chest and pushes down.

The next second, I'm flat on my back, and he's pulling down my jeans and my panties, throwing them aside. My head spins. Little sizzles of anticipation zip under my skin. I hear the hiss of his zipper being lowered, and goosebumps pop on my skin. He throws one of my legs over his shoulder, then the other. Our gazes meet.

There's a helplessness in his eyes, something I recognize because I see it in myself, too. This inability to keep away from him. This need that's a living, breathing thing inside of me; which seems to fill every inch of me and push against my skin from the inside, threatening to tear out of me. This yearning to be joined with him, to be broken by him and consumed by him, to become one with him... It seems so much bigger than me, than him, than whatever it is either of us can control. His jaw clenches, and a nerve beats at his temple. He seems to be simultaneously angry and turned on, as evidenced by something big and blunt that nudges my slit. He slides his palm up to curl around my neck, and a shiver grips me. He stays poised on the verge of entering me as he searches my features. And this... This way in which he consumes me with his eyes is almost more erotic than the act of fucking me itself. His cock throbs at my entrance. I swallow.

"Do it," I say in a hoarse voice. "Do it right now."

"You think you can tell me what to do, Little Dove?" His mouth curls. "You're not in charge here."

I open my mouth to tell him off, then cry out when he pulls away and slaps my pussy. I orgasm at once.

Little flashes of heat travel up my spine. My vision fades for a second, and I see stars, and planets, and perhaps, the entire Milky Way. Little shocks travel up and down my spine, like the flashing lights of a high striker at a fair ground. When my vision clears, all I see are his eyes.

He holds me captive with his glare and sinks an inch inside me. I groan. His chest rises and falls. His throat moves as he swallows. Something flickers in his eyes. Then he enters me another inch, and another. He grits his teeth, and his jaw clenches. He's holding back deliberately. It's more arousing than having him enter me in one smooth move.

I try to push up and take more of his length inside, but he squeezes my throat with enough pressure to cut off the oxygen to my lungs. I writhe, grab at his arm, then dig my fingernails into his wrist. He slides in another inch, and another. My channel stretches and flutters around the intrusion. I want to tell him he's so big, that he feels so good inside me, that I'll never feel like this with anyone else, that I want him to fuck me until I come again and again, and he must read my expression. He pushes the hair from my face. The gesture is tender, but when he speaks, it's anything but. "Hold your pussy lips apart for me," he orders.

I instantly shove my hands down between us, and when I squeeze the folds around my clit, the skin is so sensitive, my eyes roll back in my head.

"Look at me as I fuck you, wife," he growls.

Oh, my god, he called me his wife! Why is that so insanely hot?

I raise my heavy eyelids, and this time, when our gazes meet, his are as raw as I feel. His features are flushed, his lips drawn back as he thrusts forward and impales me. He hits that spot inside of me precisely, and another orgasm begins to build out from my core. It grows bigger and bigger until it seems to fill every part of me. Until it's bigger than me.

I whimper and wheeze, and then he's fucking me in earnest. In and out of me, as he does that thing with his hips where he tilts them and continues to hit me right there over and over again. I lock my ankles about his neck, and continue to hold myself open to him, which means my clit is exposed for every thrust. The feel of his cock stretching my channel, and his gaze pinning me down as he cuts off the last of my air is too much. The world recedes. All of myself senses are focused on where he's joined to me. To where he's pushing in and out of me, and when he commands, "Come," and releases his hold on my neck, I shatter.

The oxygen rushes to my lungs and my orgasm ignites. It roars through me like a fireball, burning me up. I combust. I'm aware of him following me over the edge with a hoarse cry. As if he's unable to hold himself back, he slumps over me. We stay that way as I float in the aftermath. His shoulders shudder. I feel his heart slam into his ribcage, the rhythm as fast as mine. When he begins to pull back, I protest. He gathers me up in his arms, and without pulling out, sits down so I'm straddling him.

"You can release your hold on your pussy lips," he murmurs.

I comply and sigh as my limbs relax. I manage to wind my arms about his neck, then sink into that massive chest. It's soooo good to be held like this. I press my nose into the skin bared between the lapels of his shirt, fill my lungs with him as my eyes flutter down. I doze off, and the sound of his phone buzzing wakes me up. I try to sit up, but he urges me to stay still. Wrapping one arm around me, he reaches over and snatches his phone.

"What is it?" he grunts.

I hear the voice at the other end say something, the tone apologetic.

"Cancel all of my meetings for the rest of the day." He shuts off the phone and tosses it aside, then goes back to holding me.

For a few seconds, we stay that way, then I clear my throat. "You're not working for the rest of the day?"

"I'm working... on you."

I blush. "Oh."

"Oh, indeed." I hear the smile in his voice. He begins to run his fingers down the length of my hair. His fingers snag on a knot, he gently loosens it, then digs his fingers into my scalp, his touch tracing a path along the strands of my hair again. I can't stop the purr that wells up my throat.

He chuckles. I still. Whoa, his entire body is as relaxed as when he was in that small room off of his closet. More relaxed than his penthouse proper, for sure.

"You don't like your apartment very much, do you?"

He pauses. *Damn, maybe I shouldn't have said that, but I'm filterless, remember?* For a few seconds, I'm sure he's going to pull me off his lap, then he continues the soothing movement of his fingers down my hair. I sigh and curl into him again. Crisis averted. Keep your lips zipped and enjoy his touch. Maybe that's pathetic, but all I know is it feels sooo right to be in his lap and in his arms like this.

"Am I that obvious?"

"To me, you are," I echo the words he said to me a few days ago. Gosh, was that only a few days ago? So much has taken place since.

He blows out a breath, and his muscles unwind further. "You know, I was taken captive by the enemy. What I haven't told anyone is that for most of my stay, they kept me confined to a forty-square foot cell,"—he swallows—"until they buried me in a space no bigger than a coffin for forty-eight hours."

"Oh, my god," I gasp.

"They kept me there without food and water. Of course, by that time, I might as well have been dead after what they did to my team. They flayed them alive in front of my eyes, then cut them up into little pieces and made me watch."

A ball of emotion obstructs my throat. A heaviness drums behind my eyes. I don't dare move or breathe. This complex, tortured man is revealing what he hasn't told anyone else before, and I feel honored. I feel like he's laying a huge responsibility on my shoulders. I feel like I can't let him down. I feel like I owe it to him to help him through whatever he's going through. I stay silent as he gathers his thoughts. His touch on my hair is almost mechanical now.

"They electrocuted me. They attached electrodes to my extremities — to *all* of my extremities—" He swallows. I try to look up then, but he grips the back of my head and stops me. "They used e-stimulation to make me orgasm against my will. Then one of my captors, who was a woman, fucked me. Over and over again."

His heartbeat picks up against my cheek. His entire body tenses again. His muscles are so hard that the planes threaten to cut through my skin.

I swallow but dare not move for fear that he'll stop speaking. I'm not sure I want to hear this, but surely, it's helpful for him to share what happened to him. It's the only way for him to start healing, after all.

"I hated my body then. Hated the fact that, despite what I'd been through, it could find a way to react and be turned on. Hated that I could get an erection, despite being beaten and cut and tortured." He laughs bitterly. "Apparently, having my own men flayed alive was not enough to douse my libido."

"That's why you didn't want to develop feelings for me? That's why you tried to stop yourself from making love to me?"

"I fucked you. I didn't make love to you," he growls.

Hmm. He looked into my eyes when he took me the last few times. In my books, that counts as making love. Also, I saw it in his eyes; he's developing feelings for me. Not that I'm going to tell him that, of course.

I stay silent, and after a few minutes, he lets out a breath that raises the hair on my head. "I'm sorry, I didn't mean for it to come out like that."

I pull back and stare at him. "Did you apologize to me?"

He scowls at me, then one side of his mouth twitches. "You're being sassy, again, Little Dove."

I flutter my eyelashes. "Does that mean you're going to punish me, Sir?"

"That means I'm going to—"

There's a knock on the door, then a woman's voice—it's the receptionist, I'm sure—calls out, "Mr. Warren, there's someone here to see you. I'm sorry but I was unable to stop her, and—"

The door swings open, then a new voice exclaims, "There you are. I've been looking everywhere for you."

"I said I wasn't to be disturbed for the rest of the day," he growls through gritted teeth.

"You promised you'd come today, and when you didn't, I missed you. I… Oh—" She must notice me. "Who is *she*?" Her voice is suspicious.

My heart slams into my ribcage like it's a battering ram trying to break its way out. Who is *she*? *Why* is she? Why is she talking to Sir like she *knows* him? *Does* she know him?

Knight's muscles tense. "I think you need to leave, right now."

"But I… I'm your wife."

55

Penny

The receptionist gasps. I freeze. Did she say what I think she did? I try to glance over my shoulder to get a good look at her, but he tightens his grip in my hair, and holds me in place.

"You shouldn't have come here," he growls.

"So you can keep fucking your... your whore?" she spits out.

I draw in a sharp breath. When he calls me his whore, it feels like the most beautiful phrase in the world. Coming from anyone else, it makes me feel dirty and used. I try to pull away from him, but does he let me? Of course, not. He presses my head into his chest and holds me in place.

Before I can say anything, footsteps sound, then a new voice cries, "There you are, Bobbie. I'm so sorry, Mr. Warren. I took her for a walk and my back was turned for just a few seconds, and she took off with my purse. Before I could get to her, she'd flagged down a cab. I managed to follow her here and—"

He must have raised his hand because her voice cuts off.

"Can you please take her back? I'll be there as soon as I can," he says in a neutral tone.

"Of course," the new arrival replies.

The woman who'd burst in earlier protests, but a moment later, I hear them leave and the door closes.

Silence descends, filled with the kind of tension I thought we put behind us. I was sure we were beginning to communicate with each other, that we were going to find a new balance, perhaps a way of becoming husband and wife in the truest sense, but this... This turn of events is something I did not anticipate.

I push against his shoulders, and this time, he releases me. I scramble off his lap. His stupid dick slides out, leaving me empty and wanting, and *Ohhh! What's wrong with me?* That woman claimed to be his wife, and I can't stop yearning for this man. *Loser. Loser. What a loser.* I manage to slip into my panties, then pull on my jeans and zip them up. I straighten my bra, then thread the one remaining button on my jacket through the eyehole, sans camisole, since he shredded that. By the time I turn to face him, he's zipped up his fly, smoothed his hair, and is leaning back in his chair.

I open my mouth, but he shakes his head. "Don't jump to conclusions. It's not what it sounds like."

"So, she's not your wife?"

He hesitates. "You're my wife."

He hesitated. Oh, my god, he paused before he said the words I wanted to hear from him.

"Who is she, Knight?"

His gaze narrows, no doubt, because I called him by his name. Too bad. Right now, I'm not in the mood to call him by the name he prefers. And if that makes him mad, then bully for me.

"Who is she?" I ask again.

"Why don't you sit down first?"

I shake my head. "Oh, no, no, no. Don't go all polite now. Don't tell me to sit down, like my knees won't be able to hold me up after I find out who she really is."

"She's the wife of one of my team members who was killed when we were taken captive. When I returned, the first thing I did was go to each of their homes and break the news to them in person. When I told her about her husband, she couldn't take it. She fell unconscious. When she woke up, she was convinced I was her husband. And I—I went along with it."

"You went along with it."

"She'd had a psychotic episode. I felt responsible for what had happened. Of course, I went along with it."

"So, you let her believe you were her husband?"

His jaw firms, but he nods.

"And she thinks she's your wife."

He nods again. "I admitted her to a hospital, made sure she got the best care. Adam and I go to see her every day."

"Adam—your friend, and the only other team member who survived. That Adam?"

"It's why I make it a point to meet him every morning. We jog, then we go and check in on Bobbie."

I wince. "That's her name? Bobbie?"

He jerks his chin. "It's the least I can do."

"And I'm not holding it against you." *Except, I am.* I don't know why, but when she said she was his wife, it was as if something inside me broke. Maybe, subconsciously, I knew something like this was going to happen. After all, for the first time in my life since my mother got sick, I'm happy. I was sure I'd found a man I could love for the rest of my life. I should have known better than to believe in that feeling. If things can go wrong for me, they will. Don't I know that by now? I square my shoulders and paste my usual bright smile on my face. I resolved not to do that again, but this situation, where I find out everything my husband has told me so far is fake, deserves nothing but a fake smile. "Right, then." I widen my smile until I'm sure my features are going to crack. "So, she's your wife—"

His jaw tightens. "She *thinks* she's my wife. You *are* my wife."

"Semantics."

He rises to his feet and keeps rising, so I have to tilt my head back to see his face. And I'm not going to look away. I'm not. I can see this through. It doesn't mean anything… Except, it does. The anticipation and excitement in her voice when she announced she was his wife… You can't fake that. She really does think she's married to him. And what he and I have is a piece of paper telling us we are. He doesn't love me—perhaps he's falling for me, but he's made it clear, he can never love me. Also, he owes it to his friend and teammate to—

"Stop, don't go there in your head."

"Excuse me?" I say in a very polite voice.

He grits his teeth. "You will not think those thoughts that are going to cause you distress."

"Oh, so now you're suddenly concerned about my well-being?"

"I've always been concerned about your well-being," he says in a hard voice that makes my nerve-endings flare. I push away the desire that coils in my belly.

"You have a funny way of showing it."

"I show you how much I desire you."

"You fucked me. Big deal." I raise a shoulder.

He shoves his hand into his pocket, and it's the first time I've seen him do that. Funny how, in a matter of weeks, I know when his body language gives away his true state of mind.

"I fuck you because that's the only way I can show you what you mean to me," he says in a low voice.

I raise my hand. "Look, you don't have to try to claim you have feelings for me, because we both know you don't."

He firms his jaw but doesn't deny what I said. He. Doesn't. Deny that he has no feelings for me. I knew it. Of course, I did. But when he confessed to allowing another woman to pretend that she's his wife — It all feels too overwhelming.

"I need to leave." I glance down at my ruined jacket. "Damn it, and everyone outside is going to know what we've been up to."

"You're my wife. Who cares if they speculate what we've been up to?"

"I'm also your employee, so I care." I jut out my chin.

"In which case,"—he widens his stance—"you're fired."

56

Penny's bucket list

- ~~Type at 250 words a minute (done!)~~
- Have 5 O's in the course of 1 night (I'll settle for 1 tbh) => Almost made this one last night when he gave me 4 orgasms. OMG 4 freakin' orgasms!
- ~~Learn to cook a gourmet meal. => I wasn't very good at it, but it's the spirit that counts, right?~~
- ~~Act in a movie or a play — I'll take a street act => It didn't go down that well. :(~~
- See the London Ice Kings play a game.
- Swim with dolphins.
- See the Northern Lights.
- Climb Uluru in Australia.
- Eat a chocolate croissant in a sidewalk café in Paris.
- ~~Be dominated. (Uh, maybe this should go up to the top?)~~
- Find a man who cares for my mother as much as I do.
- ~~Be proposed to by the man I love.~~
- Explore anal. (I'm chicken so this is right at the bottom — pun intended. Hahahaha!)

57

Penny

"He fired you?" Mira asks me with a wide-eyed gaze.

I left the office, pausing only long enough to peek in on Tiny on the first floor of the building where Knight instituted a doggy day care.

I turned down Rudy's offer of a lift and took public transport to the apartment I'd shared with Mira.

A-n-d you heard that right. The wonders of having money—you wave your hand, and up springs a day care center for pets in the building that houses your office, with qualified staff to take care of the fur babies. That move earned Knight a lot of brownie points with his staff, not that he's aware of it. Not that he did it with the view to garnering good will. He explained that this way, Tiny would be taken care of during the day, and he could peek in on the mutt. Of course, now that I'm not working, I can take care of Tiny. Assuming I'm staying with him. Which I'm not really sure about.

"Yep, gave me some bullshit about my being his wife, so it doesn't make sense for me to work for him." I peer into the glass of wine Mira poured for me as soon as I walked in the door.

"You *are* his wife—"

"Fake wife," I burst out. "Also, he has another wife."

"Eh?" She blinks. "What do you mean fake wife? And he can't have another wife. You're his wife."

Oh, ugh, I broke the non-disclosure clause in the agreement I signed. Well, too late now.

"He, uh, proposed I marry him—not for real, of course—so he could fulfill the conditions his father laid down and get full control of his company. Also because"—I hunch my shoulders—"uh, we had unprotected sex, so..." I blush a little. *Damn, I sound so stupid when I say that aloud. Who, in this day and age, has sex without a condom?*

"You're not on birth-control?" She frowns.

"Never thought about it, to be honest—" She opens her mouth, and I raise my hand. "In retrospect, it was incredibly stupid of me, but I was too focused on taking care of my mum and finding a job to pay my bills. Also, you knew I was a virgin, so I really didn't feel the need to be on it."

"And he didn't wear a condom?"

I shake my head. "He said he got too carried away in the moment."

"Hmm."

"What does that mean?"

"The same Knight who's always so wound up and tightly in control got carried away."

"You don't think he did it on purpose, do you?" I ask in a small voice.

"Hey, I'm not here to guess at his motives. Maybe it was an honest mistake. Maybe." She raises a shoulder. "Maybe it wasn't."

"Either way, I'm fucked. Literally. Because I could be pregnant with his child."

She gapes. "Jesus, I need a drink." She takes a sip of the wine from her glass, then glances at mine. "No wonder you aren't drinking now. In fact," —she knits her eyebrows—"you weren't drinking at your reception, either."

"I wish I'd been able to. When he left halfway through that lunch, I wanted to sink through the floor and hide myself."

"He's really making your life interesting, huh?" she murmurs.

I laugh. "Oh, my god, you've become so Brit in your reactions."

"Right?" She puffs up her chest. "I've been practicing how to be understated. I guess it's paying off."

"You have a Brooklyn accent," I remind her.

"Doesn't matter what I do; can't get rid of that." She takes another sip of her wine. "So, you and he have an arrangement that includes sex, and a possible child on the way."

My stomach lurches. OMG, when she puts it that way. I place the glass on the coffee table. "Don't forget the other wife."

"I thought you were joking when you mentioned that earlier," she murmurs.

"Sadly, not." My stomach makes grumbling noises, and I press my palm against it. "Turns out, the wife of one of his teammates who was killed while captive had a psychotic episode when she heard the news and now, thinks Knight is her husband."

"And let me guess. Out of a sense of responsibility, he's been letting her continue the assumption?"

"You guessed it." Bile boils up my throat. "Uh, I think I'm going to be sick." My guts churn. I jump up, head to the bathroom, and am violently sick. I empty my stomach into the commode and manage to flush before I collapse against the wall.

"Here, honey, this should help." Mira places a wet washcloth against my forehead.

I sigh. "That feels good, thank you." I rest my eyes, until my stomach seems to settle down. And when I open them, it's to find her looking at me with concern.

"What?" I take the glass of water she offers me and sip from it. "What is it, Mira?"

"Um, you puked, so you might be, you know —"

"I might be what?" I take another sip of water when realization hits. I spit out the water. "Ohmigod, ohmigod, you don't think?" My hand trembles, and the glass slips from my fingers, but she catches it.

"I can't be pregnant."

"Well, you did say you had sex without protection."

"But that was a week ago. I can't be pregnant so soon, can I?"

The concern on her face deepens.

"Shit, where's my phone? I need to check this on the internet."

"So, I could be pregnant. Damn, why can't anyone agree about how soon after unprotected sex I could get pregnant?" I scowl down at my phone.

We're back in the living room, where the two of us have been searching the Internet for some facts on my possible condition, and sadly, I'm none the wiser. I could be pregnant, or not. "Either way, it's too early for symptoms to be present," I conclude.

She tosses her phone aside, reaches for her glass of wine, and drains it. I reach for my own glass of wine, but she swipes it from the table. "I'm getting you some water."

I deflate further. "At least, some juice. Or ice cream?"

Before she returns, the intercom buzzes. I walk over and answer it.

"It's Giorgina, can I come up?"

Huh, the last person I'd have thought to see here. I buzz her in, then hold the door open.

"What's she doing here?" Mira walks into the room and places a bowl of ice cream on the table.

"Chocolate-chip! You're a lifesaver. Also, I have no idea how she obtained this address."

Footsteps approach. Giorgina must have heard me. As soon as she reaches the doorway, she says, "Knight gave me your address." She walks in and surveys the tiny space. "Apartments in London are so cozy, eh?"

"You mean, it's tiny compared to L.A."

"You said it." She walks over to the window and peeks out. "It has a certain quaintness, I have to admit. In fact, it's beginning to grow on me." She turns to us.

"What are you doing here, Gio?"

She looks from me to Mira, then back at me. "Knight sent me to make sure you're okay."

He could have come himself. *Why didn't he come himself?*

"He wasn't sure you'd be willing to see him."

She notices the look on my face and nods. "Guess he was right, huh?"

"How does he know where I am, anyway?" I frown.

"You'll have to ask him that. I tried to tell him I didn't think it would help if I met you, considering I'm not the biggest fan of how he's been treating you. But he thinks that's precisely why I should be the one to talk to you."

I begin to speak, when she cuts in with, "I'm not here to persuade you to speak with him or anything like that."

"You're not?"

She shakes her head. "Whatever it is he did or didn't do, the fault lies with him."

Mira barks out laugh. "I like your style."

"Thanks." She walks over and drops her handbag into one of the chairs. "The only thing I'd say is, don't let the lack of communication derail you. I don't know what went down, but as a PR person, one thing I'll tell you is that ninety-nine percent of disagreements are because the parties involved did not talk things through with each other. It's surprising how giving the other person some face time often puts things in perspective."

I frown. "I thought you weren't on his side."

"I'm not. Hell, I'd say whatever happened, you should not forgive him. You should make him grovel, no matter if it wasn't his fault. Nothing like a bit of groveling to put a man in his place. As you know, I'm not a fan of the institution of marriage, either, but since you can't change that, it wouldn't hurt to have an open conversation with him about what happened."

I scowl at her. "I should be pissed off with you for sneaking that reasoning past me, only you were so smooth that I'm not sure I want to be."

She half smiles. "Look, I'm a bitch, I make no bones about it. But I'll be honest, something in his voice when he called me gave me pause for thought. The man has some serious issues, but I have to admit that my cynical heart is convinced he has feelings for you."

"I do," a familiar male voice interjects.

I squeeze my eyes shut. *What is he doing here?*

"I obtained a key to the apartment. I hope you don't mind that I came in without your permission." He addresses his words to Mira with a smile on his face.

She simpers, then firms her lips. "I do mind, especially if you're here to upset her." She walks over to stand next to me.

"Sending a woman in to smooth the way, hmm?" Giorgina drawls, then glides over to bracket me in from the other side. Their protective stance makes my heart melt a little. Especially since, Giorgina doesn't know me that well... But she's all for putting up a united front against men.

"Needs must." Knight looks at me. "I'm not sorry I sent Gio here to talk to you first. I know how pissed you are with me."

"You think?"

58

Penny

"But please, can you hear me out? Please?" He raises his hands. "You're my wife. I shouldn't have kept what went down with Bobbie from you. It didn't seem like it was important enough to share it, is all."

"That's what husbands and wives do. They tell each other everything. But I guess I shouldn't have that expectation from you, considering what our relationship really is."

Gio and Mira exchange glances. "Uh, I need to be somewhere, you wanna come with me, Mira?"

Mira scowls at Knight. "Don't hurt her," she snaps.

"I won't. She means something to me, and I'm going to do my best to ensure I don't cause her pain."

"Why don't I believe a word of what you say?" I ask in a low voice.

Mira turns to me. "I think it's best if you two sort things out, but call me if you need anything, we'll be around the corner in a coffee shop."

I nod. She squeezes my shoulder, and with a last scowl at Knight, she grabs her handbag and leaves, followed at a more leisurely pace by Gio. The door closes behind them. Knight stays where he is. He shuffles his weight from foot to foot. Another sign that he's not completely assured at the moment. Another first where he is concerned.

"Can I come in, Little Dove?" he murmurs.

I flinch. "Don't call me that. And you're already in." I head over to the window and stare out. "Say your piece and leave."

The silence stretches a beat, another. The hair on the back of my neck rises. I turn and am not surprised to see him standing right behind me. I didn't hear him approach, but a part of me always knows where he is when we're in the same space.

"Is being light-footed a requirement of all you ex-soldiers?"

"Ex-royal marine, and yes. It's what's saved my life countless times."

I swallow at that. It's a reminder that the man in front of me almost never came home. And when he did, he was so damaged that the rules of the ordinary daily world don't seem to apply to him. Does that mean I can forgive him for what he did? I understand why he did it, I do, but that moment when she walked in and declared she was his wife sent a shock of such proportions through me, I'm reeling from it, even now. It's how insecure I am in this relationship—if you can call it that—that I believed a strange woman claiming to be his spouse, even though I'm the one he married.

"Our marriage is fake, isn't it?" The words are out before I have time to think them through.

He holds my gaze, then shakes his head. "The paperwork we signed is real. We are legally married. You are my wife—"

"But—"

"But—" He rubs the back of his neck. "But you know the arrangement between us. I married you because I needed to show my father I could settle down, so he'd hand over the reins of the company to me. And if I produce an heir within the year, then he'll never interfere with how I run the company again."

"And that's the only reason you married me?"

He frowns a little. "It's also because there's chemistry between us. I only have to look at you to get turned on. I love your figure, your ass, your tits, your sunny nature, how you light up a room when you enter it, how you soothe my employees after I've shaken them up."

"So, you get everything and what do I get—?"

"Money? A safe haven for your mother?"

"And what about love?"

His features grow bleak. "I'm not capable of love, or any such emotion, not after what happened to me."

"That's a copout. You don't want to explore the possibility that you could fall in love with me."

"I do care for you, Penny." He raises his hand and I know he's going to touch me, and if he does, I'll hate myself for reacting to him, and oh, god, I can't allow myself to give in to these feelings I have for him. I can't. I shrink back, and his jaw hardens. He curls his fingers into a fist, then lowers it to his side. "I'm sorry I didn't tell you about Bobbie. I truly am. Please forgive me."

"There's nothing to forgive. You did the right thing. I can only imagine how terrible it must have been for Bobbie to find out about what happened to her husband. I completely understand why you decided to play along with her assumption. I also realize you don't trust me. It's why you never told me about her."

"That's not true. I do trust you. Enough to fuck you without protection."

Wow.

"You didn't use a condom, not because you forgot, but because you purposely wanted to find a way to impregnate me. You wanted to tie me to you, thanks to some twisted sense of ownership. Since you set eyes on me, you decided I was your personal plaything. You wanted to make sure no one else could have me—"

"I—" he begins to speak but I shake my head.

"Don't try to deny it."

"I'm not denying it."

I stare. "You're not?"

"It's true, you affect me." He swallows, then draws in a breath. "Since I saw you, my life has changed. By being you, you sparked off changes in me for the better. I'm not sure what it is that you do, but this much I know, when I'm with you, I'm more like the man I was before I was captured. You make me want to become someone you'd be proud of."

My heart slams into my ribcage. *What's happening? What is he saying? How do I begin to react to this? And he's not denying that he might have purposely forgotten to wear a condom so he could try to impregnate me. A-n-d I do not find that hot. I do not. But the fact that he wanted to be with me bareback, and feel me without any barriers? That's... Sneaky, underhanded, toxic, and still hot. Oh, god, what am I trying to say to myself here?*

"You give me hope for the future. You make me feel, perhaps, not all is lost. That I could get over what happened to me and attempt to live a normal life... As long as you're with me." He moves toward me, and this time, when he takes my hand in his, I don't pull away. I can't pull away. *Told ya, he only has to touch me and I'm a goner.*

"It's not fair you have this effect on me." I swallow. "It's not fair that you can persuade me to see your point of view."

He bends his knees and peers into my eyes. "Do you forgive me?"

"Only if you promise there are no more secrets between us."

59

Knight

"You made her a promise?" Adam shoots me a sideways glance. We've jogged our ten miles and cooled down. Now, we're headed away from the Thames and toward the Shard and my penthouse.

"I didn't have a choice."

"You made her a promise, knowing you had no intention of keeping it?"

"Not true." I roll my shoulders. "I intend to tell her everything."

"Just not yet."

"Exactly." I glance at him, and yep, he's wearing a disbelieving look on his face. "What?" I scowl. "It's true. I intend to come clean with her on everything, as soon as the time is right."

"And when's that going to be?"

I rub the back of my neck. "Soon."

"I've heard that before." He comes to a stop in the middle of the sidewalk. Fucking hell, I don't want to stop. I want to get away from him and his all-seeing gaze. I want to get back to her. Except—she's no longer at the penthouse. She told me she preferred to return to the flat with Mira until she sorts things out in her head. She also asked for her old job back, and of course, I agreed. She could have asked for the moon, and I'd have plucked it from the sky and given it to her. She could have asked me to step away from the company, and I would have. *A-n-d... Whoa, hold on, what was that?* I stumble and manage to right myself before I hit the ground.

"Coming to your senses, eh?" Adam Arsehole smirks as he draws abreast.

"I have no idea what you're talking about."

"Sure you do. It's why you've gone pale and look like you're going to be sick any moment."

"I'm not going to be—" My stomach churns, my guts heave, I taste the bile that boils up my throat, and I race over to the bushes that fringe the sidewalk, where I bend over and empty the contents of my stomach. After throwing up what seems to be every last remnant of food inside me, I straighten.

"Here." Adam hands over his bottle of water. I rinse out my mouth then take a sip before splashing some of it on my face.

"Better?" He takes the bottle back from me.

"The fuck is wrong with me?" I rub the back of my neck.

"Nothing's wrong. You're rejoining the land of the living is what, my man." He slaps my shoulder.

I shake my head. "Next, you'll be saying it's the fact I'm married and halfway to falling in love with her that's bringing about this change?"

"You said it." He laughs, before his expression sobers. "How do you feel?"

"The same—" I raise a shoulder. "Yet different."

"You *are* different, compared to the man you were when you arrived back from your stint in the enemy camp. Hell, you're different from the man I knew before that. She's softening you."

"I'm not sure that's a good thing."

He scans my features. "What are you afraid of, Knight?"

I laugh. "Don't try to analyze me, motherfucker." I turn and head toward home, and he falls in step.

"Sooner or later, you're going to have to face your fears."

"Is that what you did?"

He stiffens. When he replies, his voice is thoughtful. "When I was in the enemy camp, and in the worst headspace possible, when I thought I was never going to see the light of day again, I made myself a promise. I told myself if I returned, I would not waste this second chance I've been given."

"You're a better man than me," I mutter.

"Each of us has to cope with the ghosts that haunt us in the best way we can. You'll know when it's time. Just make sure it's not too late, will you?"

"I'm sorry, I'm late. I got held up in the finance department and—"

"Take a seat, Mrs. Warren." I gesture toward the dining table that I've had put in by the kitchenette in my office. She was right when she said I'm more comfortable here than in my penthouse. The only other place I'm more at ease is the hidden room attached to the closet I had specially created. It's my comfort room, its spartan layout reminding me of my time as a new recruit in the marines. I had few creature comforts then, but the routine and structure of the training program gave me purpose. I felt more in control while I was following the rules and learning discipline.

A control I lost once I was captured. Control I'm trying to wrest back by shaping the future of my company, by creating my own destiny...by dominating Penny. It's why I feel so compelled to order her to obey my commands. She elicits this powerful need to see her bend to my will. To break her down and build her back up in a form that soothes my broken spirit. To ensure she feels safe and secure, feelings that were denied me.

All of those days when my life was not my own, when I never knew when they'd come for me and pull me out of my cell and abuse me, when I never knew if I'd open my eyes again and see another day, when I didn't want to live anymore—that's when I swore if I survived, I'd always stay in control. And if that means sleeping in my hidden room, so be it. It's bare enough that no-one can hide in corners and ambush me there. It's concealed enough that no one can track me down. *They* can't come for me there. They can't pull me out and throw me into that cavity below the earth.

A cold hand grips my chest, and my breath speeds up. I manage to push away the dread that crawls in my guts and walk over to the kitchenette.

"I hope you like salmon."

"Excuse me?" she says from inside the entrance of the room.

"Salmon, Mrs. Warren, the fish that like to swim upstream and—"

"I know what salmon is. Also, I thought we agreed you wouldn't call me that?"

"Last I checked, you were married to me."

"Last I checked, this is an office, and you're my boss."

"And you're still married to me." I hold the seat back for her.

She looks at it, then back at me. "I thought you didn't eat lunch?"

"I do now."

"What about your employees out there, who you prefer to also keep working around the clock without taking time off to eat?"

I narrow my gaze at her, then force myself to smooth out the frown on my face. I pull out my phone and type out an email. "All done."

"What's all done?"

"I've sent out an all-employee email that, from today on, everyone is required to take an hour off for lunch from 12:45 pm on."

She blinks.

"Anything else?"

"There are people here who find it very expensive to juggle childcare with jobs. You arranged for pet-sitting on the premises, so can you—" Her voice trails off when she sees I'm looking down at my phone.

I shoot off another email. "Starting tomorrow, work will begin on half of the first floor of the building to convert it to a nursery. There will be qualified childcare givers on hand to take care of the employee's children. Further, it will be free for all. And until all the arrangements for this are in place, I'll reimburse childcare costs."

"Oh." She draws in a sharp breath.

"Now, will you take a seat?"

She looks around the office as if looking for a way out, then slowly walks over and drops into the chair. I ease her in, then open up one of the containers of food. I slide some onto her plate, then fork up a morsel and hold it out. "Open."

She frowns. "Are you flirting with me?"

"It's lunch time. I'm asking you to taste this lunch that was delivered by James Hamilton's kitchen." I adopt the most innocent look possible on my face.

She opens her mouth, no doubt, to tell me off, and I take advantage and slide the food onto her tongue. Her gaze widens, then she closes her lips and licks the tines clean. The sight of her pink tongue and pinker lips sends the blood draining to my groin. A week without her presence at my home. A week during which I've used my hand to get myself off more times than I can imagine.

The only consolation is that I have Tiny for company. The mutt moped around the house, then curled up on her bed and went to sleep. I found him there, and abandoning all pretense that I did not miss her, I crawled in next to him. I woke up to Tiny trying to sit on my chest. For a few seconds I was sure I was back in the coffin my enemies had sealed me in, and that the ground had collapsed on me. Until Tiny licked my face and ensured I knew I was back in the now, and away from them. I managed to extricate myself out from under the almost 120 pounds of dog and staggered to my feet. Then, I took him out for a walk and fed him, by which time I felt more like myself. Nothing like scooping up dog-poop to bring a person back to the present. Nothing like taking care of another living thing to get perspective. Life doesn't begin and end with me. There are others worse off. I have much to be grateful for, including Penny. Perhaps, this is the lesson my friends wanted me to learn when they foisted Tiny on me?

"May I have some more?"

I bring my attention back to her.

"The food." She glances at the container. "Some more, please?"

Of course. I scoop up more of the succulent fish and offer it to her. She wipes the tines of the fork clean, then cuts up a piece and holds it out for me. I pull up a chair and allow her to feed me. She watches my mouth, her green eyes flaring. "It's good, isn't it?" she murmurs.

"Excellent," I agree.

She cuts up another piece of the fish and holds it out. This time I wrap my fingers around her wrist and bring the fork to my mouth. I lick the food off the tines of the fork, taking my time. Her breath hitches. The pulse at the base of her throat speeds up. There will never be a time when we don't feel this chemistry between us, so what are we doing apart?

"Come home with me." I slide the fork out of her hand and bring her fingers to my lips and kiss the tips. "I miss you. Tiny misses you. We can't do without you."

She swallows, and when she tugs, I release her hand. She brings her fingers to her mouth and licks the same digits I had. She closes her eyes, savoring the taste, then turns to snatch up one of the paper-napkins. "I can't, Sir."

60

Penny

"There. Looking good, Ma." I finish braiding her hair, then slide off the bed and hold up a mirror in front of her. My mother glances down at her reflection and a small smile curves her lips.

"The color suits you." I swallow around the ball of emotion in my throat.

Her smile widens.

Tears prick the backs of my eyes. Today is one of the good days. My mother replied when I asked her how her day had been. I place the mirror on the side table, then sit down in front of her.

"I miss you, Ma. I miss being home with you and Dad. I miss your attempts at trying to teach me the piano." I half laugh. "If only I had a talent, I wouldn't be bouncing around, dependent on someone else to keep you in this place. I'm sorry I couldn't do more for you, Mother, I—"

"You did good, Penny girl."

I stare. Wow, she sounds so much like her former self. Even her eyes are clear today. She takes my hand in hers. "You bring light to whoever you meet. That's your talent, honey."

The tears squeeze out from the corners of my eyes. I sniff. To not only have her sounding coherent, but to also give me the sweetest of compliments— oh, god, I don't think my heart can keep up. I bring our joined-up hands to my mouth, then kiss the back of her hers.

"I'm sorry you couldn't come to the wedding, Ma. I wish you could meet him—"

"I did."

"He's not all bad. Though his attitude is so grumpy you'd think he carries the weight of the world on his shoulders. Wait,"—I blink—"what did you say?"

"I met him."

"Who're you talking about?"

"Midnight."

"Who?"

"That's my name." A familiar voice interjects.

I turn to the doorway to find Knight standing there.

"Your real name is Midnight?"

He half smiles.

"Why didn't you tell me?"

"Why didn't you ask?"

We look at each other, and as always, the air in the room seems to light up with so many unsaid emotions, and that insane chemistry that has my nipples beading, despite the fact I'm sitting in front of my mother.

I've barely seen him since that lunch that I cut short, running out for fear I'd let him fuck me again in his office. It's only in retrospect, I realize he didn't try to stop me. He didn't use that Dom voice of his to command me. He honored my choice, respected my will, and that's so different from the man I've come to know.

To be honest, a part of me would have been relieved if he'd ordered me to stay. Better still, if he'd commanded me to bend over that table where our lunch was served, I'd have gladly done so. It's so much easier when he tries—who am I kidding? There is no "try" with this man—to make me bend to his will. I can always blame him for influencing me to give into him and then I don't have to accept responsibility. But now that he's letting me drive our interactions, I'm floundering. It confuses me so much, it's been easier to avoid him as much as possible. In fact, I haven't seen him in three days.

Now, I drink in the sight of my man in that jacket that clings to the breadth of his shoulders. He prowls forward, and I admire how those tailor-made pants outline the musculature of his thighs.

"He's handsome huh?" My ma whispers.

I nod, then swing my head around to look at her in surprise.

"What?" She giggles at the expression on my face. "I might be senile, but I'm not blind."

"You're not senile." I frown.

Her features soften. "I'm glad I got to see you settled before I go."

"Mom, please, you're not going anywhere."

"Unless you want to go to the park?" he asks as he comes to a stop next to the bed.

"The park?" Her features light up. "Are we going on that picnic you promised?"

"You promised to take her on a picnic?"

"I wouldn't have done it without running it by you first," he says as he turns to me. "I've been meaning to tell you that I've been coming to see her for a few weeks now. I wanted to come here with you right after lunch on the day we got married, but I'm afraid I lost my composure that day."

"Is that an apology I hear?" I say lightly without looking at him. Partly because the sight of my mother walking ahead holding Tiny's leash is something I'll remember forever. She's dressed in her favorite green dress, and the lines of her body are relaxed.

We had a picnic lunch earlier on Primrose Hill. The lunch was delivered to us courtesy of—you guessed it, James Hamilton's kitchen, complete with wine glasses and crockery. Also, as soon as we were done, someone came by to pick up the remnants. Don't ask me how he arranged for that. Guess the rich don't do anything by half, huh? But I don't begrudge Knight his money anymore. How can I when he's used it to make my mum happy. I've never seen her so in her element. Not since before my father died. A ball of emotion fills my throat and I swallow around it.

"I'm sorry I ran out on you at our wedding lunch." He slows to a halt. So do I.

I can't look at him, though. Not with the waterworks threatening to spill over. This is what happens when I'm on my period. I get overly-sensitive to everything. I stiffen. "There's something I need to tell you."

"What is it?"

His voice is so gentle, so unlike Knight, and yet also, so like the Knight he is underneath that alphahole exterior he loves to show the world. It only makes my heart beat faster. My palms grow clammy, and I lock my fingers around my handbag.

"You can tell me anything, Little Dove." He clasps his big warm fingers around my colder ones, and his touch is gentle and arousing. My toes curl, my scalp tingles, and my heart drops down to my feet, then bounces up to tangle in my throat.

"Sir, Knight... I—" I swallow. *Don't cry. Don't cry.* "Knight, I—"

He cups my cheek. "Tell me, baby."

A-n-d, that endearment is enough for a tear to spill over.

He pales. I kid you not, the color fades from his cheeks. He bends his knees and peers into my eyes. "You're scaring me, honey, and that's the only reason I'm going to order you to tell me what's on your mind." His voice lowers to that remembered beloved hush. "Right. Now." Before he completes the sentences, the words burst out of me, "I'm not pregnant."

61

Knight

"You're not pregnant?"

She shakes her head. "I got my period yesterday, and I was so upset. But I was also relieved. I'm not ready to be a mother, yet, you know? Not until I've lived life a little, and traveled, and crossed some items off my bucket list. Paris, for sure. It's only two hours from here by Eurostar, and I've never been. Can you imagine? And I haven't swum with dolphins or seen the Northern Lights or climbed Uluru. Of course, there are a few things I know you're going to help me tick off, like having five orgasms in one night, I mean you're the master of orgasms, so I know this is bound to happen at some point. And then, you said we'd have anal—" She squeezes her eyes shut. "Did I say anal aloud in the park? Ignore that." She draws in a breath. "Not that I should be embarrassed to say that aloud, and I know we haven't done it yet, but you should know, I've been practicing with a plug in my bum like in the fanfic stories and, aargh—" She slaps her forehead. "Now I said bum. How could I say bum?" She buries her forehead against my chest. "Can we start again? I'm nervous—"

"Penny, it's okay."

"—no, you don't understand. I'm really nervous. I wanted to tell you. I should have told you yesterday. But I had a good cry, and Mira was there to console me, and then we ate ice-cream together and watched a chick flick, although I really did want to call you and talk to you instead—"

"You should have."

"—but I was worried you'd be upset. I know how much this means to you and—"

"Penny, you're more important."

"—now, your dad's going to be upset and—"

"Fuck my dad."

"Did you say F your dad?" she asks in a small voice.

I notch my knuckles under her chin, so she has to look up at me. "You heard me. I will not let him control my life anymore. Everything I've done so far in my life has been to get a reaction out of him, and that includes joining the Royal Marines." I wince. It's the first time I've said the words aloud.

"Wow, that's quite a confession," she murmurs.

"All those months of being stuck on my own provided me enough time to think over my past. When I returned to London, I was confused about what I wanted. I lost faith in the goals that guided my life until then. I joined the military—not only because I wanted to serve my country, though that, too—but also because it was a giant fuck you to my father's lifestyle. He spent his time pursuing money and power, and I swore not to be like him. But then I got captured, and my world turned upside down. So, when I returned, I figured what I had to do was embrace that materialistic part of me, if that makes sense?"

She nods. "And now?"

"Now, I know you're the most important thing in my life—" Tiny's bark reaches us and a few seconds later he bumps into me from behind. I manage to hold my stance and keep her upright at the same time. I laugh. "And this boy, of course."

"You make a great dog-parent. You'd have made a great dad, too."

"There's time."

She swallows. "Is it horrible that I was relieved not to be pregnant. I do want kids, just not yet."

"I want what you want. And if we never have kids, having you with me, by my side, in my life, is enough."

"Oh, you two remind me of me and your dad," Michelle pauses between us. Tiny barks again and tugs on his leash.

I release Penny and grab his collar before her mother overbalances. "Down boy." He instantly plants his butt on the floor and pants up at me.

"You've been such a good boy; you deserve your treat." I pull out the packet of doggy treats I've taken to carrying around and toss him one of the biscuits. He flicks out his tongue, snatches it out of the air, then looks at me with pleading eyes.

I laugh. "One more, but that's the last one, okay boy?"

Tiny woofs, then snaps up the next biscuit and pants up at me.

"No more for you," I say in a warning voice. He whines and drops his head, and a melting sensation squeezes my chest. I close the distance to him and rub him behind his ears. "Who's a good boy? You're a good boy, is who." Tiny bumps his head against me. I scratch it, and he purrs. Honest to god, this dog sometimes behaves like he's a cat. "You'll have dinner soon enough, okay?" I step back, then turn to find Penny staring at me.

"What?"

Her lips twitch, then she shakes her head. "Nothing."

"You lying, hmm?"

She flushes. "I was thinking how much you've changed since I first met you."

"Funny how the love of a good woman can do that."

Her flush deepens. She looks around, then back at me. "Uh, it's getting late."

"Eric, there you are." Michelle tugs on my sleeve. "What took you so long? You're late for dinner. We need to get back to the house before Penny returns from her friend's house."

I frown.

"Eric, didn't you hear me. Let's head back home."

"She thinks you're my father," Penny murmurs.

"Ah." I hook Michelle's arm through mine. "You're right, time we headed back."

"Thank you," Penny says in a soft voice as I drive her back home. I gave Rudy the day off. He deserves some time with his grandkids. Funny how I never thought about that before today. That's how much she's changing me. Bit by bit, she's transforming me. No one has had such a profound impact on my life, not even my parents. My father was solely focused on his business, and my mother, while she made sure we were cared for, wasn't the most open emotionally. It's why Abby and I turned to each other. And I haven't spent as much time as I should with her since my return. I've shirked my duties as a brother.

And as a husband? I can no longer fool myself into thinking our relationship is fake. It might have started out as an arrangement, but it's become so much more. *So, tell her that. Why can't I tell her how I feel about her? Why can't I tell her about the other thing I've hidden from her? Will she judge me for it?* It's the one thing I haven't dared tell any of my friends so far.

"Today was a good day for her, thanks to you." Penny turns to me. "It wouldn't have been possible without you. Thank you for playing along with her illusions."

"I know all about illusions," I murmur.

She gives me a strange look. "Sometimes you say the weirdest things. And I don't know if you mean it in jest or not."

I focus on the road, not sure what to tell her. I don't want to lie to her anymore, but sharing more with her— *Am I ready for it?* It would make me vulnerable to her in a way I've never been with anyone else. She continues to stare at me, no doubt, expecting a reply. My throat closes, my skin prickles, and I grip the steering wheel with such force, the skin of my knuckles turns white. The tension in the car thickens.

She opens her mouth to say something, but that's when Tiny chooses to bark from his doggy seat that I've fitted into the back. He paws at the window, then presses his nose into it. She turns to see what's gotten his attention and laughs. "Oh, so cute, Tiny's found himself a girlfriend."

"A girlfriend huh?" I ease the car to a stop at a red-light, then glance over my shoulder. Sure enough, the boy's staring through the window at a poodle. The little dog is strapped into a doggy seat in the adjacent car. She has a bow clipped behind her ear and must be less than one-quarter of Tiny's size. She looks at him, then haughty as can be, looks straight ahead.

Tiny barks and places his paw against the window. The light changes. The car drives off, and Tiny whines.

"Aww, poor baby, did she blank you, huh?" Penny laughs.

"Better get used to it, boy. You have a lifetime of groveling and giving in to female demands ahead of you."

I take my foot off the brake and guide the car forward. We ride in silence for a few minutes, then she asks, "Is that how you see it moving forward? You giving in to my demands?"

"When needed," I agree.

"And groveling?"

"I haven't started, if that's what you're alluding to."

"Is this a precursor of the groveling phase, then?"

"What do you mean?"

"Checking in on my mom, then taking us out on a picnic, getting the picnic basket delivered, playing along with my mother's delusions."

I pause, then flip on the indicator before I answer, "Your mother and I have a lot in common."

"How's that?"

"Both of us suffered a shock—she, when your father died; me, when I was tortured. Both of us began to lose our minds. Only difference is, I hide it well."

62

Penny's bucket list

- ~~Type at 250 words a minute (done!)~~
- Have 5 O's in the course of 1 night (I'll settle for 1 tbh) => Almost made this one last night when he gave 4 orgasms. OMG 4 freakin' orgasms!
- ~~Learn to cook a gourmet meal. => I wasn't very good at it, but it's the spirit that counts, right?~~
- ~~Act in a movie or a play — I'll take a street act => It didn't go down that well. :(~~
- See the London Ice Kings play a game.
- Swim with dolphins.
- See the Northern Lights.
- Climb Uluru in Australia.
- Eat a chocolate croissant in a sidewalk café in Paris.
- ~~Be dominated. (Uh, maybe this should go up to the top?)~~
- ~~Find a man who cares for my mother as much as I do.~~
- ~~Be proposed to by the man I love.~~
- Explore anal. (I'm chicken so this is right at the bottom — pun intended. Hahahaha!)

63

Penny

"I'm worried about him, Abby." I pace the floor in front of the desk in my friend's office. Abby only comes into work a couple of times a week. The rest of the time, she prefers to work from home.

After Knight dropped me off last night at my apartment—he didn't insist I come home with him, something that both surprised and relieved me, but may have left me a bit disappointed. I want to spend more time with this man who's showing such a different side of himself. And yet, I can't completely forget what an ass he's been to me in the past. Also, his cryptic comments in the car disturbed me. I believe he was trying to tell me something, without saying it openly. It's almost as if he wants me to dig in and find out what is bothering him.

Is it something related to his capture and the time he was tortured? Probably. So, why doesn't he come out and share with me? Especially after he agreed not to keep any more secrets from me.

I thought we were past the hiding things from each other phase, but maybe not? He asked me to give him time, and I understand why he'd say that, and I do want to be patient. But a part of me wants to push it. To find out everything there is to know about this man who intrigues me, frustrates me, and makes me want to slap him and demand he tell me everything, then jump him and kiss him.

"Argh!" I throw up my hands. "I don't know what to do. I can't sit behind my desk while he's locked up in his office doing whatever it is he does and pretend he's my boss and I'm his assistant and everything is okay."

"It's probably why he told you not to come into the office anymore. He wanted to spare you the going crazy whenever you see him."

"And if I don't catch glimpses of him on a daily basis, that's worse."

"But you don't want to move in with him, do you?" She taps her fingers together.

"Not yet. I mean, I do, but if I did, it's like I'm giving in. And I don't think I'm ready, yet."

"And why is that? You know the truth about Bobbie. Is that still holding you back?"

I shake my head. "I understand why he did that. And I'm proud of him for helping out his friend."

"Then what is it?"

I bite the inside of my cheek, "I can't help but think he's hiding something else from me. It's nothing I can put my finger on. It's just an instinct, you know?"

She nods slowly. "When you're married, you sense these things about your spouse, so you're probably right."

Of course, what I have with Knight did not start out as a real marriage. And now? Now, I'm not sure what it is I have with him.

"Knight's been through a lot. Marrying you has changed him, though. He's calmer, better adjusted to civilian life. For someone who, until a month ago, was held behind enemy lines, it's a sea change in temperament."

I lower my chin. "You're right. Of course you are. Maybe I'm expecting too much from him? Maybe it's unreasonable of me to think he's ready to share all of his secrets with me?"

"Or maybe, he hasn't been able to voice what happened to him yet. He may not be willing to face things himself. And until he comes to terms himself with what happened… Perhaps, there are things he can't tell you because he hasn't acknowledged them to himself yet?"

I draw in a breath. "Everything you say makes a lot of sense. And I want to be patient. I do. I'm sure, given time, he'll be willing to share more, it's just—" I hitch a shoulder. "I don't know; I'm not ready to move back, is all."

"When do you think will you be ready?" She leans forward in her chair. "Not that I'm putting pressure on you or anything. In fact, I'd prefer you figure things out completely before you see him again. These men,"—she nods toward the door—"they tend to screw things up in your head when you see them. You're probably better off taking a job somewhere else and putting distance between the two of you as you work through your feelings for him."

"But if I do that, if I move out of the picture completely, wouldn't that send a signal to your father that all is not well? Wouldn't it make him want to change his mind about handing over the company to him?"

"You're not living with him anyway," she points out.

I stab the toe of my pink ballet flats—yeah, I decided to switch it up from heels today. I woke up feeling like everything that could go wrong would today. In a bid to self-soothe, I opted for comfort over style. Pink baggy jeans and a loose top with my most comfortable cardigan over that complete my casual ensemble. Too bad, if I don't look as polished as the stupid receptionist, or Georgina, for that matter. Right now, it's time for some self-care, and if this is what I need to feel good, then so be it. I'm not going to deprive myself of what my instincts say I need.

And what about what he needs? He's your husband. No longer fake husband. I don't know what's happening between us, but this relationship which twists my guts and makes me want to puke every time I think of future without him is not a fake one. Not at all.

"I'm not pregnant," I burst out.

She stills. "Did you think you were pregnant?"

I pop a shoulder, unable to look at her.

"Hold on"—she stiffens—"is that why Knight married you? Because he thought you were carrying his baby?"

"That might have been one of the considerations, yes. But forget about that. You know how your father was hoping for him to have a child within the first year of marriage? Guess that's not going to happen, either. When I told Knight, I thought he'd be upset, or angry, or disappointed, but he was very understanding. He told me not to do anything I don't want to do. That if I'm not ready for a baby, he's fine with that."

"He did?" She seems taken aback, then a small smile curves her lips. "He did, huh?"

"It took me by surprise, too. But then a lot of what he's doing of late seems to be out of character."

"Not if you knew him before he was taken by the enemy. My brother is one of the warmest, most generous, most easy-going people I know. It's why, though he went against our father's wishes, my parents didn't disown him completely. Not like me."

"It hurts, huh?"

She half laughs. "To their credit, once I got married, they did make up with me and welcomed Cade to the family."

"They did?" I frown. "No one else from your family has met me yet."

"Oh, I'm so sorry I brought that up." She rises from the table and rushes around to embrace me. "I'm such an ass for bringing that up."

"Not that it matters, except I'm floundering a little right now. I'm so pleased I can talk to you, though. It helps me understand him better, you know."

"In which case, I'm sure talking to me will help you." A new voice interrupts us.

Abby and I turn to the door. An older man walks in. He's almost as tall as Knight, but leaner. His hair is greying at the temples. His shoulders are not as broad as Knight's, but the way he wears his suit, the way he strides in with that arrogant confidence clinging to him, it's clear, it's his father.

He walks over to me and holds out his hand. "I'm Knight and Abby's father."

"I gathered." I shake his hand. I heard through the office grapevine that their father prefers to work from home. Knight had not invited either of his parents to our wedding. So, I haven't had the chance to meet him before this.

He turns to Abby. "How's Cade? It's been a while since I saw the two of you."

Abby nods. The look on her face is half-polite, half-resigned. It's almost like she's not sure how to act toward her father. Which is a pity. I'd do anything to speak with my father one more time. To have him in my life and be able to pick up the phone and talk to him at any time? That would my dream come true.

Her father's features seem to soften. He moves forward and pats her shoulder. "You can stop looking so wary, I merely wanted to meet the woman who agreed to marry my son."

"Hmm." She looks between us, clearly unconvinced of his intentions.

"Five minutes; that's all I want. She is my daughter-in-law, after all?"

64

Knight

"You left her with him?" I round the table and race for the door of my office. I fling it open and am greeted by the empty desk. "They're in your office?"

"That's where I left them."

"You should have stayed."

As I'm about to walk out the door, Abby calls out behind me, "He wanted to catch up with her. It didn't seem wrong. After all, he is our father."

"He's a shark. The only thing he understands is money. He has no idea about feelings and emotions and that there's life beyond the business."

"And you do?" she cries.

I pause, then turn to look over my shoulder. "What are you trying to say?"

She closes the distance between us. "You love her. Why don't you tell her that?"

"Because—" I shake my head. "You wouldn't understand."

She touches my arm. "What I understand is you have feelings for her. That you might have secrets you're holding back from her."

I begin to speak, but she holds up her hand. "I'm not judging you. I'm not. You've been through so much Knight, and it can't be easy for someone in your position to trust another with your emotions. But she's not 'anyone.' She's your wife, and you need to tell her everything, or else you're going to destroy the trust you've built so far with her."

The blood drains from my features. Sweat pools under my armpits. I can't lose her trust. I can't lose *her*. I can't.

She takes in my features, then lowers her arm. "Go to her, brother."

I run out the door, down the corridor, and I slap at the button of the elevator, but of course, the car is nowhere close to arriving. "Fucking fuck." I race toward the stairs, tear open the door, then leap down the stairs. That military training I went through is being put to good use. Down one floor, then the other, through the doorway, up the corridor. I reach Abby's office, fling the door open, step in... and come face to face with her.

Her features are pale, her lips red like she's been biting down on them. Her eyes glitter—with tears? With anger? With both?

"Penny—" I reach for her, but she steps around me.

"Don't touch me." She pushes past me.

I turn, grab her arm.

She stares down at where I have my fingers locked around her wrist, then up at my gaze.

The hurt in them sends a piercing pain through my chest. "Penny, please, give me a chance to explain."

"How many chances should I give you, Knight? You lied to me. And after I asked you if you had any more secrets to share with me, you said no."

"Penny, it's not what it sounds like."

She laughs, the sound is so bitter, my heart threatens to break apart. My lungs burn. This beautiful, innocent, sunny, happy girl... Look what I've turned her into. I should have known I would corrupt her. Take her joie-de-vivre and leave her with that cynical look in her eyes. The one thing about her that attracted me to her is the very thing I destroyed.

"Penny—"

"No, you don't get to tell me what to do. Never again. You hear me. I don't want to see you. I wish you'd never come back alive." Her features twist. She gasps. "Oh, my god, I didn't mean that. Why did I say it? What's happening to me?"

"It's me." I swallow. "It's all my fault."

She looks at me with an anguished expression on her face, then she slips off her wedding and engagement rings and holds them out to me.

"No—" I shake my head. My heart leaps into my throat. My blood is pounding so hard in my ears, I can barely hear myself speak. "Don't do that, Penny."

"Take it, Knight, please," she pleads.

"You're my wife—"

"—your fake wife."

"It's always felt real to me. More than real." I swallow around the ball of something that's blocking my throat.

"And I thought so, too." She hunches her shoulders. "I hoped it was more than what the contract between us was about, but it's clear, you don't trust me. If you did, you'd have told me about Bobbie. If you felt anything for me, you wouldn't have hidden something so big from me. Now I understand, there was nothing real between us."

"There was... There is," I snap.

"Whatever there was, you destroyed it by your actions. Me wearing your ring is making a mockery of the kind of marriage I'd hoped to have one day. One in which my husband would have enough confidence in me to share his secrets, as I would with him. That's not what we have, Knight. What we have is…" She swallows. "Nothing." She holds out the rings. "You've hurt me enough. Please don't make this more difficult for me. Please take back your rings."

I try to draw in a breath, but my lungs burn. My scalp feels too tight. My skin feels like it's being flayed off my body. Is this how it felt when the rest of my team were being tortured? Why does this feel so much more painful than when I was being abused by my captors? Why does it feel like I'm dying, like there's nothing left for me to live for?

She looks at me with glittering eyes. "If you feel anything for me, if you have one iota of respect for me, you'll hold out your palm and take back your rings."

Fuck! "Penny, I—"

"No, don't try to convince me or order me to obey you because we know I'll end up doing what you want, but that's not what I want."

"What is it you want?"

"I want you to take back your rings, Knight. Please." She looks at me with so much pain in those eyes, so much beseeching, so much everything, that inch by painful inch, I find myself raising my arm. I hold out my palm, she drops her rings in it, then she turns and takes off running.

And I let her go. My thigh muscles spasm, my feet hurt, every part of my body insists I follow her, but I hold back. I twist my fingers into fists, let the rings dig into the flesh of my palm, let the pain of the separation sweep through me, but I don't go after her. She's better off without me. She is.

He, on the other hand— I turn in the direction of my father's office. His door is closed. Fuck him. I barge in, slamming the door behind me.

The sound crashes through the space. My father looks up.

Before he can react, I cross the floor, round the desk, then grab his collar and haul my sperm-donor to his feet. I raise my fist and swing, only to stop less than a hair's breadth away from his face. To his credit, the old man doesn't flinch. Nerves of steel, he has. The same quality that made me such an asset on any mission. Cool under pressure, able to dissociate myself from reality and do what was needed in the moment. And I paid the price for it later. Just like he's going to pay the price for causing distress to my sweet wife. I tighten my hold on him, then clench my fist. The rings dig into the palm of my hand and blood squeezes out from between my fingers. His gaze widens. For the first time in my life, he appears shaken.

"Son, you're bleeding," he whispers. His eyes—so like mine—darken with empathy, and goddamn, but I can't stomach it. I can't handle the pity in his eyes. I don't want him to understand what I'm going through. I don't want anyone to realize the depth of the wound I'm carrying around inside me—no one except her, that is.

I release my father, and he stumbles, but he doesn't back away. He grabs my fist. I allow him to pry open my fingers. He sees her rings, and the color fades from his features. He pulls a handkerchief from his pocket and holds it out. I drop the rings into it. He wraps the bloodied rings with care and hands it over to me. I take it with my unhurt hand, but he doesn't let go.

"Let me help you," he insists.

"The way you did by what you just told her?"

"I didn't think I was telling her something she didn't already know. She's your wife; she should know your secrets. How long did you think you'd be able to hide it?"

"That's my problem. She's *my* wife; *I'm* the one who gets to tell her *my* secrets. "

"The only way to have a healthy relationship is by starting out on the right foot; something you, evidently, haven't done."

"And you have?"

He releases his hold on the handkerchief, and I slide it into my pocket. Then he grabs some tissues from his desk. When he reaches for my torn-up palm, I don't pull away. I allow him to press the tissues into the lacerated skin, then he folds my fingers around them. He releases his hold, and the two of us stare at each other.

The silence extends, then he blows out a breath. "If you're referring to your mother, she's aware of my past. She's aware of what I had to do to keep my family in the style they were accustomed to."

"And all we wanted was more of your time. We could have done with far less and a father who was present at mealtimes, at school plays, and at graduation ceremonies."

He winces. "I accept, I wasn't perfect. I accept, I didn't come close to it. But I tried my best. When you come from nothing, you realize the value of money. It's the one thing I was determined my family would never suffer for want of."

"And when you have an absentee parent, you realize you'd rather have their presence in your life than all the money in the world."

His features twist. He rakes his fingers through his hair, then seems to get a hold of himself. "I'm sorry I wasn't there for you and Abby. But I'm not sorry I interfered in your life. I'm not sorry I put down a deadline for you to get married and settle down. And I'm not sorry I told her that you're planning to adopt Bobbie's child. I only wish you'd told her first."

65

Penny

"How can he think so little of me? Does he think I would stop him from adopting a child who needs his help? Why couldn't he tell me earlier? Why did I have to find out this way?" I stare into the depths of my Ben & Jerry's Cherry Garcia ice-cream. It's a classic, and one my mom loves.

After my father passed away, and before she started losing her mind, it was our ritual most Friday evenings—the one day she didn't hold down a third job—when we'd share a tub and watch her favorite classic movies on TV. My normal go-to for comfort is wine—don't judge. But the fact I turned to ice cream today shows how upset I am. It's one way I feel connected to my mother, but it's also something I try to avoid, as it makes me feel so nostalgic, and that only makes me wallow in self-pity.

But today, I want to wallow. I want to roll around in my distress. I want to squelch through all the emotions and bury myself in my misery. A tear rolls down my cheek and plops into the ice cream. I scoop it up, tears and all, and plop the spoonful in my mouth. Tasting the slightly salty taste only makes me feel worse. Which was the entire point... right? I sniffle, then hunch my shoulders. "I can't believe he didn't tell me."

"Maybe he thought it'd upset you more?" Mira ventures.

I'm in our flat and sprawled out on the couch wearing my favorite pair of fuzzy slippers and pajamas. Good thing I didn't take any of my old clothes when I moved in with Knight. Not that I needed to, since he filled the closet in my room with brand-new clothes for all seasons, and with footwear to accompany it. All my size, too. Of course, he must have had a professional stylist do it, but still. He not only guessed my size correctly, but also the colors I like. And the cuts of the clothes? They were perfect and flattering and always showed off the best parts of me, too. It's another sign of how thoughtful he can be. Another thing that confuses me about this man.

"It's upsetting me anyway. I specifically asked him if he had any more secrets and he—" I frown. "And when he didn't reply... I thought there couldn't be anything else. And I understand why he's doing it. Bobbie is his dead teammate's wife, and he feels responsible for his family. If he'd only told me, I'd have stood by him."

"So, you don't mind that he wants to adopt their child?" Mira asks slowly.

I shake my head. "The child doesn't have a father, and the mother is not in any state to be their caregiver. I think it's an amazing thing that Knight is doing. If only he'd trusted me enough to share."

"Maybe he was working up the courage to tell you, but his father beat him to it?"

I jerk my chin up in Mira's direction, and she raises her hands. "I'm not defending him or anything. And you're right to be upset with him. If I were you, I'd have done the same thing—"

"But?" I swallow.

"But—" She hesitates, then rises to her feet and begins to pace. "The guy loves you—"

"He's never said so."

"He has feelings for you—"

"Not enough to trust me with his secrets, apparently," I say bitterly.

"And you love him."

I deflate. "Is that so obvious?"

"Both of you have a connection that's clear to see. It's the only reason to give him time to come around."

The intercom buzzes. We glance at each other, then Mira walks to the doorway and answers it. She speaks in a voice that's too low for me to make out the words, then buzzes whoever it is in. She turns to me. "It's Gio. I guessed you'd be okay with my inviting her up?"

I nod.

Mira opens the door, and a few seconds later, Gio enters. "Hey!" She greets Mira, then turns to me. "Thanks for letting me in, especially as I'm not the person you probably want to see right now."

I half smile. "You're always welcome here, Gio."

Her features soften. She walks into the room, takes one look at my features and bursts out, "What's he done now?"

I choke out a laugh. "You're something else, you know that?"

She walks over to me in her six-inch heels, places her designer handbag and a paperback on the coffee table, then sits down next to me. "Mind sharing?" She glances at the ice cream.

I hand over the tub, and she takes a mouthful. She makes a humming sound and swallows. "Sooo good. I always forget this is my favorite flavor, until I taste it."

"Right?" I wipe away my tears. "And to answer your question, he hasn't done anything wrong —"

"Just wrong by you?"

I glance away. "I'm not sure."

"That's my fault. I'm the one who thinks she should give him a chance, but I'm sure you think otherwise. Gio?"

Gio looks at Mira. "You think I'm heartless, don't you?"

Mira rolls her eyes. She walks over, takes the ice cream tub from Gio, and scoops out a spoonful. "I didn't say that. But I also know you don't have as soft a heart as me."

"Those with the hardest exteriors hide the most emotions," she murmurs.

Both of us look at her. A frown appears between Mira's eyebrows. "Beneath that ball-breaker persona you portray to the world, you're a romantic, aren't you?"

She scoffs, "I was talking about Knight."

"Hmm." Mira seems like she's about to say something, then changes her mind.

"What?" Gio scowls at her.

"Nothing." Mira's lips twitch.

I pull my knees up and rest my chin on them. "Did Knight call you again or —"

"I wrapped up work, wanted to hang out with undemanding company, so—" she raises a shoulder.

"Gee, thanks, you have a way with words," Mira murmurs.

"Oh, please, bitch, you know what I mean." Gio reaches over and grabs the paper bag, then pulls out a gold-colored package with a familiar brand-name of very expensive chocolate. Only the best for this woman.

"Godiva!" Mira cries.

"The only chocolate brand worth eating." She rips open the package, flips open the cover, then proceeds to drop a few of the pieces into the ice cream tub that Mira holds.

"Try that." Gio gestures.

Mira fishes out one of the ice-cream covered chunks, licks it off the spoon, then moans. "Ohmyfuckinggod, that is orgasmic." She swallows. "Not as orgasmic as some of the O's that man has, no doubt, given you"—she stabs her spoon at me—"but I'll wager it's close."

I chuckle, take the tub from her, and bite down on one of the chocolate-covered morsels. "Mmm, almost as sinful. Almost."

"Bitch," Gio says without heat. "I've resigned myself to being BFF's with Steely Dan."

I choke on my next mouthful. "Steely Dan?"

"That's what I call my vibrator."

Mira blinks, "I don't want to be gauche, but I still don't get it."

Gio blows out a breath, "Steely Dan is the name of a very famous Seventies rock band who named themselves after an oversized, steam-powered, strap-on dildo in William S. Burroughs' novel *Naked Lunch*."

My jaw drops.

Mira's gaze widens, "Jeez, would have never guessed you're a closet nerd."

"You mean, because I am well-groomed and love my designer brands, I shouldn't have a brain?"

Mira reddens. "Sorry, I that was presumptuous of me."

Gio's features soften. "You're good. I quite like disarming people with my"—she points to herself—"looks and fashion-sense, and then I lower the book—I mean, the boom—on them." She cackles.

"I think I'm developing a serious girl crush on you," Mira says slowly.

"Aww honey, you're so good for my ego." Gio laughs. "By the way, came up with that nickname after a rather intimate session too. Steely

Dan has made me come more times than I can count, and faster and harder than any man ever has…and I suspect, ever will."

"Hmm." I contemplate taking another mouthful of the gooey ice-cream. *I shouldn't, should I? Oh, what the hell? Besides, the ice cream is doing what I intended with the brain-freeze settling over me. And if it adds another layer to my plentiful behind, I'm not complaining. And neither will he. Assuming I let him squeeze my flesh. Will I though?*

"I'll take your Steely Dan and raise you my BBF," Mira murmurs.

"You mean BOB don't you?" Gio tips up her chin.

"Nope, I meant Book Boy Friend." Mira smirks.

"I'll stay with Battery Operated Boyfriend, thank you very much," Gio retorts.

"BBF's are superior."

"And imaginary."

"Don't mock 'em 'til you try 'em." Mira scoffs.

Gio taps her chin. "I could, of course, take on a BBF and tag-team with a BOB."

Mira stares at her. "TBH, when you have a BBF, you don't need a BOB."

"Next, you'll be saying you've never wanted to try DP." Gio smirks.

Mira looks at her with speculation. "Something you wanna share with us?"

"Don't mock it 'til you try it. Not that I have… Yet."

Mira and I exchange an amused look.

"You're such a badass, I can totally believe you need a very special man — or men — to satisfy you," I tease.

She laughs. "Good thing I'm not in the market for one. Happy with my Danny boy, thank you very much. Also, we were talking about Knight and you."

I hunch my shoulders. "Not sure what to make of it. I'm a little pissed at his father for telling me something Knight may have told me in his own time. But also, I can't be pissed because I'm glad I know. I think he's doing the right thing, but I wish he'd just told me. We could've found a solution together. I'd have stood by his side. I'd have done anything for him, if he'd only let me. But the man doesn't want to give me a chance."

"I thought things were improving between the two of you," Gio says slowly.

When I glance at her, she shrugs. "Abby told Solene, who told me.

We're all concerned about the two of you. I know it seems like we're all up in your business, but—"

"I like it." I smile a little. "I miss having siblings, and after my mother fell ill, I felt ungrounded, so it's nice to know there are people who care about me."

Gio's expression softens. "See, I would be pissed if I were in your shoes. I prefer to face things on my own. But that's that darned independent nature of mine, which has gotten me into more trouble than I care to admit. Not that I'm going to change or anything. But that doesn't change the fact that you are a sweetheart, and he doesn't deserve you."

"Hear, hear." Mira reaches for one of the remaining wedges of chocolate and raises it. "You're not a complete bitch, Gio."

Gio laughs. "You're not too bad, either."

"High praise coming from you." Mira grins, then turns to me. "So, you going to give him a chance to explain himself?"

66

Knight

"If only she'd give me a chance." I rub behind Tiny's ear, and he yawns, then clambers onto the sofa next to me. The mutt's the size of a pony, but he clearly thinks he's a poodle. He prefers to curl up on the settee in the living room and thrust his nose into my lap.

The first time, he took me by surprise. I admit, I'd been worried the sectional wouldn't bear his weight, but it held up. Also, when I tried to push him off, he sulked until I relented and allowed him up. And so most evenings, after my run with Adam—we've taken to running twice a day, once in the morning and once after work, now—I sprawl out on the sofa and watch gardening shows with Tiny.

Y-e-p, you heard that right. The man who used to hold a gun has found an affinity to holding flower bulbs. In fact, I've taken to culti-vating them in pots on the balcony of my penthouse. Something about the undemanding routine of working with your hands in the earth, surrounded by greenery and nature, seems to soothe the churning in me. Something only she'd been able to do previously. Thoughts of her are never too far away from my mind. Especially because I know I've hurt her again. Why didn't I have the courage to tell her about

Bobbie's daughter? I haven't seen her yet, and the social worker who's been assessing me for the adoption hasn't been impressed by me. I wasn't surprised, at first, considering I was a single man. But as far as they know, I'm not anymore. Of course, it doesn't help that they've never met my wife, and I'm also an emotionally wounded man with too many issues. Hell, I'd be the first to say I'm not fit to be a parent.

In a way, that's why I was relieved when Penny told me she wasn't pregnant. Not that I wanted the disappointment I glimpsed on her face, but considering I had to figure out the details of how I was going to push through the adoption, it seemed prudent not to rush into being a father of another child. *So why didn't you tell her about it?* Bobbie escaping from the hospital and her caregiver that day and walking into my office provided the opportunity to clear the air with Penny, but I didn't take advantage of it.

Fact is, I was a coward. It's not that I don't trust her, but I didn't want her to feel burdened by the promises I made to my friend and teammate. That's *my* burden to bear. *But isn't that what marriage is about? Sharing your burdens? Sharing your most intimate secrets? Are you ready to share yours with her? Besides, how long did you think you'd be able to hide a child living in your house from her?*

The absurdity of trying to keep this secret from Penny doesn't escape me. I'm an idiot.

I slump back into the cushions, legs kicked out on the sectional. I've turned down the volume on the television, so there's no commentary. The screen shows images of the English countryside in autumn. Greens and browns and golds. The color of her eyes when she's angry or when she's experiencing high emotion. Everything reminds me of her. Pink roses of her favorite color, sunflowers of her sunny nature, dahlias of her delicate beauty, the symmetry of her features, and sweet, star-shaped asters of her good-nature. I took advantage of her.

She's the very opposite of me. She lights up the corners of my existence, and I never once told her how much I appreciate it. Instead, I wanted to bury myself in her, draw from her grace and beauty and kindhearted nature. I was greedy and selfish. I was drawn to her because I needed her to heal myself. And what did I given her in return? Secrets, disappointments...and orgasms... Which would have been so much more fulfilling if I'd told her I love her. If I'd opened myself up, mind and body and soul, and made love to her.

It's not too late. You can tell her everything. You can drop the final walls you've put up between the two of you. You can trust her. You can —

Tiny begins to bark.

"What's wrong, boy?"

He barks again, then whines.

"It's okay boy, there's no one here but you and me, and —"

His ears perk. He jumps onto the floor and bounds toward the elevator doors. He barks even louder, then prances about in front of the elevator.

I frown and rise to my feet. "What's up boy?"

I walk toward him and glance at the indicator to find the cage is on its way up. Tiny jumps up and plants his paws on the elevator doors, which are still shut.

"Sit, boy," I grab his collar and manage to coax him back. He whines, begins to plant his butt on the floor, then changes his mind, and once again, straightens. He barks so loudly, the sound reverberates off the walls. It stabs that part of your ear that only responds this way to barking dogs and screaming children.

"Whoa, quiet down," I yell. "Whoever's coming up will here soon enough and —"

The doors slide open, and he straightens and leaps forward with such enthusiasm, my hold on him loosens. He half skids forward with a joyful bark as she steps into the hallway.

"Hey, boy, did you miss me? Uff—"

Tiny bumps his head against her, and she staggers back.

"Penny!" I move so quickly my feet don't seem to touch the floor. I reach her and grab her waist, then draw her to me before she can fall over.

"Tiny, sit," I scold him.

His ears droop. I swear, his jowls hang more than normal, and with a whine, he plants his butt on the floor.

"Aww, poor baby. You didn't mean it, did you?"

Tiny's tail thumps with enough force that the ground seems to shake.

She pulls away from me; I release her. She steps toward Tiny, and bending only a little, throws her arm around the big brute.

So, the mutt gets a hug, and I— I'm greeted by the sight of her perfect, heart-shaped behind clad in sweats—pink, of course. She scratches him behind his ears, and his eyes roll back in his head. I know the feeling. *Lucky bastard. He gets to feel her touch, to be at the receiving end of her limpid gaze, to feel her warmth as she hugs him, and whoa... Hold on, are you jealous of a dog? Get a grip, man.* I shuffle my weight from foot to foot; she ignores me. I clear my throat.

Tiny woofs, and she makes an "awww" sound and pats his head. He, of course, plays it for all it's worth. He places his paw on her shoulder and looks into her eyes and —

"Okay, that's enough."

I step forward and glare at the mutt. "Down, boy, and I mean it."

He looks from me to her, then back at me, before he lowers his head and lies down on the floor. He continues to watch us with those big, melting eyes, and that gets the intended reaction from her.

"Why did you do that?" She turns toward me. "I was petting him."

"And you're done now."

She scowls. "I'll say when I'm done."

"Oh?"

She firms her lips. "And I thought you'd changed."

Clearly, not enough. I throw up my hands. "You walk into my place. Then, you ignore me. You walk past me without acknowledging my presence and then, you shower this—this—mutt with affection."

She blinks. "He's cute."

"I'm cute."

"Ha!" She laughs. "You and cute." She shakes her head in disbelief.

"I can be cute." *I can be anything you want, if you give me a chance, baby."*

"There are many adjectives I associate with you, but cute is not one of them."

"So, there are adjectives you associate with me, hmm?" I try to keep the gloating out of my voice, but I don't think I succeed; her brows knit.

"They're really not anything to be proud of."

"The fact that you spend time thinking of me at all is something I'm proud of."

Her gaze widens. She seems taken aback, then with a last pat on Tiny's head, walks past me and toward the view of the city from the floor-to-ceiling windows. She pauses halfway. "There's an armchair by the window," she murmurs.

"Indeed."

"And a bookshelf next to it."

"Mmm-hmm."

"With books."

"Don't you want to see what they are?" I murmur.

She reaches it and runs her fingers across the spines. "These are fantasy novels."

"Romantasy," I correct her.

She whips her head around to stare at me. "Did you say—"

"Romantasy?" I walk over to stand next to her. "There are also fantasy romance novels, all spicy and with the tropes you love."

"Wait, hold on"—she gapes—"you know about tropes?"

"I might have done a bit of research to understand them, but yes, I do know about tropes. Also,"—I pick up a tablet and hand it to her —"take a look."

She shoots me a confused look.

"Go on. You're going to love it, I promise."

She pulls up the screen, browses for a few moments, then gasps. "Oh my god, this has all my favorite apps where I can read Dramione fan fiction?" Her fingers fly across the screen. "And a lifetime subscription, too?"

"Also—" I hand her another device.

"A brand-new Kindle paper white?" She places the table aside and snatches the Kindle from me. She switches it on, then stills. "You filled it with my favorite smutty fantasy romance authors?"

"Those whose books are very similar in themes to Dramione. I also took the liberty of adding some enemies-to-lovers contemporary romance novels, which I'm told remind readers of Dramione."

She swallows, then blinks rapidly. "You didn't have to do this."

"I did." I round the armchair then place my palms on it. "Have a seat, milady."

She half laughs. "You know what? I think I will."

She drops her bag to the floor, then slides in. I reach forward and touch a lever and the chair reclines back. Then, with a smooth mechanism, the lower half extends out so she's able to stretch out her legs.

"Whoa, this is so comfortable."

"The best on the market. Also..." I press another button and one of the arms extends out. "Now you have a place for your devices and books to be close at hand."

Her eyes round. "I've never seen anything like this before."

"And you shouldn't have. This was made for you."

"For me?"

"I called up the best designer in the world, gave her my expectations, and—"

"She delivered it so quickly."

"I asked for it to be."

"Oh." Her lips part. A myriad of expressions flit across her features. She opens her mouth to say something, but I shake my head.

"Not yet. Let me savor this feeling; it's not one I'm used to."

"You mean doing something nice for someone?"

"Doing something for you." I squat down next to her, so we are at eye level. "I'd do anything for you, Little Dove. I'm sorry for not telling you about Bobbie or her child. I feel responsible for what happened to my team. If I had been more vigilant, she wouldn't have lost a husband, and her child, a father. Those men trusted me, and I let them down. My teammates put their faith in me, and I couldn't save them. I'll never be able to forgive myself for what happened."

She peers between my eyes. "So, are you going to go through the rest of your life beating yourself up for what happened?"

67

Penny

"If that's what it takes to atone, yes."

"And what about us?"

"You're important to me, more than anyone else has ever been. More than any of my team. But, I also have to live by the promise I made my friend."

"And I'll be the first to admire you and encourage you to do that. It just hurts that you didn't tell me earlier."

"I've been a fool. For the first time, I wasn't able to recognize what my instincts were trying to tell me. I should have trusted you from the very beginning. I should have told you everything."

I place the Kindle on the side-extension, then reach over and cup his cheek. His eyelids flutter down, and tension seems to release from his shoulders. He turns his face and kisses the palm of my hand. A shiver runs down my spine while a melting sensation grips my chest and my stomach. My arms and legs weaken. It's a sinking feeling that tells me I'm well and truly a goner.

"Sir," I whisper.

His lips curve. He wraps his thick fingers around the nape of my neck and places his forehead against mine. "I didn't think I'd ever hear you say that again."

"Me neither," I confess.

He stills, his muscles turn rock hard, but he doesn't react. He searches my features. "What changed your mind?"

I shake my head. "It wasn't one thing." I slide my fingers down his throat to the part of his chest where I can feel his heart beating against his ribcage. "Or maybe, it was. I always knew this—the man you are at heart is a gentle, sensitive, perceptive soul who cares for others more than himself."

He scoffs, "You sure you're not talking about Tiny—the first half, at least?"

I shake my head. "You tried to hide it, but I saw through it. You were cornered and made to fight for your life. You saw unspeakable things done to your teammates, your friends, the people you considered closer than brothers."

"And they were. Every single one of them."

"What you went through would have broken anyone else."

"It did break me, too," I remind her.

"But deep down, you wanted to survive. You wanted a way out."

"You," he says simply. "You were my way out. I saw you and knew it. And fought it every step of the way. But you carried me along, kicking and screaming. I resisted, knowing I wasn't going to win this fight." He lowers his chin to his chest and presses his hand to the spot above my heart. "I wanted to win your heart but had no idea how to go about it. Indeed, the more I tried, the more it seemed I pushed you away. The more I wanted to win you over, the more I resisted that instinct. The more I wanted to be like your book boyfriends, the more I seemed to act more like the villain in a story."

"My favorites." I sigh.

He starts. "Don't think I heard that right."

"Haven't you realized by now, I'm drawn to the bad boy? The alpha-hole, the badass hero who's possessive to a fault and who'll do anything for his woman."

He raises his head and looks into my eyes. "You don't have to humor me, Little Dove. I've been worse than a villain toward you. I've been obnoxious and mean, and someone who should be covered in red flags."

"Stop. If you say anymore, I might have to jump you right now, and that would be embarrassing."

He shakes his head. "You're a strange girl, Little Dove. I'm trying to tell you all the reasons we shouldn't be together."

"And you forget that I fell for Draco. He's far more interesting than Harry Potter."

He frowns. "Meaning?"

"I have a thing for toxic boyfriends in not only my book life, but also in real life."

His lips twitch. "You realize, I'm not going to be like Draco anymore."

"Just as long as you're Draco in bed, and Harry Potter everywhere else."

His forehead crinkles. "I think I understand what you're saying. You should know one thing, though."

"What's that?"

"I'm not ready to sleep with you… Yet."

"Wha—"

Before I can say anything else, he's hauled me to my feet and is striding through the apartment, Tiny dogging his steps. He walks into his bedroom, then glances over his shoulder. "Sit, boy."

Tiny sinks down on his haunches, and Knight kicks the door shut in Tiny's face. "Aww, you could have let him in."

"He's had his fill of you; it's my turn now," he growls.

"Are you jealous of Tiny?" I choke out a laugh.

He huffs, "Of course not." He heads straight through to the ensuite, where he places me on the counter next to the sink.

"Stay." He points a finger at me, then hesitates. "Please." He shakes his head, the muses, "I think I've been spending too much time around Tiny."

I nod, slightly amused by how hard he's trying and how out of character it seems. I don't want him to carry this new side of himself too far. I did say I want a Draco in bed, didn't I? Do I need to be clearer about what that means? Surely, he understands I like that dominant side of him, and the kinky side of him too, when it comes to fucking me? I do want him to make love to me, but I also want him to take me so hard, I see stars. I squeeze my thighs together.

He arches an eyebrow at that but doesn't comment. Instead, he pulls out his phone, and swipes the screen. The next second, a familiar tune begins to play over the speakers.

"Is that—?"

He nods. "The motion picture soundtrack from *Harry Potter and the Deathly Hallows, Part Two.*"

The familiar strains of Hedwig's Theme fill the space. Goosebumps pop on my skin. The hair on my forearms rises. He tilts his head, and the expression on his features indicates he understands how deeply this music affects me. It reminds me of a time when I was young and inno-cent, when everything was possible. Everything is possible now, with him, in this space. With this complex man who hides his sensitive heart, I can have anything I want. He leans in, kisses my forehead, then moves away. I watch as he lights the candles he's dotted around the bath, then retrieves a jar of bath bombs, tosses them into the bath, then runs the water. The scent of roses fills the air, infused with subtle notes of coconut and vanilla.

"You found the ones I love," I murmur.

"I had some help."

"Mira?"

He nods. "I reached out to her and told her how much of an ass I'd been. I begged her for help. She didn't agree, at first; I had to persuade her." He pretends to wipe sweat from his brow. "That woman put me through the wringer with her grilling." He lowers his hand. "I've been interrogated by the enemy, but her questions were far more difficult to answer."

I chuckle. "She's protective."

"She's a good friend."

"So is Gio. I may not know her well, but she's turned out to be someone I can rely on."

"I'm glad." He turns off the tap and switches off the lights, leaving the space bathed in the warm glow of candlelight, then walks over and holds out his hand. "May I?"

68

Knight

She places her hand in mine. It's so slim, so fragile, once again I'm struck by how much smaller than me she is. I tug, and she falls toward me. Instantly, I wrap my other arm about her waist and pick her up. She wraps her legs about me, twines her arms around my neck and nestles in. I carry her over to the bathtub, but she doesn't let go.

"Sweetheart, you need to release me."

She shakes her head.

"The bath will help you relax so you can sleep well."

"But I don't want to sleep, I'd rather—" She rocks her pelvis into the crotch of my sweatpants. No surprise there. Of course I'm aroused. Doesn't mean I'm going to act on it.

"This is about you, baby. I need to make up for all the times I've been an asshole to you."

"Hmm." She fits her core over the bulge, and my knees threaten to buckle. I manage to stay upright and try to school my expression into one of disapproval. She merely curves those beautiful lips, then pushes her breasts into me. Her nipples are little bullets of delight that threaten to tear into my flesh. A wound I'd accept gladly. "I prefer you be an asshole in bed. In fact..." She tilts her head. "Part of your appeal is that you are this mean, moody, glowering, grumpy alphahole."

I laugh. "Only, I've promised myself I'm going to change. You deserve to be treated like the queen you are. You deserve to have all of your wishes fulfilled. You deserve to have a life where you can get anything you want. I promise you, I'll ensure no one ever hurts you again, including me. I promise to protect and love and cherish you, and keep you in the style you deserve. I promise —"

"To fuck me?"

I smile wider. "Not today."

Her lips turn downward.

"Let me indulge you, baby. Let me show you how good I can make you feel."

"Since you're being so persuasive..." She hesitantly releases her grip on me, and I lower her to the floor. Then, I reach for her cardigan and slide it off her shoulders, followed by her T-shirt, then her pink sweatpants. When she stands naked in front of me, except for her bra and panties made of some frothy pink lace, I almost forget about my promise. Almost. This time, I'm not going to be greedy. This time, I'm focused on her to the exclusion of everything else. When I'm with her, my needs don't count. The only thing that counts is her.

I nod toward her lingerie, a question in my eyes.

She swallows, then nods. I reach behind her and unhook her bra, which slithers to the floor. Then, I loop my fingers into the waistband of her panties and glide them down her silky, thick thighs. She steps out of them. I glance up at the prettiest pink pussy ever. I know now how it tastes. Know how it feels to have her tight hole squeezing down on my cock. Know how she makes those little noises when she comes. I lean in until my nose brushes her cunt. I draw in a deep breath, and my head spins. My balls tighten. If I smell her one more time, I will snap and take her right here. I rise to my feet, then scoop her up in my arms and into the bath. She sighs, then leans back against the special bath pillow I placed earlier to protect her neck.

Bit by bit, her muscles relax. "This is nice."

"It's going to get nicer."

I head out and return a few minutes later with an ice bucket in which nestles a bottle of champagne. I place it next to the bath, then hand her Kindle over.

Her gaze widens. "Wow, you want me to read in the bath?"

"I believe it's the one thing all of you readers agree on is the most relaxing thing in the world?" I pop the cork on the champagne and pour it into the two flutes I managed to carry, as well.

She takes the glass I offer. "You think of everything."

"Just getting started, baby."

We clink glasses. She takes a sip and makes a noise of satisfaction which goes straight to my cock. Sweat breaks out on my forehead, and it's not only because it's warm in the space. I take in her lush curves, how her nipples peek out through the bubbles, the flare of her hips and the flash of her thigh as she bends her knee, and it sends a pulse of such agonizing lust through my body that I have to shake my head to clear it. When I look at her again, she's staring at me with a question in her eyes.

"You okay?"

I chuckle. "Never been better." I sink down to my knees next to the bathtub, then cup some of the water and pour it over her breasts. She shivers. I trace my finger down to her belly button, and she gasps. "I thought you weren't going to fuck me?"

"Doesn't mean I'm not going to make you feel good, baby. Part your legs for me."

She does.

"Now go back to reading." I jerk my chin toward her Kindle.

She blinks. "You're kidding, right?"

"I want you to have the full experience."

"What's that?"

"Having an orgasm and at the hands of your real-life husband, while you're reading your spicy Dramione inspired fiction."

She swallows, and her eyes glitter with unshed tears.

"What's wrong?"

She shakes her head. "Everything is so right."

"Good, now focus on your written word."

She slowly turns her gaze back to her screen. "Oh you cued the device to the smutty bits, you—" She gasps for I've slid my fingers between her thighs. And when I slip my fingers inside her, a whine slides from between her lips. Her fingers tremble, then clutch at the Kindle. I weave my fingers in and out of her, and a soft groan spills from her lips. I bring my other hand down to pinch her clit, then curve my fingers inside of her. She cries out and her back arches. The Kindle slips from her fingers and falls into the water.

69

Penny

"No, no, no, my Kindle." I try to sit upright, but he pinches my clit, and I detonate. The orgasm flows through me like the water slithering between my thighs. My toes curl. I throw my head back and into the pillow that cushions me from hurting myself. I come and come, dimly aware that he's continuing to work his fingers in and out of me. With his free hand he, pinches a nipple, and a second orgasm rips through me. He twists the nipple, and a sharp flash of pain zips down to meet the spot where he's thrusting his fingers in and out of me.

He adds a third finger and a fourth, and oh, god, that feels so good. I squeeze my thighs together, holding his hand captive. Then reach down and grab at his broad wrist. It only spurs him on, for his movements become more frantic. He brings his head down and bites down on my other nipple, and I cry out. "Oh, my god, I'm coming again!"

He continues to pinch my nipple, sucking on my other one while his wicked fingers press down on that secret spot between my inner walls, and my eyes roll back in my head. This time, the orgasm arrives with no warning. One minute, I'm panting; the next, I'm flying through the air. Black spots cloud my vision as I scream. I begin to slump, and he slides his arms under me and lifts me out of the bathtub.

"My Kindle," I manage to gasp out.

"It's waterproof," he murmurs.

Of course it is. I try to say it aloud, but my limbs are so heavy. The combination of the bath and the orgasms has relaxed me to the extent I can't keep my eyes open anymore. My last recollection is of him drying me gently, then slipping me between the covers. He turns me over on my side, and when he spoons me, any remaining tension in my muscles dissolves. I shut my eyes and allow sleep to claim me.

———

A soft sucking sensation between my legs penetrates my haze. I push up my pelvis, trying to chase the sensation. A warm chuckle fills the air, and I know why.

He's between my legs, with his head on my thigh. He blows on my center. I shudder. He licks up my pussy lips and slurps on my clit. I moan. I feel his lips curve against my core, then he slips his tongue inside me. My nipples ache, my scalp tightens, and every cell in my body awakens. That awareness, combined with the sleep that dulls my senses, is a contradiction that turns up my arousal. He traces the outline of my clit with his tongue, drags the stubble of his jaw over my sensitive core, and goosebumps pop on my skin. I reach down blindly, grab at his hair and tug. A growl vibrates over my center. Sensations crowd my skin. He nips at my clit; I cry out. He cups and massages my breasts while licking into my cunt and slurping on my pussy lips, and a rainfall of pleasure courses through my blood stream.

The climax whispers over my nerve-endings, sparking the happy parts of my brain. I can't stop the smile that tugs at my lips as the orgasm embraces me in its warmth.

I drift off to sleep again. I wake up two more times, and each time, he makes me come. The first time, I'm on my side and he's behind me with his cock inside me as he stretches me around his girth. He slides his hand between my legs and plays with my clit until the orgasm settles over me like a veil, seeps in my blood, and passes through me like a summer shower.

The last time is when I flutter my eyelids open to find him hovering over me. The first rays of dawn stream through the windows and bathe him in a blue-gold light that turn his green eyes into pools of need so powerful, my breath catches. My entire body is aflame with an answering desire. My bones have turned to jelly. I can only hold onto his probing gaze as he drives into me. I clamp down on his dick with my inner walls as he fills me. Open up my heart and let all of my feelings for him come to the fore as, with one final thrust, he hits that spot deep inside me that only he knows how to find. This time, the orgasm engulfs me and carries me away, over the edge, to a place I haven't visited before.

Now, I open my eyes to find I'm alone.

My throat hurts a little. Guess I must have cried out when I shattered that last time. I stretch and, inch by inch, my muscles relax. A pleasant heaviness lingers between my legs, but otherwise, I feel so refreshed.

I glance around, and literally, everything around me sparkles. Whoa, if this is what it means to be taken care of and given five O's in one night, then sleeping with the hard-muscled, chiseled body of my husband curled around me does to me, I'm not complaining. I throw off the covers, push my legs over the side of the bed and sit up, then spot the note on the nightstand.

Gone running with Adam. Tiny is with me.
 -your husband

PS: I've set up your phone so you can track my location anytime.

A happy sensation bubbles up my chest. I'm grinning again, and I'm not going to control it. My husband. My husband. My h.u.s.b.a.n.d. Gah! I loooove, love, love the sound of that. That's how he referred to himself last night, too. A blush creeps up my skin. He didn't made love to me, but he pleasured me. He paid attention to me and touched me and made me very, very happy. My brain cells are definitely wearing big grins today, and my pussy is purring. Definitely.

I glance around and miss him. He'll be back soon, but you know what? It's my turn to surprise him. I grab my phone, which he's placed next to the note and plugged in—that man, swoon! And my handbag is on the floor next to the nightstand. Whoa, he's so thoughtful. And I knew he would be. I knew he was the real thing. The one. My other half. And he's acknowledging it, too—by actions. The words can't be far off, right?

I snatch up my phone, and when I unlock it, I see the app. Oh wow, he pulled it up for me on the screen so I wouldn't miss it. My eyes begin to sting. This is such a huge step forward. The fact that he trusts me with this information? A warmth blooms in my chest. He's showing me, through his actions, how much faith he has in me. And that, combined with how attentive he was toward me last night—my breath catches. This...is everything I dreamed for but didn't dare to hope would happen.

What a change a month has made, though? This complex man is slowly sharing parts of himself with me, parts he hasn't shown anyone else, and damn, but it's real and emotional and heart-rending and... I love him, and I want to tell him so again. This time, I know he'll respond in kind. I jump out of bed, run to my room and pull on my as-yet never used running gear that appeared in my closet. I race out of the penthouse.

I confess, I slow to a brisk walk very soon—I'm not a runner. I'm not going to pretend I am. But I've always loved walking, and this city, with its parks and the many woods dotted around the boroughs, is perfect for it. The dot on the phone that pinpoints his location comes to a stop up ahead. Guess he's stopped by the bank of the river for a break? I hasten my steps. It takes me ten minutes of power walking to round a bend and spot him. He's sitting on a bench, one hand on Tiny's collar. Both man and dog are staring ahead. My heart leaps in my chest.

I break into a slow jog. Guess I lied. When there's incentive enough, I can run, apparently. My breath comes out in puffs and sweat beads my forehead as I close the distance to him. As I come up behind him, he turns and says something. I know he's speaking because I can see his lips move in profile. But there's no one next to him. Adam must have left. I guess he's speaking to Tiny. Only... Tiny is on the other side of him, lying down in the grass, also facing away from me. I'm too far away to make out what he's saying. As I near him, he faces forward again.

Tiny is the first to scent me. He jumps ups and barks. Knight turns and spots me. His features soften. He releases Tiny, and the big Dane lumbers toward me. He pauses, and when I reach him, brushes his head against me very gently. Both dog and man have learned how to interact with me without hurting me. For some reason, that makes my eyes sting. I greet Tiny, then continue past him toward Knight. When I come to a stop in front of him, he widens the space between his legs, and I step forward. He plants his big hands on my hips and looks up at me.

"Missed you," he murmurs.

"Me, too." I lower my head and brush my lips over his. He doesn't pull back. I whisper my nose up the side of his cheek, drawing in the scent of sea breeze tinged with the musky notes of his sweat. "You always smell so good," I murmur.

He chuckles. "I'm all sweated out."

"I like that." I press a kiss to his temple, then straighten. "Where's Adam?"

"He left."

"So, who were you talking to?"

He blinks. "What do you mean?"

"I saw you turn and say something as I was walking up."

He swallows. "You did?"

"But there was no one here; guess you were talking to Tiny."

He releases his hold on my hips, then slowly shakes his head. "It wasn't Tiny."

"Eh?" I tilt my head.

"I was talking to Adam."

70

Knight

She chuckles. "You told me he left."

"He left a long time ago."

"He did?"

I force myself to speak through the knives' edges that seem to line my throat. "He was never here."

She frowns. "I'm not sure I follow."

My heart begins to pump so hard, I can feel the blood slam against my temples, my wrists, my ankles. Every pulse point in my body speeds up. *This is it. You're going to tell her the truth. No more holding back. You're going to share with her the one thing you've never said aloud to yourself.* I curl my fingers into fists and take a deep breath. "Adam never made it back to London."

"Eh?" Her frown deepens. "So, he was taken captive with you... But he didn't return with you?"

I swallow around the lump in my throat. "He was hacked to pieces in front of me."

She gasps.

"My best friend. My brother in every way, the one who had my back in every one of my missions, was murdered in front of my eyes, and I couldn't do anything." I dig my fingernails into the palms of my hands and break through the skin.

"Oh, my god, that must have been so traumatic for you, Knight." She throws herself at me, straddles my lap, and wraps her arms and legs around me. Tiny walks over to plant his butt on the ground next to me. He whines, and goddamn, but the sound is as forlorn as I feel.

"He was the last to die. The bastards took out the other three in our team, one by one. Adam and I kept each other going. We promised each other that we'd make it out alive. But as the days wore on, he began to sink first. It got to him, I guess. They realized his weak spot was his wife and his daughter. They used it to break down his mind. I, of course, had no such blood ties. Not even Abby, as I knew she was safe with her husband. I was the emotionless one. The strong one. The unbreakable one. They kept at it, though. They tried everything, and when it was clear Adam was sinking, they used him against me. And when they realized our friendship was my weakness, they killed him. Slowly. His cries, his begging for mercy, his voice as he screamed for his life haunts me at night. Before he died, he made me promise I'd take care of his wife and child."

"Oh, Knight." Her tears bathe my throat as she tucks her face under my chin and weeps.

"I'm sorry I didn't tell you earlier, Penny. There were so many times when I wanted to, but I couldn't bring myself to say it aloud. I knew if I did, I'd never see Adam again. But I also knew I had to tell you. It was the only way to show you how much you mean to me. It was the only way to move on."

She sits up, and moisture clings to her cheeks. "Is that why you came out today, to bid him goodbye?"

"That's what I was doing as you walked up." I nod.

"That's why you left me a note with details of how to find you? You knew I'd come in search of you?"

"I hoped." I tuck a strand of hair behind her ear. "I didn't want any more secrets between us. I wanted to tell you everything."

"Even though it meant you'd lose your friend for good?"

The ball in my throat grows bigger, until it seems to fill my chest and twist my stomach and turn my guts into a seething mass of hurt. I nod, then swallow to dislodge it. "I need to move forward. You make me want to move forward. To move toward you. I cannot lose you again. If I did, there'd be no coming back from that. I have to let go of Adam because you are my life."

She cups my cheek. "So, all this time when you said you went running with Adam, you were—"

"Running alone, sometimes with Tiny. And Adam would join me. We'd talk, I'd reassure him I'd do everything possible to adopt his daughter and ensure his wife was cared for. Of course, he'd also give me advice about us—" I nod at the space between us.

"Wait, you told him about us?" she cries.

"Of course I did. There are no secrets between us, and now"—I place my palm over the one she has on my cheek—"there're none between us, either."

Another tear squeezes out from the corner of her eye. I bend and lick it up because it's too precious to be wasted. "Don't cry for me, baby. I knew I had to deal with what I was going through. I knew I had to face up to what happened to me. I was waiting for the right time. I was waiting for now."

"I'm sorry for your loss, Sir, truly."

"All I need is you." I kiss her forehead. "Your beauty, which gentles my soul. Your love, which fills all the emptiness inside me. Your sunny nature, your joie-de-vivre, which gives me life. Your heart, which speaks to me and tells me I'm yours."

"You're mine." She stares between my eyes. "Mine."

"Mine." I place a kiss over one eye, then the other, then on each cheek, and brush my lips over hers. "I love you, Penny. My Little Dove. My savior. My redeemer. You threw me a lifeline. And while it took me a long time to admit how much I needed it, I'm glad I latched onto it."

"I love you, Sir," she whispers against my mouth. "You were an asshole—still are an asshole—but you're my asshole."

"I do prefer alphahole," I drawl.

She chuckles. "Promise me you'll never change how you fuck me. Promise me you'll never hide anything from me again. Promise me you'll always love me."

I wrap my fingers around the nape of her neck and haul her close enough that our eyelashes entwine. "I love you. I adore you. I'm nothing without you."

Her breath hitches.

"I love you a million times over, and I'll never apologize for it."

"Oh." Her pupils dilate.

"I will die before I let anything happen to you."

Her lips tremble. "Promise me you'll live."

"I live to see the light in your eyes, to hear you sass me and defy me, and to drive me a little crazy with your rambling thoughts, and your chatter, and your laughter. I live... for you, only you."

She half laughs. "And I thought you didn't have a romantic bone in your body."

"Including this one?" I lower my hands to her hips and fit her snugly over that ever-excited part of me that tends to stand up whenever she is around.

"Technically, that's a muscle."

"Technically, you could call that my third leg, but whatever."

She makes a gagging sound. "That was terrible."

"Some parts of me are never going to change, but I hope they won't deter you from what I'm going to ask you for next."

She swallows, and the pulse at the base of her neck speeds up. "What is it?"

I slide my hand into my pocket, pull out her wedding ring, then take her left hand in mine. "Will you be my wife, to love and love and love and love and love some more? To worship with my soul. To cherish with every cell in my body. So not even death may part us."

"You took some liberties with those vows, huh?"

"I did." I try to smile, but my lips refuse to cooperate. My heart drops down to my feet, then bounces up and into my throat. I hold her gaze. "What do you say, Little Dove? Will you give me another chance?"

71

Penny's bucket list

- ~~Type at 250 words a minute (done!)~~
- ~~Have 5 O's in the course of 1 night (I'll settle for 1 tbh) => Almost made this one last night when he gave 4 orgasms. OMG 4 freakin' orgasms!~~
- ~~Learn to cook a gourmet meal. => I wasn't very good at it, but it's the spirit that counts, right?~~
- ~~Act in a movie or a play — I'll take a street act => It didn't go down that well. :(~~
- See the London Ice Kings play a game.
- Swim with dolphins.
- See the Northern Lights.
- Climb Uluru in Australia.
- Eat a chocolate croissant in a sidewalk café in Paris.
- ~~Be dominated. (Uh, maybe this should go up to the top?)~~
- ~~Find a man who cares for my mother as much as I do.~~
- ~~Be proposed to by the man I love.~~
- Explore anal. (I'm chicken so this is right at the bottom — pun intended. Hahahaha!)

72

Penny

Abby strides up the corridor; her footsteps echo around the almost empty building.

It's seven p.m. and most people have gone home. But not me. I have a demanding boss who's obsessed with taking his company to new heights. Especially now that his father has handed over the full charge of the company to him. If you thought that'd slow down Knight, you thought wrong. Now that he has full control of the destiny of this corporation, he's in a hurry to shape it into the vision he has. One he's shared with the entire company at the "town hall" he held this morning.

The employees were energized after the meeting — it might also have to do with the fact that he announced a twenty percent increase in salary, across the board. And that he's setting up a café on one of the lower floors where the food will always be free. That, combined with the childcare and the pet-sitting facilities, is sure to make his company one of the most sought-after to work for in this part of the world. It's resulted in tons of positive media coverage that Abby shared with me.

So, I'm taken aback when she stomps over and slaps her palm on the desk in front of me. "You could have told me."

"What are you talking about?"

"Knight told me. And I'm glad my brother feels he's close enough to share things with me, but you're one of my closest friends. I'd have preferred to hear it from you."

Did he tell her about Adam? That isn't mine to share anyway. Also, considering how things have shaped up between us since, it's not something I'm comfortable talking about with anyone else.

I lean back in my chair. "I really don't know what you're referring to."

She walks around my table, then leans a hip against it. "Don't pretend you don't know."

"Know what?"

"That you and Knight are back together. That he confessed his feelings for you. That he's woken up to what the rest of us could see all along." She rolls her eyes. "And thank god for that."

"Oh, that?" The tension leaves my shoulders.

"That?" She narrows her gaze on me. "Isn't that enough? Is there something else you were thinking of?"

"What? No. Of course not." I look away, then back at her. "I guess I'm still getting my head around everything. It happened so quickly, you know? One second, I was upset with him; the next..." I shake my head. "The next, he bowled me over."

"So, he groveled, huh?" she asks, a knowing look on her face.

"Is that what Cade did? Is that what brought the two of you back together?'

Her eyes gleam. "Let's just say, he was very persuasive. He literally went down on his knees to beg for forgiveness, and he did it so well, I had to return the favor."

I burst out laughing. "OMG, I can't believe you said that."

"Yeah, it's something I could have done without hearing," a very familiar voice says in a droll tone.

"Knight." Abby straightens, then walks over and hugs him. "Why are you making your wife work so late in the office?"

"Do you think I can make her do anything she doesn't want to do?" He shoots me a look from under hooded eyelids. "Except, in bed, of course."

"Eww, I could have done without hearing that."

"Payback's a bitch, little sis." He smirks.

Abby steps back and looks between the two of us. "I came by to say

I'm so happy my brother and my friend are together, this time for real. And I'm looking forward to seeing the two of you this weekend at my place."

Knight pales. "You're organizing another party?"

She smirks. "I am, and you're coming."

He cracks his neck. "I can't say no to you, Abby. But I'm not comfortable hanging out with so many people all at once."

"They're our friends." She arches an eyebrow at him. "They're *your* friends. And after you skipped out on your wedding luncheon..."

"And it's not like I don't want to see them —"

She stares at him.

"Okay, so maybe I'd prefer to spend that time with my wife?" He looks at me with a plea in his eyes. A-n-d that's how much this guy has changed. He doesn't hesitate to show his real emotions to me and ask me for help when needed. Which is so completely different to the way he was a week ago. Telling me about Adam seems to have lifted a weight off his shoulders. That was a week ago, and since then, he seems to open up more to me every day.

I moved back in with him, and we're taking the time to get to know each other all over again. We travel to work every day with Tiny, and he cooks dinner every night and breakfast in the mornings. With every passing day, he relaxes more, talks more with me, smiles more... It feels so natural, so normal to be with him. And the fact that we work together only enhances our relationship. Our understanding of each other deepens with every passing moment. And while he still hasn't made love to me, he holds me close every night, and I wake up with him wrapped around me every morning. I've never been this happy and content, and so much in love.

She looks between the two of us, and her expression softens. "Aww look at the two of you. Aren't you cute?"

Her brother seems taken aback. "I'm not sure that adjective applies to me."

"You should see the look on your face as you stare all lovestruck at your wife." She pats his shoulder. "It's okay, Knight. Happens to the best of us. I can't tell you how happy I am to see you not fight the connection between the two of you."

He winces. "Am I that easy to read?"

"I'm your sister. Of course, I could tell what was happening. As for the chemistry between you two. I noticed it before either of you."

"Really?" I turn on her. "You mean, that first time when Knight came to tell you he was leaving on his mission, you realized there was something between us right then?"

"I know Knight did a double-take when he saw you. And I know your gaze kept tracking back to him. I wanted to introduce the two of you then, but I was preoccupied."

"You were so upset that I was leaving, and with good reason," Knight murmurs.

"Call it a sister's intuition. I was so scared, and I didn't know why. I was convinced I was never going to see you again. Not that I could tell you that. I didn't want to upset you. Not before you left on such an important assignment, too." She bites the inside of her cheek. "Knowing now what you do, would you have gone?"

"Absolutely. Knowing what I do now, I'd have made doubly sure that nothing stopped me. I was there for Adam, and for the rest of my team. And while I'll never completely get over what happened, now I know it wasn't my fault. I know I may never get over the trauma, but it will fade with time."

She swallows, then turns to me. "I have you to thank that he's going to therapy, huh?"

I blink, then nod at Knight. "It was all him. He's the one who told me he was ready. I helped him find someone who I thought would be well-suited to his needs. But the initiative to start the sessions and to do the work, that's all Knight."

It's only been a few days, but it's amazing how the will to move on from the trauma is accelerating the process of healing.

"I couldn't have done it without Penny." His lips curve, and the look in his eyes is so possessive and filled with so much adoration, I'm sure my heart literally stops, then starts again.

"The incentive to be the kind of man she deserves spurs me on to do better every day," he says in a low voice.

"You guys... My work here is truly done." She sniffles.

Knight tears his gaze from mine. "Hey sis, didn't mean to make you cry."

Abby fans herself. "These are happy tears, you goofball." She leans up on tiptoe to kiss his cheek. "You make me so proud to be your sister, Knight. You're the best big brother anyone could have asked for. Also"—she inclines her head in my direction—"if you hurt her again, you'll have me to contend with."

"I'd kill myself before I do that," Knight murmurs. And the tone of his voice indicates he's not kidding.

"Please, can we not say the K-word again?" I rise up from my chair and walk over to him.

Knight instantly wraps his arm about me and pulls me into his side. "Whatever you say, baby."

Abby chuckles. "On that note, I'm off. Don't forget—tomorrow, six p.m." She levels a final glance at Knight before she saunters off.

"Is it me, or is my sister's confidence in herself growing?" he murmurs.

"The love of a good man." I slide my palm over the soft material of his suit jacket then, because I can and because he's there, I bury my nose in his shirt and sniff. His sea-breeze and pepper scent fills my senses, and I melt into him.

"I don't deserve you, baby, but I've never been as at peace as in the last few days. Seeing you first thing in the morning and the last thing before I go to bed... Not to mention, whenever I start missing you—which is always, by the way—I only have to walk out of the office, and there you are. It makes me feel like the luckiest man in the world." His phone buzzes. He ignores it and holds out his palm. Without question, I place my hand in his. He brings my fingers to his mouth and kisses them. Then, he notches his knuckles under my chin and peers into my eyes. "It's not that I can't live without you."

"No?" I frown.

His lips twitch. "It's that I don't want to try. I love you, Penny." He lowers his head and places his lips over mine. "More than myself. My life is worth living because I found you. I know what love is because of you, baby." He presses his mouth to mine, and his kiss is so sweet, so tender, so everything, I melt into him.

I wrap my arms about his shoulders and tug on the short hair at the nape of his neck. I press myself to him, open my lips, but when the phone buzzes again, I stop. "I think you need to get that. Whoever it is has been trying to reach you for a while."

He presses his forehead into mine and draws in a breath. Then, without releasing me, he pulls out his phone and presses it to his ear. "Hello?" His arm around me tightens. "We're on our way."

73

Knight

"It's going to be okay." She places her hand over my joined ones.

We're at the social services' office, waiting to meet Adam's daughter Bianca. She's been staying with a foster family the last few months. All of my money hadn't helped me fast-track the process of adopting her. I suppose that says something positive about the foster care system — they won't allow just anyone to adopt, regardless of how much money they have. On the other hand, it can't be healthy to delay the placement of children with their adoptive families.

In the end, Bobbie's passing away accelerated the process. She went to sleep and never woke up. The nurse at the hospital told us she passed peacefully. The call I received was from the hospital, and when we arrived, they told us the news. They mentioned she'd had lucid moments over the past few months, when she was aware I wasn't her husband, but her husband's friend. Unfortunately, she flitted in and out of reality. Luckily, one of those lucid moments also resulted in a letter to child protective services specifying her wishes that Penny and I be permitted to adopt her child.

She said she couldn't think of a better couple to step in for her and Adam.

She also said she hadn't wanted her daughter to see her in the state she was in, so she'd made the decision not to see Bianca, even though it broke her heart. This was right for her daughter. She was leaving the stage wide open for Penny and me to walk into Bianca's life as her parents.

The letter gutted me. I'm not ashamed to say I found a tear running down my cheek. Thankfully, my wife was there to console me. We held onto each other, and I allowed myself to absorb comfort from her. After all, that's what marriage is about, right?

I'm not hiding my weaknesses from her anymore. I now realize there's courage in sharing. There's bravery in baring my deepest fears. Leaning on her doesn't take away from my manhood; it adds to my grit, my guts, and my depth. And allowing her to comfort me, to recognize the man I truly am, is the most satisfying sensation. Almost as fulfilling as making her happy in every way. As fulfilling as allowing her to hold my hand as we wait for the three-year-old who's going to change our lives to join us.

We'd arranged for a small private burial for Bobbie and came to the social services office from the cemetery. I threw all of my power and influence at the system, and also took Sinclair's help in moving the paperwork along. I didn't want my daughter to be spending another night away from her family.

I hear footsteps approaching, then the voice of a little girl exclaiming, " Are we going to meet my… new parents? Do you think they'll be okay for me to take my little Kitty along?" She walks in with her foster caregiver, a middle-aged woman with a kind face.

When Bianca spots us, her blue eyes grow round. She has dark blonde hair which has been braided on either side of her cherubic face. She's wearing a pink dress that falls above her knees, and on her feet, she has sparkly, pink ballet pumps. She's holding a soft toy in the shape of a kitten in her hand. Her footsteps slow and she trails back.

Her foster mom turns to her and says, "It's okay, honey; they were friends of your mummy and daddy. They're going to take care of you now. Do you remember what we talked about?"

She nods slowly, as she takes in both of us.

Her foster mum comes to a stop in front of us. "Do you want to say hello to your new mommy and daddy?"

Her lower lip trembles. She looks from Penny to me, then back to Penny, and her big eyes grow teary. "They don't look like mommy and daddy."

"Oh, sweetheart, don't cry." Penny drops to her knees and holds out her arms. "Your mommy and daddy asked us to take care of you because they can't be here anymore. We love you so much, darling."

She sniffs, then takes a step forward, another. She releases her hold on her foster mother, and instead, grips the kitten with both of her hands. She walks toward Penny. "Are you my *new* mommy?"

"I am, baby."

"And you won't leave?"

Penny's chin quivers. "No, we won't leave you. We'll be here for you forever and ever and —"

She throws herself at Penny, who hugs her close.

Penny buries her face in Bianca's hair. "I have you, baby, I have you."

I look down at the two shiny blonde heads, so similar to each other, and my heart expands in my chest. I blink back tears as a warmth fills me, and a tingling shivers up my spine. It's a sensation that tells me I have everything I want. Everything I didn't realize I was looking for, and it's been given to me. This time, I'm not going to screw it up. This time, I'm going to ensure I hold onto it and be grateful for it every day that I'm alive. This is why I came back. This is why my life was spared. So I can do my best, every single moment, for the rest of my life, to become the kind of human who makes them proud. I squat down until I'm on eye level with both of them.

"I'm Knight. I was your daddy's best friend."

Bianca steps back, one hand now gripping Penny's. "You're my new daddy?" She looks at me with those big blue eyes, and for the second time in my life, I'm a goner.

"I am, honey. And I'll make sure you're always cared for. I'm here to take care of you from now on."

She slowly closes the distance to me, then reaches up and touches the scar on my cheek, the one I almost forgot about. "Did it hurt?"

I nod. "But I'm okay now, thanks to your mama."

Penny smiles at me. A real smile. No more fake smiles for my woman. I plan to give her every reason to mean each one of them. Bianca looks at me from under her eyelashes, a shy expression on her features. "My kitty also has a scar." She holds up her ragged, soft toy and sure enough, there's a tear on her face that was stitched up.

"Do you want me to kiss it better for her?" I ask.

When she nods, I lower my head and carefully, and with utmost seriousness, press a kiss to the kitten's forehead.

She brings her kitten to her ear and pretends to listen to it. "Kitty says she's feeling much better now."

My lips quirk. "What else does she say?"

"That I'm going to be very happy."

"Is she asleep?"

"Out like a light." Penny sinks down onto the sofa next to me. "She couldn't stop telling me how much she loves her room and her new toys. I'm sure she'd have loved Tiny, too, if he were here."

"It would have hurt her when he moved back with Isla and Liam. We did the right thing in asking Rick to dog sit him until they return."

"That's true." She cuddles into my side. "That little girl has seen enough loss in her life. She needs stability and routine."

It's why we moved out of the penthouse and into a townhouse before bringing Bianca home. No more glass and chrome, this place is wooden floors, high ceilings, and sunshine pouring in through the big bay windows. And there are no hidden rooms. I don't need one. I'd be lying if I said I don't wake up with nightmares about my ordeal, but their frequency has decreased. The sessions with the psychologist have helped, and curling my body around my wife's in our bed at night ensures I sleep well most nights. She supplies the comfort I seek. As for the control I'm searching for? Isn't it obvious? I get it when I dominate her. This compulsion to keep her safe and secure, and above all else, to care for her feeds my need to stay in charge.

From the moment Penny entered my life, it began changing for the better. It's thanks to her, and now, Bianca that this place feels like home. We chose a house with a big back garden with a swing-set and a slide so Bianca can keep herself entertained. And the bonus? It's next-door to Cade and Abby's. And it's within walking distance of the Seven—who've all purchased homes in the neighborhood—and Michael's, as well as JJ's—on Primrose Hill. When Abby told us this place was going on the market, it was a no-brainer.

She lifts my arm, then nestles in under it. "It's nice to be close to everyone. And with so many of us here, it feels like we own all of the Hill."

I laugh. "Today Primrose Hill; tomorrow the world," I laugh, do my best impression of a comic book villain.

Penny joins my laughter. "That reminds me, has Rick accepted his role as the Captain of the London Ice Kings?"

"Not yet, but he's considering it."

"I have to say, it came as a surprise. I didn't realize he played ice hockey professionally."

I nod, "For the NHL, no less. But he had a falling out with his manager. Lost his temper, beat up the guy, and was expelled from the team."

"Rick?" She frowns. "You mean the same Rick who barely speaks, and went on to join the Royal Marines?"

"Guess he grew up. He was drafted in at seventeen, amongst the youngest ever, played until he was twenty-one, until this unfortunate incident, then quit, returned to the UK, joined the Marines, and went on to serve with me. He's older than me and was a captain when I joined. "

"Why did he leave?"

I frown. "That's not my story to tell."

"Was he injured?"

I shake my head. "Can't reveal that. What I can say is that he was awarded the Victorian Cross, the highest decoration in the British honor system, and then he retired."

"Wow, how old is he?"

"Not too old to lead the team, and with Finn on there, as well, he has all the support he needs."

"Not to mention Gio."

I nod. "Your friend is perfect for the role of Marketing and PR Director for the London Ice Kings."

"Hmm." She scowls up at me. "You realize, she and Rick don't get along, right?"

74

Penny

"All right, everyone, settle down." Abby taps a fork against her champagne flute. The people in the room gradually quiet. I glance around and take in JJ with his now-fiancée Lena—yep, he proposed—talking with that other silver fox, Philippe, in a corner of the room. Their heads are bent, and JJ whispers something to Philippe, who barks out a laugh.

Next to them, Sinclair sits with Summer. There's a bassinet next to them in which their daughter snoozes. Sinclair pulls Summer into his side, and she cuddles in. On the opposite side of the room, Michael and his wife Karma are absorbed in each other. They've gotten a babysitter for the evening and are, undoubtedly, enjoying their free time. That is, until Karma's next one comes along. At three months, she's not yet showing, but there's no doubt she's pregnant. She's glowing; also, Michael has his big palm cupped over her belly—a dead giveaway—and the other around her shoulder. He kisses her forehead before turning his attention to Abby.

Mira is working tonight and couldn't be here, much to her disappointment. The celebrity factor is covered by #Declene. Solene is curled into Declan, while he's sprawled out on an armchair not far from Summer. The two were shooting in New Zealand but took their first break in weeks and decided to come to London to catch up with their friends before they whizz off to one of the islands in the Mediterranean for a much-deserved break.

Edward, the only one of the Seven who doesn't live in London but who happens to be visiting, stands next to the bar. He has a drink in his hand. Rick stands next to him. Tiny pants at his feet, his gaze fixed firmly on the bottle of champagne Cade holds in his hand. Cade, for his part, has his gaze locked on Tiny. There's a warning look on his face. Tiny whines, and Cade shakes his head slowly. Tiny lets out a big sigh, then sags to the floor and cradles his big head on his paws. He hasn't taken his eyes off the bottle of champagne, though. Yep, the mutt has a taste for champagne. He's been known to pour an entire bottle down his gullet. Or so Isla warned me in one of her calls. No wonder, Cade has one arm around Abby and the other is fixed to the bottle of bubbles. He's not giving it up easily.

"Thank you everyone for being here today. I can't tell you how wonderful it is to see all our friends and family in one room. I know we are all busy people, but I wanted to properly welcome the newest addition to our family."

"Is she talking about me?" Bianca whispers from where she's seated on the sofa between me and my husband. Her dress is pink, of course, a twin of the one I'm wearing. She transformed into a mini-me practically overnight. In fact, she's taken to us and us to her so quickly, I almost can't remember how it was without her.

"Of course she is, Princess." Knight takes her hand in his and brings it up to his mouth, kissing her knuckles.

Bianca giggles. "I'm not a real Princess, Papa."

"You're the princess of my heart." He flashes her an adoring smile. Knight's entranced by Bianca, and she has a case of hero-worship. Not that I blame her. He has that effect on all females.

"We are so proud and grateful to have you with us, Bianca. Welcome home." Abby raises her flute.

That's when Giorgina breezes in on her six-inch high heels. "Hello everyone, sorry I'm late." She takes in the scene, and in a very dramatic gesture, pops out her hip and plants her hand on it. "Hope I'm not interrupting…" She arches a delicate eyebrow.

Across from me, Rick stiffens. He glares at the newcomer with something like longing, before quickly disguising the expression.

If Giorgina notices him, she doesn't pay him any heed. She spots the bottle of champagne Cade holds and exclaims. "Aha, so you're the guardian of the bubbles?"

She struts toward him, snatches up a flute from the bar, and taking the bottle from him, examines the label. "Dom Pérignon, excellent. I think I might have found my tribe after all. I—"

Tiny leaps to his feet. She blinks and watches him, mouth open as he prances over to her. For a big dog, he can be very graceful and purposeful when he has his sights set on something. Before she can move, he rears up. Gio screams, and her eyes bug out. Tiny snatches the bottle of champagne from her hands, tips the bottle down his gullet, and plants his paws on the floor next to Gio in one smooth move. He releases the empty champagne bottle, which rolls away, then brushes past her. The momentum makes her stagger back. Her heels catch in a crack in the wooden floor, and she begins to tip over. She yells out, throws up her hands, and her handbag goes flying. Before she can hit the floor, Rick is there. He catches her around the waist.

For a second, Gio is plastered from back to hip to thigh against Rick's front. Her gaze widens, and color flushes her cheek. She pulls free from Rick, then spins around and raises her hand. "How dare you touch me, you oaf."

To find out what happens next read Gio and Rick's story in The Ice Kiss

Read an excerpt:

Giorgina

"On your knees. Mouth open. Tongue out." He wraps his fingers around my throat and leans in until his breath raises the fine hair on my forehead. "You're such a good girl. You take everything I give you so beautifully."

My breath hitches. My belly flutters. When Shane East says 'good girl' I'd do anything he wants, even if it causes pain. Especially, if it causes pain. He can train my holes anytime.

A-n-d… Don't you dare tell my friends I'm listening to *The Billionaire's Fake Wife* by L. Steele, instead of *How to Win Friends and Influence People* by Dale Carnegie. After all, as everyone knows, I only listen to motivational speakers and only read self-help books. And… I have my life organized by the minute—if not, the second, which I would if I could, and I have tried, but it's counterproductive. Managing by the half-hour works a lot better. It allows me to deliver on my tasks, so everything is perfect. Just how I like it. Which reminds me, I have precisely thirty minutes to get this shindig over with. The only reason I'm here is because my friend Abby invited me and I couldn't say no. I flounce into the room, hitch my Hermès bag over my shoulder and declare, "Hello, everyone, sorry I'm late."

Silence descends, broken only by Shane's baritone in my ear which growls, "Come for me now. Right now." Oopsie, best to shut off my audiobook for the time I'm here. I slide out my phone from my handbag, stop the audio, then pull out my earphones and drop them into my bag.

When I look up, my gaze arrows in on the man hulking by the bar. He's six-foot-six—no kidding—the tallest, hunkiest man I've ever met— outside of my spicy novels, though I'll never tell him that—with shoulders that fill my vision. And that chest of his, clad in a black T-shirt which is threadbare and outlines every single ridge and divot of his pecs, and that throat—OMG, that gorgeous, sinewed throat, with veins that pop in relief for he's pissed.

Of course, he's pissed, as evidenced by the set of his jaw, the nerve that flexes at his temple, and those dark brows drawn down over his eyes. Blue eyes. Icy and frosted, and downright glacial, they chill me to the bone even as the sight of his luscious, pouty, lower lip makes me want to dig my teeth in and draw blood. *Argh.* These conflicting emotions where Rick Mitchell is concerned always give me whiplash. *How can you hate a man and yet, be attracted to him so much?* His gaze intensifies.

He raises a bottle of water to his mouth. His biceps bulge, the veins on his forearms stand out in relief, and my mouth waters. *Ugh, why does he have the most deliciously sculpted arms?* And that narrow waist, lean hips, and thick, powerful thighs that contract as he walks, and between them, that bulge —which indicates he's packing something mean and big and— He widens his stance, and I jerk my head up. His lips curl, and oh, my word, that smirk. It's hot and mean and so very annoying.

So, he caught the staring. Big deal. It's a free country, last time I checked. So what, if this city is dull and grey and the rain gets on my nerves? I'm not one to complain. I'm going to work with the cards I've been dealt. My life has been nothing if not preparation for me to meet challenges head on. It doesn't stop heat from flushing my cheeks, though.

His grin widens, then he wraps those succulent lips around the bottle of water and guzzles from it.

I will not stare at his throat as he swallows. Will not allow myself to salivate at the thought of licking my way up that hard column and tasting the salt on his skin. Will not.

He raises the glass in my direction. Caught again. Twice in two minutes. What a disaster. I toss my hair over my shoulder, pop out my hip—clad in the latest Max-Mara creation, by the way and tip up my chin, then force myself to tear my gaze away from that gorgeous, irritating hunk of a man.

"Hope I'm not interrupting." I arch an eyebrow at the room in general and spot the bottle of champagne Cade—my friend, Abby's husband—holds in his hand.

"Aha, so you're the guardian of the bubbles?" I say brightly. *Guardian of the bubbles? What. The. Hell? Clearly, I've been spending too much time in the company of Hollywood personalities. Couldn't come up with anything better? Also, to hell with that. I'm funny and charming, and outgoing. Stay positive. Fake it till you make it, remember?* I strut toward him, procure a flute from the bar, and taking the bottle from him, check out the label. "Dom Pérignon, excellent. I think I might have found my tribe after all, I—"

Suddenly, a pony—no, it's a dog, a massive mutt, a Great Dane, by the looks of it—leaps up to his feet. He must have been crouched down by Rick's legs, and I didn't notice him because, of course, I was focused on the man to the exclusion of everything else.

Seriously though, am I that taken in by this man that I missed this... this... Enormous beast who now prowls toward me? There's a glint in his eyes, as he takes me in—like I'm his next meal. The hair on the nape of my neck rises. His jowls shiver. He opens his jaws, and drool drips from them. His teeth are so sharp. I swallow. He's moving toward me with such intent. Is he going to bite off my head, or maybe, a hand? Doesn't anybody else see this? Why isn't anyone stopping him?

My pulse rate spikes. Ohmigod. I should cry out for help. I should. I open my mouth, but nothing comes out. He draws closer, and every cell in my body seems to freeze. He gathers speed as he nears, then rears up, and believe me when I say, he's taller than I am.

I whimper. That's right—brave, confident, takes-no-prisoners Giorgina whimpers. My heart fights to escape my ribcage. The blood pounds at my temples. He snatches the bottle of champagne from my hands, upturns it so the contents empty down his gullet, then plants his paws back on the floor, drops the bottle, and pushes past me to the sound of several voices yelling in unison, "Tiny!"

Seriously? Tiny?

I stumble back. The six-inch high heels of my Louboutin's catch in a crack in the wooden floors. *Oh, no, no, no.* I begin to tip over.

I throw up my hands to try to find my balance, and my handbag goes flying. *This is it. Death by Great Dane. Ugh! That's not the kind of headline I want to make.* I squeeze my eyes shut and brace for impact, only something strong and hard bands around my waist. The breath whooshes out of me. The next second, I'm hauled to an upright position. I know who it is before I sense the heat that leaps off of him and lassoes around me. I know who it is before that scent of fresh snow and cut grass teases my nostrils. I know who it is because I'm plastered from back to hip to thigh against his front and his sizable thickness stabs into the curve of my butt. I know who it is because no one but he could sport such arousal so big, it feels like a hockey stick has slapped me in the rear.

Jesus. Of course, my brain goes to hockey sticks. He's likely to be the new Captain of the London Ice Kings, so he'd better know how to wield a hockey stick. I mean, not the one between his legs — nope, not going there in my head. Obviously, I'm sure he plays with that one, too — the one between his legs, I mean. And ohmigod, the image of his big, fat fingers squeezing his monster cock is something I'm not going to forget in a hurry.

His grasp around my waist tightens, and he pulls me so close, said hockey stick — is it curved at the end, too? — throbs against me. It seems to grow longer, thicker, larger... *Gah, that's your imagination. It has to be.* No one has such a big dick, except maybe, porn stars. And Rick's not a porn star. He's a freakin' ex-NHL player, who did a stint with the Royal Marines, did some moonlighting as a bodyguard, and is now back to playing hockey. That's all he is. He's human.

He may look like a god, avenging angel, and devil, all rolled into one, but he's a man. A man who's larger-than-life, and built, given no inch of him gives while I'm plastered to him, including his cock, which is now happily nestled in the cleavage between my butt-cheeks, and... *OMG!* My flush deepens, and spreads down my chest to my extremities. A thousand little fires spark across my skin.

Someone clears their throat, and I glance around the room to find every single gaze is on me. *Oh no, no, no. Nice way to make an impression on your new employer.*

"Let me go." I pull free from Rick who, thankfully, releases me, then spin around. "How dare you touch me, you oaf?"

Rick

She raises her hand, and I sense she's going to slap me, but I don't stop her. Instead, I welcome her palm connecting with my cheek. I welcome the sting of pain that zips out from her touch and down my spine. I welcome the throb in my balls, the twitch of my dick which has only grown harder thanks to the contact of her skin with mine. I welcome the flash of anger in her golden eyes, the red stain of her cheeks, the pulse that beats at the base of her throat. When I don't react, her gaze grows stricken, she firms her lips.

"I don't need your help," she hisses at me.

"What you *think* you need and what you *need* are two entirely different things," I drawl.

She huffs. "I'm not sorry I slapped you." Her gaze flicks to my cheek where her palm-print is, no doubt, in evidence.

"I'm not sorry I caught you," I murmur.

"Good."

"Good," I agree.

She tips up her chin, then turns to leave, and promptly stumbles on the same gap in the wooden floor. If I were a bastard, I'd let her fall. If I were the asshole she thinks I am, I'd allow her to hit the floor on her knees and hurt herself, but the thought does funny things to my guts, so I catch her around her waist again—because that's going to piss her off to no end—and right her. Then, before she can turn and tell me off, I step back.

Looks like you can't do without me, after all." I brush past her and snap my fingers at Tiny who, having emptied the champagne bottle down his gullet—don't ask—jumps to his feet and prances over to me to hand it over.

I stare into the bottle—nope, not a drop left in it—then back at Tiny, who pants up at me with a happy smile on his face. The mutt smiles, I kid you not. He has what must be the biggest and most satisfied smile in the doggy world on his face. And I'm stuck with him for the foreseeable future. "Can't take you anywhere, eh?" I murmur.

In response, Tiny thumps his tail on the floor, and the ground seems to shake a little. Or maybe, that's from the gnashing of teeth I can hear coming from Giorgina's direction. I ignore Little Miss Spoiled Brat and walk toward my friend and new boss, Knight Warren. He recently married Penny, and they've adopted his friend Adam's little girl Bianca. She jumps to her feet and races toward us. "He's sooo cute." She throws her arm around Tiny's neck. The Great Dane stays still and lets her fuss over him.

"He also polished off a $4000 bottle of champagne," I say in a low voice to her parents.

Knight chuckles. "Doesn't seem to affect him at all. Besides, Cade can afford it."

As if hearing his name, Cade Kingston, captain of the English cricket team prowls over to us. "What are you ladies whispering about?"

"That you're going to have competition for rabid fans, now that the London Ice Kings has him as the captain." Knight nods in my direction.

Cade does a double-take. "You're accepting the offer?"

"I haven't said yes, yet," I admit.

Knight's wife Penny rises to her feet. "You going to make that a habit?" She jerks her chin toward the palm-print I wear on my cheek.

I shrug. "It was worth it."

She frowns. "Gio has a good heart. I know she can come across as haughty and disdainful, but she's a loyal friend."

"So am I."

"Go easy on her, okay?" She reaches up and pats my cheek.

"I don't plan on having anything to do with her," I murmur.

"Hmm." She turns to Knight. A look passes between them, then she bends and kisses his cheek. "Time I get Bianca to say goodbye to everyone."

"I'll be right behind you, baby." He wraps his hand about the nape of her neck and pulls her back for a thorough kiss. By the time Penny straightens, she's flushed and blushing, and her eyes are sparkling. With a giggle, she bends and puts her arm about Bianca's shoulder. "Come along, honey. Let's say our goodbyes to everyone."

"Do I have to say goodbye to Tiny?" The little girl pouts.

"You'll see him again soon," I point out.

"Promise?" She holds out her palm.

"Promise." I place my much larger palm over hers and squeeze gently. She seems satisfied. Enough to pull her hand from mine, and with a last hug for Tiny, she allows her ma to lead her toward the others.

Knight turns to me. "Right, then, I do need to go as well. But first, I need to point out that hockey is your first love. Not a day went by in the army when you didn't follow news of the sport from around the world. You're the only man I know who tunes in regardless of who is playing."

"So?" I raise a shoulder.

"So, I don't know of anyone else who lives and breathes the game as much as you. You're perfect to take the team into the League."

The League is the European equivalent of the Cup in the U.S. Competition is fierce. The very fact that he thinks I... The man who hasn't competed professionally in well over five years, stands a chance of playing, let alone leading the team to victory, shows how deluded this man is.

I open my mouth to tell him so, but he shakes his head. "You know that's the only reason you were on the military's ice hockey team."

"It was the best way of working out." I raise a shoulder.

"Bull-fucking-shit," Knight and Cade say at the same time.

I chuckle. "Fine, so it's also because I did like playing on ice. That doesn't mean I want to compete on a professional level again."

Knight scans my features. "Think about it. Think what you really want, mofo. After all these years of doing what is expected of you, do the thing you really want to do in here—" He slaps his palm into the space over my heart, and I hesitate.

"Where is this coming from?" I crack my neck. "And how do you know I'm not doing what I want right now?"

"You mean babysitting Hollywood stars—"

"It's called being a bodyguard," I snap.

"And not that I don't love our resident silver screen icons,"—He nods to where Solene, the biggest popstar since Taylor Swift and her fiancé Declan, the leading superstar of Hollywood, are currently sucking face in an armchair across the room—"but you have to admit, it doesn't hold a candle up to the feeling you get when you mow down the opposition and you swing the puck home."

Images of the last time I was on ice at the final of the Cup, as the centerman of my team, controlling the pace of the game, impacting the offensive and defensive positions, helping the players on my team, winning face-offs, leading breakouts, throwing that final puck towards the goal... Then, walking off the ice and never looking back. What happened that day is something I don't like to revisit. It's the reason I've avoided the ice since. Am I ready to go back and face the ghost of what happened that day? I'm not sure, to be honest.

I open my mouth, but Knight claps my shoulder. "Don't answer yet. Also, there's one more thing you should know—" He breaks off to look over my shoulder. "Giorgina, you're just in time."

Giorgina

"In time for what?" I strut over to them—because that's the only way I can walk in these heels, which seemed to be a good idea when I spent half a month's salary on them, but which I'm now wondering was a good idea, but I have them on, so might as well as make the most of them, right? "What are you gentleman conferring about?"

Cade flashes me a smile. "Heard so much about you from Abby, but we've never been formally introduced. I'm Cade."

"Giorgina." I hold out my hand. "You can call me—"

"—Giorgina," Rick snaps.

I shoot him a shocked glance. What's wrong with the man? He's more angry than usual.

"Gio, is it?" Cade's grin widens. He reaches for my hand, but Rick snaps his fingers, and the Great Dane lumbers to his feet and steps between me and Cade.

"What the—?" I gape.

Cade laughs. "Sending a mutt to do your dirty work, hmm?" He shoots Rick an amused glance. "I'm off to kiss my wife. Haven't done so in nearly ten minutes; need to remedy that." He tips his head in my direction. "Nice to meet you, Giorgina. Don't let Rick's bad attitude color your opinion about the rest of us."

Rick glowers.

Knight chuckles.

Cade swaggers off, and I follow his progress. He reaches Abby, draws her in, then bends her over in a theatrical move and kisses her. By the time he straightens, Abby's laughing, as are their friends. Then Michael and Karma approach them and the four begin an earnest conversation. There's an ease among this group of people, one which hints at shared experiences. One I'm not part of and might never be.

I've never had the time to focus on building friendships. I've been too focused on my career. And the one time I did let my guard down and trust someone... Well, let's just say, that didn't turn out well. Nope, those warm, fuzzy feelings are not for me. Besides I don't need friends. I'm here to focus on building my new career and developing a healthy relationship with my new boss. I turn to Knight, the owner of the London Ice Kings. "I can't wait to start work on the marketing and PR for the team."

Knight smiles. "We're very lucky to have you on board, Giorgina."

Rick mutters something under his breath that sounds suspiciously like, "That makes one of us."

I shoot him a glance. "What was that?"

"Who, me?" He stabs a thumb into his chest. "I didn't say anything."

"Hmm," I firm my lips.

"I'm glad the two of you already know one another; you'll be working closely together."

"We will?" Rick scowls.

"He's not yet the captain of the team," I remind Knight.

"That's true," Knight slowly nods. "If Rick doesn't accept the position, you'll work in *close proximity* with whoever replaces him."

That draws a low growl from Rick. His nostrils flare. A vein pulses at his temple.

"Something you want to say, Mitchell?" Knight murmurs.

Rick scowls at him. "I know what you're doing."

Knight chuckles. "Is it working?"

Something passes between the two men. "What am I missing, someone care to fill me in?" I burst out.

"Just that you'll have a dotted line reporting into the captain. This being a new team, a lot of the attention will fall on him, so you'll need to not only work closely with him but also take your cues from him in terms of building up his image." Knight interjects in a smooth voice.

"O-k-a-y," I nod. It's unusual but not unheard of.

"Also, Priest has agreed to take on the role of the General Manager —"

"Edward has?" Rick arches an eyebrow.

"Given his background and the challenges he's overcome, he was the perfect choice for the role. I have to admit, I was surprised when he accepted, but he has his reasons," Knight cuts the air with his hand. "All in all, things are shaping up well. But it's going to take a lot of effort on the part of everyone to pull things together. This means the captain will need to not only get the team working together as a unit, but he'll also have to pull his share when it comes to the marketing and publicity."

"Makes sense." I nod.

"As the PR manager you'll need to have daily meetings with the captain, and work intimately with him on crafting the details of the publicity strategy for the team."

"That's what I do best." I square my shoulders. "In no time at all, I'll have whipped the image of the captain and the team into shape."

"In the initial days, you'll have to work in very close quarters with the captain."

I frown. "I understand. I'm not one to shirk from hard-work, and since Rick is not the captain"—*thank god*—"things should run smoothly, and—"

"I accept the role," Rick interjects.

"What?" I slingshot my head in his direction. "You're doing it to get on my nerves."

"I'm doing it because Knight needs me."

I slap my hand on my hip. "Until a few seconds ago, you were positive the role wasn't for you."

"That was then."

"So, what changed?"

"I realized Knight was right all along; I'm the man for the job."

"You are." Knight nods.

"I don't want to work with you," I snap.

"Are you saying you're not accepting the role?" Knight frowns.

"Umm..." I turn to him. "That's not what I'm saying." I need this job. I ran out of L.A., breaking the lease on my place, without any savings—which means, my cashflow is almost non-existent at the moment. And the Ice Kings' salary is more than generous. To be honest, I don't have an option. But if it means I'm going to be working closely with this asshole, well... Do I have a choice?

"Good, so you're on board as PR and Marketing Manager, and you"—he turns his gaze on Rick—"are Captain." Knight's face breaks into a smile. "About fucking time." He claps Rick on the shoulder. "I'll leave you two to get better acquainted and come up with a plan." With a last nod that encompasses both of us, he heads off.

"Shit." I curl my fingers around the strap of my bag.

"Fuck." Rick rakes his fingers through his hair.

"This is all your fault." I stab a finger at him. "Why couldn't you have said no to the role?"

TO FIND OUT WHAT HAPPENS NEXT READ GIO AND RICK'S STORY IN THE ICE KISS

WANT A BONUS EPILOGUE FEATURING KNIGHT AND PENNY? USE THIS QR CODE

How to scan a QR code?

1. Open the camera app on your phone or tablet.
2. Point the camera at the QR code.
3. Tap the banner that appears on your phone or tablet.
4. Follow the instructions on the screen to finish signing in.

READ SUMMER & SINCLAIR STERLING'S STORY IN THE BILLIONAIRE'S FAKE WIFE

READ AN EXCERPT FROM SUMMER & SINCLAIR'S STORY

Summer

"Slap, slap, kiss, kiss."

"Huh?" I stare up at the bartender.

"Aka, there's a thin line between love and hate." He shakes out the crimson liquid into my glass.

"Nah." I snort. "Why would she allow him to control her, and after he insulted her?"

"It's the chemistry between them." He lowers his head, "You have to admit that when the man is arrogant and the woman resists, it's a challenge to both of them, to see who blinks first, huh?"

"Why?" I wave my hand in the air, "Because they hate each other?"

"Because," he chuckles, "the girl in school whose braids I pulled and teased mercilessly, is the one who I—"

"Proposed to?" I huff.

His face lights up. "You get it now?"

Yeah. No. A headache begins to pound at my temples. This crash course in pop psychology is not why I came to my favorite bar in Islington, to meet my best friend, who is—I glance at the face of my phone— thirty minutes late.

I inhale the drink, and his eyebrows rise.

"What?" I glower up at the bartender. "I can barely taste the alcohol. Besides, it's free drinks at happy hour for women, right?"

"Which ends in precisely" he holds up five fingers, "minutes."

"Oh! Yay!" I mock fist pump. "Time enough for one more, at least."

A hiccough swells my throat and I swallow it back, nod.

One has to do what one has to do... when everything else in the world is going to shit.

A hot sensation stabs behind my eyes; my chest tightens. Is this what people call growing up?

The bartender tips his mixing flask, strains out a fresh batch of the ruby red liquid onto the glass in front of me.

"Salut." I nod my thanks, then toss it back. It hits my stomach and tendrils of fire crawl up my spine, I cough.

My head spins. Warmth sears my chest, spreads to my extremities. I can't feel my fingers or toes. Good. Almost there. "Top me up."

"You sure?"

"Yes." I square my shoulders and reach for the drink.

"No. She's had enough."

"What the—?" I pivot on the bar stool.

Indigo eyes bore into me.

Fathomless. Black at the bottom, the intensity in their depths grips me. He swoops out his arm, grabs the glass and holds it up. Thick fingers dwarf the glass. Tapered at the edges. The nails short and buff. *All the better to grab you with.* I gulp.

"Like what you see?"

I flush, peer up into his face.

Hard cheekbones, hollows under them, and a tiny scar that slashes at his left eyebrow. *How did he get that?* Not that I care. My gaze slides to his mouth. Thin upper lip, a lower lip that is full and cushioned. Pouty with a hint of bad boy. *Oh!* My toes curl. My thighs clench.

The corner of his mouth kicks up. *Asshole.*

Bet he thinks life is one big smug-fest. I glower, reach for my glass, and he holds it up and out of my reach.

I scowl. "Gimme that."

He shakes his head.

"That's my drink."

"Not anymore." He shoves my glass at the bartender. "Water for her. Get me a whiskey, neat."

I splutter, then reach for my drink again. The barstool tips in his direction. This is when I fall against him, and my breasts slam into his hard chest, sculpted planes with layers upon layers of muscle that ripple and writhe as he turns aside, flattens himself against the bar. The floor rises up to meet me.

What the actual hell?

I twist my torso at the last second and my butt connects with the surface. *Ow!*

The breath rushes out of me. My hair swirls around my face. I scramble for purchase, and my knee connects with his leg.

"Watch it." He steps around, stands in front of me.

"You stepped aside?" I splutter. "You let me fall?"

"Hmph."

I tilt my chin back, all the way back, look up the expanse of muscled thigh that stretches the silken material of his suit. *What is he wearing? Could any suit fit a man with such precision?* Hand crafted on Saville Row, no doubt. I glance at the bulge that tents the fabric between his legs. *Oh!* I blink.

Look away, look away. I hold out my arm. He'll help me up at least, won't he?

He glances at my palm, then turns away. *No, he didn't do that, no way.*

A glass of amber liquid appears in front of him. He lifts the tumbler to his sculpted mouth.

His throat moves, strong tendons flexing. He tilts his head back, and the column of his neck moves as he swallows. Dark hair covers his chin —it's a discordant chord in that clean-cut profile, I shiver. He would scrape that rough skin down my core. He'd mark my inner thighs, lick my core, thrust his tongue inside my melting channel and drink from my pussy. *Oh! God*. Goosebumps rise on my skin.

No one has the right to look this beautiful, this achingly gorgeous. Too magnificent for his own good. Anger coils in my chest.

"Arrogant wanker."

"I'll take that under advisement."

"You're a jerk, you know that?"

He presses his lips together. The grooves on either side of his mouth deepen. Jesus, clearly the man has never laughed a single day in his life. Bet that stick up his arse is uncomfortable. I chuckle.

He runs his gaze down my features, my chest, down to my toes, then yawns.

The hell! I will not let him provoke me. Will not. "Like what you see?" I jut out my chin.

"Sorry, you're not my type." He slides a hand into the pocket of those perfectly cut pants, stretching it across that heavy bulge.

Heat curls low in my belly.

Not fair, that he could afford a wardrobe that clearly shouts his status and what amounts to the economy of a small third-world country. A hot feeling stabs in my chest.

He reeks of privilege, of taking his status in life for granted.

While I've had to fight every inch of the way. Hell, I am still battling to hold onto the last of my equilibrium.

"Last chance—" I wiggle my fingers from where I am sprawled out on the floor at his feet, "—to redeem yourself…"

"You have me there." He places the glass on the counter, then bends and holds out his hand. The hint of discolored steel at his wrist catches my attention. Huh?

He wears a cheap-ass watch?

That's got to bring down the net worth of his presence by more than 1000% percent. Weird.

I reach up and he straightens.

I lurch back.

"Oops, I changed my mind." His lips curl.

A hot burning sensation claws at my stomach. I am not a violent person, honestly. But Smirky Pants here, he needs to be taught a lesson.

I swipe out my legs, kicking his out from under him.

Sinclair

My knees give way, and I hurtle toward the ground.

What the—? I twist around, thrust out my arms. My palms hit the floor. The impact jostles up my elbows. I firm my biceps and come to a halt planked above her.

A huffing sound fills my ear.

I turn to find my whippet, Max, panting with his mouth open. I scowl and he flattens his ears.

All of my businesses are dog-friendly. Before you draw conclusions about me being the caring sort or some such shit—it attracts footfall.

Max scrutinizes the girl, then glances at me. *Huh?* He hates women, but not her, apparently.

I straighten and my nose grazes hers.

My arms are on either side of her head. Her chest heaves. The fabric of her dress stretches across her gorgeous breasts. My fingers tingle; my palms ache to cup those tits, squeeze those hard nipples outlined against the—hold on, what is she wearing? A tunic shirt in a sparkly pink... and are those shoulder pads she has on?

I glance up, and a squeak escapes her lips.

Pink hair surrounds her face. *Pink? Who dyes their hair that color past the age of eighteen?*

I stare at her face. *How old is she?* Un-furrowed forehead, dark eyelashes that flutter against pale cheeks. Tiny nose, and that mouth— luscious, tempting. A whiff of her scent, cherries and caramel, assails my senses. My mouth waters. *What the hell?*

She opens her eyes and our eyelashes brush. Her gaze widens. Green, like the leaves of the evergreens, flickers of gold sparkling in their depths. "What?" She glowers. "You're demonstrating the plank position?"

"Actually," I lower my weight onto her, the ridge of my hardness thrusting into the softness between her legs, "I was thinking of some-thing else, altogether."

She gulps and her pupils dilate. *Ah, so she feels it, too?*

I drop my head toward her, closer, closer.

Color floods the creamy expanse of her neck. Her eyelids flutter down. She tilts her chin up.

I push up and off of her.

"That... Sweetheart, is an emphatic 'no thank you' to whatever you are offering."

Her eyelids spring open and pink stains her cheeks. Adorable. Such a range of emotions across those gorgeous features in a few seconds. What else is hidden under that exquisite exterior of hers?

She scrambles up, eyes blazing.

Ah! The little bird is trying to spread her wings? My dick twitches. My groin hardens, *Why does her anger turn me on so, huh?*

She steps forward, thrusts a finger in my chest.

My heart begins to thud.

She peers up from under those hooded eyelashes. "Wake up and taste the wasabi, asshole."

"What does that even mean?"

She makes a sound deep in her throat. My dick twitches. My pulse speeds up.

She pivots, grabs a half-full beer mug sitting on the bar counter.

I growl, "Oh, no, you don't."

She turns, swings it at me. The smell of hops envelops the space.

I stare down at the beer-splattered shirt, the lapels of my camel colored jacket deepening to a dull brown. Anger squeezes my guts.

I fist my fingers at my side, broaden my stance.

She snickers.

I tip my chin up. "You're going to regret that."

The smile fades from her face. "Umm." She places the now empty mug on the bar.

I take a step forward and she skitters back. "It's only clothes." She gulps. "They'll wash."

I glare at her and she swallows, wiggles her fingers in the air. "I should have known that you wouldn't have a sense of humor."

I thrust out my jaw. "That's a ten-thousand-pound suit you destroyed."

She blanches, then straightens her shoulders. "Must have been some hot date you were trying to impress, huh?"

"Actually," I flick some of the offending liquid from my lapels, "it's you I was after."

"Me?" She frowns.

"We need to speak."

She glances toward the bartender who's on the other side of the bar. "I don't know you." She chews on her lower lip, biting off some of the hot pink. How would she look, with that pouty mouth fastened on my cock?

The blood rushes to my groin so quickly that my head spins. My pulse rate ratchets up. Focus, focus on the task you came here for.

"This will take only a few seconds." I take a step forward.

She moves aside.

I frown. "You want to hear this, I promise."

"Go to hell." She pivots and darts forward.

I let her go, a step, another, because... I can? Besides it's fun to create the illusion of freedom first; makes the hunt so much more entertaining, huh?

I swoop forward, loop an arm around her waist, and yank her toward me.

She yelps. "Release me."

Good thing the bar is not yet full. It's too early for the usual office-goers to stop by. And the staff...? Well they are well aware of who cuts their paychecks.

I spin her around and against the bar, then release her. "You will listen to me."

She swallows; she glances left to right.

Not letting you go yet, little Bird. I move into her space, crowd her.

She tips her chin up. "Whatever you're selling, I'm not interested."

I allow my lips to curl. "You don't fool me."

A flush steals up her throat, sears her cheeks. So tiny, so innocent. Such a good little liar. I narrow my gaze. "Every action has its consequences."

"Are you daft?" She blinks.

"This pretense of yours?" I thrust my face into hers, growling, "It's not working."

She blinks, then color suffuses her cheeks. "You're certifiably mad—"

"Getting tired of your insults."

"It's true, everything I said." She scrapes back the hair from her face. Her fingernails are painted... You guessed it, pink.

"And here's something else. You are a selfish, egotistical jackass."

I smirk. "You're beginning to repeat your insults and I haven't even kissed you yet."

"Don't you dare." She gulps.

I tilt my head. "Is that a challenge?"

"It's a..." she scans the crowded space, then turns to me. Her lips firm, "...a warning. You're delusional, you jackass." She inhales a deep breath before she speaks, "Your ego is bigger than the size of a black hole." She snickers. "Bet it's to compensate for your lack of balls."

A-n-d, that's it. I've had enough of her mouth that threatens to never stop spewing words. How many insults can one tiny woman hurl my way? Answer: too many to count.

"You—"

I lower my chin, touch my lips to hers.

Heat, sweetness, the honey of her essence explodes on my palate. My dick twitches. I tilt my head, deepen the kiss, reaching for that something more... more... of whatever scent she's wearing on her skin, infused with that breath of hers that crowds my senses, rushes down my spine. My groin hardens; my cock lengthens. I thrust my tongue between those infuriating lips.

She makes a sound deep in her throat and my heart begins to pound.

So innocent, yet so crafty. Beautiful and feisty. The kind of complication I don't need in my life.

I prefer the straight and narrow. Gray and black, that's how I choose to define my world. She, with her flashes of color—pink hair and lips that threaten to drive me to the edge of distraction—is exactly what I hate.

Give me a female who has her priorities set in life. To pleasure me, get me off, then walk away before her emotions engage. Yeah. That's what I prefer.

Not this... this bundle of craziness who flings her arms around my shoulders, thrusts her breasts up and into my chest, tips up her chin, opens her mouth, and invites me to take and take.

Does she have no self-preservation? Does she think I am going to fall for her wide-eyed appeal? She has another thing coming.

I tear my mouth away and she protests.

She twines her leg with mine, pushes up her hips, so that melting softness between her thighs cradles my aching hardness.

I glare into her face and she holds my gaze.

Trains her green eyes on me. Her cheeks flush a bright red. Her lips fall open and a moan bleeds into the air. The blood rushes to my dick, which instantly thickens. *Fuck.*

Time to put distance between myself and the situation.

It's how I prefer to manage things. Stay in control, always. Cut out anything that threatens to impinge on my equilibrium. Shut it down or buy them off. Reduce it to a transaction. That I understand.

The power of money, to be able to buy and sell—numbers, logic. That's what's worked for me so far.

"How much?"

Her forehead furrows.

"Whatever it is, I can afford it."

Her jaw slackens. "You think... you—"

"A million?"

"What?"

"Pounds, dollars... You name the currency, and it will be in your account."

Her jaw slackens. "You're offering me money?"

"For your time, and for you to fall in line with my plan."

She reddens. "You think I am for sale?"

"Everyone is."

"Not me."

Here we go again. "Is that a challenge?"

Color fades from her face. "Get away from me."

"Are you shy, is that what this is?" I frown. "You can write your price down on a piece of paper if you prefer." I glance up, notice the bartender watching us. I jerk my chin toward the napkins. He grabs one, then offers it to her.

She glowers at him. "Did you buy him, too?"

"What do you think?"

She glances around. "I think everyone here is ignoring us."

"It's what I'd expect."

"Why is that?"

I wave the tissue in front of her face. "Why do you think?"

"You own the place?"

"As I am going to own you."

She sets her jaw. "Let me leave and you won't regret this."

A chuckle bubbles up. I swallow it away. This is no laughing matter. I never smile during a transaction. Especially not when I am negotiating a new acquisition. And that's all she is. The final piece in the puzzle I am building.

"No one threatens me."

"You're right."

"Huh?"

"I'd rather act on my instinct."

Her lips twist, her gaze narrows. All of my senses scream a warning.

No, she wouldn't, no way—pain slices through my middle and sparks explode behind my eyes.

To find out what happens next read Summer & Sinclair Sterling's story in The Billionaire's Fake Wife

Read Michael and Karma's story in Mafia King

Read an excerpt from Mafia King

Karma

"Morn came and went—and came, and brought no day..."

Tears prick the backs of my eyes. Goddamn Byron. His words creep up on me when I am at my weakest. Not that I am a poetry addict, by any measure, but words are my jam. The one consolation I have is that, when everything else in the world is wrong, I can turn to them, and they'll be there, friendly, steady, waiting with open arms.

And this particular poem had laced my blood, crawled into my gut when I'd first read it. Darkness had folded within me like an insidious snake, that raises its head when I least expect it. Like now, when I look out on the still sleeping city of London, from the grassy slope of Waterlow Park.

Somewhere out there, the Mafia is hunting me, apparently. It's why my sister Summer and her new husband Sinclair Sterling had insisted that I have my own security detail. I had agreed... only to appease them... then given my bodyguard the slip this morning. I had decided to come running here because it's not a place I'd normally go... Not so early in the morning, anyway. They won't think to look for me here. At least, not for a while longer.

I purse my lips, close my eyes. Silence. The rustle of the wind between the leaves. The faint tinkle of the water from the nearby spring.

I could be the last person on this planet, alone, unsung, bound for the grave.

Ugh! Stop. Right there. I drag the back of my hand across my nose. Try it again, focus, get the words out, one after the other, like the steps of my sorry life.

"Morn came and went—and came, and... and..." My voice breaks. "Bloody asinine hell." I dig my fingers into the grass and grab a handful and fling it out. Again. From the top.

"Morn came and went—and came, and—"

"...brought no day."

A gravelly voice completes my sentence.

I whip my head around. His silhouette fills my line of sight. He's sitting on the same knoll as me, yet I have to crane my neck back to see his profile. The sun is at his back, so I can't make out his features. Can't see his eyes... Can only take in his dark hair, combed back by a ruthless hand that brooked no measure.

My throat dries.

Thick dark hair, shot through with grey at the temples. He wears his age like a badge. I don't know why, but I know his years have not been easy. That he's seen more, indulged in more, reveled in the consequences of his actions, however extreme they might have been. He's not a normal, everyday person, this man. Not a nine-to-fiver, not someone who lives an average life. Definitely not a man who returns home to his wife and home at the end of the day. He is...different, unique, evil... Monstrous. Yes, he is a beast, one who sports the face of a man but who harbors the kind of darkness inside that speaks to me. I gulp.

His face boasts a hooked nose, a thin upper lip, a fleshy lower lip. One that hints at hidden desires, Heat. Lust. The sensuous scrape of that whiskered jaw over my innermost places. Across my inner thigh, reaching toward that core of me that throbs, clenches, melts to feel the stab of his tongue, the thrust of his hardness as he impales me, takes me, makes me his. Goosebumps pop on my skin.

I drag my gaze away from his mouth down to the scar that slashes across his throat. A cold sensation coils in my chest. What or who had hurt him in such a cruel fashion?

"Of this their desolation; and all hearts
Were chill'd into a selfish prayer for light..."

He continues in that rasping guttural tone. Is it the wound that caused that scar that makes his voice so... gravelly... So deep... so... so, hot?

Sweat beads my palms and the hairs on my nape rise. "Who are you?"

He stares ahead as his lips move,

"Forests were set on fire—but hour by hour
They fell and faded—and the crackling trunks
Extinguish'd with a crash—and all was black."

I swallow, moisture gathers in my core. How can I be wet by the mere cadence of this stranger's voice?

I spring up to my feet.

"Sit down," he commands.

His voice is unhurried, lazy even, his spine erect. The cut of his black jacket stretches across the width of his massive shoulders. His hair... I was mistaken—there are threads of dark gold woven between the darkness that pours down to brush the nape of his neck. A strand of hair falls over his brow. As I watch, he raises his hand and brushes it away. Somehow, the gesture lends an air of vulnerability to him. Something so at odds with the rest of his persona that, surely, I am mistaken?

My scalp itches. I take in a breath and my lungs burn. This man... He's sucked up all the oxygen in this open space as if he owns it, the master of all he surveys. The master of me. My death. My life. A shiver ladders along my spine. *Get away, get away now, while you still can.*

I angle my body, ready to spring away from him.

"I won't ask again."

Ask. Command. Force me to do as he wants. He'll have me on my back, bent over, on my side, on my knees, over him, under him. He'll surround me, overwhelm me, pin me down with the force of his personality. His charisma, his larger-than-life essence will crush everything else out of me and I... I'll love it.

"No."

"Yes."

A fact. A statement of intent, spoken aloud. So true. So real. Too real. Too much. Too fast. All of my nightmares... my dreams come to life. Everything I've wanted is here in front of me. I'll die a thousand deaths before he'll be done with me... And then? Will I be reborn? For him. For me. For myself.

I live, first and foremost, to be the woman I was... am meant to be.

"You want to run?"

No.

No.

I nod my head.

He turns his, and all the breath leaves my lungs. Blue eyes— cerulean, dark like the morning skies, deep like the nighttime...hidden corners, secrets that I don't dare uncover. He'll destroy me, have my heart, and break it so casually.

My throat burns and a boiling sensation squeezes my chest.

"Go then, my beauty, fly. You have until I count to five. If I catch you, you are mine."

"If you don't?"

"Then I'll come after you, stalk your every living moment, possess your nightmares, and steal you away in the dead of night, and then..."

I draw in a shuddering breath as liquid heat drips from between my legs. "Then?" I whisper.

"Then, I'll ensure you'll never belong to anyone else, you'll never see the light of day again, for your every breath, your every waking second, your thoughts, your actions... and all your words, every single last one, will belong to me." He peels back his lips, and his teeth glint in the first rays of the morning light. "Only me." He straightens to his feet and rises, and rises.

This man... He is massive. A monster who always gets his way. My guts churn. My toes curl. Something primeval inside of me insists I hold my own. I cannot give in to him. Cannot let him win whatever this is. I need to stake my ground, in some form. *Say something. Anything. Show him you're not afraid of this.*

"Why?" I tilt my head back, all the way back. "Why are you doing this?"

He tilts his head, his ears almost canine in the way they are silhouetted against his profile.

"Is it because you can? Is it a... a," I blink, "a debt of some kind?"

He stills.

"My father, this is about how he betrayed the Mafia, right? You're one of them?"

"Lucky guess." His lips twist, "It is about your father, and how he promised you to me. He reneged on his promise, and now, I am here to collect."

"No." I swallow... *No, no, no.*

"Yes." His jaw hardens.

All expression is wiped clean of his face, and I know then, that he speaks the truth. It's always about the past. My sorry shambles of a past... Why does it always catch up with me? *You can run, but you can never hide.*

"Tick-tock, Beauty." He angles his body and his shoulders shut out the sight of the sun, the dawn skies, the horizon, the city in the distance, the rustle of the grass, the trees, the rustle of the leaves. All of it fades and leaves just me and him. Us. *Run.*

"Five." He jerks his chin, straightens the cuffs of his sleeves.

My knees wobble.

"Four."

My pulse rate spikes. I should go. Leave. But my feet are planted in this earth. This piece of land where we first met. What am I, but a speck in the larger scheme of things? To be hurt. To be forgotten. To be taken without an ounce of retribution. To be punished... by him.

"Three." He thrusts out his chest, widens his stance, every muscle in his body relaxed. "Two."

I swallow. The pulse beats at my temples. My blood thrums.

"One."

Michael

"Go."

She pivots and races down the slope. Her dark hair streams behind her. Her scent, sexy femininity and silver moonflowers, clings to my nose, then recedes. It's so familiar, that scent.

I had smelled it before, had reveled in it. Had drawn in it into my lungs as she had peeked up at me from under her thick eyelashes. Her green gaze had fixed on mine, her lips parted as she welcomed my kiss. As she had wound her arms about my neck, pushed up those sweet breasts and flattened them against my chest. As she had parted her legs when I had planted my thigh between them. I had seen her before... in my dreams. I stiffen. She can't be the same girl, though, can she?

I reach forward, thrust out my chin and sniff the air, but there's only the damp scent of dawn, mixed with the foul tang of exhaust fumes, as she races away from me.

She stumbles and I jump forward, pause when she straightens. Wait. Wait. Give her a lead. Let her think she has almost escaped, that she's gotten the better of me... As if.

I clench my fists at my sides, force myself to relax. Wait. Wait. She reaches the bottom of the incline, turns. I surge forward. One foot in front of the other. My heels dig into the grassy surface and mud flies up, clings to the hem of my £4000 Italian pants. Like I care? Plenty more where that came from. An entire walk-in closet, full of clothes made to measure, to suit every occasion, with every possible accessory needed by a man in my position to impress...

Everything... Except the one thing that I had coveted from the moment I had laid eyes on her. Sitting there on the grassy slope, unshed tears in her eyes, and reciting... Byron? For hell's sake. Of all the poets in the world, she had to choose the Lord of Darkness.

I huff. All a ploy. Clearly, she knew I was sitting next to her... No, not possible. I had walked toward her and she hadn't stirred. Hadn't been aware. Yeah, I am that good. I've been known to slit a man's throat from ear-to-ear while he was awake and in his full senses. Alive one second, dead the next. That's how it is in my world. You want it, you take it. And I... I want her.

I increase my pace, eat up the distance between myself and the girl... That's all she is. A slip of a thing, a slim blur of motion. Beauty in hiding. A diamond, waiting for me to get my hands on her, polish her, show her what it means to be...

Dead. She is dead. That's why I am here.

A flash of skin, a creamy length of thigh. My groin hardens and my legs wobble. I lurch over a bump in the ground. The hell? I right myself, leap forward, inching closer, closer. She reaches a curve in the path, disappears out of sight.

My heart hammers in my chest. I will not lose her, will not. *Here, Beauty, come to Daddy.* The wind whistles past my ears. I pump my legs, lengthen my strides, turn the corner. There's no one there. Huh?

My heart hammers and the blood pounds at my wrists, my temples; adrenaline thrums in my veins. I slow down, come to a stop. Scan the clearing.

The hairs on my forearms prickle. She's here. Not far, but where? Where is she? I prowl across to the edge of the clearing, under the tree with its spreading branches.

When I get my hands on you, Beauty, I'll spread your legs like the pages of a poem. Dip into your honeyed sweetness, like a quill pen in ink. Drag my aching shaft across that melting, weeping entrance. My balls throb. My groin tightens. The crack of a branch above shivers across my stretched nerve endings. I swoop forward, hold out my arms, and close my grasp around the trembling, squirming mass of precious humanity. I cradle her close to my chest, heart beating thud-thud-thud, overwhelming any other thought.

Mine. All mine. The hell is wrong with me? She wriggles her little body, and her curves slide across my forearms. My shoulders bunch and my fingers tingle. She kicks out with her legs and arches her back, thrusting her breasts up so her nipples are outlined against the fabric of her sports bra. She dared to come out dressed like that? In that scrap of fabric that barely covers her luscious flesh?

"Let me go." She whips her head toward me and her hair flows around her shoulders, across her face. She blows it out of the way. "You monster, get away from me."

Anger drums at the backs of my eyes and desire tugs at my groin. The scent of her is sheer torture, something I had dreamed of in the wee hours of twilight when dusk turned into night.

She's not real. She's not the woman I think she is. She is my downfall. My sweet poison. The bitter medicine I must partake of to cure the ills that plague my company.

"Fine." I lower my arms and she tumbles to the grass, hits the ground butt first.

"How dare you." She huffs out a breath, her hair messily arranged across her face.

I shove my hands into the pockets of my fitted pants, knees slightly bent, legs apart. Tip my chin down and watch her as she sprawls at my feet.

"You… dropped me?" She makes a sound deep in her throat.

So damn adorable.

"Your wish is my command." I quirk my lips.

"You don't mean it."

"You're right." I lean my weight forward on the balls of my feet and she flinches.

"What… what do you want?"

"You."

She pales. "You want to… to rob me? I have nothing of consequence.

"Oh, but you do, Beauty."

I lean in and every muscle in her body tenses. Good. She's wary. She should be. She should have been alert enough to have run as soon as she sensed my presence. But she hadn't.

I should spare her because she's the woman from my dreams... but I won't. She's a debt I intend to collect. She owes me, and I've delayed what was meant to happen long enough.

I pull the gun from my holster, point it at her.

Her gaze widens and her breath hitches. I expect her to plead with me for her life, but she doesn't. She stares back at me with her huge dilated pupils. She licks her lips and the blood drains to my groin. *Che cazzo!* Why does her lack of fear turn me on so?

"Your phone," I murmur, "take out your phone."

She draws in a breath, then reaches into her pocket and pulls out her phone.

"Call your sister."

"What?"

"Dial your sister, Beauty. Tell her you are going away on a long trip to Sicily with your new male friend."

"What?"

"You heard me." I curl my lips. "Do it, now!'

She blinks, looks like she is about to protest, then her fingers fly over the phone.

Damn, and I had been looking forward to coaxing her into doing my bidding.

She holds her phone to her ear. I can hear the phone ring on the other side, before it goes to voicemail. She glances at me and I jerk my chin. She looks away, takes a deep breath, then speaks in a cheerful voice, "Hi Summer, it's me, Karma. I, ah, have to go away for a bit. This new... ah, friend of mine... He has an extra ticket and he has invited me to Sicily to spend some time with him. I... ah, I don't know when, exactly, I'll be back, but I'll message you and let you know. Take care. Love ya sis, I—"

I snatch the phone from her, disconnect the call, then hold the gun to her temple, "Goodbye, Beauty."

To find out what happens next read Mafia King

Want to find out more about Karma and Summer's babies and Isla's child? You'll find this and more in The Agreement.

Read Cade and Abby's, brother's best friend, fake relationship romance in The Agreement

Read Daddy JJ's, age-gap romance in Mafia Lust

Read Olivia and Massimo's second chance romance in Mafia Obsession

Did you know the Seven and The Sovranos are part of the same world and their stories intertwine from The Proposal onward.

You can find the suggested reading order on http://www.authorlsteele.com

From L. Steele

PS – I want to hear from you!

Hello I'm L. Steele and I love watching movies and writing books. I live in London with my family.

Please do review the book on Amazon, Goodreads, and Bookbub, as well as on TikTok and in Facebook reader groups. Reviews and recommendations from you entice other readers to pick up the book, too, and that encourages me to write more and faster!

Want to be the first to know when my next book is out? Sign up for my newsletter on my website http://www.authorlsteele.com

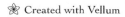 Created with Vellum

Printed in Great Britain
by Amazon

39596175R00215